THE ASH'BANI

Book Two
of
The Five Angels Trilogy

KIMBERLY M. RINGER

Kisy Kane Publishing, LLC

Contact Information: www.kimberlymringer.com

ISBN Hardback: 978-1-7373358-3-2

ISBN Paperback: 978-1-7373358-4-9

ISBN E-Book: 978-1-7373358-5-6

First Edition: December 2021

AUTHOR NOTE TO READERS:

THE FIVE ANGELS HAS been a heart project of mine for longer than I care to admit. Megan and CJ's story has always been on my mind and begged to be told. I hope you have enjoyed the story so far, and are looking forward to what comes next.

A special thank you to **Barb, Elisabeth, Holly,** my **husband** and **little human**. You have helped keep me sane. Thank you for letting me vent, throw spaghetti at the wall to see what sticks, and all you have done to help me through. I love you and thank you so very much.

YOUR MENTAL HEALTH MATTERS

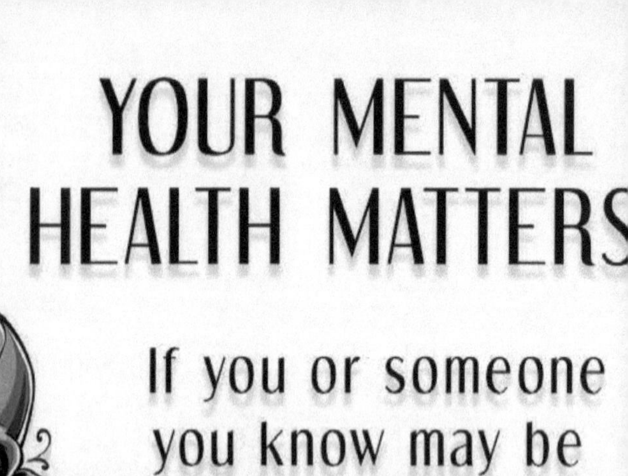

If you or someone you know may be struggling with suicidal thoughts, you can call the U.S. National Suicide Prevention Lifeline by simply dialing 988 or the full phone number: 800-273-TALK (8255) any time, day or night, or chat

Crisis Text Line also provides free, 24/7, confidential support via text message to people in crisis when they dial 741741.

CONTENT CONSIDERATIONS

Family Death
On Page Death
Emotional Violence
Physical Violence
Politics
Religion
Profanity
Sexually Explicit Scenes
Torture

Misogynistic Society
Narcissistic Persons
Magic System
Genocide
Bones
Child Abuse
Manipulation
Skeletons
Destitute Society

DEDICATION

For My Little Human, Catalina
Your bravery and strength are beyond measure.
The entire trilogy is for you.
Boop Snoot.

CONTENTS

MAPS

x

NALSAR WORLD MAP
LANSKER FROZEN ISLANDS
CURTAILS OF THE NORTH
LANSKER SEA
NALRIN
VEX ISLE
CINDER
THE WHISPERING CHANNEL
CELTIC MARSH
THE GLEAMING OCEAN
OBSCURITAN
ENCHANTED CANAL
SOUTHERN ISLES

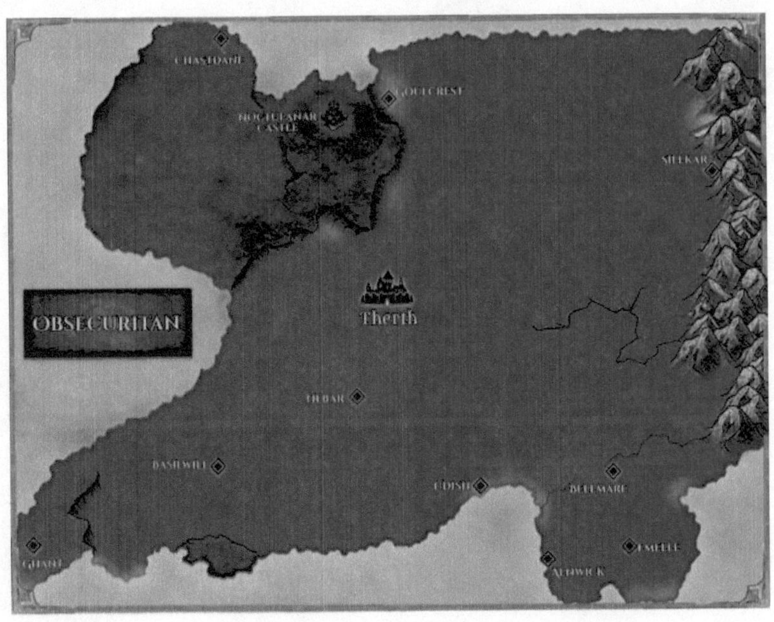
CHASEDANE
GOULCREST
NOCTURANAR
CASTLE
SEEKAR
OBSECURITAN
Therth
THBAR
BASILWILL
UDISH
BELLEMARE
GHANT
EMEELE
ALNWICK

Pronunciation Guide

Characters

Megan	Meg-an
Cory	Core-E
CJ	See-Jay
Ansel	An-sell
Symatha	Sim-a-tha
Julian	Jewel-e-in
Jean	Gean
Owen	O-en
Lindy	Lin-dee
Clarice	Clar-eece
Mickel	Mick- El
Erina	Er-ena

Other

Vernadali	
Vern-a-dal-e	
Maltal	Mal-tall
Syth	Saith

Locations

Noctulanar	Nock-two-lan-ar
Nalrin	Nal-ren
Obsecuritan	Ob-see-cure-e-tan
Manusia	Ma-new-sha

CHAPTER 1

CJ

"ANGELS, IT'S COLD," I cursed as I stepped off the ferry and pulled my jacket tighter around my chest. The icy wind blew right through me, and if I didn't get inside, I was going to become a meat popsicle. A man a little taller than my own six-foot two stature, with brown hair and vivid blue eyes, walked up and held his hand out. While he looked to be in his early 40s, he was probably 120–130 years old considering how people age here in Nalsar.

"You must be Cory James Mathewson," he said with a deep bass of a voice, slipping a glove off to shake my hand.

"CJ, please," I said, taking his warm hand in mine, not sure what else to say. Everyone would know who I was. I was the Angels Blessed Vernadali with no family history in Vernadali culture and, most of all, the human, not Sangra like everyone else.

"Vernadali James. Vernadali Samuel asked me to meet you and take you to his office," he explained. "Do you have any other belongings on the ferry?"

"No, sir. Julian said I should pack light." My fingers were going numb and blew into my hands to keep them warm.

"I'm sorry?" he asked, a little taken aback.

"Julian told me to pack light. I didn't pack anything because he said I could get anything I needed here," I expounded, rubbing my hands together.

"You use Head Julian's name so casually. May want to fix that while you're here," he said with a bit of annoyance.

"Is that how he should be titled?" I genuinely asked. "I'm sorry, I don't mean to be disrespectful, but we worked so closely with him over the last year and neither my family nor he corrected me. He has always just been Julian."

"You're serious?" he said, looking at me. When he realized I really didn't know any better, he replied, "Yes. His proper title is Head Julian."

Yeah, this was going to be a joy. I nodded and pulled my hands up under my armpits to stay warm.

"Bit cold, are ya?" Vernadali James said, a snide smile on his lips.

"Just a little. I'm not dressed for this weather. If I had realized it would have been so cold, I could have brought my warmer jacket... and beanie... and gloves... and scarf. I lived in Chicago, in the Manusia, so with the right gear, I don't shy away from the cold, but a little warning would've been fucking nice, Julian. I mean..." I said, smiling in apology at him at the last bit. I knew Julian was probably laughing his ass off, thinking of me showing up in a lightweight jacket and sneakers. We made our way toward the gate, and I tried to keep from turning into the aforementioned meat popsicle.

"I think I like you, CJ. You'll get used to the cold again soon enough," he said with a laugh. "Once you're done with Vernadali Samuel, I'll take you to get your gear and set up your classes."

"What exactly am I going to be learning in those classes? When Julian said all my aptitude tests confirmed I was a

Vernadali, he didn't give me much information as to what I'll be doing here."

"I bet that was some conversation," James said.

"What do you mean?"

"With Head Julian. Everyone knows what you, Lady Megan, and the others have done for our world." He walked up to the security gate, raised the sleeve on his arm where a scanner scanned a tattoo of a crest, and beeped. The gates opened with a creak and squeal that would've been the best setup for walking up to a haunted house. James motioned for me to catch up with him.

"We are, of course, eternally grateful, but even after everything that you guys have done, Head Julian tells you that The Five Angels blessed you, and you've become one bad ass bodyguard." He whistled. "What I wouldn't give to have been a fly on the wall during that conversation."

"It wasn't the conversation with Juli... I mean Head Julian that you would want to be a fly on the wall for. That was full of shock, planning, and just trying to absorb something else in my life that had drastically changed in the last year. Now the one with Megan?" I said, smiling at the memory. "The scariest part of it was that she never yelled or raised her voice. Let's just say that was a very long and quiet trip back home. Let me tell you; if your partner ever just goes silent on you, that's when you know they're mad."

"She didn't react at all? Just accepted it?" Vernadali James questioned, looking perplexed.

"Angels, no. After I told her I was the Vernadali assigned to her, Head Julian slowly backed out of that hospital room, leaving me to deal with her. Fucking coward," I muttered. Vernadali James laughed hard at that. "Sorry. Really. I will try to show some respect."

"Obviously, you know him well if you're brave enough to say that about him," he chuckled. "So, what happened? If you don't mind me asking."

"Clarice and Lindy, two of our family, first thought there was something abnormal about the way I moved during hand-to-hand combat practice. We knew Megan was enormously powerful for many reasons, and one of them was the way she moved. Clarice had marveled at how fast Megan was. When Lindy started training me, she had mentioned to Clarice how I was moving and thought it odd. They did some investigating and, without me knowing, gave me the at-home assessments. When I passed those, they arranged for the full aptitude tests in Nalrin."

"And Lady Megan never knew? No one ever mentioned it to her?" Vernadali James asked.

"No. I asked everyone not to. Megan had so much on her mind. We had so much going on and I didn't want to add to it. Clarice had me studying as much as Megan had been for her trials. That was the hardest part. It was so hard not to tell her that when I went to Nalrin without her, that not only was I working on getting my paperwork to stay here in Nalsar, but that I was also taking the aptitude tests." I let out a long, long breath at the memory.

"When we got back from Noctulanar Castle, I found out that I blew all the tests out of the water. My blood work came back with all the markers off the charts, so when we returned, they redid the blood work. The second round came back the same. Now, here I am an Angels Blessed Vernadali freezing my ass off."

I hadn't been able to tell her. Her whole world had been turned upside down again, and I couldn't bear the thought of adding another worry to her long list. So, I had taken the brunt of the ire from her.

"She wasn't pissed about you being a Vernadali? It's not an easy life," he said, his voice low.

"Megan took that in pretty good stride, actually," I said, blowing into my hands again, trying to keep them warm. "Megan. No, Megan was pissed it had been kept from her. She lost control of her power for a split second, and the entire room sparkled with her electricity."

"She has a temper, huh?"

I bellowed in laughter. "You could say that. I could tell you stories of us in high school where, luckily, I wasn't the recipient of that anger. Short story?"

"Please!" Vernadali James responded, intrigued. We still had a way to go, and talking about it eased some of the pain of leaving her back home.

"Back in the Manusia, at least where we lived, there used to be dress codes in school. One particular day, it was unusually hot for our area. She was wearing shorts and a tank top. One of the teachers tried to give her a write-up for it and make her go home to put different clothes on to cover up. He thought what she was wearing was indecent for a high schooler and that her clothing was distracting to the other students." I rolled my eyes dramatically. "You couldn't even see her bra straps, and her ass didn't hang out of her shorts. She dared the school to call Ansel and Symatha, and she went off on the head of the school. Kids stopped in the hallway, recorded it on their phones, and posted it all over social media. When the teacher tried to take it to the school board, they wouldn't hear of it because they had all seen the social media posts about it. They knew exactly what had happened."

"What did she say to scare off a council like that?"

"Basically, she said that any of her friends had seen her in less clothing outside of school, and that the only person who was distracted by her clothing was the male teacher trying to write her up. She called him a pedophile for it. Let's just say that she never got a write-up again for her clothes. That was just over a write-up. Let's not even discuss what happened when she had a vision of an ex-girlfriend cheating on me. When it came true, Megan laid into her like she had cheated on her." I thought back to that day and chuckled. I also vividly remembered the look Amber and Becca had given me a few days later when they suggested that Megan cared for me as more than a friend.

"Good thing you're Angel Blessed then?" he said, wincing.

"At least it *might* level the playing field," I said, smiling, then sighed. "Look, I know it's absurd, but I don't want to draw attention to myself. I know that isn't truly a possibility, being the only human and the only one of my line here, but I just want to learn what I need to learn and get back to her."

"You love her immensely, don't you?" he asked. There was no judgment or cynicism in it—just the truth.

"In every lifetime. I have walked very dark roads with her, both in the Manusia and here. I will walk whatever is thrown at us with her to the very end. To my very last breath," I said seriously.

"You left everything behind and are embracing being a Vernadali for her." This time, there was awe in his voice and a touch of longing.

"I am," I confirmed, wondering just how long I was going to be away from her. "Because she is worth it. I honestly don't know what I would do if the Angels thought to take her from me." The thought alone hurt.

We reached the edge of the cliff at that point, and the only words out of my mouth were, "Oh, Holy Fuck."

CHAPTER 2

I LOOKED OUT OVER the compound. All the buildings were made of glass and stone, but deep into the ground. It was like the whole city and training area had sunk 300 feet into a crater with steep cliff faces. In the center, there was a large courtyard that I suspected was more for training instead of social gatherings.

"Wow," I said this time.

Vernadali James smiled. "Yeah. That's what I said, too, when my dad and grandfather brought me here for the start of my training. Amazing, isn't it?"

"Yeah," I said. "How do you keep tsunamis and flooding out?"

"The whole island has a variety of incantations cast upon it. We don't rely solely on our power to keep the compound safe, though," he answered, reading the question on my face. "There are very elaborate drainage systems in place that process any salt intrusion from the surrounding ocean and recycles all the wastewater in the compound."

"So, we drink our own pee?" I asked, a little put off.

"Is it any different in some parts of the Manusia where you recycle your water?" he said curiously.

Even after everything we have been through this last year, to hear of my home as the Manusia was weird. It had always been Earth, the United States, Monterey Bay, Chicago. But no, since Megan dimension jumped, it was now the Manusia.

I sighed. Megan. Angels, I missed her already. We had only been home for a little over a month before Julian said I needed to report to the Curtails of the North to start my Vernadali training. I let out a long, slow breath. At least Julian arranged for me to take some leave during the Manusian Christmas Holiday in a few months. Christmas would likely be the only time I could see her until I was done.

I just have to keep it together until then. I'll see her soon, and then once all this training stuff is completed, we will be married and able to live our lives in peace. I smiled at the thought as I continued to look out over the compound—a lifetime with the woman I love, have loved for longer than I had realized it. Gods and Angels, I was a stupid fuck.

"CJ?" Vernadali James called, pulling me out of my thoughts.

"Oh, right. Sorry," I said, shaking my head. "The pee water. No, I guess it isn't all that different."

"The recycled water is filtered through that building over there to the right. Vernadali Kilan isn't the most hospitable of people, so I suggest staying away from that area. The water system is very efficient. What water isn't recycled back as drinking water is filtered through the fountains and used for the crops that grow on the outer parts of the isle," Vernadali James explained as he led me to an elevator off to the left.

Before stepping inside, James turned to me and said, "After you get inside, there is no turning back. You must complete the Vernadali Training. There will be no opportunity to leave. Once training is completed, you will be formally assigned your Charge and protect your Charge for the rest of your life. Is that understood?"

Maybe he didn't know after all. "So, you don't know..." I said so quietly, I hardly heard the words.

"Know what?" he asked, watching as others walked by who were trying to eavesdrop on our conversation.

"About my Charge?" I replied, still keeping my voice low.

"You will be assigned your Charge after you complete your training and obtain your herald," he said as a few other people walked by. "Just like the rest of us."

"Herald?" I asked.

James lifted the sleeve on his arm and showed me the tattoo he had put under the scanner to let us in the gates. Only the tattoo wasn't a crest like I thought it was, but three swords alternating directions vertically, surrounded by a laurel. Underneath the laurel was an unrolled scroll that was empty. It was the same as the pin I had seen the Vernadali in Nalrin wear. I hadn't noticed a tattoo on any of them, though.

"When you pass all your training, you will get this symbol on your right forearm. Once you are assigned your Charge, their name will be put on the scroll underneath."

"What happens if your Charge dies? Do they add another scroll?" I asked as we waited for the elevator to come back up.

"Yes. A new one will be etched just below once you're assigned a new charge but," a shadow crossed his face. "Many Vernadali take it as a life failure to have their Charge die. Most die for the shame of it."

"So, finish training, and her name will be there," I said, more as a statement than a question as I looked down at my forearm and ran my finger over it. I couldn't help but smile slightly. A tattoo of Megan's name. I never thought of myself as one to get a tattoo, but this was one I could stand behind... proudly.

"Or his name. No one knows who their Charge will be until after their training is complete."

"Not exactly, but let's go." I moved toward the elevator, but just as I was about to step past him, he grabbed my arm.

"What do you mean, not exactly?" he said, staring at me.

I didn't say anything. Maybe he knew what we had done over the last year, but apparently not that I was already sworn to Megan, and more than just intimately. People who walked by were staring at me, and my shoulders sagged a bit. I didn't want to be a freak show here. I just wanted to get my training done, get back to Megan.

"I already know my Charge," I said as quietly as possible and breaking eye contact.

"I had heard the rumor, but rumors are just that. Rumors. Vernadali Samuel told me, you're the Angel Blessed Vernadali and everything, but... WOW," he said as quietly as he could so that everyone who walked by wouldn't hear. His grip on my arm loosened slightly, and I pulled my arm back. "To know your Charge, before you're trained. That's something indeed."

"Look, like I said, I don't want to be special. I just want to get my training done and get back to Megan. There are things we still need to do. Can we please not make it common knowledge? I'm already getting looks from everyone else," I said, looking around.

"I won't say anything. Your secret is safe with me." Smiling, he added, "I think it will cost you a drink, though."

"Deal!" I said, relaxing slightly. Maybe I wouldn't be the outcast here. Then I laughed under my breath. Of course, I was going to be. Just from the boat to this elevator, there were enough stares.

I took a deep breath as my heart raced. These guys have been doing this for generations. They're light years ahead of me in knowledge and have probably known each other since they were born. Then I realized that even though it was rare, I do have something that they don't. I have the comfort of knowing who my Charge is already.

And Megan is worth this.

All of this. For Megan.

"Let's go," I said, stepping into the elevator and looking at James, who followed me in. He slipped a key into a hidden slot and hit the bottom-most button on the elevator.

"Welcome to the Curtails of the North, Vernadali C.J.," James said with a smile as he turned the key.

Then I was free falling to my destiny.

CHAPTER 3

MEGAN

"WHY ARE THERE SO many forms!" I complained, but I could see Lindy smile a little from across the table. "Stupid bureaucracy. They're just trying to make an example out of me."

"Well, you did bring them here unauthorized," Lindy said, half paying attention.

"They thought we were playing an April's Fool's joke on them... at Christmas. What was I supposed to do?" I smiled and giggled at the memory.

Julian had arranged for us to go to his parent's house in Chicago for Christmas. When CJ told them we were planning on getting married in July, the first words out of Logan's mouth were, and I quote, 'It's about fucking time you pulled your head out of your ass!' Then there was the barrage of questions. CJ's Mom, Annie, pressured us about a date, where we were living, etc. There was so much we couldn't tell them.

After hours of hounding and giving them what information we could, they eventually wore me down, and I just transported them all here to Nalrin. Of course, the bad news was that the Nalrin council was keeping a pretty close eye on what I was doing in case Ansel, my father, decided to show back up, so they knew I had brought them here within a few minutes.

My new family was, of course, the most gracious of hosts, but Lindy had warned me the council would give me hell about it later. She was right, too. They showed up about forty minutes later, handed me a large stack of paperwork, along with a reprimand from Julian himself. The documents from Julian, I had to fill out immediately and submit the other huge stack the next time I showed up for vocation.

When I was done with the Council, I headed back into the house and found that CJ's father, George, was still looking around the living room for a console to turn the hologram off because he didn't believe me or anyone else that this wasn't the holodeck from Star Trek. He thought that was a more believable answer than multiple universes. He also suggested that we had drugged him, and this was all a bad hallucination. He even went as far as to say that if we had, and CJ and I weren't getting married, he would never forgive us.

Annie and CJ's brother, Logan, both took it smooth and seamless. I think they were just so happy that CJ and I were getting married that they would accept just about anything. Annie continued to pepper us about the wedding, and Logan started asking non-stop questions about what life was like here.

"Megan?" Lindy said, pulling me out of the memory. She continued hesitantly, "A Vision?"

I flinched, "No. Still nothing."

That was the other thing; I hadn't had a vision since we were at Noctulanar Castle in that fight against my parents that left my mother dead, and Ansel vowing vengeance upon us all. Not of someone cooking breakfast. Not of Ansel. Not of me working in the garden. Nothing. Not a single one in over six months. "Was just remembering Christmas is all."

"That was pretty funny. The look on their faces when they showed up in front of the house was great."

"They didn't believe us. George was getting kind of mad and insulted we wouldn't tell them where we were living. I tried to just tell him in Nalrin, but when they pressed for an address, well, that's when I had to tell them it wasn't necessarily in the Manusia. After trying to explain to them that it was actually in a different dimension, well, how else was I going to get them to believe me!"

"Oh honey, I know. You don't have to convince me, but the council is not too happy about it. I love Annie, though. She's so easygoing."

"Well, Logan is a great guy too," I teased her.

"Gorgeous too," she interjected before realizing what she said, as her face turned beet red.

I just smiled. The way they had flirted when he was here, I knew there was something more between them. She hadn't told me there was, but I wasn't completely stupid. On most of my trips back to the Manusia, she accompanied me to see them and my best friend, Amber.

"Just be careful with him," I said softly, and her eyes snapped up to meet mine. "I'm not dumb, Lindy. I know you two are gaga over each other. I'm happy for you both. It's just, I know it's going to be hard with everything going on, and he's had some serious heartache."

"Rebecca," she breathed. I nodded. "He told me. I don't know how he didn't kill him for that."

"Me neither. I'm not sure how any of us didn't," I said through gritted teeth.

Rebecca, Logan's high school sweetheart, was killed by her father in one of his drunken rages three weeks after graduating high school. Logan had tried and tried for years to get her to move in with him, to get her away. He had called the police. He had reported it to the school. He had even arranged for child protective services to do welfare checks. Hell, when we all found out about the sexual abuse and beatings afterward, we tried everything repeatedly. The system failed her, and none of it worked. Unfortunately, this was one situation where it took him killing her to get him off the streets. He now sits in San Quentin with no possibility of parole.

"Megan, I really do care for him," she divulged shyly. It was so unlike her. "The last thing I want to do is hurt him. He is loving, kind, and loyal. He makes my heart sing, and I didn't think anyone would be able to do that again."

"Then enjoy life, Lindy," I said, putting my hand over hers. "Go sneak off as often as you can to the Manusia to see him. Bring him here whenever you can, and enjoy life."

"You really are okay with it?" When I nodded, she smiled brightly and said, "Thanks. You're the best."

I shrugged, "I know."

It still amazed me at how laid back she was. While dealing with my parents' last year, she had always just been in deep thought, so I thought that's just who she was. Instead, she was trying to help us put pieces of the puzzle together and find out what the next step was. I know we wouldn't have been able to get half as far as we did if it were not for her.

Since we got back from Noctulanar, she had relaxed and returned to what Jean called her normal dingbat self. She was my best friend this side of the Manusia. Lindy took my side when we discussed wedding plans, what we should have for dinner, or anything, really. She had also stayed up way too late at night when I just needed to talk, just needed to get something off my chest or cry it out. Not to mention she was insanely worried about me not having any more visions. I'd had them since I was a kid, and now... nothing.

It had been almost a year since my parents, who I had previously thought dead, tried to build the weapon of The Five Angels. We had fought so hard and failed so drastically, so many times, that when they kidnapped CJ, I had questioned whether any of us would come out alive. I had only focused on saving CJ. It was only the fact that they hadn't had the piece needed for the Angel of Healing, the Golden Medallion of the Sa Ra, which still hung around my neck, that we were saved. It was during that fight that my mother was killed, and I had blacked out.

Blacked out. That seemed like an oversimplification. I ended up in a coma. Again. It was CJ that had brought me back from the black weight, only to find out that somewhere along the way, the Angels had blessed him with the abilities of a Vernadali. Not just an ordinary Vernadali, as if that wouldn't have been enough. No, he was an Angels Blessed Vernadali. I hadn't been able to yell at him about it. I hated the fact he was being dragged further into this mess, but it wasn't his fault.

No, what made me furious was that not only had he not told me about it, but Clarice and Lindy figured it out and didn't tell me. Not to mention that Jean and Owen just *conveniently* forgot to mention it. That entire hospital room had had my electricity filtering throughout it after he told me. I had lost control of my power and there were still lines on those walls to prove it. Julian had casually mentioned that even after cleaning and painting the room, they couldn't remove the echoes of my power. However, I couldn't bring myself to even feel bad about it, either.

I sighed and went back to filling out the forms for CJ's parents and brother to have free transportation rights to and from Nalrin to visit us. Not that they had any other reason, but we had to declare it on the forms. Since CJ wasn't here, there wasn't much reason for them to come to Nalsar before now, but I still visited them back in the Manusia regularly, just to keep them from worrying. I usually went to visit CJ and mine's friends at the same time during my off weeks. Now, we need to get those rights signed off because if I know my soon-to-be mother-in-law, which I do, she will want to put in her two cents on my wedding.

My wedding. I never thought that I would be planning my own. Let alone planning my wedding to CJ. Some things were already decided, like the flowers, which had to be red tulips. They are my favorite, and I wanted to carry a big bouquet of them down the aisle and have them at the end of each aisle of chairs. There was also the fact that it had to be outside, though we hadn't decided exactly where.

CJ and I talked about getting married back in the Manusia, but decided that if we are going to make our lives here in Nalrin, why not start it out here. Jean and Owen offered Grandma's garden, which I considered, since it was my favorite place on the property. There was also the waterfall about half a mile or so into the forest that had a beautiful open meadow at the base that I could almost see everything laid out. CJ was concerned about the noise from the waterfall drowning out everything, but Clarice demonstrated how the waterfall could have a silence incantation put on it so that the beauty of the falls could be seen but not heard. Neither CJ nor I could make that decision yet when he was only home for Christmas. Jean and Lindy had pushed, but I wasn't making that decision alone.

Then there was the wedding party. CJ said that was the easiest decision out of everything. Logan would be his best man, and Owen, his groomsman. Neither of us wanted a big wedding party, as we wanted to keep the whole thing small and quaint, but that wasn't going to happen. Julian was making it a dimensional affair, even with my objections. I was still holding out on asking Lindy. I knew she would, but I just hadn't dared ask her yet.

"Lindy?" I was surprised at the hesitation in my voice.

"Hum?" she asked, half paying attention as she was figuring out how to fill in her forms.

"WouldyoubemyMaidofHonor?" The words came out fast, mumbled into one word, but she completely froze. I saw a smile cross her face as she looked up at me, and I could see tears swelling up in her eyes. "Really? You want me?"

I completely relaxed. "No, the other Lindy in the house. Of course, you, silly!"

"Of course, I will!!!" she squealed as she threw her hands up to cover her mouth. "I just assumed you'd want Amber since she's your best friend in the Manusia."

"Well, she is, but you're mine here, and this is where we are starting our lives. I want it represented in every facet. Amber will be right behind you. She and I already discussed it when I told her we wanted the wedding here. She said strategically it was a good idea since the wedding was here. Besides, between school and work, she worried she wouldn't be able to help with the planning like she should if she were Maid of Honor, but she was thrilled and honored to be a bridesmaid."

"How did she react when you told her you and CJ were getting married?"

"Pretty much how Logan did." I giggled. "All of our friends back in the Manusia thought CJ, and I needed to be together and that it was just a matter of time. There had also been bets on who would step up and ask the other. Apparently, Becca won a lot of money when they found out CJ had risked everything to ask me out on that date."

"And Nalrin?" she asked hesitantly. "Or did you not tell Amber about that part?"

"Like I could keep that from her. She's studying to be an astrophysicist, Lindy. How do you think she reacted? She started asking me all these questions with really big words that just made my head hurt listening to them. I tried to tell her I was sure that some scientist knew, and likely some were from Nalrin, but she just gave me a look. She started parsing out all these formulas and started again with a lot of big words that, again, hurt my brain. It took some convincing and some serious pouty faces from her before she swore she wouldn't tell anyone."

"And by convincing, you mean you threatened to banish her to the Ralvins?" she said, leaning back with an eyebrow cocked almost to her hairline.

I feigned hurt. "WHY LINDY! I don't know what you're talking about?! I would *never* do such a thing!"

Lindy just shook her head and went back to finishing her paperwork. I smiled, filled in the last question on the form just as she was finishing hers, and we headed into the living room to relax. I'd fill out Amber's paperwork later tonight. I just needed to make sure I take them with me when I return to Nalrin City tomorrow.

I wasn't looking forward to that commute. Every other week, I headed back to Nalrin to work with Julian. He seemed to think that I have a knack for diplomacy. I kept reminding him of how I blew up at the council, but he still thought I could handle it. For now, he had me doing background checks and other research for him until we could decide what my vocation should be. To be honest, there isn't anything that sounded too appealing. I had a degree in legal studies, and before everything happened, I was planning on going to law school in a couple of years. That wasn't exactly transferrable to Nalrin.

Lately, though, my mind is too consumed with trying to figure out what to do about my father and wedding plans. I usually finished up background checks and whatever else Julian needed me to do by mid-week because there weren't many positions in the higher ranks that were open right now. Julian had also seemed to back off on some of the research projects he had me doing. Clarice and Lindy often came into town to spend time researching Ansel's heritage, the Ash'bani, in the Nalrin library.

After CJ left for his training in the Curtails of the North, they finally told me that my father was half Ash'bani, who were abnormally sturdy. They recovered from injuries faster and had a high pain tolerance that would knock just about anyone else down to the ground. They suspected that was how and why I had lived through the explosion at their house when they faked their death in the Manusia. The problem was that there wasn't much commonly known about the Ash'bani. The Ash'bani were tight-lipped about themselves and stuck to the dark parts of Obsecuritan. Only the diplomats, whom I have met on rare occasion, ventured into the Nalrin province.

The Ash'bani diplomats, Chyss, the Head diplomat, and Zamph, his Take Over, and I didn't get along very well when we met. I hoped they would help me find out more about myself, and hence my father, but no luck yet. I had continued to try and even pleaded with them by bringing up my father, but they avoided me at all costs. Not easily done, considering I'm usually hanging around all the high-ranking conferences.

They would see me in the Council Chamber or the halls and eye me with such hatred and loathing. I was told not to worry about it, that they don't like anyone, but this was different. It wasn't until my bodyguard that Julian required I had while in Nalrin told me he had overheard them saying that I was the plague bringer of the Ash'bani that I backed off trying to meet with them.

Plague bringer. They thought I was the plague bringer to their race. I have zero plans on destroying any race. I took a deep breath and reached into the bookcase to pick up a book from my favorite book series from the Manusia. I just want to marry CJ, and live a safe, quiet life here in Nalrin.

"You're reading that series again?" Lindy asked.

"Yes, and what's wrong with that?!" I said as I plopped down in my favorite chair.

"It's only like the fifth time you've read it since we moved your... extensive book collection from the Manusia," she said when I raised an eyebrow at her. Only once did she make the mistake of dissing my book collection. She had ended up hog-tied with one of Clarice's whips. It was a sight I will never forget.

"I've only read it five times since we brought it over? Well, that doesn't compare to the probably twenty times I've read it before that. You really should read it," I told her as I tossed the first book of the series at her.

She caught it with one hand and instantly tossed it back to me. "I have no interest in reading for pleasure. Give me books with educational value. Stuff I can use later. I'm not one for escapism."

I rolled my eyes and just smiled as she sat down and read a book on ancient incantations of Noctulanar, then giggled. "I swear, Lindy, what am I going to do with you."

"Love me forever! I'm sure," she said, shrugging.

CHAPTER 4

IT WAS A BRIGHT, sunny day as I ran through the forest. After lunch, I had an ass beating in hand-to-hand combat with Clarice and then studied more incantations. Sure, I had passed the trials, but that didn't mean I wasn't still grossly behind in my Sangra education. Controlling the power was still a struggle, and I still had to use a cocoon to keep my power in check.

Not to mention that the more time passed, the more I felt the charge of that electricity and the pressures of it. I wasn't sure if it was just settling within me as more time passed or if it was indeed growing. Once, and only once, had I let it all out since we returned from Noctulanar Castle. I had let it out that one time, because I felt like my bones were being crushed by the pressure.

While I hadn't felt like I was on fire, the electricity didn't want to listen to me. The more I tried to control it, the wilder it got. I panicked, and that certainly didn't help things. I ended up burning CJ's hands and arms pretty bad as he helped ground me. It had taken over an hour before I could contain it in its cocoon. Now it was going to stay there until CJ got back. I didn't trust myself to be able to re-contain it without his help.

So, I practiced and studied a lot. Overall, I just tried to keep my mind off the fact that CJ wasn't here. He left about a month after we got back from Nalrin for Vernadali training up in the Curtails of the North. It's been ten months and only being able to see him at Christmas, well, I missed him terribly.

Running regularly again helped wear me out. Even on the days that I felt ambitious and let half of my power out of its little cocoon, the pure physical exertion had helped kept it contained. Today was no different. My power was super jumpy. I had resorted to cocooning all but a tiny bit of it during my combat training with Clarice, after zapping her a bit too harshly. Something was tickling it awake, making it edgy, and I needed to take the edge off. Hence the long, hard run.

I allowed my mind wandered as I ran down the path I had worn in the forest behind the house. I took a deep breath as I remembered the fight CJ and I had had in the hospital when he told me he is a Vernadali. Not just any Vernadali, but *my* Vernadali. He was a fucking Angels Blessed Grand Protector!

Once I had let some of my anger go, knowing there wasn't any point in fighting him over it, we dove right into trying to find out more about them, though there wasn't much more than what he had already found out since we had left Nalrin. Vernadali were from a few select ancient bloodlines and have always been from those bloodlines. Never a deviation, until now, which made some people, well, very uneasy.

There were theories, of course. Lindy said the best-suggested theory was he was blessed when we were in the Garden of Beauty. The way the flowers had lifted and surrounded us after he asked me to marry him, the fact that when he held my hand, and we used the Golden Amulet of Sa Ra we could heal people without pain, was all just way too coincidental. The Angel of Beauty had even told us we had been blessed. My problem with it was that the Angel of Beauty said that he was blessed with the affinity of soothing, the ability to heal without pain when used with me and the Sa Ra. She said nothing about making him a Vernadali.

It's been five months, twenty days, and twenty-eight hours since he'd been home, and I couldn't wait for him to be back. We had talked a couple of times via LightCall, a video conference technology that was only available to the council and other high-ranking members across Nalsar. Julian set it up for us for when I was in Nalrin. Scheduling was tricky though, because it couldn't conflict with his training, and I had to be in Nalrin. Even though we had talked a few times, they were nowhere near long or private enough.

No one could tell me when he would be back, either. They'd just say, "*When he finishes his training.*" The hard part was that, technically, he was so far behind. Vernadali usually start training at five years of age. CJ, however, well... he was thrown into it all! *Here, you're an amazing protector. Now, go be that kick-ass protector we made you!*

Being in Nalrin around Julian and other Vernadali had its perks. I was able to gather that his instructors in the Curtails of the North thought the only way he could learn his lessons at the speed he had been was because he was Angels Blessed. Book courses that usually took a couple of years for normal Vernadali to finish, CJ had completed after only four months.

They didn't know CJ like I did. If he were determined, he would be the sponge that absorbed every ounce of information to finish up early. He would forego sleep and food if it meant he could reach his goal sooner. It was exactly how he got his bachelors in only three and a half years, and his masters only a year later. He just didn't stop; well, that and strategic class scheduling.

Since finishing the classroom work, he had spent the last couple of months in combat bootcamp. The last time I talked to him, he said that the martial arts classes were the hardest, but he knew that those took years to be any good at because it was really about muscle memory. Fighting was just something that took practice, but he said he very much looked forward to beating Clarice in a match.

Suddenly, I felt as though ice water had just been dumped over my head and seeped into my veins. My whole left hand and arm up to my elbow had gone completely numb. I stopped mid-stride to catch my breath. The cold gave me a splitting headache, and I sat down on a log next to the trail. The ice water turned into something dark, heavy, and shattering that washed over me in waves.

This wasn't the first time I had strange feelings flow over me, and each time left me tired and worn out. It had started like a dark cloud hanging over me, and I thought it was just depression from missing CJ. Lately though, it was becoming more frequent.

I had wondered if it had to do with Ansel, and that alone filled me with dread. After all we went through last year, I knew there had to be another way for him to enact his revenge against the council and me, but having to wait until he showed his hand to see how he would do that was driving me crazy.

"Well, I guess my run is over," I muttered to myself. I rubbed my arms and legs, and they felt warm to the touch, but I was still so cold. I felt out and couldn't see anyone's ember.

I put my head in my hands and rubbed small circles at my temples. I could have sat there for minutes or hours, but slowly, the headache dissipated. The cold throughout my body had not, and while I knew I wouldn't be able to continue my run, I wasn't sure I could make it back all the way, so I pushed to Jean and Lindy, *"Heavy. Help. On my way back."*

"Megan." Lindy in relief when she found me about a quarter-mile from the house. Worry lined her face, and she half-carried me back to the house.

When we got to the front yard, I stopped and bent over on my hands on my knees. I focused on the ground, reached into my cocoon for my power, and found it falling into a black abyss. I tried to force it back up to where I could reach it, but it kept shying away from whatever was making me feel this way.

When we reached the house, Jean met us there, and I felt her put her hand on my back, "You ok sweety?"

"Yeah. I think so. While running, I felt like I had fallen into the Southern Isle waters. Still feel cold and heavy."

"Clarice is feeling something similar, but she won't talk about it. I've been with her the last few minutes," she said. "Let's get you inside and under a warm blanket."

"Clarice too? Really?"

She just nodded her head as we headed inside.

Inside, Clarice had her head in her hands, sitting in a chair with some papers in front of her: More letters from her dad, which had been sent through Nalrin. He had been writing to her a lot, but she wouldn't discuss what they said. She just sighed every time another one came. I never saw her write back, but it always affected her mood for a few hours after one arrived.

"Clarice, Megan's feeling the same feeling that you are," Jean said quietly.

"How often Megan?" Clarice pushed, barely above a whisper and without looking at me.

I had to think about it. "Well, today was the worst of it, but occasionally, for about a month?"

She nodded her head.

"Why isn't anyone else feeling it? Why didn't you mention it before? Do you know what's causing it?" I asked as I sat down on the ottoman in front of her.

"It's the darkness from Obsecuritan. You're connected to it because it fed on you at Noctulanar Castle. I, however, am born with it in me."

"I don't understand. Why are we getting this feeling? Owen was touched by the darkness, too. He doesn't seem affected by it," I said, pulling a blanket tight around me.

"Owen wasn't stupid enough to offer it blood. You did. The blood you gave connected you to it. Frankly, I didn't think that was possible unless..." Clarice shook her head like she was trying to distract herself. "I feel it because I was born with it. It's calling me home."

"Calling you..." I raised my eyebrows and said the words like she was a little crazy, though not too crazy, because, well you know, we live in Pychoville.

"Yes, calling me Megan. Remember when the boys from Gendril showed up and wanted me to come back?" I nodded my head, and she continued, "While my father sent them out to find me, he claims he doesn't know where I'm living, but I don't believe him. It isn't like I'm hiding. Anyway, my father wants to see me. He has even resorted to telling me I don't have to take over his position and that he has already arranged for my sister to take over. She'll be better at it. She's narcissistic and enjoys other people's pain."

"And you don't want to go?" I asked her, consciously ignoring the comments about her sister. Jean and Lindy looked at each other, and there were a lot of questions in their eyes. There was so much that we didn't know about Clarice's history. She may have to release those secrets soon, but we still respected her privacy.

"It... is... Complicated," she intoned.

"Well, if you want to go, I'll go with you. I'm going to go do my chores. Horses aren't going to clean up their own shit."

"Thanks Megan," she said as I got up and headed to change.

By the time I was done with the stables and my shower, the feeling had mostly worn off, and I went to finish up the paperwork for Amber. I heard Lindy follow me into the kitchen and grab something to eat, but she didn't touch it when she sat down at the table. She just sat there, staring off into space.

"You're doing it again, Lindy," I said as I filled in Amber's address in the Manusia.

"Hum? What's that?" Shaking her head and looking at me, she took a drink of her orange juice.

"That deep thought thing you do when things get crazy around here."

"When?" she said, raising her eyebrows and laughing. I just leveled a look at her.

She didn't say anything for a moment again and just looked down at her glass. So, I put down my pen and took her hand. "Seriously, Lindy. What's going on in that pretty little head of yours?"

"I'm just thinking about Clarice. She never talks about her father. Like ever. She has practically kept her whole life before coming to Nalrin some sort of secret. Then, last year Gendril boys came to 'bring her home,' and now all these letters are coming." She looked at me pointedly. "Something isn't right."

"I know." I sighed. "I think the time is coming when she will have to let us in on that part of her life, but she will tell us when she is ready. We just have to trust her."

She agreed and then turned her whole body toward me excitedly and started in, "SO! Your wedding!"

"You're going to give me whiplash with that mood change, girl, but yes, what about it?"

"Well, we only have the date," she said hesitantly.

"Yup, July 2nd. And the flowers. And a few other things."

"We still need to find you a dress. I can't believe that the wedding is less than two months away and you still don't have your dress! Julian is presiding over it, so that's covered. We need to get the tulips ordered from the grower in the northern part of Nalrin since they aren't going to be available from the Manusia this time of year. The guest list went out a few months ago..." she rattled off.

"Wait. When did the invites go out?" I asked.

"A few months ago," she drawled. "People have to know about it well in advance so they can make sure to get here. I worked on it with Jean and Annie."

"So, you already sent out the invites. CJ and I didn't even get to finalize the invitation list?" I said, raising my eyebrows.

Her eyes widened a little, and there was an ounce of fear there. Snapping her fingers and waving her hand up, papers showed up in her hand as she slowly handed it over.

I read it over, and there were a lot of people I didn't know on it. "Lindy, CJ, and I wanted a small wedding. Just family and friends," I said quietly as I scanned more and more names. I knew we weren't going to have the real small wedding we wanted, but this list... All the Heads and their TakeOvers were on the list for the Nalsar Council as well as all of the Heads of each department in the Nalsar Council.

"I know, but Julian made demands, so a lot of people on that list are on the Council," she sighed and said in an apologetic voice. "Then George wanted some of his business partners there. It snowballed."

"And you didn't think to talk it over with the people actually getting married?" I said, without looking up at her. I was too busy running over the list and contemplating how to tell Julian to shove his demands up his ass, but didn't see any way to avoid everyone showing up anyway. If we didn't invite the entire Council, this would be the wedding that everyone crashed.

"Fine," I said, sighing heavily. I didn't have it in me to fight this. As long as CJ and I were married at the end of the day, I could give them a few concessions. "What else still needs to be done?"

"Then there are the guy's suits, the chairs, place settings, seating arrangements, you and CJ need to decide on a location. With CJ being gone, the planning hasn't been happening. There is just so much to do! Two months! JEAN!" Lindy yelled out into the living room. "We have to plan the rest of this extravagant wedding in less than *two months*."

She continued rambling under her breath about this and that, making notes on a notepad that Jean had come in and placed in front of her. I shook my head and focused on finishing up Amber's paperwork while she babbled on making some of the decisions for me. Some of them just didn't matter. I mean, seriously, I don't care where everyone sits. As far as I'm concerned, we are becoming one family, just let everyone sit where they want.

"What about the wedding bell flowers?" Jean asked.

"Megan, what do you think?" Lindy asked.

"I'm sorry, what are wedding bell flowers?" I questioned. Jean gave me a strange look, but Lindy chimed in.

"The flower, well it's not really a flower. It is, but it isn't. It is a lot like... Oh, what is that stuff called to help fill up a bouquet in the Manusia... Baby's breath... That's it. Everyone is given a piece to throw when you walk back down the aisle. It's tradition. You have to have that."

"Um okay, if you insist." I hadn't looked up from the paperwork. I just wanted to get this done, but I slowly looked up at them when they didn't move onto the next item on their list.

They looked at me like I was from another planet. Technically not another planet, but I am from another dimension; at least, I grew up in another dimension.

"If... you... insist?" Jean said, crossing her arms.

"Ok, what am I missing here?" I asked.

"That is a Nalrin tradition, and since Julian is presiding over the wedding, traditions need to be followed," Lindy tried to explain to keep Jean from exploding.

"Well, if it's a hard and fast rule, why is this up for discussion? However, remember two things, please. First, CJ and I came from the Manusia, and those wedding customs are the only ones we know. Second, it is our wedding. You have already taken over the guest list, so tread carefully," I warned, narrowing my eyes slightly. They both looked a little astonished I was so firm about this.

"Sorry," Jean said.

"Look, we want to incorporate Nalrin traditions, but we just don't know them. We grew up with American customs, which did not include baby's breath being chucked at us as we walked back down the aisle. Traditionally, that was rice, but some people did flower petals, bird seed, or bubbles, but after the reception as the couple left."

That made them relax a little, and I saw Lindy's eyes brighten. "Bubbles?!" she turned to Jean. "I love the idea of bubbles. Is there a way we could do both?"

"Does Megan even want bubbles?" Jean asked. I think she was secretly hoping I didn't. Jean wants a traditional Nalrin wedding. The problem is, CJ and I are not traditional.

"Bubbles would be cool, but..." Ok, I know it's my wedding, but I need to keep everyone happy, too. "How about modifying both traditions? We cover the entire aisle with the wedding bells and use the bubbles for when we leave on our honeymoon as husband and wife?"

Lindy immediately agreed, and after a minute, Jean relaxed and apologized for being so demanding. I, of course, let her off the hook, and the three of us worked on ironing out several more details and compromises on traditions.

"Where are you going for your honeymoon?" Jean asked, looking over the list of things that still needed to be determined.

"I don't know. CJ said he was handling that." I sighed. "I don't care. As long as we can get away and just spend some time together, preferably alone."

"Megan?" Lindy said as she looked at the list again. When I looked up at her, she asked, "Do you want to abide by Manusia tradition of having someone walking you down the aisle."

I looked at them carefully. "I guess I could ask George to walk me down the aisle. I've been sort of thinking of breaking that tradition completely, though, and just walking it alone." Then I wondered, "Would Julian be mad if I don't have someone walk me down the aisle?"

They looked at each other. "No," they said in unison.

I blinked. "What?"

"Nalrin tradition is to walk down the aisle alone," Jean said carefully.

"Okay then. Easy answer to that one. Solo walk according to Nalrin tradition," I said, smiling.

CHAPTER 5

THE NEXT MORNING, I was running late. Really late. I should have been on the road back to Nalrin an hour ago, but the bed just seemed like a much better place to be. Just as I was getting ready to head out, a knock on the door made me jump out of my skin. I really must be out of it this morning. I always sense someone coming before they get here.

I felt out to get a sense of their ember and shook my head in the middle of the living room when I realized who it was. If anyone could sneak up on me, it was him.

"Ya know, Mickel, I'm perfectly capable of getting myself to Nalrin safely," I told the six-foot-four Guard who was standing there looking very smug. I eyed him carefully, then checked the clock. What time did he leave this morning? I looked back at his horse, and it was sweaty and needed to rest. I'd have to make sure that we got Owen's mare ready for him to use.

My eyes trailed over his face, and I noticed his light brown curly hair had fallen out of the tie in the back in places. It framed his green eyes and hit just above his strong jawline. "What time did you leave this morning?"

He shrugged and his broad tanned arms were crossed against his chest, making him look more like a mountain standing in front of me.

"I've been doing fine on my own for months. Now *he* decides you need to escort me to and from vocation?"

"That may be Lady Megan, but Julian's orders," he said, smiling and smirking at me.

"Who is at the door, Megan?" Clarice said as she walked into the living room wrapped in nothing but her towel.

"It's only Mickel," I told her over my shoulder, glaring at Mickel. He held my stare, and a corner of his mouth lifted. I shook my head. "Come on in and have a seat. I'll be just a couple of minutes."

When he got inside, he plopped down and leaned his head back in my favorite chair. I thought I saw Clarice blushing and hurrying back to her room, but there was no way. That can't be possible. Clarice doesn't get embarrassed.

"Um, I need to check on something in the other room," I told him over my shoulder as I headed to her room.

When I got there, I didn't even bother to knock. I just walked in. "What in the name of the Underworld, Clarice?"

I stopped when I looked at her face. She was actually blushing. Clarice was blushing.

"Do you know who that is in our living room?" she asked, utterly flustered.

"Ah. Yeah! I believe I even called him by his name. Julian is a little overprotective right now, so he sent Mickel to go back with me." Do I know who he is? GEESH! Does she think I'll just let any man walk into the living room?

"You said you had a personal bodyguard, but you didn't say it was Mickel de Seduisant! The most decorated and sexiest guard in all of Nalrin!" she said as she threw on some clothes.

"I'm sorry, what?" I asked, my temper rising quickly.

Lindy came bursting in. "Someone mind telling me what Mickel de Seduisant is doing sitting our living room... alone?"

"He's my bodyguard." I sighed. "and no, I didn't know that he was the most decorated guard in all of Nalrin."

It shouldn't surprise me, considering that the only reason I'm working in Nalrin is at Julian's insistence. Overprotective... Overbearing... I mentally grumbled several slurs at the thought.

"Umm, you forgot sexiest in that description," Clarice said as she put a hand on her hip. "Angels, the things I would do to that man." She slowly licked her lips, and the smirk and tone of her voice was leaving not much to the imagination.

"Oh, stop it, you two!" I said, looking between the two of them. Then I heard Owen in the living room. "Mickel! What are you doing here?!" Of course, the whole house was now going to be giving me crap.

"For Angels' sake!" I groaned as I stomped out of Clarice's bedroom. I could swear I heard Lindy say something about her guarding that body behind me. Those girls *really* needed to get laid. "Go see Logan, Lindy. Your horny is showing."

I stomped down the hallway and passed Jean's office just as she was coming out.

"What in the Angels is going on out here?"

"Everyone is in an uproar over my bodyguard," I huffed. She was right on my heels.

"Why is your bodyguard here?"

"Apparently, Julian thinks I can't get to Nalrin by myself, and so he sent Mickel to go with me. I mean, it's not like I haven't been going to Nalrin on my own for months already." I stepped into the living room, but Owen and Mickel weren't there. Checking the kitchen, they weren't there either. "Where did they go? I swear! If Owen thought he needed to create a shrine to him, I got two girls who would gladly help him. UGGG! I so need to make sure I get up on time if this is going to happen all the time."

"Wait," Jean said, grabbing my arm and stopping me. "Mickel? As in Mickel de Seduisant? He's here?"

I sagged my shoulders, put my hands over my face, and groaned again. "Not you too. He is just my bodyguard. You all knew that my bodyguard's name was Mickel. Why is everyone acting like this!?"

I think she just understood. "Oh! You think I'm all hot and bothered like Clarice and Lindy?!"

I eyed her carefully. "They were undressing him with their eyes, THROUGH THE WALLS! Then Owen was all excited to see him."

Jean laughed hysterically. "Oh, honey! Trust me, it isn't like that. Not at all! I hadn't realized you had been assigned *that* Mickel. It's a common enough name. I just didn't put it together. Come on, let's get Owen and Mickel. I have a feeling I know where they went."

We headed outside and, sure enough, they were in the garden. Only Owen had Mickel hanging upside down in the flowers, just as I had done to him almost a year ago. I couldn't help but laugh.

"Owen, put Mickel down!" Jean hollered. They both looked over at her, and Mickel fell to the ground with a thud.

"Ahh, the almighty fall!" Owen said, laughing.

"I'm so confused," I mumbled.

"I bet you are. Come on. This should be fun. I haven't seen Mickel in years." She laughed.

She walked over there, hands on her hips, and put on her best mad face. I knew she wasn't really, so I had to work hard to keep from laughing.

"Mickel... Anatole... de Seduisant! How dare you show up here like this!" she yelled at him.

As Mickel picked himself off the ground and looked at Owen, both of them had the same confused look on their faces. Lindy and Clarice were now standing at my sides, looking just as confused as I felt, so I just shrugged at them and turned my attention back to Jean.

"After all these years, you just show up! No call! No anything. Just walk on into my house, like it's no big deal, and disappear with Owen?! What the Underworld am I? Fucking chunk meat?!"

I could see Mickel trying not to laugh, but not one to be outdone, he said, "Well, what about you? You just ran off and ditched me in the lion's den?"

"The lion's den! Is that what you call it? That was your career choice."

He just looked at her pointedly with his arms crossed across his chest, making himself look that mountain again, and stared her down.

"Seems like you've made that lion's den work for you. Cushy little job of following my niece around."

"Cushy? Do you have any idea what a huge pain in the ass that niece of yours is? She just walks around from meeting to meeting," he said.

"Hey! I've told you plenty of times you don't need to follow me around!" I snapped back at him. "But, noo. You just said, *I have orders, Lady Megan,*" I said, trying to imitate his voice.

He was trying not to laugh and was pointedly avoiding looking at me, and just continued as if I hadn't said a word. "There is no one to fight. No one's ass to kick. No, Jean's to pick up and toss over my shoulder into the mud."

Owen and Mickel sputtered and burst into laughter. Mickel practically ran over to Jean and picked her up in a huge bear hug, swinging her around as she squealed in laughter. "Looks like you have been taking good care of her, Owen. Wouldn't want to have had to put you in line."

"Do you want me to put you back upside down again?" Owen said.

"Okay, someone care to explain things here?" I asked, looking between the three of them. "How do you know each other and why when I told you that Julian had assigned me a full-time bodyguard in Nalrin, even said his name was Mickel, you didn't tell me you know him?"

Jean and Owen looked at each other knowingly. It was Mickel that explained.

"Lady Megan, I have known Jean since before she had her Maltal. We grew up next to each other. My family used to have property about five miles from here. Not to mention that we have worked on a lot of missions for the Council in the past. Some fun. Some, not so much," he said as a few shadows crossed his face. His eyes had flickered to both of them quickly as he looked back to me.

"Oh, don't you, Lady Megan me," I said, doing my best impersonation. Just to make a point, I punched a small thread of my power at him, zapping him in the butt. He rubbed it, and then I continued, "You've been with me non-stop while I'm in Nalrin for months and months. Not once did you even mention that you knew them. I've talked about them loads of times. You've had the opportunity, Mickel."

I wasn't mad, just more annoyed than anything else. I stood there looking at each of them.

I tried to keep from smiling, especially since Mickel had blue pollen on the very tip of his nose and wasn't doing a thing to remove it.

"Mickel," I said, "we need to get on the road. That is, if you're done horsing around with Owen."

"As you wish, Lady Megan," Mickel said with a formal bow. I just rolled my eyes and went inside to grab my things for the week. When I got back outside, and we headed for the stables, I said, "Your horse is exhausted, so we will use either Jean or Owen's mare ready to take instead. You can get Damilea next time you're here."

I secured my bag as he prepped Owen's gray mare, Starstrike.

When he was done, I glared at him again. "Anything else you would like to tell me about my family and how you know them. Anything at all?"

"No, ma'am," he said with a huge smile.

"Wipe your hair and face off. You have pollen all over it still," I said, rolling my eyes. I swung myself up into the saddle as my mare pranced a moment. Mickel climbed into the saddle next to me and adjusted the reins. I glared at him once again and then put my heels to the mare's sides, chirped, and we took off.

Behind me, all I heard was, "Angels be Megan."

CHAPTER 6

APPARENTLY, JULIAN NEEDED TO see me this afternoon and sent a private ferry for Mickel and me ahead of the usual ferry schedule. So the fact I was running late already this morning would not win me any points with him.

When we got to the ferry, it took a few minutes for the men to get the horses settled. There were reporters and camera personnel who, immediately upon recognizing me, took out their cameras and started taking pictures of Mickel and I.

I sighed heavily, and Mickel gave me a look and said, "What did you expect?"

"It's getting worse by the day, though. Every time I make my way back, there is more and more media. Why can't they just leave me alone?" I grumbled, throwing my pack down onto the deck.

"They've been hunting for information on the wedding location too," Mickel said in a way that was more of a heads up than any kind of warning.

"Well, good thing we haven't decided where it's going to be then, right?" I said, smiling at him, and he just shook his head and smirked. "I'm going to go see how Madame Winters is doing."

"Lead the way, Lady Megan." Mickel nodded and followed me toward the tent as I dramatically rolled my eyes.

Last year, when my family had come through, she had given me the warning to follow the darkness, which ended up being super helpful in the end, but she had collapsed, and her ember flickered a lot. I've worried about her ever since, and she hadn't been here the last few times I'd been through.

When I started making the trip to and from Nalrin, I checked in on how she was doing with her granddaughter Coletta. Madame Winters had recovered a month later and now only comes once a month. I was hoping she had felt up to coming today. I've missed her. In the last few months, we have had long conversations while I waited for the ferry to arrive, and occasionally, when I knew she would be here, come early, just to spend that time with her.

I bounced into their tent and almost ran right into her granddaughter.

"Oh, I'm sorry, Coletta," I mumbled, and caught her by the shoulders to keep her from falling over.

"Megan! I wasn't expecting to see you so early today."

"Early? Underworld Coletta, I'm already over an hour behind schedule, but Julian sent Mickel."

"Mickel... Must want to see you quickly if he sent your bodyguard to meet you at the house instead of just here," she said, concern lining her face.

I just shrugged. "I only have a few minutes. He even sent a private ferry for us."

"She's in the back. She isn't doing very well and she shouldn't have come, but said she wanted to see you one last time. I don't think she will be able to make the trip anymore," Colletta said, heavy with meaning.

I nodded in understanding and went into the back.

"Madame Winters?"

"Ms. Megan. I didn't expect you until later."

"I'm running later than I had planned, but Julian needs to see me this afternoon. Besides, I thought you would've known exactly when I would arrive," I teased her as I sat down. Madame Winters could see things to happen, but in a very different way than I used to.

"I'm heading to the Angels, sweety. I'm not able to see things as I once did, but I saw something."

"Oh?! And what was that?" I purposely kept it light and carefree. I didn't want to wear her any more than the trip already was going to.

"I did." She sat up, put my hands in hers, and smiled. It was big and toothless on a worn and wrinkly face, but one of warmth and friendship. "I saw you with your very special Vernadali, who was kneeling in front of you."

I smiled and sighed contently at the thought. "Sounds wonderful."

"There's more though," she said, worry creeping into her tone. "As I said, he was kneeling in front of you so you were facing each other. I'm not sure where you were, though, but you were hand in hand, a sad smile on your face, and there was a bright light growing between the two of you that burst and pulsed in every direction. It was a very warm and powerful cleansing light."

I didn't know what to say.

"I don't know if it means anything to you. It took me two weeks to recover from seeing it."

"Oh, Madame Winters. I'm so sorry. You shouldn't waste your energy on me." I felt horrible that it took her so long to recover.

"Oh, don't you worry, child. I searched it out using rainroot," she said as if it was nothing at all.

"Your last one! Those are so rare." She had mentioned that she had one months ago. So for her to use it to look for something in CJ and I's future was a little shocking.

"Oh pfffff! I wanted to see if there was anything I could see to help before I left this world, since you aren't able to see right now. I'm not sure it is really helpful for what you're searching for, but I am taking it to mean that you and your Vernadali will be happy for many more years to come. That makes it worth using my last rainroot."

I searched her face for any trace of worry. She was still smiling, and her face still radiated the same warmth and love I have seen from her every month. It showed in her ember too. While it was weaker than the last time I saw her, I could see it was steady, and she wasn't hiding anything from me. She was truly happy.

"Lady Megan," Mickel called on the other side of the tent, "the ferry is ready when you are. I will wait out here with Ms. Colette."

"You should get going. Don't want to keep Mickel waiting too long," she said.

"I'm going to miss our talks, Madame Winters," I said, trying to hold back tears, and choking on a sob.

"Oh, dear. I'm nothing but an old woman. Don't waste your tears on me. Now, go. I'll watch over you with the Angels soon," she said and gave me a huge hug. I held her tight.

"All the same, I will miss them greatly. Thank you for everything," I said as a tear rolled down my cheek. She was so sure and comfortable with her upcoming death.

She smiled, wiped my tear away, and said, "No, thank you. Now, if you don't go, that ferryman is going to be very upset."

I turned and ducked under the tent flap, hugged Collette, and told her I would see her next week if she was here. She nodded, said that she planned on it, but warned me to be careful.

Mickel and I walked in silence to the ferry. Once we were on board, I turned to him and apologized for how I acted earlier.

"Megan. Please don't worry about it."

"I'm sorry, regardless. I'm not sure why I acted that way. It just kind of annoyed me that you guys all knew each other, but no one bothered to tell me. Not even Julian. Is there anything else you're keeping from me?"

"I'm sure there are plenty of things, but I am sorry if you feel like we betrayed you," he said.

I paused for a minute. I needed to make things right with him. He has been an amazing confidant for me while I'm in Nalrin. "It's just... I feel solely responsible for stopping the horrors that my family is inflicting upon this world."

"You shouldn't though."

"Well, no one else stepped up to the plate when Ansel and Symatha were trying to create the weapon. We were the only ones who even tried to do anything about it." I looked out and saw the Bluchree dancing in the ferry's wake. "Think about it. They left the world in the hands of someone who didn't even know this world existed until a couple of months before. Then they sent her off to face the people threatening to destroy it?"

A long silence stretched before us. He was just letting me rant. I sighed heavily before I continued, "To be honest, I'm not sure how I lived this long. I wouldn't be alive if I'd shown up and not met up with the family. I know I shouldn't bad mouth the council, but it seems like all they did was try to tighten up security and amp up their armies."

"And that they did." His voice was laced with annoyance as he continued, "The Curtails of the North showed a hand that others had not seen before. There is more of a military holding there than anyone knew. Not all Vernadali, but a military holding, nevertheless."

"Doesn't surprise me since they train all Vernadali."

"I suppose you're right," he said. "And for the record, you're privy to information that others in Nalrin only wish they could get their hands on. If information is being kept from you, then that information isn't getting to Julian. He tells you everything. I think he thinks of you as his own daughter."

"That would explain why he sent me you," I said, elbowing him. "The most decorated Nalrin Guard, and you get assigned to that same little girl. Don't give me compliments. I've heard it all before." I said, then continued in a whiney mocking tone, "You're so much more powerful than any other Sangra. You have an Angel blessed Vernadali to be assigned to you, which is the love of your life. Your conviction is stronger than anyone else in Nalrin."

He gave me a look and then rolled his eyes. "Megan."

"You know what conviction gets you? A one-way ticket in a pine box. That's what. I am serious when I say I'm shocked I haven't died yet. Angels, if I make it out of this without killing myself I'll be surprised." I turned to look at him, and he was trying so hard to keep from laughing. "It's all true anyway, and speaking of truths. Why didn't you tell me you were so decorated?"

He shrugged. "I've just done my job the best I know how. I don't care about being decorated. Sure, it has moved me up the ladder, and I get to work with the highest-ranking officials, but I've never wanted fame, fortune, or to have a bunch of medals that just collect dust and rust in a vault. I just want to do my job. To feel a sense of accomplishment. To feel like I'm doing something good with my life."

I could see he meant it. He shifted his weight awkwardly and wouldn't look at me. Add that to the list of reasons I liked him. He isn't in it to be known. He just wants to do what is right and to keep his Charge safe. I decided to just leave it at that and change the subject.

"So, what was Jean like as a kid?" I asked him.

"Feisty! Once those powers of hers came in, watch out! We used to practice with, well, I should say *on* each other," he said.

"Oh really? Do tell! I so need dirt on my aunt."

"Well, you're not going to get any from me. I will tell you she has always been a very honorable and powerful woman." Then he thought for a minute and continued, "Ok, so, one time she and I were out in the forest behind my parents' place. We took my sister's favorite doll and were making it grow as large as we could, then shrink it down to the size of a pebble, whenever she came out to look for it." His voice trailed off, and he giggled.

I could see that he cherished those memories. his expression changed, and there was sadness in his eyes. "Then there was the accident with her father."

"What happened?" I asked. "Symatha had told me to ask Jean about it, but I haven't been able to. Just seems like something that she wants left in the past now that Symatha is gone."

"I don't suppose she would want to talk about it, even if you asked. What happened, well, that depends. Jean's story? Symatha's story? Or for something completely different, do you want the official story?"

"There is that much discrepancy?"

"Sadly, there is. Basically, from what I gather, Symatha and Jean were practicing. Since Symatha was much older, her powers were more refined and stable. Jean's were not. Symatha cast something too strong for Jean to reflect, and her father stepped between them. The problem was he was holding an elixir that hadn't stabilized yet, and it blew up in his chest. It killed him instantly. Symatha and Jean never really got along, but Symatha thought Jean was holding back how much power she had and purposely reflected it, sending it flying into their father. Jean thinks Symatha was trying to hurt her, and their father died saving her."

"Which do you believe? Symatha's or Jean's?" I queried.

"I always have and will continue to side with Jean," Mickel said with conviction and earnest that only a loved one would receive. Right then, he betrayed himself, because he blushed hard when he realized just how he said that. It was more that blushing reaction that told me anything than what and how he said it. He could have easily flung it off as him treating her as a little sister, but that clearly wasn't the case.

"I see that," I said, smiling. When a concerned look crossed his face, I added, "Don't worry, secret is safe with me."

We looked out over the harbor as the ferry was waiting for its turn to come into Nalrin Harbor.

After a few moments, he said with his voice low, "I would appreciate it. I have always loved her. I just wasn't even on her radar. For her, it has always been Owen."

"I... I don't know what to say."

"Don't worry about it. I have come to terms with it." I studied him, looking for the sincerity in that statement, when he added, "No, really. I rather have her in my life as a very dear and close friend than not at all; besides, Owen is very good to her. Owen is my brother in every sense of the word. I would go through hell for him. Have been through hell for *both* of them, and I would do it all again to keep them safe."

I nodded.

"Megan," he turned me to face him, "I'm very serious about this. It is good between us. I've had relationships. They were fun, but nothing held my interest. It isn't that I'm holding out hope for her. I just have never felt like I have when I'm around her or think of her," he said softly.

"You know that every time you fall in love, it won't be like her, right? No one will feel the way it does with Jean. It's different dynamics, different history, or non-history. Maybe that's what you need is some non-history." He looked at me for a long moment before I asked, "Does she know?"

"I don't know. I think she knew at one point when we were teenagers, but at this point in our lives, I don't think she knows that I still do. I would rather keep it that way." Even though his voice wasn't pleading, I could see in his eyes how important it was for him she never knows. "Please promise me."

"Mickel, I am probably the one person who understands how you feel more than anyone. There was a time, not that long ago, when CJ and I were just friends, the best of friends. I truly believed that having him in my life was more important than taking that step. I promise I will never say anything."

"So how did you two become who you are now, then?"

"He ambushed me over pizza." I smiled at the memory. "He was so nervous. I thought he was going to tell me he had cancer, or his parents were dying, or Logan was dying. Instead, he looked at me, took a shot of courage and said, that we had been friends for a really long time, we did everything together, that we got along so well, blah blah blah, then asked why we had never gone on a date?"

"And that was that?"

"Not exactly." I laughed. "I was in such shock I asked him if he was fucking with me. I had honestly thought he only thought of me as a little sister. I never imagined that he would actually care for me the way I cared for him. Then we went out on one single date. When we sat by the beach, he slipped up and told me he loved me. That same night, everything, and I mean everything in our lives, changed. The rest is literally, Nalrin history."

He just stared at me.

"What?"

"Just like that?" he said, laughing in astonishment.

"Just like that. If you want to call it that. So, as I said, your secret is safe with me. We never had this conversation."

"Thank you," he said, still shaking his head. "Can I ask you something else?"

"Anything. I told you months ago that if Julian was going to have you shadowing me, that there has to be total trust between us."

"I remember, but it's not like that."

"Ok, what is it?" Now I was totally intrigued. The ferry was settling into the dock now, and we headed back to get our packs.

"How and when did Owen learn to flip and dunk people into flowers for enjoyment?" he asked with a smile on his face.

"Guilty," I said, pointing to myself and laughing.

"Seriously! You taught him to do that? Why on earth would you do that! I'll be sneezing pollen out of my sinuses for a month."

"I didn't directly teach him to do it. I did it to him last year when I was training for my exams. He must have been practicing, which is good to know. You know that man holds a grudge."

"Oh, yeah, he does," he said as we stepped off the dock and headed to the train to take us to Nalrin Center.

It sounded like there was another story there, but I thought he had said enough for one day. "Remind me to ask you later what you did to deserve that one."

"Oh, I'll tell you now. I dunked him in a bath of rotting fish three nights before he and Jean got married," he said, letting out a huge belly laugh. "I don't think I will ever get paid back enough for that one."

I laughed. "Oh no, I imagine you won't. Good luck surviving that one."

CHAPTER 7

WHEN WE GOT TO Nalrin Center, there were more guards than usual at the checkpoint. I handed them my bag and identification card, which allowed me to be pushed through security without so much as a pat-down, but they told me that today, everyone was being put through normally. This did not make Mickel happy, but I assured him they were only following orders. When Mickel opened his mouth to object, I gave him a pointed look, and he gave me one back that clearly said that he was their supervisor and shouldn't be subjected to this. After a momentary silent conversation between the two of us, he sighed and went through the motions.

"Sorry, Lady Megan," the guard who cleared us said. "Security has been increased. If you have been beyond the second wall, we are required to do a full security check. We are pushing back any media that is here." The Guard jerked his head toward the throng of reporters, and I wrinkled my nose in disgust.

"No problem," I said, as I took my bag from him. The media had clearly worked out how often I was coming to Nalrin, or there was a leak in Julian's office which let them know when Julian needed me there.

I turned and faced Mickel, who was double-checking the contents of his pack. He hated people going through his things, which was ironic considering that he will be the first to rifle through your bags if he thinks you're a threat to his assignment.

"Lady Megan! Lady Megan!" I turned to see a Council runner sprinting towards me, which immediately put Mickel on alert, and he dropped his bag to stand in front of me. Sometimes I forgot how fast he could be and how big of a presence he can create when he needs to. The runner skidded to a halt just in time to keep from running full bore into Mickel.

"Lady Megan, a message from Head Julian," he announced, holding it out for me, but Mickel took it and dismissed the runner.

As he hands me the message, I told him, "You didn't need to cut him off. It's the same runner that always delivers Julian's messages to me."

"Sorry, Lady Megan."

"So, we are back to formals?" I teased him.

"We are back in Nalrin and in public. And since we never had those previous conversations..." He eyed me with a smile on his face.

"What conversations?" I laughed.

"The extra security is just putting me on edge," he said formally when a group of five guards walked by us. "What does Head Julian want?"

I open the note and sighed, "I am not going to my residence first. Julian wants to see me immediately. Maybe he will tell me what all this is about." I tipped my head to security and headed for the Chambers building.

"I'll take your stuff to the residence building and meet you at Julian's office. They gave you back your syth's, right?" Mickel said, taking my bag.

"Yup," I answered, patting my thigh. I felt bare without them here, well, anytime I'm not at home. "See you in a few."

He nodded and took off.

Every time I came to Nalrin, I was always amazed at the beauty of the buildings. I had admired the ancient Greek buildings back in the Manusia, and the architecture in the city center was very much the same. I couldn't help but run my hand along the stone as I walked past. If it were not for all the politics and the fact there were so many people, I could see living in a city like this.

When I got to the fountains, the water displays weren't running, but maybe later tonight I could sneak out and get lost in the movements. They were so mesmerizing at night. The way the moons reflected off the water with the lights and movement...

There was just something so peaceful about them. The reflections so clear that the gentle ripples from the breeze today the only evidence that they weren't really mirrored.

I heard a commotion behind me. People running against the cobblestone courtyard. As I turned, I saw Mickel and, shit. I hadn't noticed how much time had passed. I got up and turned toward him. I must have zoned out.

"Meg... Lady Megan. You were to meet me at Head Julian's office immediately."

"I'm sorry, Mickel. I zoned out," I apologized.

"When Head Julian's guards said you hadn't shown up yet—" he stopped and tried to make his voice more professional around the other two guards he had brought with him. "Well, you're safe. Let's go."

I had worried him, and he wasn't supposed to show emotional attachment to his assignment. Which I thought was a bit of a silly rule, considering if you're going to be watching over someone for as long as he has been, how are you not supposed to worry about that person? "Can you two give me and Mickel a moment, please?" I asked the extra guards.

"I'm sorry I worried you," I said, just loud enough for him to hear.

"You're my charge, Lady Megan."

"This isn't a Lady Megan conversation, Mickel." I eyed him, hoping he understood my meaning. "I'm just saying I'm sorry that I got lost in the water and didn't realize how much time had passed."

"I was running later than I intended as well. I dropped our bags off in our residences, and then I think I was purposely delayed on the way to Julian's office. So, when I got there, and you weren't there..." He looked over his shoulder and dropped his voice, "Yes, I was worried that something had happened. Rumors are swelling about Ansel, but no one knows where he is. I'll let Julian explain."

We rushed to Julian's office, where he knocked and announced my arrival. That was something that I still have not gotten used to. Someone is only announced when they are someone of importance. A Queen, King, President, Julian, you know, someone important. I sighed and went in.

Julian was sitting on the couch, but got up and gave me a warm, welcoming hug when he saw me. "Megan. How was your travel?"

"Fine as usual. Though, was it really necessary to send Mickel?" I said, putting just a tad sass in my tone.

"I thought you could use the company. It's a long and lonely way to come by yourself."

"Julian," I drew out his name.

"What?"

"So, sending Mickel has nothing to do with all the extra security and the deliberate delaying of Mickel from the residential building to your office?"

"Mickel was deliberately delayed?" He looked at Mickel, who just nodded. "Hmmm."

I waited a moment to let him think, but I've never been one to be patient if I don't have to be. "Julian, are you going to tell me what's going on?"

"Have a seat, please."

My heart started raced.

My breathing picked up, my power starting to tingle in anticipation at the thought. CJ... I haven't heard from him in a little over a month—OH ANGELS, what happened to CJ? I took a second to take a deep breath and tried to center my power. Then, before I could chicken out, I blurted, "Did something happen to CJ?"

He giggled. "No. Nothing at all. He is progressing very well in the Curtails of the North and should be home in plenty of time for your July 2nd wedding."

"Thank the Angels. Julian, you can't scare me like that!"

"I'm sorry, my dear," he said lightly.

"Speaking of the wedding. You will officiate it, right?"

"Are you finally formally asking?"

"Sorry," I stood up, and as I formally bowed, I continued, "Julian, would you do CJ and I the honor of officiating our wedding on July 2nd?"

I could hear Mickel snicker and try not to bust up laughing. I looked at him sideways, and he straightened up.

"First of all, what did I tell you about bowing to me. Second, of course. It has been on my calendar since you set the date," he said, laughing.

"Then why?"

"Why did I ask if you were formally asking? Because I felt like giving you a hard time."

"Jerk," I said lightly and sat back down, much more relaxed now that I knew CJ was okay. "So, what pray tell, is going on that you needed to see me before tomorrow morning?"

"As you know, we have been keeping our ears open, so we can get an idea of what Ansel is going to do next." I nodded, and he continued, "We don't know what he's doing, but there have been rumors of him hiring assassins and paying people off for information on exactly where you are."

"He is out to get me for killing my mother. Though it's not that hard to find me. I would think it would be obvious where I am. I'm not exactly hiding." I sighed. "I don't know why he can't just disown me and forget I ever existed. That's what I want to do.

Just forget he existed, and move on to live a happy, quiet life with CJ."

"There is more," he said quietly. I could see Mickel perk up a little by the door out of the corner of my eye. "The Ash'bani Head and Take Over were assassinated."

"Chyss and Zamph are dead?" I asked.

"They are. I'm surprised by your reaction. You didn't like them, and since they thought you were the plague bringer to the Ash'bani race, I would think you would be ok with it."

"I'm never ok with someone being assassinated," I told him sternly. "Just because I don't like someone, doesn't mean I wish them serious ill will or harm. A cold that lays them out for days, the raging shits in the middle of rush hour traffic, or a thousand plagues upon their privates... sure, but never assassination or serious harm."

"Never?" Julian said pointedly.

"My parents?" I asked. "You're asking if I'm okay with someone assassinating my parents?"

He raised his eyebrows at me and said, "Aren't you assassinating your parents? In a manner of speaking?"

"First of all, when I went into Noctulanar Castle, there were two objectives: get CJ before my parents killed him, and stop them from creating the weapon, which, if the first one was done... domino effect," I said smiling. "Now, I am trying to stop Ansel from killing everyone. I had no intention of Symatha dying at Noctulanar Castle. I have no intention of killing Ansel either. We don't even know what his next move is. I don't want him dead. Just stopped."

"What if killing Ansel is the only way to stop him?" Julian asked. He didn't say it in a judgmental way, just straightforward. It wasn't something I had to give serious consideration to, but if I were honest...

"Again, I don't want him dead," I said carefully, and he raised an eyebrow. "If killing him was the only way to stop him from destroying an entire world? I don't know. Sure, it might have to be done, but even if that's the case, I don't think I'd be 'okay' with it."

"Fair and true. Now, back to the matter at hand." Julian reached down and looked for a file on his desk and opened it. "There are replacements nominated for the Ash'bani Head and TakeOver. The territory vote produced five candidates. I need you to do their background checks and see what you can find before tomorrow mid-day when they are supposed to arrive. Then we can do clinicals and I can make my decision."

"Mid-day tomorrow? On a full-scale background check?" Was he nuts?! A full-scale background check like that would usually take me over a day!

"You're the best," he said encouragingly and smiled.

I just sighed and put my hand out for the files. "Ok, hand them over. I'll get started right after I go drop off some paperwork at the Transportation Bureau."

"Who for?" he asked.

"CJ's parents, brother, and Amber, all from the Manusia."

"Can they be trusted to keep our world a secret from the humans? We work so much in that dimension, that we can't afford for what the humans would call a witch hunt, which ironically would not be good for the witches who do in fact, deal in the Manusia. There is a reason we try to keep the same calendar as the Manusia you know," he said, smiling.

"I wouldn't submit the paperwork if I didn't think I could trust them. Don't you trust me?" I gave him a sly smile. I knew he did. He had told me that repeatedly.

"Of course I do," he said to me and then turned to Mickel. "Mickel have those documents brought from Megan's residence to me. I'll approve them all for immediate use, with a binder on them."

"A binder? Which one?" I asked hesitantly. Sure, I trusted they wouldn't say a word, but was a binder necessary?

"A silence binder," Julian said carefully. That made me feel better. It just meant they wouldn't be able to speak about it to anyone who didn't already know about Nalrin or the Nalsar dimension. Julian broke through my thoughts and continued, "In fact, have a Lark Messenger sent to Jean and Owen advising them of the approval and advise our associates in Manusia know."

"Sir, I'd like to take Lindy with me to get Annie, Logan, and Amber when I get back this weekend. I was thinking of bringing Lindy, Jean, Annie, and Amber to Nalrin next week to do some planning and shopping."

"Very well," he said, as a mischievous smile crossed his face. "You can head back immediately after the background checks are completed, and you have delivered your results."

"You..." I started to say, but as he raised an eyebrow, I shook my head and stood up. "I will be in my residence if you need me. Going to be a full pot of coffee night tonight."

I started to head out, and just as Mickel opened the door for me, Julian said, "Oh, and Mickel will be with you around the clock until further notice. When you're done with the background checks, Hurgo said she got your test results back."

"Did she say she found anything?" I queried hopefully. He knew how to hide news. Sneaking in that I was stuck with Mickel the entire time, then telling me that the Head Physician had news about my brain scans. Sneaky bastard.

"No, just that when you had completed your tasks for me, to send you her way," he said, already turning his attention to the next thing on his calendar.

"Okay, I'll see her," I said, a little deflated, and headed to my residence.

Hurgo, the Head Physician in Nalrin, and I had been doing test after test after test, trying to figure out why I hadn't had any visions. So far, nothing had come up. The last time I was here, I had my brain mapped, and they were going to send it to the 3D room to look at it more closely. It felt a little weird knowing that people were standing in a room with a 3D projection of my brain before them. To be honest, I wasn't sure they just didn't want to try out their new toy. But then again, if it was a chance at answers, I'd take it.

CHAPTER 8

WHEN I GOT TO my room, I set up my desk and called the kitchen to have some food sent up. I was lucky I had access to an actual computer. Technology in this realm was reserved only for health officials and record keeping. Julian had... Well, he's Julian. He ordered a laptop be delivered to my residence, and it happened. When they delivered it, I explained to them I'd been working with computers my whole life. It's the only way I know how to do anything. I practically had to sign away my first born's first born to keep it here permanently. Nevertheless, I had one and could do my vocation.

After much discussion regarding Julian's orders for Mickel to basically never leave my side, I ordered Mickel to go to bed.

"I'll be up most of the night going through this," I said, shaking the file that Julian had given me. "Seriously. Go. To. Bed."

"Fine. I'll grab a pillow and blanket and sleep on the couch," he said, making his way to the closet next to the bedroom.

"No. Go to your residence, which is only next door, and get some solid sleep," I ordered.

"But—" he tried to say.

"No buts! You have been going since before sunup. So get some sleep. You will be out in point two seconds, and next thing you know, it will be morning, and you can do all that body guarding stuff," I said, mocking him as he narrowed his eyes at me. "Seriously. Go. You'll know if I need help."

He shook his head and said, "Thank you."

"Good night, Mickel," I said, pushing him out of the room and closing the door. He looked exhausted. When Julian had initially assigned him to me, I fought it, but Julian was right about one thing. Having Mickel around didn't make things so lonely.

After I ate, I got to work. There were five candidates being considered for the Ash'bani leadership position. I ran them each through the Nalrin security systems and could throw one out immediately. How was she even able to make it this far in the nominations? There is no way she should have even been on this list. There were rules and guidelines as to who could be the representatives.

The rules were strange. You can't be a representative if there was a dead-end in your family tree anymore recent than five generations back. All five generations had to be born in Nalsar. No skips, no less. Experience told me it usually meant that they had just moved to this dimension from another realm, or more likely, that there was criminal history and the person was erased. I found it unfair and ridiculous that you were immediately disqualified for criminal history in the family line.

Is it their fault if their Great Great Grandfather was Jeffrey Dahammer? No, it isn't, but those are the rules in place. At least it cut the numbers down on potentials. Since that was the first check I did, it meant I didn't have to dig any further on her, thus saving me some time.

By about five the next morning, I had culled the number of five potentials down to three. The last one I ruled out had some sketchy bank records, so I crossed him off the list. In the last three, I started running through an algorithm that I had one of the technology vocation supervisors create to itemize out their political agendas. Based on past decisions, friends, family, known life experiences, it wasn't a foolproof way to determine what someone may decide to do in the future, but it was a computerized estimate of what that person's decision could be. There were thousands of questions in the system that had to be computed. If the computer could feedback a likely answer quickly, it usually meant they weren't swayed by influence and made decisions more so on what they believed. If the computer couldn't make a determination, it may mean that they haven't been consistent in their decisions and may be more apt to be corrupted or bought out for their vote. Yes, it could place only those with certain decision tendencies on the Council, but since I'm the only one with access to it, I would deal with that later down the line when I trained a replacement. Besides, I only have to give my recommendations. It's ultimately Julian's decision.

Since the process usually took a few hours, and there were three of them, I lay downed for some sleep.

CHAPTER 9

I WOKE SITTING STRAIGHT up, my scream still in the air. Mickel barreled in before I was totally awake in his sleeping shorts, hair in every direction, sword in hand.

"Lady Megan!"

"I'm fine. Bad dream." I looked at him, rubbed the sleep from my face, and chuckled at him. "Get dressed. I'll be ready in a bit."

He blushed, realizing how little he was wearing. "Yes. Of course," he said, stammering as he bowed out of the room.

I shook my head, trying to shake the dream. I had been pulled toward the edge of a cliff by a chain wrapped around my waist. No matter how much I fought it, I kept sliding toward the edge. With every inch, my head felt heavier, like it had last year while I was in the hospital after Noctulanar Castle. What was worse was that when I got to the edge, I saw Ansel pulling on the chain, and with a final tug, he pulled me over the cliff and into the black abyss. The falling was what had actually woken me up. It was just a bad dream.

I flopped back onto the bed.

It had felt so real. If I had any inkling that it could have been a vision, I would have been worried. Hell, I still hadn't had one! I was *really* looking forward to being able to talk to Hurgo about it this afternoon. Since I was little, I had visions. I had gotten so used to them. So, while it was weird not to have any, it was a nice reprieve.

Damn, it sounded like I couldn't decide if I want them or not. They come in handy, and yes, I probably relied on them too much, but it was nice to finish a sentence without having to pause because my mind and eyes had gone somewhere else.

I threw the blankets back and got up, stumbling for the kitchen. For the Angels sake! I felt like I'd been drinking all night. I took a glass from the cupboard, turned the handle to the sink, and filled the glass.

Looking out at my home here in Nalrin, the 900 square feet of residence was slowly becoming my own. Over the last few months, I had been decorating it and replacing the furniture with more comfortable pieces. My one statement piece was the bright teal couch that had a pull-out bed in the living room with big oversized light gray chairs next to it for when my family was here. I had lots of natural light because of the large windows on the other side of the living room, which was open to the kitchen. I also got three white and teal bar stools that matched the couch to line the counter to the kitchen. I loved the large open space. I was spending just as much time here as I was at the house, that this was feeling like home as well.

Three flittering chimes came from my laptop, which was set up next to the floor-to-ceiling doors that opened out to the balcony. The windows and balcony were probably my favorite thing about the residence. They made the space look much larger than it was.

The last candidate had just finished up, and I sent them to the printer. I looked at the clock and was surprised it was only 10 in the morning. I still had eight hours before mid-day, when these had to be turned in. I guess Julian was right; I am the best.

"I just don't have to sleep, and I can meet his deadline!" I said mocking.

I reviewed the results and was surprised that most of the decisions could be answered in about the same time for each candidate. There, in one of the candidates, some answers contradicted each other. I reviewed the others in more detail and reviewed the work I had done the night before, writing up my recommendations. I didn't know any of the candidates personally, so it made it hard for me not to think which one might give me some answers about my father. I pushed the thoughts from my head and printed the document.

I went down the hall, jumped in the shower, and by the time I was out and dressed, Mickel was knocking on the door.

"You have perfect timing," I told him as I opened the door.

"I heard you get out of the shower, so it was easy to time," he said lightly. "Oh, wait, I'm working. I mean, that's my job, Lady Megan."

I just shook my head and went to take the reports off the printer. The shower helped, but I still felt like a mule had kicked me. I read through my report and recommendations again, because well, I felt like shit. It would not be good to have a ton of typos and accidentally recommend the wrong person because I hadn't slept.

"Thank you for coming to my aid earlier," I said, signing the bottom of the page and putting it in the file.

"Lady Megan, it's what I do."

"I didn't realize you were so fast. Will CJ be that fast?"

He grinned. "Faster."

I smiled back, and his expression was different this morning. More reserved. "Did I push you too far on the ferry?"

"No. You just caught me off guard, is all. No one had ever figured it out, or at least I don't think they had. I don't know. Maybe they did and just didn't say anything. Let alone so quickly." He was fiddling with the buttons on his jacket—such a typical male. Super macho and ready to jump in front of a bullet for you, but they get all fidgety and uncomfortable when you mention feelings.

"Well, I like not having to be perfectly formal with you all the time." I stopped when I realized how much of a come on that sounded. "I mean, since we have been working together for so long now... I mean, you have been thrown into my crazy life, and I am just not a formal person. I feel like in the last few months we have gotten very close. I mean... UGGG!" Why does everything I say sound like I'm flirting with him! I blame Clarice and Lindy.

"I know what you mean. Don't worry," Mickel laughed, and then he surprised me by pulling me into a big bear hug. "Megan, in my mind, you're part of my family. So are Jean and Owen. It is just that my job requires me to keep a distance emotionally. That's very hard for me to do, considering my history with your family."

"I know that. Do you want to ask for another assignment? I understand if you do," I asked him, hoping he wouldn't take me up on it.

"Yeah, you will have another bodyguard over my dead body!"

"CJ may have something to say about that," I teased him.

"Well, he is your Vernadali and soon your husband. I'm your bodyguard. While their job descriptions are similar, I think he has rights to guard your body in ways that I just wouldn't feel comfortable with," he teased back.

"Agreed!" I said as we headed to the kitchens to grab something to eat.

CHAPTER 10

"OHHH, CHILDAR EGGS! I haven't had those in ages!" I said as I grabbed a big spoonful of the bright blue scrambled eggs, along with the bagel-like bread and orange juice.

The kitchens were mostly empty, except for a few workers and guards. Mickel sat down across from me and we ate in silence until one of the guards came over and whispered something in Mickel's ear that made him smile from ear to ear. Then he looked at me and thought for a moment.

"Spill it Mickel," I demanded.

"No way," he said, trying to rearrange his face as professionally as he could.

I picked up a spoon full of eggs and aimed it right at him. "Tell me, Mickel, or you're going to be wearing childar," I warned.

"Okay, Okay. I give. I give. That was Remie, and he just came from the Curtails of the North." I instantly became more attentive. "He said that soon-be husband of yours can kick some serious ass and that if I was going to stay your bodyguard, I would need to brush up on my skills."

"Is that so?" I couldn't help but swell with pride. Of course, it wasn't much, but it made me feel so much better hearing something about how he was doing.

"Hey, Remie!" I shouted and waved him back over.

"Yes, Lady Megan," he said, bowing formally. I made a face. I still hadn't gotten used to everyone bowing at me like I was some kind of royalty. And Lady. I hated Julian for giving me that title.

"So, you saw CJ?"

"I did ma'am. I like him," he said with a smile. "That boy can fight."

I smiled from ear to ear, but Remie's head ducked a little lower. "What happened?"

"Some of the other guards and I had overheard them talking about you and your parents. When Vernadali CJ found out, he did the responsible thing by waiting to kick their ass during practice so he wouldn't get into trouble. He wants to get home," Remie said respectfully.

"Wait, they were talking about me?" I felt deflated and small. Must have been pretty bad if CJ went ballistic like that.

He nodded, hesitated, and waited for Mickel's approval before continuing. "They were talking about how much you must be a screw-up coming from parents like that. The guards know better, though. We saw you last year when you were here in front of the Council. The way you stood up to the Council and what you did against your parents. After that, there is no way that you could be messed up."

I didn't know what to feel. Anger because people assumed I'm a mental case, or pride knowing that the guards think so highly of me. Just above a whisper, I asked, "How did CJ find out about it?"

"He walked around the corner when they were talking, and one of them said something expressly inappropriate for me to repeat. I think that if Vernadali Brennen, his team leader, hadn't just walked around the corner at the other end of the hall, he would've killed them right where they stood. I hadn't seen CJ that mad the whole time I was stationed there."

I knew how he could get. He had a tendency to be overprotective of me. I put my head down and played with my eggs. CJ shouldn't have to deal with this shit. Because of me, his whole life has changed 500%, and now he has to deal with that?

"Lady Megan." he leaned down on the table.

"Yeah," I mumbled, still playing with my eggs.

"Don't worry about it. After that particular practice, there isn't a person in that compound that's going to mess with you or CJ. I'm not kidding when I say that boy has skills. They would be impressive if he were Sangra, the fact he is human, Angel blessed, or not." He whistled, "He just might put Mickel here out of a job."

"Thanks, Remie," Mickel said, and Remi headed back out of the room.

When I didn't say anything, Mickel looked at me and said, "Look, I know what you're thinking. That CJ getting in that fight is all your fault and that if it weren't for you, none of this would be going on, right?"

I nodded. It's amazing how well he knew me in such a short period of time. "CJ should only have to think about training up there. Not standing up for me too." I sighed and pushed my tray away, having lost my appetite. "But... I'm not sorry Ceej kicked their asses. I am thankful for some news on what is going on up there."

Mickel just nodded, and I waited while he finished his breakfast in silence.

CHAPTER 11

WHEN WE GOT TO Julian's door, eight additional guards were standing outside. Mickel and I looked at each other with silent questions written all over our faces. When we got closer, Mickel looked at me and moved to walk in front of me.

"Lady Megan Keller is here to see Head Julian," he said when we got to the doors.

"I'm sorry, Mickel. Head Julian is not available," one of the non-regular guards said.

"He will see me," I said, stepping out from behind Mickel. When they saw me standing there, it was like they had seen a ghost. Not one of them said a word. "Mickel, can you please move these gentlemen aside so we can go in?"

"Lady Megan. There are potential diplomats in there. We are not to admit anyone," the blond guard said.

"The potential Ash'bani diplomats that I have just spent the last 16 hours doing background checks on and getting next to no sleep to complete? Those potential diplomats?" I said, trying to sound nice, but all it did was come off snarky. I *really* needed some sleep.

"As you wish, Lady Megan," the blond guard said, and opened the door.

There were five Ash'bani standing across from Julian when we walked in, all wearing long black robes with long purple corded necklaces with a medallion at the end resting just above their navel and a cloche style hat. All who, when I walked in, focused their large eyes on me, freezing me in place.

Five versions of my father stood before me.

It took every ounce of restraint to keep from going for my syths. I felt Mickel put his hand on my shoulder, tight and alert. I took a half step back and bumped into Mickel, standing there solid as a wall. My power coiled faster in its cocoon, and my heart raced.

I blinked again, but five versions of my father still stood there.

Five versions of my father smiling wickedly at me.

My reaction had set Mickel off, and he was in bodyguard mode. "You okay?"

I didn't say anything. As I looked at them, each of my father's smiles spread into wide grimaces. Each one showing way too many teeth and eyes filled with hatred and loathing. Mickel squeezed harder on my shoulder.

It's not Ansel.

There cannot be five Ansel's standing in front of me.

It is not Ansel.

It is *not* Ansel.

I blinked, shook my head, and slowly the five versions of my father faded away, becoming the faces of the five potential diplomats that I had been researching.

"Ahh, Lady Megan," Julian said, covering my discomfort.

"Good day, Head Julian," I said, trying to keep my momentary fear out of my voice as I formally bowed. He wouldn't object here in front of dignitaries.

He smiled a knowing smile as I stood up. "Do you have the research and declaration completed?"

"I do," I put my professional big girl voice on.

"And your results? Are all five fit for duty?"

"No, Head Julian," I told him, and as I did, all five of the dignitaries got very stiff. I didn't like this part of my job. Giving the results of my research. They wondered which ones would be dismissed immediately and which ones would be allowed to proceed to clinicals. They had come such a long way from home, and I wished I could have done the background checks before they had made the trip. I sighed and continued. "Elden Hite and Gertl Perok'o do not meet all the preliminary requirements for service."

I saw the tallest on the end, and the one in the middle right, step back and stride out of the room. The three left standing adjusted, so they stood shoulder to shoulder, and I continued, "As'nal, Tarol, and Titus. You are hereby directed to report to the Nalrin Diplomat Center for full Physicals and Psychological testing by the end of the week. Head Julian will have decisions one week before the next council meeting in one month where you will need to bring yourselves up-to-date on current matters and be ready for said meeting. You are excused."

I turned to Julian, who smiled proudly. I sighed and rolled my eyes as they walked out the door. "You know I hate doing that."

"I do, but you do it so well," he said, trying to comfort me.

"I walk in, some pathetic girl who does a computerized background check on them and dashes their dreams of being a leader. I don't like it," I told him.

"This appointment is significant, though. They're replacing assassinated predecessors, and more importantly, they're of the race, where you need their cooperation."

"Oh no, Julian. You're handling all the political crap. How many times do I have to remind you of me mouthing off to the Council last year?"

"You've grown so much since then," he said lovingly, with a smirk on his face. "Don't you have a legal studies degree in the Manusia?"

"Yes, but that doesn't mean politics. It's reading laws, interpreting them, and defending my client in court. Well, at least that's what would've happened if I had stayed there."

"Many of those skills translate into the position you currently hold. It means you can help write the laws here. You can make a difference."

"Doesn't change my feelings about politics any. That's kissing ass and being in the right person's pocket," I said, glaring at him.

"So be a broker for change, Megan," Julian said, standing tall. It was more of a command than anything, and the presence this five-foot man gave still astounded me.

"I'll always be the little girl who just found out about this world and made friends with the Council Head to get a leap ahead in life. No one will listen to me," I begged him to understand. "Besides, that isn't what I want. You know that."

"You just want to have a peaceful, quiet life. I know, I know. You've reminded me plenty of times," he said, grinning from ear to ear. I thought I heard Mickel giggle behind me.

"And I will keep reminding both of you until you get it through those skulls of yours," I said with laugher in my voice. "Is there anything else you need, Julian?"

"In such a hurry to get home?"

"Well, I need to stop by and see Horan, but, yes, yes, I am. Lindy so very kindly reminded me we only have two months to the wedding, and then she brought Jean in to explain just how much I have been slacking in that department." I pinched the bridge of my nose and sighed.

"Why have you been putting it off to the last minute?" Julian asked.

"It just doesn't feel right planning for CJ and I's wedding when he isn't here to give input on it. However, I've put it off long enough, and since I don't know when he will be home and for how long before the date, we need to get it done," I said.

Julian smiled warmly at me. "Go. I'll see you soon."

"Does poor Mickel have to travel with me?" I asked hopefully so that Mickel could have some time off.

"Megan, I'm not budging on this." His voice was soft but strong.

"Ok. Fine, but I have been making these trips on my own, you know, for months," I tried to fight back, just a little.

"Megan." He sounded just like a father asking his kid to stop trying his patience.

"Yes, Julian. Mickel will join me in my travels. He can stay here in Nalsar, right? He doesn't need to go to Manusia with me, does he?" I turned to Mickel, "No offense."

Mickel just laughed. "Oh no. I understand completely, Lady Megan."

"I'm not budging," he said, standing tall, like he, in fact, wouldn't be budged from that spot.

I just stared at him, eyes narrowing. I knew how much to push him. I already toed the line. I sighed and said, "Fine. I was just trying to give poor Mickel a break."

"Here are your identification cards giving Annie, George, Logan, and Amber free access to Nalsar," he said as I took the passes from him. "Now, go see Horan."

"Thanks," I said, practically skipping out the door. I couldn't wait to see what Horan found out. I heard Julian chuckle as Mickel closed the door behind me.

CHAPTER 12

"Okay, Megan. All loaded," Horan said.

We walked through the double doors, and once they were shut, a 3D projection of my brain appeared in the room. There were three other doctors in the room looking through their charts and adjusting the view of what was before us.

"I'm not a scientist, let alone a doctor. I have no idea what I'm looking at other than it looks like the picture of a brain in a book," I finally told her.

"Right, sorry. We have reviewed the documents from the Manusia doctors and their films from your various scans there. Your brain wave patterns have completely returned to normal, well, as normal as they were. They were never the same as a humans, because you aren't one. They are more in line with Sangra, but there are differences."

"Differences? How so?" I asked.

"They... I can't explain it. They're just different from any being in Nalsar." I could tell she was uncomfortable not having the answer, so I let it drop and let her continue, "Anyway, when we compared them to the records from when you were at the hospital after the explosion, to the ones we have taken here... Well, here, let me show you."

She walked over to one of the other doctors and adjusted the model in front of us with the wave of her hands on the screen to show one particular area. "See, this part of the brain here is part of your subconscious, and here is what it looked like when you were in the Manusian hospital after your parents faked their death."

She walked into the projection and pointed and outlined the area. "See how it is slightly darker than the rest of the brain?"

"Yes," I said hesitantly.

She took the tablet from the doctor again, and the room projected four pictures. "The top two are from the Manusia. The bottom two from here in Nalrin. The ones on the left are from just after your accident when you were in a coma. The ones on the right are six months after you woke up. What do you see?"

"The ones on the left look identical."

"Yes, that is correct, with one small exception. The one on the bottom is slightly larger."

"The ones on the right, they look similar too, but the one from when I was in a coma here, it is slightly larger and this time darker," I said in understanding.

"Correct. Basically, all this tells us is that the part of your brain that caused you to go into the coma both times healed and healed the same as last time. We don't know why after you returned to Noctulanar, it was darker, and affected a larger area."

"So, what does that all mean?" I asked, not entirely sure I wanted to hear the answer.

"It means that we don't know why your visions haven't come back. All the tests show everything to be fine. You couldn't be in better health. You still have all your power, you can still talk to people silently, and you can still kick some serious butt."

"That doesn't have anything to do with power."

"Not my point. My point is, there isn't much else we can try to do to figure out why your visions haven't come back. They may come back in time; they may never return," she said softly.

All the air in my lungs came rushing out in a huge huff like I'd been kicked in the gut. While I liked having a reprieve from them, I certainly didn't want to give them up.

"They may never come back?" I asked slowly.

"I'm sorry, Megan. We just don't know. There have been so few citizens who are both Seers and Cogniti in our history that we just don't know very much about how they interact. We also don't have brain scans like this of other people who have your abilities."

"But why would the Angels give me such gifts and then take them away?" I said, trying to keep the panic at bay.

"I'm a physician, Megan, not a spiritualist. I don't know the answer to that. What I do know, though, is that the Angels have blessed your family, and I want to believe, for your sake, that they will return. It may just be your mind resting," Physician Horan tried to encourage.

"Thank you, Horan." I walked outside and ran directly into Mickel.

"Lady Megan," he said before I could apologize. His voice was soft and considerate. "Our things are ready to go when you are."

"Let's go," I said, and made my way out of the building. I could feel tears boiling in my eyes. "Mickel, I need a few minutes."

"As you wish. I will get your bag and meet you at the bridge."

I nodded and went and sat at the edge of the fountain pools and cried.

Yes. It seemed silly to cry over losing my visions.

Yes. It was actually very stupid because with everything else going on in the worlds, my visions were but a small thing.

Still. They have been a part of me and who I am for as long as I can remember. We would never have gotten very far without them last year. I'd come to rely on them to help me out when I didn't know where to go. I wanted them back. Now that I was being told they really may never... I stared at the fountains, then as the tears started to fall hard and fast, I put my head in my hands and sobbed.

It was midafternoon when Mickel found me still staring at the fountains. I hadn't realized I had sat there for so long.

"I sent a page to you a couple of hours ago to let you know I was going to stop by the library and pick up some things for Lindy," he said.

"Sorry, I don't remember seeing one."

"Lindy sent a message asking if we could bring home some books on Ash'bani. So I went and retrieved them from the Librarian," he said, holding them out for me.

I took the books and made our way to the tram to take us down to the harbor. "Makes sense. We need to figure out as much as we can about them."

"Megan," he said tentatively.

"Hum?"

"I know what Horan told you, but whether or not your visions come back, what I have seen in the months you have been my assignment," he shook his head smiling, "you're a very talented, remarkable, strong, and powerful woman. Visions or not. With all that, plus the power of your family and an Angels Blessed Vernadali, you will conquer anything the worlds throw at you."

When I looked up at him, he was standing proud and tall.

"Doesn't matter if I have visions or not. We have to stop Ansel eventually," I said with more conviction, and I needed to change the subject, or I was going to start crying again. "Right now, though, I just want to go home and make sure Lindy hasn't completely run away with my wedding plans."

"Sounds like a great idea. Julian is keeping the ferry on permanent standby for your use. Once we reach the harbor, the horses will be loaded, and we can leave immediately."

"I'm going to get spoiled by Julian. He is giving me free will to do whatever I want. Snap my fingers and I get it. Even things I don't need or ask for," I said with a giggle.

"Don't worry. I'll help CJ keep you in line."

"Speaking of Ceej. When you were talking to Remi, did he give you any idea of when he would be home?"

"I'm sorry, Megan, he didn't," he said—my heart fell just a bit. "But I did some asking around at the Vernadali office here in Nalrin."

"AND?" I asked, my heart jumping.

"They couldn't give me an exact date but said that if he keeps progressing the way he has, it shouldn't be more than a couple of weeks, and not to worry, he would be home in time for the wedding."

That kept a smile on my face the whole way home.

CHAPTER 13

"ROCK PAPER SCISSORS FOR who puts the horses up?" I asked. I had taught him the Manusian game a few months ago, and he loved it probably because he won more often than not.

"1. 2. 3," I fisted my hand up in a rock while his became scissors. "HA! I won."

I tossed the reins to Mickel, stuck out my tongue, and snuck into the living room as quietly as possible. They were standing in front of a table set up in the middle of the living room with a bunch of different place settings set up.

"Megan would like this one," Jean said, pointing to one on the table.

"But this one seems more like CJ," Lindy replied to her.

"Megan would like to know what in the Angels you two are talking about," I said, crossing my arms across my chest.

They both looked up with surprise, and Lindy ran up and gave me a huge hug.

"You're home early!" Jean said.

"Don't sound too panicked, Jean. I had a crazy 18 hours there, then I met with the doctors, and then Julian said I could come on home. I wanted to get some things done and then head back for some wedding planning." Then I looked pointedly at the table. "That is, unless you guys have planned every last detail without me?"

Lindy looped her arm in mine and led me to the table. "Not everything, though. Since you're back early, I'll get a message to the dress shop to move your appointment up. And we didn't plan everything, just things we know you won't care about too much. Like the dishware for the reception. I like this one for you," she said, pointing to a white set of dishes with a few small red and black starburst patterns on them. "But Jean says you would like this one better." She pointed to some simple white dishes with a silver ribbon along the outside edge, with a bow printed on just one side of the lip.

I liked them both, but I also liked the red and ivory set and the set with the twigs and birds on them. Next, there was a set like the silver ribbon one, but in gold, a red set that was way too traditional for us, and finally a set that was so fancy and formal, I was afraid to touch it.

"You're right. I do like the black and red starburst one, and CJ would probably pick the silver ribbon one. However, that might be because it's more traditional looking than the starburst. That is, if he was required to pick something. I don't think he cares what we eat on." I laughed. "So, to keep y'all from fighting. I pick... the silver ribbon set. I want to have a formal, relaxed, fun feel. Plus, it will tie in with the outdoor venue."

"No contradictions there, are there?" Mickel said as he walked in the door.

"I am one big contradiction." I turned to look at him, and he was covered in mud from head to toe. "Ahhh, what happened?"

"Yeah, I'm headed to the shower. The horses and I just had a little disagreement. They won," he said, giggling.

"Apparently." I looked him over from head to toe.

"Don't you track mud through my house, Mickel! I will beat you within an inch of your life if you do," Jean scolded him.

"I wouldn't dare, Jean. Is my old room available?" he asked, blushing slightly.

Jean snapped her fingers, flung her hands out and down. "It is now. Second from the end of the hall. CJ and Megan like being at the end of the hall," she said with a wink, as Mickel smirked and headed to take a shower.

When he was about halfway down, my fingers twitched and may have zapped him on the butt. A chunk of mud fell onto the floor and I giggled.

"Mickel! I told you not to leave a trail of mud!" Jean yelled at him.

"Blame Megan," he growled back, rubbing his butt. I just smirked at him as he made his way into his room.

"Mickel is staying with us?" Lindy whispered. She hadn't moved a muscle since he walked in.

"Julian thinks he needs to be my bodyguard 24/7 now," I told her.

"24/7?" Jean said.

"Sorry, Manusia expression. I guess here it would be 36/7. 36 hours a day, 7 days a week," I explained.

Nodding, Lindy asked, "What about when CJ gets back?"

"Mickel is sticking around. Julian's orders." I shrugged. "So, what else did you decide on while I was gone." Changing the subject. I didn't look forward to having to tell CJ that Mickel was permanently assigned to me, or me to him, or whatever. I guess I understood it for now, but once CJ was back, it didn't make any sense. CJ is a Vernadali. How much more protection can one get?

"We got the red tulips ordered from the grower up north. Owen got the rounds of woodcut for the end of the aisles. Clarice got the wedding bellflower pieces made for those, and we started on the guest seating chart for dinner, but we haven't gotten the list from CJ's family back yet to see who is coming from that side."

"No seating chart," I told her.

"First, you don't want Bride-Groom seating at the wedding. No wedding bell flowers being thrown. Now no seating chart for the reception? Is there anything traditional you *are* doing?"

"Sure, the dress, bridesmaids, walking solo down the aisle..." I ticked each off on my finger when she interrupted me.

"Walking solo down the aisle isn't traditional for you," she said, but she cut herself off when she saw the look on my face.

I took a deep breath. "Look, I just feel that as we are getting married, it's the joining of two families. So why make them sit separately? So, no Bride-Groom seating and NO SEATING CHARTS. For the wedding or the reception. Someone will end up mad they got to sit with so and so, or got stuck with someone else at their table. I don't want to deal with the family or dimensional politics of that one. Let people sit wherever in the underworld they want."

"Okay," they both said, defeated.

"Now, show me what else you have done," I said, trying to lighten the mood, "or would you like to wait to go over it when Annie, Amber, and Logan get here tomorrow."

Lindy froze. "Wait, Logan's coming tomorrow?"

I smiled. "Well, technically, you and I are going to get Logan and Annie. Jean, can you get Amber? Owen can go with you."

"Owen got called out on an assignment shortly after you left. He'll be back tomorrow sometime," Jean said. "I'll make Mickel go with me. It will be good to catch up. It's been ten years. At least, I think it's been ten years. Could be more since I saw him last. I take it you got their passes?"

"Yup. Julian himself signed them. They have access to Nalrin for as long as they can keep the secret of Nalrin." I pulled the passes out of my jacket pocket and gave Jean Amber's. When I looked back at Lindy, she had a smile on her face that I could tell she was trying to hide, but her blushing cheeks were giving her away.

"Lindy, are you going to be able to keep yourself together until the morning?" I didn't think her face could get any redder, but it did.

"Yes. I just haven't seen Logan in three of our weeks. It's longer for him, and well." She looked down, "What if he decided he doesn't want to be with me. What if this 'long-distance thing' and the whole different dimension thing is too much for him?"

"Stop doubting it. Sure, that's all a possibility, but frankly, Logan's just as stubborn as CJ. More so in some ways. I am willing to bet he would move the Angels out of the way to be with you. Logan is loyal and determined to a fault," I said, trying to make her feel better.

That made her face drop a little, instead. I saw Jean eye me to tread lightly; then she ducked out of the room.

Lindy answered slowly as she went to go sit down on the couch. "I feel weird for even having feelings for him. I don't know if it would even work."

"Why is that? Just because he's human? CJ is human. I'm Sangra. Okay, I guess CJ and I aren't the best examples," I said as lightly as I could.

"Auturno. We gave each other our hearts. Mine died with him. I still carry his. I will never love anyone truly again." She hiccupped a bit as a tear rolled down her cheek. "In fact, it's only been after seeing what you and CJ and Jean and Owen will go through for each other, does it even remind me that love can still exist. When the one you give your heart to dies before their time, it breaks something in you. I can't explain it, Megan. I'm not whole anymore."

"Okay, look. I understand that. I think because he did die before his time, you still have some of your own heart to give. You're right about one thing, though." I sighed. I had to word this just right, or she'd brush me off.

"What is that?" She sniffed back more tears.

Funny how I had just had this discussion with Mickel, but said, "You will never love anyone like you did Auturno again. That doesn't mean that you can't go on and live a happy life. To love again. Don't you think Auturno would've wanted you to be happy? If Logan makes you happy, then why stop it."

"I guess. It's just, well, it brings back all those memories, and what if I sabotage everything with Logan because I find myself thinking it doesn't feel like it did with Auturno?" She wiped away a tear to keep from messing up her make-up.

"I'll say it again. You won't feel for Logan the way you did with Auturno, if it goes that far. Different people, different loves. You just don't love two people the same way. I love you different than I do Clarice, or Jean, or Owen, and for sure different than C.J."

She nodded and took a deep breath, still studying her hands. "So, tomorrow?"

"First thing in the morning," I beamed. "I'm beat, and I need a good night's sleep."

CHAPTER 14

IT WAS NICE TO visit the Manusia again. We had to wait for Logan to get off of work, so Annie took us to Cecilio's, her favorite place in the city, to get deep-dish pizza. Lindy was beside herself. I think she found her new favorite Manusia food. Everything went off without a hitch, and Annie, Logan, Lindy, and I were soon back standing in Grandma's garden at home.

"Man! I don't think I will ever get used to the feeling of the world falling from underneath my feet," Logan said.

"Oh, stop being a baby!" Annie teased him.

"Let's go inside," I said, but before I could get to the front door, I was overcome with a dark and heavy feeling. "Wooo."

"You ok?" Annie asked.

"Yeah. Fine." I straightened up and headed into the house. I didn't want to worry her. After all, she didn't know about all the crazy stuff that was going on. "Go ahead inside. Jean, I'm sure, will want to fill you in on everything she and Lindy have been up to. Plus, she can better explain some of the tradition blending we have done."

She nodded and headed inside. I stood outside for a bit longer and just took some deep breaths. I centered myself and felt out, but there wasn't anything out there. Why am I getting this feeling? A few minutes later, I felt a hand on my shoulder.

"Lady Megan? Are you feeling ok?" Mickel asked.

"Just have a dark feeling come over me. I don't know what it is, or how to explain it." I shook my head and looked at Mickel. "Is Amber here? Any trouble in the Manusia?"

"I had to explain who I was. She was a tad hesitant going with me even though Jean was with us." I looked at him. He was blushing. "Though she was fine once I gave her your note."

"Why are you blushing?" I teased him.

"She's in the kitchen. She had us stop by the grocery store to pick up some things. She is insisting on making something called enchilada pie for dinner?" he said, successfully avoiding the question.

"No way! Enchilada pie! Ohhh, I haven't had that in AGES!" I practically pushed him out of the way to get into the house. I know I just had pizza, but my mouth was already watering. I already couldn't wait for dinner.

It was mid-afternoon when Owen got home, completely riled up, and I noticed he tried to hurry his way to the bedroom to change out of some clothes that were pretty bloody. Once he changed, he decided that sparring with Mickel was a good idea. I watched Mickel kick his ass every time. Annie, Clarice, and Jean were going over the menu, and guest list for the wedding, and Lindy and Logan had disappeared off to who knows where. Amber and I sat catching up on everything that had been going on in the Manusia. It felt so normal.

"David and I broke up shortly after," she said. "Then we got back together, but we are over and done with for good now," she said with conviction.

"How can you be sure? I mean, I know how much you cared for him. Maybe things will work out," I said.

"Oh no. I'm positive. There is no way I could be more positive." I eyed her questioningly. "No, seriously. I'm the kind of positive that comes from when you get off work early and come home to see him neck–deep between her legs. Did I forget to mention she was screaming his name, riding his face? I'm that kind of positive."

"Are you fucking serious!?" I asked, my eyes bulging out.

"Wish I wasn't. If we had discussed it before, it might have been different, but I found out he had been with her for months. I moved out that night. That's why Jean found me at Becca's. She's letting me rent the spare bedroom until I can get a deposit together for my own place again. Justin seems to be fine with it, but it's a little awkward when I have to be at work early in the morning and he's walking around naked and wood flopping all over the kitchen."

I laughed hard at that.

"Becca has torn into him few times about it, but I think he secretly does it on purpose. Though, to be fair, Becca has taken to walking around the house naked too. Hard for me to say something when it's their house."

About that time, Lindy, Logan, Owen, and Mickel came into the living room.

"The extra horses arrived last night. They're rested and ready to go. We should probably be on the road in an hour, Lady Megan," Mickel said, and I winced.

"Lady Megan?" Logan said with a bellowing laugh. Annie and Amber were giggling, too.

"Oh, shut it, guys. In case you weren't given the memo, Mickel is my..." Well, hell, how am I supposed to tell them he's my bodyguard, without stating that he is my bodyguard because

Ansel is trying to kill me. I looked at Mickel, and he picked up for me.

"Bodyguard. All high–level consultants in Nalrin have one," he said. I could have hugged him right then and there.

"Ok, fine, he's your bodyguard. Megs, that isn't why we are laughing. Lady!?" Logan said. "He doesn't know you like we do, does he?!"

I threw a pillow at him. "Asshole!"

"Come on Megs," Amber said, laughing. "We all know you can burp and be as coarse and rude as any sailor on a ship! Lady isn't necessarily what anyone would call you."

Mickel smirked, and when he opened his mouth to say something, I threw another pillow at him, which he caught way too easily. He got the memo, shut the Underworld up.

"I can be a Lady if I wanted to," I said, but couldn't keep a straight face when I saw the look on Amber's. "Okay. Okay. Fair enough. It's just a title! If either of you tell any of those stories, I'll dunk you in the flowers." I love my family, but they can be such pains in the ass.

I really should have warned Mickel about the formal titles. Oh well. They would've heard them in Nalrin anyway.

CHAPTER 15

I KEPT A FEEL out for anyone we could come across on the road, and Mickel's head and eyes were on a swivel the entire time. We were getting closer to the Nalsar River, and there seemed to be more travelers joining us on the main road. Of course, people would come to the marketplace for supplies, but that heavy dark feeling had settled over me again, and something didn't feel right.

"You feel it too, don't you?" I pushed to Clarice, Owen, Jean, Lindy, and Mickel. Each of them had imperceptibly nodded their head, and I saw Owen and Clarice keep their hands within very easy reach of their weapons the whole way.

I found myself discreetly, but carefully, watching anyone and everyone who joined us on the road. How they fell in line, what they were watching, what they were wearing, everything. I was getting paranoid. I tried to tell myself I was being silly, but between what Julian said and the fact that I have CJ's family and Amber with us, I knew I was feeling more than a little bit protective. They're human, and while Logan was well versed in martial arts, none of them have power like everyone else here. I concentrated on listening to Annie and Amber's chit-chat to take my mind off of it.

I gave Mickel the reins to my horse when we got to the river and turned to the ferryman. "I'll be just a few minutes. I want to go talk to her."

"Madame Winters isn't here, madam," the ferryman told me. "She left yesterday afternoon and didn't look so well."

"Collette?"

"She is. Her brother came and retrieved Madame. Go ahead. No rush," he told me.

"I'm going with you, Lady Megan," Mickel said after securing our horses.

"It's ok, Mickel. I'll only be a few minutes," I tried to reassure him.

"I'd like to see Collette too," Lindy said.

"And Megan, you know how much I love flea markets! I have to check this place out." Annie's eyes were pleading, and it was just not fair. How are you supposed to say no to your soon-to-be mother-in-law when she looks at you like that?

"Ok, fine. Let's go." Why did I feel like it was soon going to be like herding cats in a room full of rocking chairs?

We made our way over to Collette and when she saw me, she stepped out of the tent and pulled me away from everyone else, and whispered, "What are you doing here?"

"We are heading back to Nalrin. What's wrong?"

"There are whispers in the dark. Whispers of Ja'Nee coming," she said with her eyes wide.

"Ja'Nee?"

"Assassins. Hired assassins from darkness." There was a pop, and her eyes shot wide open in surprise as she pushed me out of the way. Someone cloaked in black plunged a konarak blade right through her ribcage. I felt my scream rip through my throat more than I heard it. Mickel was at my side in a heartbeat and caught Collette's limp body as it slid off the blade.

It must have realized who I was, because it turned toward me and hissed. I could hear Mickel and my family pull their syths out behind me. Clarice pulled her whips out with a crack. It was that crack of her whips that brought me back to reality and pulled my concentration to Collette laying on the ground, staring into nothingness.

My syths were instantly in my hands, and my power was crackling at my fingertips in anticipation. When I saw the ember of the being that just murdered my friend, I was thrown.

There was no glow to it. It was solid black, fading at the edges. I whispered, "Ja'Nee?"

"Clarice, Owen, Jean. Get them out of here!" I shouted.

"No, I'm staying with Lindy," I heard Logan shout behind me.

I could see Lindy smirk beside me, but I shook my head at her.

"No, you aren't staying here," she said.

"I'm not leaving you," he shouted to Lindy.

"Lindy, go with them if you fucking have to. Keep them safe. Jean and Owen can go with you, too. Clarice and Mickel can stay with me," I said. We were completely surrounded by Ja'Nee now. They circled us, and I felt their darkness pull at me.

The Ja'Nee in front of me lunged and the blade of his konarak, still dripping with Collette's blood, narrowly missed my side. I mentally pushed him back and concentrated on the negative space. Only, there was too much negative space. It lunged.

I moved just in time to twist around and land a hit on his side. I pushed some of my electricity through my syth, but when it reached the Ja'Nee, it just dissipated.

"Get them out of here! Get everyone onboard the ferry and let's get out of here!" I shouted. I could hear Lindy's syths clanging behind me. Logan reached over and slid one of Lindy's extra syths from her belt, twisted, and landed a blow to one of the Ja'Nee. That slight distraction allowed Mickel to jump up over the top of it and slide his sword through its neck. As its head slid from its body, it disappeared in a puff of smoke.

I ducked under the Ja'Nee's swing and drove my syth into the small of his back. The Ja'Nee faded slightly, but its whole body twisted to face me from the ground. Its hands reached out toward me like the tendrils of darkness I had seen in Noctulanar, but just before the tendrils reached me, Mickel grabbed my arm and I felt the world fall out from underneath my feet.

Ice cold, musky air surrounded us, then we were in the courtyard in front of the Nalrin building standing before about fifty Nalrin Guards. Our weapons were still out, and I thought I saw a few guards twitch at the sight of us.

Mickel was the first to speak. "I am Mickel de Seduisant. Head Guard of the Nalrin Special Units and Guardian assigned to Lady Megan Keller. Sanction Code 42B66NSU2. The others are of our party. You may stand down."

In unison, all the Nalrin Guard sheathed their weapons and stood at attention. I looked at Mickel with a question on my face. He gave me an apologetic look. There were a few Vernadali that lowered their weapons but did not fully yield to whatever that code meant. I took a breath.

Lindy was checking Logan over to make sure he was ok. I turned to Annie and Amber, and there were a few superficial wounds, they were shaking, but otherwise okay. We had gotten out of there before the Ja'Nee could do any serious damage.

"What the fucking hell, Megan?" Amber said, her voice hardly above a whisper and shaking so badly that it was everything she could do to keep from crying. Of all of us, she is the one I was worried wouldn't be able to handle all this mentally.

"I'll explain when we get to my residence." I strode to her, put both hands on her cheeks and looked her square in the eyes, "I promise. You are 100% safe here."

"You have two homes?" she replied. Of all the things to say, and she said that.

I forced a smile on my face, shoving my worry inward, and shook my head. "Yeah. I do."

"Mickel. Let's get them to my residence," I told him while looking over Annie. She had a minor bump on her head and a scrape on her arm, but it wasn't oozing anything it shouldn't, so I wasn't too concerned.

He nodded. When I looked up, the two rows of guards parted, and when I saw who it was, I sighed with relief as I saw Remi making his way to us.

"Lady Megan, Mickel. Head Julian requires your presence immediately. Vernadali, stand down," he said with authority.

"I suppose he does," I said curtly. "Remi, can you please get everyone to my residence? Oh, and Horan to look at Vernadali CJ's mother," I said with an extra pointed look at Remi, hoping to get my point across.

Remi's eyes widened just the smallest, insurmountable bit, and I bit back a smirk of amusement. They trained Vernadali to keep their emotions in check and if I hadn't been looking straight at him, I would've missed it completely. I put my arm around Annie. Her slightly plump five-foot-six frame straightened a bit.

"Of course." He bowed formally, looking at me with a careful expression. Then he turned to another guard, "Send Physician Horan to Lady Megan's residence immediately?"

"Thank you." I told him, then turned to Annie. "Please go with Remi. He will make sure that someone looks at that cut. I have to go meet with... Someone, but I promise I'll be there soon, okay?"

She looked at me then and cocked her head to the side and said, "What did you call CJ? A Verna what?"

Remi chuckled. "Vernadali."

I glared at him. "Vernadali, Mom." I took a deep breath. "I have no doubt I'm about to be in a lot of trouble, but I need you to go with Remi and get that arm looked at, okay?"

"Megan?" Logan asked, thick with meaning. I could see the rage, frustration, and the millions of questions that were on his face. He tried to hide them from everyone else, but I saw it clear as day and Annie would have noticed too if she wasn't in so much shock right now.

"Logan. I need you to take care of Mom and Amber," I said with a bite that left nothing to be argued, then added through my teeth, "Please."

Logan gave me a look to mean that he would have his answers, but nodded.

"Mrs. Mathewson, please come with me, and let's get that gash looked at," Remi said as he led them toward my residence.

"We are in a heap of shit, aren't we, Mickel?" I said, watching them, Logan glaring at me over his shoulder. Mickle just nodded in confirmation as we turned and hurried to meet with Julian without another word.

CHAPTER 16

WHEN MICKEL AND I got to Julian's office, there were two rather pissed-off-looking guards standing out front. I didn't even stop to acknowledge them; I just walked past and opened the door.

Julian was sitting at his desk and writing furiously. "Both of you sit down."

Mickel and I looked at each other and sat down in front of his desk. Yup. We were in a great heap of trouble.

"Sir," Mickel tried to explain, but Julian put his hand up to stop him from saying any more.

He was silent for a very long time; well, it felt like it. I felt like I was six years old and my parents were just sitting there looking at me after I'd done something wrong or stupid. Underworld's being! I would rather do that right now than sit before Julian as he wrote feverishly with that disappointed look on his face. Mickel and I just kept looking at each other and then at Julian, but neither of us dared say a word.

Time seemed to slow, and slowly the realization that Collette had just been killed sank in. Tears welled in my eyes, and Mickel reached over and squeezed my hand. Collette. Angels. Poor Madam Winters. Her brother was going to be devastated. I sniffed, and Julian just waved his hand and a box of tissues floated over toward me.

"Thank you," I mumbled, and he nodded his head, still writing as quickly as he could.

It couldn't have been more than a couple minutes before Julian called, "Garrett!"

"Yes sir," a guard who I vaguely recognized answered.

"Deliver this immediately." When the Guard had left, he turned and faced us.

"First. Are you ok?" We nodded. "Second. Mickel, do you know how much trouble you guys could be in right now?"

"Yes sir," Mickel mumbled.

"Teleporting directly to the courtyard of the Nalrin Council?! You know it is strictly forbidden to teleport anywhere within a realm. Do you know how lucky you are that you aren't laying in a pile of your own blood right now or floating in the inbetweens?" His voice reverberated against the walls, shaking our eardrums. I had never seen or heard him so mad.

"Wait, could be?" I asked Julian. "You mean we aren't in trouble."

"Very much not the point, Megan. You *are* in trouble, believe me. I'm doing everything I can right now to protect you and your family. Now, Mickel, what in the Underworld happened that you would break such major protocol?"

Mickel explained how everything was going as usual until Collette mentioned the Ja'Nee.

"The Ja'Nee?" he said in a low and confused voice.

Mickel's voice was slow and careful. "Yes, sir. The Ja'Nee are the ones who attacked us. We were able to kill one of them by beheading it, and Megan injured one, before-"

"I don't think I injured it. It turned around and projected darkness at me, which is when you grabbed me and we landed here in Nalrin," I interrupted.

"Sir. I think this was a direct attempt on Lady Megan's life. There was no genuine attempt at trying to hurt the rest of us. The Ja'Nee were completely focused on Megan," Mickel told him.

"I also believe that Mickel." He started to pace the floor. "The question is more, how did Ansel get access to the Ja'Nee. They don't work for anyone. You have to literally have darkness under your control for that." He sighed heavily.

"Ansel? Why are you so sure it was Ansel?" I asked.

"Is there anyone else you have pissed off so royally, as you would say, since you arrived here?" he responded, pacing behind his desk.

"No. Well... But, I think he would want to do that himself. Why hire assassins of darkness to do it?"

He pondered that for a moment. He jumped slightly when a high-pitched honking came from a portal that appeared behind him. He sighed. "Angels save me. You're excused. However, you're confined to your residence until further notice. I have to clear some matters up before you can proceed about your business here."

"Julian." I was nervous for even asking, as that high-pitched honking continued. "I need to explain why I was attacked at the river to those from the Manusia. They're part of my family, though only by marriage. Well, soon anyway. But they deserve to have a reason, and not a bullshit one either. I don't want to start my new life with them on a foundation of lies."

"You may tell them, but please, be discrete."

"I will, Julian. Thank you," I said, taking a deep breath.

"Go. Check on them," Julian said. "Again, you're confined to your residence until further notice. Mickel, you are confined to Lady Megan's residence with the rest of the group. I will not have you unprotected right now."

Mickel and I nodded and hurried to my residence, neither of us saying a thing.

CHAPTER 17

WHEN WE GOT BACK to my residence, four Vernadali were stationed at my door. They merely nodded at us as we went in. Mickel insisted upon going in first, despite my objections. Remi and another Vernadali were just inside the doors, and when Remi saw me, he gave me a consoling look.

I sighed as Mickel said, "Owen, Jean, Clarice, and Lindy, can I talk to you for a moment please out on the balcony?" without looking at anyone, and headed straight outside to the balcony.

"Thank you, Remi," I breathed as I made to stand next to him. Horan was still mending Annie's wounds and looked like she probably had some kind of painkiller in her, too. Amber, on the other hand, was wrapped up in a blanket with her knees to her chest. Logan was sitting next to her with his elbows on his knees and his hands clasped tightly together, but looking straight at me. Those million questions in his eyes being speared right for me. Oh, this was going to be so much fun.

Remi nodded toward Annie. "The one Horan is working on. That's really Vernadali CJ's mother?"

"She is, and the doof between her and the other girl, is his brother, Logan," I said, smiling brightly, as Logan narrowed his eyes at me.

Remi smiled. "He looks like him. Older?"

"He is. Bigger pain in the ass than CJ is, too," I said, smirking at Logan. He got up, strode over—trying not to make it look like he was in a hurry—stood in front of us, and his arms crossed, trying to look intimidating.

"Megan, what is going on?" he said.

"Logan, the doof, let me introduce you to Remi," I said, a smirk on my face.

Remi bowed his head down in greeting, but Logan just kept staring at me. "Nice to meet you too, dude. Megan. Answer me. What kind of shit is going on?"

I sighed. "Logan. Patience. I will tell you, but let Head Physician Horan finish patching up Mom, ok." He relaxed a little at that and I tried to change the subject. "Remi here, used to be stationed where Ceej is training until just what, couple weeks ago?"

Remi's eyes narrowed and the right side of his mouth turned up, trying to suppress a grin. "That's true. He is doing very well."

"What is he learning at this training camp we can't have any information about?" Logan probed, his voice rough and annoyed.

"He is learning what all Vernadali learn. History, Physics, Combat training. It's much like your military training in the Manusia, just with information relevant to Nalsar," Remi said easily. I was thankful he wasn't going into all the other magical Angel stuff. Although, honestly, I wasn't sure what he was learning up there, either. Angels! I was to be his Charge, and I didn't know. I took a deep breath, looked at where Mickel and the others were coming back in, and groaned.

"Come on, Logan." I grabbed him by the arm and went to check on Annie and Amber. I was just reaching the couch when one of those waves of darkness flowed over me, and I missed a step and caught myself on the couch. I took a breath and tried to push it away. Great. Great fucking timing. I glanced over my shoulder, showed Clarice struggling with it too. She nodded her head and so I moved forward and asked Horan, "They okay?"

"They are. Annie here is going to need to see me again before you leave Nalrin though. Understand? I want to check out that scratch on her arm. Make sure it isn't..." she glanced over at her, "Infected."

I read between the lines and reassured her I would make sure Annie stopped by for a follow-up. Finishing up, she let herself out.

"Megan. Now, will you tell us what the hell is going on?" Logan said. He was sitting back between Annie and Amber and looked at me with eyes that were full of questions and fear.

"Ok, look. CJ and I decided that there are just some things that, well, you shouldn't be concerned about. Now, you have a right to know, and if he were here, I'm sure he would agree." I was stalling. I knew it. I turned to glance at Remi, and he gave me a short, curt nod in agreement.

It was Annie who spoke next, but her words were slow and deliberate. "Why do you think we shouldn't know what is going on here?"

"You know how as a parent there are things you don't tell your kids because you don't want to freak them out, or because it isn't their problem, or because sometimes ignorance is just bliss?" I asked her.

"Yes. I do," she said with a faint smile as her eyes flicked to Logan.

"Well, this is exactly that sort of thing. Now, please understand that part of your ability to continue to come see us hinges on you not telling anyone about our world here. That includes what I am about to tell you. Most of the dimension does not know what I am about to tell you. You can't talk about it outside this room. Not in the halls, not even once you're back at home." I waited a moment for it to sink in for each of them before I asked, "Do you still want to know?"

"Absolutely! CJ is going to be living here with you, and so, yes, I want to know what the hell is going on," Annie said immediately. I had to smile. While her voice made it sound as though she spat the words, she knew that this was just the life her son chose and she accepted that.

Logan nodded his head, and when I turned to Amber, she looked at me and I could tell she seriously considered saying no. "Amber. I know you're freaking out right now. If you would prefer to go home and forget all about this, I can arrange that."

"You have an awful lot of power here, Megs," she whispered, her eyes not leaving mine.

I heard my family chuckle behind me, and Remi tried to stifle a laugh. I looked down at my hands, allowing some of that power to weave between my fingers. She smiled slightly, even though there was shock in her eyes. I chuckled and said, "In more ways than you know."

"Why didn't you tell me?"

I raised my eyebrows and gestured to everything around us. "I will tell you if you can abide by the rules I laid out. Can you do that?"

She took a really deep breath and then sat up straight. "I reserve the right to have a complete mental breakdown later, which will include cookie dough ice cream and a cheesy rom com and, or have you make me forget later? Or so help me Megan, I'm taking all your jewelry."

"Of course," I told her. Glad to hear her make a joke.

"Seriously though," I asked her, and she nodded. "Ok, well, it all started with my parents a little over a year ago."

Annie, Logan, and Amber looked at each other. "Um, Megan sweety," Annie said carefully.

"Yes, I know. They died about three years ago."

"Exactly. You were in the hospital in a coma. CJ rarely left your side, and only did if I promised to stay," Amber said.

"Ok, so I guess I do need to back up. This is going to be a cliff notes version ok." They nodded again.

I sighed and started in. "That explosion where they died? They didn't die. They faked their death and came back here to

Nalrin. Basically, a long, long time ago they did some things that were against the rules here and they got into trouble for it."

"Megan, you have to tell them. To say they just 'broke the rules' doesn't do anyone any justice. And frankly, will just piss me off," Lindy said, crossing her arms as they came back into the room.

"Have you told Logan yet?" I asked her.

"Told me what?" he asked, and I shushed him.

She hung her head. "No, I haven't."

"Well, if I don't give the cliff notes version then Logan hears about Auturno from me. Is that what you want?" I asked mentally.

"Not really," she said, shaking her head. I looked at her pointedly.

"You should have told him. He told you about Rebecca," I said out loud.

"What does this have to do with Rebecca?" I shooshed him again and looked at Lindy.

"I know," she said. She thought for a moment, sighed, and said, "Well, it's not really how I wanted you to find out, Logan. I should have told you already but..."

"I was trying to give them the cliff notes version!" I said, but the look Lindy was giving me made me change my mind. "Ok, basically they were looking into how to create the weapon of the Five Angels, which is not a weapon you can easily defeat. It is against the law to look into how to create the weapon, and when they were confronted by the council, they fought and council members died. One of which was Auturno, my father's brother..." I looked at Lindy, whose eyes were filled with tears. "And Lindy's husband."

Logan looked at Lindy. "OH BABE!" He got up and grabbed her in his arms and just held her while she sobbed. It was at that moment, I knew that Logan was in it for the long haul with Lindy, no matter what. It was the way he comforted her and told her none of it mattered. He loved her. He truly loved her. Even if I hadn't heard him say it. I looked back at Annie, and she knew it too. She gave me a look that conveyed both happiness and sadness. Realization that both sons were going to move to another dimension filled her eyes, yet there was a gratefulness that warmed my heart as well.

"My parents retreated to the Manusia, well, our dimension... your dimension... oh whatever," I continued. "There, they built a life and had me and Matt. Everything was fine until Matt died. Amber, you remember how after that my father basically had a psychotic episode."

Amber nodded, saying, "Yeah. You would meet Beth for coffee just so you could see her for a while."

"Here you will hear everyone call her Symatha. She went by her middle name back home. So, if you hear it, it's the same person. Anyway, they faked their deaths, and came back here," I said, and found myself pacing in the living room. I heard Mickel making a pot of hot water. I smiled slightly; he knew me so well that he was already preparing the hot cocoa. I pushed to Mickel to make enough for Amber, too.

"Yes, ma'am," he said, just like a soldier. They each looked at me and cocked their head to the side in unison. It made me smile.

Focusing Logan, Annie, and Amber again, I continued, "Life went on and then the night of CJ and I's first date, I transported CJ and me here. From there, we found out that they had succeeded in getting the information on how to build the weapon of the Five Angels. Once we figured out that was what they were trying to do, we tried to stop them. We failed repeatedly." My voice caught as I remembered how they had taken CJ in the library.

"They had all the pieces... they needed, and went to a castle in one of the southern regions. They had..." I looked up and saw Annie paying very close attention and skirted around the little details, "their sacrifice ready. Only one of the pieces they thought they had, they didn't. I did. So, it failed."

Owen coughed at my oversimplification, and Jean's eyebrows were raised. Clarice stood there unmoving, and when I looked at her, there was a look of understanding on her face.

"I'm not telling his mother and brother that CJ almost died a year ago!" I shouted at them mentally.

"Megan. What aren't you telling us?" Annie demanded.

"Lots, and I won't tell you everything," I said firmly. She stared me down. She was all mom demanding answers. "No, Mom. I will not tell you everything."

She huffed, and I continued, "When the ritual failed, a fight broke out and my mother was killed. My father blames me for killing her, and has decided that I have to pay for her death."

I looked up and saw the look of shock on their faces. Each of them studied me closely, but Amber looked to Mickel, who had taken position behind me and I saw him give her a quick small nod out of the corner of my eye. The corner of my mouth turned up, and I looked at her with raised eyebrows and there was just that slight reddening of her cheeks.

"When you said that you and CJ were dealing with your parents' stuff, you weren't kidding," Annie said.

"It was close enough to the truth," I said, my attention going to her. "I'm sorry I can't tell you everything, but-"

"There are things you don't tell us so we don't worry," she said, finally understanding. It was silent in the room for a few minutes before Annie asked, "Did you kill Beth? I mean, Symatha?"

"Yes. I think I did," I said quietly, but Annie just nodded and sat back, trying to process everything. Whatever she had played out in her mind, I don't think it had come anywhere close to the truth.

"Not really, Megan. You were busy fighting Ansel. It was me and Owen fighting with Symatha," Lindy said, trying to not make me look like the guilty party.

"Technically, it was my body that Ansel had thrown against the pillar that created the domino effect, that caused Poseidon's trident to pierce through her chest," Clarice tried to clarify. She said each section with a point and, by the end, had a smile on her face.

Annie, Logan and Amber looked to each of us for a long moment.

"That story is so crazy, and you say it like it is nothing. You can't be making that crap up," Amber said, her eyes big as saucers. They bounced between us for a moment. "Seriously, Ansel wants to kill you because your mom died?"

"Yeah," I said with a chuckle as I realized just how crazy it sounded when it was said like that.

"Well, damn, and here I was having a hard time figuring out how to tell you I totaled your car," Amber said. Her eyes went wide, and she clamped her hands over her mouth after she realized what she had said.

Annie was staring at her bug eyed and jaw dropped to the floor and Logan said, eyes wide, "OH, you fucked up."

"You totaled Betsy! I gave her to you to love and cherish. Not to destroy!" I shot back at her, my power bouncing to my fingers, and a slight hum filled the room at my anger. Mickel moved behind me and put both hands firmly on my shoulders. Twisting my head around to look at him, I narrowed my eyes, and he gave me a look of warning. I had the feeling he would jump between me and Amber had I made one move to hurt her. Smart man. I loved that car. I love her too, but... Betsy.

"It wasn't my fault. A drunk sped onto the highway in Sand City and I swerved, missed him, but the semi in front of us didn't, so I ended up under the trailer," she explained.

"Oh, my Betsy." I sighed, a tight knot in my chest.

"Your poor car?! I could have died Megs!"

"But you didn't, because otherwise you wouldn't be here freaking out over the fact that I told you that I killed my mother and my father is trying to kill me!"

"Guess we're even?" she teased.

I met her eyes, and it was all I could do not to laugh, but still sighed, "Poor Betsy."

Lindy, attempting to change the subject, said, "Hey Megs. When can we get back to wedding planning?"

"Seriously, after what we went through, you want to know when we can get to the dress shop? Don't you think we need to give Annie, Amber, and Logan just a little bit of time to absorb all that shit I just spewed?" I asked. I would be surprised at the attempt, but this was Lindy. I should have expected nothing less from her.

"Well, I'm not taking this bridesmaid thing lightly. And I think that if you ask Amber, she would like to know also," Lindy said, standing tall and arrogant.

"Oh, don't bring me into this," she blurted, but when I looked at her evenly, she broke down. "Ok, yeah, I was really excited about going dress shopping. It is your wedding. To CJ! We are so excited for you and CJ to get married, you have no idea. Besides, you know that I'm a sucker for shopping!"

I couldn't help but laugh, but then I had a thought. Was it really safe to have a wedding, considering the guest list? What if Ansel showed up and slaughtered everyone? "Maybe we should put off the wedding." I mumbled.

You could have heard a pin drop in that room. Everyone turned and looked at me like I had rocks for brains.

"I'm sorry, what the fuck did you just say?" Logan said. The look on his face was one of pure hilarity. It was twisted in confusion, but the way it was placed on his face made him almost look like a Picasso painting.

"I'm serious. If it was Ansel behind the Ja'Nee, then is it safe to bring half of the Nalrin Council and a bunch of humans to the middle of Nalrin?" I asked.

"The wedding is not being postponed," Owen said. "CJ would agree."

"Agreed," Logan said. "I think he would say that now, more than ever, it should continue. Prove that, well, love is stronger than anything else. Did you not hear Amber? Everyone in this room is excited to see you and Cory get married."

"Since when did this wedding become about everyone else? It's about us! Me and CJ. Not you guys, and I'm trying to keep everyone safe, Logan," I said, more than just a little annoyed.

"It is about you two. We have waited a very long time for you two to be happy together. You finally are, and we want to celebrate that with you," Logan said, crossing his arms across his chest, daring me to fight him.

"Besides, as Mother of the Groom, and your future Mother-in-Law, I forbid you to cancel or postpone this wedding," Annie said, standing up and pointing a finger at me.

I felt like I was in middle school again. "Like Logan said, we have waited too damn long for both of you to pull your heads out of your asses and get married. You have finally realized what everyone else has seen since you were sophomores in high school. Until Ansel shows up himself, the wedding will not be canceled. Even if he did, I'd love to have some words with him. That asshole will not impede your and CJ's happiness. I forbid it," Annie said, stomping her foot.

The room was deathly silent before Logan, Amber, and Lindy snickered. I just looked at her for a long moment, trying not to laugh, and dared to say, "Annie, do you realize how Mother-in-Law from hell you just sounded?"

"Yeah, Mom, that was pretty wicked. Didn't know you had that in you," Logan said.

"Well, if someone's got to be the bitch, it will be me. I can handle it," she told him. She turned to me, pointed her finger at me again and said, "You *are* marrying my son on July 2nd, rain, shine, Ansel, or Satan forbid!"

At this point, the only thing I could say was, "Yes, Mom."

Not Logan, Amber, Lindy, or even Mickel or Remi, dared to say a thing. This was a mother giving a tongue lashing and order. You did not cross the mother.

"So, since that's settled," she said, "when do we get to the dress shop?"

"Well..." Mickel and I looked at each other. "We are sort of confined to the residence until further notice. House arrest as they say."

"Why?" Logan asked.

"Transporting directly to the front of the dimensional headquarters isn't something that they take too kindly to. So, while Julian sorts out what to do with us, and potentially not throw us all in Nalsar's version of solitary confinement, we are not to leave my residence. That means that Clarice, Jean, Owen and Lindy, you cannot go to your Nalrin residences. He was specific about us all staying here." Luckily, they nodded in understanding.

"What about food?" Logan asked. Owen let out a belly laugh at that.

"Are you forgetting what Amber said earlier. I have an incredible amount of power here." I stood up tall, trying to act like I was all that and a bag of chips. When Mickel, Lindy, Jean, and Clarice laughed, I broke down. "Nah... it's called room service. So, food is on me."

CHAPTER 18

WE ORDERED, AND IT came about an hour later. While we waited, we started reading through some books I had sent up on the Ash'bani. We already knew that they lived in one of the darkest parts of Obsecuritan, in a province called Samuria. Their capital, Ghant, was a highly religious place for them. The temple was where each Ash'bani conducted all things spiritual for the entire Samurian Providence.

As for the race themselves, we knew their eyes changed to match their mood, and their eyes were slightly larger than a Sangra's. While their mouths didn't initially look larger than ours, they could unnaturally unhinge their jaw to show the extra teeth they have.

"I also found through talking to various Heads of Territories, or from what I could find in the library, that there weren't that many full-blooded Ash'bani left. Full-bloods are virtually immortal, and couldn't be killed except by old age or by the Angels themselves. They could easily live to be over 800 years old. It was also extremely hard for them to have children. Now, there are very few full-blooded Ash'bani left," I said.

"So, they could be the basis of stories of vampires in the Manusian world?" Logan asked.

"Possibly," I said, shrugging.

Clarice continued, "Half-bloods aren't impossible to kill, but it is extremely difficult for one to die, much like a full blood. It depended on what the other half of their genetic make-up is. They could still heal insanely fast, as we saw when that syth was put into your father's knee."

"Likely, but that room had a strange power going through it. Remember, Megan had that spear go through her shoulder, and after CJ ripped it out, there was no way she should have healed that quickly," Jean said. I reached up and rubbed at it. It bothered me sometimes, but she was right. I hadn't passed out from the pain, and there was no way I should have had use of the arm after that happened.

"Wait. You had a what now?" Logan interjected. When I turned to face him, his eyes were wide, and both Annie and Amber's looked like they weren't even breathing. I cringed.

"Some things we don't tell you?" I said, wincing.

Logan came over and pulled my shirt down over my shoulder and ran his finger over the light pink scar that was just to the inside of the joint. "You had a spear through your shoulder? You have full use of your arm? No surgery? And all you have is this small spider-webbed circle of a scar?"

"Like Jean said, there was a strange power going on in that room. Not saying more," I said, pulling my shirt back into place. I turned to Clarice and asked, "He's half?" Clarice nodded her head. "Well, that will be all kinds of fun."

"But if it's so hard for them to conceive, how did your mom have both you and Matt within just a couple of years?" Annie asked.

"A half-blood could produce children much easier than a full-blood, but it would still be difficult. Maybe Symatha was just that fertile?" I said, shrugging.

"Since Ansel is a half-blood, we don't know exactly what Ansel could die from. None of us know what his other half is. Aurtuno and I looked into it. We couldn't find anything on their mother, other than she died when Ansel was born. His father faded to the Underworld a century before I met Aurtuno," Lindy said.

"If they're supposed to be so hard to kill, then how did she die during childbirth?" I asked.

"She wasn't Ash'bani," Lindy said as Clarice picked up a book and was studying it carefully. "We have been trying to figure out what that other half is so that we can see if there is anything there to exploit to at least get him to stop this madness. None of us want to resort to murder."

"Why not?" the question came from Annie, and I whipped my head towards her.

"Mom, are you condoning us killing Ansel?" I said carefully. Even Logan, Mickel, and Owen were looking at her strangely.

"He's a twat. Boohoo, you couldn't have some information you wanted. Get over it," she said every inch a mom. Logan and I looked at each other, then back at her. Shock on each of our faces.

"I think I found something," Clarice said, pointing to a section in the book she was reading. "Why wasn't I made aware of this. My tutors should have taught me this." She was staring in disbelief.

"You had tutors?" Logan said, genuinely. There was no judgement in his voice. "You didn't go to a school? You had tutors? Is that how all children learn in this dimension?"

"Yes, I had tutors. Whether you went to a school or had tutors really depends on where you grew up."

"Not the point, Loog," I said, elbowing him.

I smiled at Clarice, and she explained what she found. "There was a major civil war that erupted between two factions of the Ash'bani. Because they were virtually immortal, the war raged for over a thousand years. The world was severely scarred and scorched by the wars that were fought between the two factions."

"When it appeared as though the war was going to exterminate all other races in the world, the Five Angels intervened. They banished them to the darkest parts of Obsecuritan, which is where later generations developed the slightly larger eyes. The Ash'bani pleaded with the Angels to spare them when the Angel of Death appeared. The Angel of Death, who was the only one who could take their life force, listened to their pleas and offered them a deal."

"Making a deal with Death?" Logan whistled under his breath, but Clarice continued.

"He would not change them as a race but required them to complete a Purification Ritual, which they called the Ardith. The Ash'bani would mediate and travel to the Five Angels and the Angels would then expel all darkness from within them to lead a normal life without the tortures of darkness, thus ending their need for war. If an Ash'bani did not complete the ritual by their 100th birthday, then the Angels would take their life force from them. The Ash'bani haven't fought in or started a war for over 4,000 Nalsar years."

The room was silent. Who would've thought there was something that dark in their past? Let alone something where the Angels intervened and put conditions upon their lives!

"I don't understand. Humans have light and dark in them. We turned out mostly ok," Logan said.

"But we have had our dark moments, too. Julius Ceaser, Emperor Hirohito of Japan, Adolf Hitler, Genghis Khan, Josef Stalin, plus some could and would argue that Saddam Hussein should be added to that list," Amber offered.

"But they're the ultimate Switzerland. Never even fought in a war for over 4,000 years?! That's crazy!" I said.

Logan whispered under his breath, "Think about that time table. That's so far into our written history... Do we even have any written history that old?"

"I hate to think morbidly, but we need to know. Does it say anything about what their weaknesses are?" Jean asked.

"Just that they're sensitive to climate changes, are overly stubborn, and the fact it is hard for them to create offspring. Pretty much what we already knew," Clarice said.

"Damn!" Owen cursed, kicking a chair, sending it scrapping against the floor. "Not anything we can use."

"Not unless you can freeze him to death," I said, only half joking. Logan muttered something about how it explained why I was so damn stubborn, but I did my best to ignore him.

"So you think killing him may be the answer," Annie said, smirking.

"Mom, I don't want to kill anyone. Ansel needs stopped, but let's try to find an answer that doesn't result in the death penalty?"

She smirked at me before saying, "I don't think this dimension would condemn you for killing him, sweety. Just do it here and not back home," she shrugged.

I stared at her as she got up and went to the kitchen to get some water. I could not believe what she just said. So casually. Who was this woman? She couldn't be the Annie I knew.

Turning my gaze to the floor, I chewed on my thumb and debated whether that was a thought I could even entertain. On the surface, I could say, "Yes, Ansel must die," but, on the other hand, could I do that? Could I actually be the one to physically and directly cause his death? Could I live with myself knowing that I killed my father? I mean, sure, I blamed myself for my mother's death, but it was an accident. I didn't walk into that room intending on killing her. I didn't go into that room intending on anyone dying. My only thought was to stop them from killing CJ and to get him back.

The guards came in with cots and blankets for the night and we were told Julian would speak to us in the morning. I gave my bed to Annie and Amber, with Owen and Jean sleeping on the couch's pullout bed. Everyone else picked a cot each and took blankets from the closet.

"Lady Megan, there will be two Nalrin Guard and four Vernadali stationed just outside your door," Remi said. "Just let us know if you need anything."

"Bit of an overkill, don't you think?"

Remi just smirked at me in a way that meant it was orders. "I'll see you in the morning, Lady Megan."

When Remi left, I curled up in a corner, but I couldn't sleep. My mind kept reliving the attack. The Ja'Nee had concentrated on me, but they had said nothing. It didn't help that every time I would close my eyes, I saw my father's exaggerated face back in Noctulanar cursing me.

Close to morning, Jean came and sat down next to me. "Megan, what's bothering you?"

"Nothing. Everything," I said, not able to look at her. "My mind just won't shut off. It's bouncing around. CJ, Ansel, the Ash'bani, how cool everyone took the information about my parents. I mean, I'm glad they're taking it in stride, but what if when they wake up they freak out because they realize it wasn't all just a dream?"

"Just be there for them. I have to admit, I admire how Annie doesn't want any of this craziness to impede you and CJ getting married," she said.

"How do you know she won't wake up and be the one freaking out?"

"Because we talked about it when you and Mickel helped get the cots set up. She figured something strange was happening when CJ told her he had to go to special training, but there was no way that she could come visit, send letters, or even a care package to him. When we picked her up, she asked if he was back yet, and she was disappointed, but understood."

I looked over to where Annie was sleeping down the hallway and into the bedroom, and she was out. She hadn't moved much, which made me feel better because it meant she wasn't overly restless, or the pain meds Horan gave her knocked her out. Either way, she was sleeping. "So, what woke you up?"

"Been thinking about the Ash'bani. Why would the Angels create a race that only they could kill? Or by growing old, and then give them such a long-life span? I just don't get it," she said, thinking it through.

"I don't get it either. I mean, humans on a really good day live to be a hundred, with a few exceptions. Most die between 80 and 100. And there are lots of ways for us to die," I whispered back to her.

"I just think there has to be a loophole," Jean said.

"Wish I knew what it was."

CHAPTER 19

THE NEXT MORNING, AFTER everyone had cleaned up, I had the kitchens send up some of my favorite breakfasts; Childar eggs, Cinder omelets, waffles, pancakes, and potato pancakes. After we all filled our stomachs to the point they felt like bursting, the guards hauled the cots and blankets off.

We were just settling back down when the doors burst open and Julian came in. Dark circles under his eyes, the braids in his beard looked like he had been fiddling and picking at them all night, and his hair was just a bushy mess. Did he even sleep last night?

My family was on their feet and formally bowed within seconds, but I didn't. Julian looked at me at first with a questioning look, but when I looked back at him and crossed my arms, he laughed.

"Lady Megan, you surprise me at the most bizarre times," he remarked.

"Lady-Megan. That's going to take some getting used to," Logan said as he and Amber giggled.

"A title she earned through bravery and respect by those of us in the highest ranks of the council," he said with authority.

Logan opened his mouth to say something stupid, but I interrupted before he could fully lodge his big foot in his mouth. "Annie, Logan, Amber. This is Julian. HEAD of the Nalrin Council. He is also technically Head Julian, Head of the Nalsar dimension, aka, the one who can instantly revoke your ability to be here and can probably wipe your memory of all things Nalsar," I told them as they instantly straighten up like they were standing in front of the President. In a way they were, but the President didn't have anything on Julian.

"So, Julian, when can we leave? Megan has an appointment at the dress shop in one hour," Lindy said, practically bouncing.

"You may leave after this meeting. However, there are some rule changes that Megan needs to be strictly made aware of," he said.

Nodding, I wondered how much security clearance I had lost with transporting here. I would be lucky to still be allowed to clean the stables here in the center of the city.

"I have spent the better part of the night with the Heads of all the realms." I saw Mickel flinch, and Julian's eye flicked to him quickly. "I don't think I need to explain just what kind of an uproar you caused transporting intra-dimension. And to the dimensional headquarters at that." His frustration was thick in his voice and you could see the red anger creep up through his black beard into his cheeks to his hairline.

"I'm sorry, sir. Since we are from the Manusia," Logan began, "could you please explain?"

"Ahh yes, America, having the right to know what you're being accused of. Very well. There is an agreement with all the realms... dimensions that you may transport between realms. However, transporting within the same realm without prior approval from the Head of said realm is strictly against the rules. Effectively, once Owen and Mickel transported you here, all travel in and out of our dimension was halted."

"Julian..." Owen started to say in apology, but Julian raised his hand to stop him.

"It is all sorted, and they agreed that considering the circumstances, it was justified. They have also approved Mickel and Megan for teleporting directly to Nalrin and your home."

"What of her family? The wedding plans?" Amber asked.

"If they're transported on the same trip as Lady Megan, you are covered," Julian explained.

"Sir, what if she is somewhere other than home and attacked? For instance, we were at the Nalrin River market when we were attacked," Mickel said, ever the bodyguard.

"I'm afraid the Heads weren't willing to give her permission to transport freely."

"Very well," Mickel said, as I looked at him knowingly. We were being left to defend ourselves.

"That's not all, however. The Heads determined there needs to be a punishment for those who actually cast the transportation incantation." I looked at Owen and Mickel. Owen's face went completely still and Mickel arranged his face hard as a rock and stood at attention. "Owen Kayl Tudor and Mickel Anatole de Seduisant, your powers are hereby frozen for one 36-hour cycle."

Mickel's jaw dropped slack, but snapped back up a moment later, and Owen was trying not to smile.

"One day?" Owen said, bordering on jumping up and down with excitement. "One day without our power? That's what the Heads sentenced?"

"Actually, no. They sentenced you to one year in *The Betweens*, but I told them considering the safety of our dimension, and possibly theirs, lies with the safety of Lady Megan, we needed to have you here, so I told them I would suspend your power. They agreed with no other questions," Julian explained, with a smile on his face. "They just didn't ask for how long your power would be suspended."

"*The Betweens?*" I asked.

"It's the place between dimensions. A vast area of nothingness where there is no one and nothing around you. It's the equivalent of solitary confinement in your world, but much worse," Lindy explained with horror and sadness in her voice.

"Now, Mickel, Owen, place your hand over the stone," Julian said as he waved his hand off to the left, and a microphone appeared, sticking out of a portal. A bunch of heads showed up beyond the rim of the portal, and when Julian saw what he was looking for, he said, "Owen Kayl Tudor and Mickel Anatole de Seduisant, you are hereby sentenced to the loss of your power for the time period previously discussed. At the end of said period, your power will be returned to you.

Within power to be held,
Time shall be your payment.
Upon the circle of the suns,
Within power returned."

As Julian spoke, you could see a light travel up from their torso, down their outstretched arm, pool into their hand and slowly drip onto the stone that vibrated and glowed gently before settling in Julian's palm. Mickel's looked different somehow as it dropped onto the stone. Like it didn't want to be absorbed, more like oil than Owen's. It took much longer for Mickel's power to be pulled from him than it did Owen's, and there was a light breeze that swirled around him before it would drop onto that stone. Jean flinched, and Julian's eyes narrowed at Mickel.

I looked at their embers, and they were dim and flickering. If we had been in a fight, I would've thought that they were seriously hurt. Their bodies slightly slumped, and didn't stand as tall as they normally would've once the last drops had fallen onto the stone. Julian turned to the microphone and said, slightly annoyed, "Sentence has been issued. Good day to the Realms." Flicking his finger, the portal closed.

"Angels, I really hate those guys!" Julian said with a smile. "Now go. I'm sure that Madame Sinclair won't be happy if you're late in her shop. Mickel, you shall stand guard outside the shop with Owen and Logan. I do not think Ansel would dare to attack her in Nalrin, but we cannot be too careful."

"Me, Sir?" Logan said, surprised.

"You're Vernadali CJ's brother, are you not?" Julian said as he was walking to the door.

"Vernadali CJ? I mean, I am CJ's brother, but—" he stammered.

"Then I think the Angels will look upon you favorably. Good day," he said as he walked out.

"Verna- Vern. I don't think you explained what that Vern-a-dolly is," Annie asked, as I flinched. She had sounded it out so slowly, it sounded like different words.

"It's a type of guard, a special sort of bodyguard," I explained.

"Oh, it's much more than tha..." Mickel started, but trailed off when he saw the look on my face.

She looked from me to Mickel and back to me. "Does this fall under, 'we don't tell you because there are things that we don't want you to worry about'?" she asked.

"Yeah, it does. We tell you the basics, but there are a lot of details that we just can't share. We don't want to scare the family. Whether they're good or bad things," I tried to plead with her. "Trust me when I say that he is going to kick Logan's ass halfway to Sunday and back."

"PFFF, whatever! That kid has never been able get the upper hand on me," Logan defended.

Mickel intervened, "Do you think I could kick your butt right now, even without my power?"

"Yes, because you're trained," Logan said quickly.

"Those who have watched your brother training have come to me and told me to brush up on my skills because that brother of yours is that good. Without any power like us Sangra," Mickel said.

"Remi said something about that too." He looked from me to Mickel and back. "Really? CJ is going to be able to kick my ass?"

"Oh yes, he will. I can promise you that and I will be in the front row to watch it," I said, and looked back at Annie. "Seriously, Mom. He is going to be able to take care of himself and me. Plus, he will have all of us watching his back. And don't think for one moment I'm going to let anything happen to CJ once he gets back."

"Okay, sweety. It's just the craziness we have seen and what you have told us... Well, I am his mother. It's sort of in the job description to worry," she said as she let go of my hand. I'm not even sure when she grabbed it.

"You know guys, Julian wasn't wrong when he said that Madame Sinclair would be mad if we were late. Tick. Tock," Lindy said, and Amber jumped up excitedly.

"I'm going to head down to the library to see if I can find anything else on the Ash'bani. Maybe even see if I can get time with Chyss or maybe even Zamph," Clarice said.

"Um... Clarice," I said, stopping dead in my tracks. I looked to Mickel and mentally asked him, *"Can I tell her? Is it even my place?"*

Mickel shrugged.

"She's going to find out, anyway. It would be better to hear from me," I told him.

He nodded in agreement.

"So, what's with the cogniti with Mickel, Megan?" Clarice caught on quick. "What aren't you telling me?"

"Wait, what is that?" Logan and Amber said at the same time.

I sighed. "Cogniti. It's like telepathy, only I can't read your thoughts. I can only put my voice in your head," I told them and before they could launch into a ton of questions, I continued, "and no, I'm not going to talk about it now."

"But," they said in unison.

"Later!" I pushed to them and their eyes went wide.

"Megan," Clarice said with a worried look on her face.

"Chyss and Zamph were assassinated," I said. "I did background checks on the replacements this week."

Clarice's face went from shock to methodical in seconds. I could see the wheels turning a million miles a minute.

"Yes, Julian thinks it was Ansel's doing. No, I don't know anything else."

"Who are the replacements?" she asked after more thought.

"Titus, As'nal and Tarol. They're to have their physicals and psych reports by week's end. Julian will decide and announce it one week before the next council meeting."

"Okay. I will see if I can get time with any of them. I'll start with Titus. He and my father go way back, so he will likely give me an audience. Thanks," she said as she stormed out of the room.

"Assas—" Jean started to say, but I cut her off.

"Not now. I rather not waste the time I have with Annie, Amber, and Logan here talking about politics. We will talk more when we get home. Clear?" I said pointedly. Without waiting on an answer, I looked at Lindy, "Ready?"

"You. Politics?" Amber said. I sighed heavily. "Damn, Megs. Your life really has changed in the last year. I didn't think you would've touched politics with a ten-foot pole."

"Trust me, if I had it my way, I wouldn't. I try to remind Julian that I'm not cut out for it, but..." I said, trailing off.

"What Julian wants, Julian gets," Owen, Jean, and Lindy said in unison. I just smiled and nodded.

"Alrighty then. Come on, Megan, let's go find a dress that will make CJ DROOOOOOL!" Amber said, pulling me out the doors. I couldn't help but smile.

"I'm not sure who is more excited, you or Lindy? You guys have me beat, and I'm the bride!" I said, as I tried to keep my arm from getting ripped off.

CHAPTER 20

IT WAS ACTUALLY REALLY hard not to bust up laughing at Owen and Mickel as we made our way to the shop. I had seen them strong and proud every day I had known them, and here they were tripping over their own feet. Jean even had to catch Owen to keep him from falling down the stairs to the bridal shop. When we got to the doors, the girls went inside, and the boys stood guard outside. Mickel and Owen really tried to look formidable, but their shoulders sagged, and they just didn't stand as tall. I saw Logan say something, giggle, and Mickel smacked him upside the back of the head.

Lindy practically skipped up to the desk, and when the girl looked up and saw Mickel standing guard outside, her eyes got big as saucers. "Welcome to The Budding Blossom. Home of the flawless Madame Sinclair. What can we do for you?"

"We have an appointment. It's under Megan Mathewson," Lindy told her. I looked at her strangely. "I figured if we made the appointment under Megan Keller, there would be a line a mile long of people wanting to see what you were choosing. It worked, since there was no one outside. Plus, since that's going to be your last name sooner than later, I figured; why not?"

I rolled my eyes at her. "No one is going to be that interested in what I'm wearing for my wedding."

The attendant bristled at that and said, "Lady Megan, I can assure you, people are very much interested in which dress you wear. When Madame Sinclair heard that you and Vernadali CJ were getting married this year, she hoped you would choose our shop. There wasn't a shop in the capital that wasn't hopeful you would choose them to find your dress. When Lady Lindy made the appointment with us, Madame Sinclair made us all sign confidentiality agreements bound to our power. If we break the agreement, we lose our power for a year."

"I'm nobody."

"Lady Megan, you saved our dimension once. We know that fight isn't over. Besides, we are very good at keeping information private here. We deal with many of the diplomats," she explained as she brought up our appointment on the tablet. "Okay, I have everything prepared. I'll get Madame Sinclair."

When Madame Sinclair came out, she brought in a bunch of dresses for us to look at. I told her to remove anything with long sleeves. This was a summer wedding, and I refused to be sweating for long hours in long sleeves.

I ruled out all mermaid-style dresses, since my butt was big enough. I didn't want to have it scream, "Here is my butt!" After trying on about a hundred other dresses, I had it down to three sleeveless with corset closures. Mostly because Annie and Amber said they liked the way it brought out my shoulders, which have been defined with all my training, and accentuated my waist.

The first dress was straight across the neckline, A-line silhouette, with white satin underneath a chiffon ruffle. The beading on the bodice had intricate flowers and leaves, and at the center of every flower were just a few red beads. It was beautiful, though this time, as I stood on the platform in front of the mirror with everyone looking at me, I noticed something I didn't before.

"Is it me or do my boobs look non-existent?" I asked as I repositioned the top and looked at it from the side.

"Totally flat," Lindy said after she studied the dress for a moment and let out an enormous sigh as Jean and Amber laughed. "Too bad too. I liked that one."

"It's beautiful, though. I just don't like how it makes me look like I have no chest. Not that I want to be all Boob-a-rilla or anything, but if I got it, I might as well not hide it," I said to Madame Sinclair.

"Very wise choice, Lady Megan," Madame Sinclair agreed. "Let's get the next dress on you."

The second one had a sweetheart neckline, which for sure didn't let me hide my chest, and the bodice had pleats that really helped show off my waistline. The rest of the dress was satin and taffeta with lace appliques and hand-sewn beading that dotted the skirt and gathered around the bottom edge. When I stepped out onto the platform again, we all agreed this was a much better choice.

"I have to admit, I feel a bit like Cinderella in this one," I said, smiling.

"Just a moment. Let me make some adjustments," Madame Sinclair said as she waved her hand and pinched here and there, making the dress fit perfectly. "There. How's that feel?"

"Like the dress was custom made for me!"

"That's why Madame Sinclair is the only place to shop for your wedding dress," Jean said excitedly.

I stood there looking at myself in the mirror, attempting to imagine myself walking down the aisle, and I suddenly felt a little old. Not old, like in age, but traditionally old. "Let's try the next dress," I said, getting down and heading back to the dressing room.

I put the last dress on, which was my favorite on the hanger. It also had a sweetheart neckline, but a faux satin wrap cinched across my waist. It started just from under my right breast and waist to a smaller point on my left hip. The top bodice portion had very intricate beading which matched the underneath of the white satin beak-front skirt that started at my left hip. The back was lower than the others and fell a little further than halfway between my shoulder blades and my hips. Madame Sinclair cinched the corset tie in the back and pinned my hair up into a loose French twist.

"Madame Sinclair, could you make the modifications like you did the other one before we go out there?"

"Absolutely," she replied and immediately started on the chest and working her way down and then added. "You know this shows off your Maltal beautifully." She added an extra inch to the bottom and a foot to the train. The more she worked, the more I could feel it fitting perfectly. When she was done, I asked her to change the corset ribbon to red and when she was finished, I didn't dare look in the mirror. I just walked out and walked onto the platform.

When I looked up, it was perfect. Flashes of the vision I had last year flittered through my mind. How had I forgotten about that vision?

Here I stood, looking just as I had at the end of the aisle, waiting to marry CJ. I looked at Lindy, and she was beaming with her hands clasped in front of her. Annie and Jean were smiling from ear to ear. Jean handed Annie a tissue, who dabbed her eyes.

Amber had her jaw fully on the floor and was gaping like a fish. Finally, she screamed, "If CJ doesn't marry you in that dress, I will. Megs, THAT'S THE DRESS!"

"I know," I breathed as I looked at myself. It was perfect. A movement in the front windows caught my eye, and I saw Logan looking through. He had his hand over his mouth and the other reached over to slap Owen and Mickel to get their attention. "THE BOYS! They can see!"

Madame Sinclair threw her hands up and the windows went black. "Not anymore, they can't," she said with a mischievous grin.

I sighed. "I almost hate to ask, because I'm not really sure it matters, but how much is it?" I asked, holding my breath.

"It is much more than the others, but you're right, it doesn't matter. The dress is already paid for," Madame Sinclair said.

"Excuse me?" I said, looking at Jean and Lindy, who were just as shocked as I was. "Who?"

"I am not at liberty to say, Lady Megan. Also, there is no point in arguing with me. This is not someone I am at liberty to say no to."

"Julian," I said, hissing his name, narrowing my eyes. "I'm gonna kill him."

I looked up and saw myself in the mirror. The dress really was perfect. I turned to see the back, and Madame Sinclair was right. The back cradled and highlighted my Maltal, and the red cinch was perfect to set it all off. This dress was elegant, clean, sexy, and just me. "Ok, let's get this off before I stain it with tears."

"Wait, I want pictures!" Amber cried, pulling out her phone and taking a few of the dress and details. "You know my mom is going to want to know what you're wearing. Don't worry, I won't show them to anyone else, but I have to have some for my scrapbook as well."

"What about a veil?!" Annie asked.

"I hadn't thought about using one?" I said.

"It's up to you, Megan," Jean shrugged.

"What is Nalrin tradition?" Annie asked Madame Sinclair.

"Traditionally, Nalrin brides don't use a veil, but we have them available as they're becoming more popular with the younger brides," Madame Sinclair told us.

"What do you have that's just plain and sheer? I don't want to distract from the dress. Especially in the back," I asked her and she went to see what she had.

When Madame Sinclair came back, she placed a tiny comb in my hair and placed the veil in. There was only the slightest shimmer when the light caught it. When Madame Sinclair took a step back after placing it, she studied me for a moment, then went to work making changes. She waved her fingers and arms, pulling and shortening until she got it where she thought it looked best.

"I like the look in the front," I said, turning to look at the back. Madame Sinclair had elongated it to reach to the floor, and because you could hardly see it, it only complemented the dress.

"You look perfect," Amber said, as Madame Sinclair ushered me into the back so that she could make any other modifications and I could change.

When I came out, Amber and Lindy were critiquing a knee-length, solid black retro 50s style dress with a sweetheart neckline that had a sash that went from under the breast and up to create straps up around their neck. The dress was adorably cute on them, but they had one more they wanted to show me. I thought I had only been gone about 10 minutes, but apparently, with the extra sizing and tweaking Madame Sinclair had spent on me in the dressing room, the girls had about an hour of discussing dresses.

I had told them that as long as they were black, red, or fit with the wedding, I didn't really care what style they were, as long as they were comfortable in them. That hadn't made Amber happy, but I spun it that if they got a black one, she could wear it to whatever she wanted in the Manusia, which won her over. If they decided on something hideous, I was going to tell them so.

"I like that one," I told them.

"I think you will like this one better, and I like them both equally, anyway. So, bride's choice," Amber said over her shoulder.

A few minutes later, they walked out in a 3-tone sleeveless, sweetheart neckline, knee-length dress. The top was white and pleated, the section between under the breast to the high waist point was red bunched satin, and from the waist down solid black. Amber was right. I did like this one better.

"So, what do you think?" Lindy said, bouncing out of the dressing room.

"I do like it, but I like the other one too."

"Well, which one do you like better?" Amber pressed.

"Like I said, whichever you're more comfortable in."

"This one fits in with the color theme of the wedding perfectly, but the other would give the wedding party a more uniformed look," Lindy contemplated.

They stood there, discussing it with Madame Sinclair, and when they finally decided, it was the solid black retro dress. Madame Sinclair made note of the measurements and adjusted the length on Amber, since she was shorter than Lindy, to make the dress look the same on both of them.

I went to the door to get the boys and when I opened it, the courtyard was packed with people.

Fuck. The media had shown up, and I had to squint against the flashes of light. The Nalrin Guard had been called in to help regulate the crowd. Mickel, Owen, and Logan slipped inside the shop, and we locked the door behind them.

"They showed up about an hour ago," Mickel said. "I called the guard office and asked them to send some help."

Sighing, I asked Mickel, "What tipped them off?"

"That was sort of my fault," Logan said, pointing to himself. "When I saw you in your dress, I was trying to get their attention, and I also grabbed the attention of a few passersby. They recognized Mickel as your bodyguard, Owen as your uncle, and well, before we knew it, there were people everywhere."

"Good thing I lowered the barrier," Madame Sinclair said, as she had finished up with Amber and Lindy. "Now, Owen, Logan, let's get your suits picked out. I sent word to my assistant in the Curtails of the North to get CJ's fitted, so I will have his suit ready with the others."

Lindy followed her to get the boys set up. There was no way Lindy would not have a say in what they wore.

"Lindy sure is obsessing about this, isn't she?" I said to Annie, Jean and Amber.

"She loves it. I think she would make a great event planner," Jean said.

"For her only knowing you for a year, Lindy knows you well enough to know what you will like," Amber said. "When the rack of bridesmaid dresses came out, she instantly went through the rack and pulled eight off and we went from there. There were a couple she pulled off that I shook my head at knowing that you wouldn't go for it. One looked a lot like Becca's prom dress, and we all know how that turned out," she said as she motioned how Becca's boobs had fallen out of the top dancing. Luckily, James had put his jacket over her quick enough that not everyone in our class saw. While we all laughed about it now, it was horrifying for Becca.

"Then there was one that I liked that was a wispy one shoulder piece, but she said the chiffon didn't meld with the look of the dress you chose. She just has an eye for it. It's almost like she can see it all in her head."

"Oh, I do not doubt that."

Once the boys were set, we signed for the purchases. Once again, I was told that I wasn't allowed to pay. I got a glimpse of the final total, and there were a lot of zeros involved. I tried to do the math, and unless the bridesmaid dresses were over 10,000 kinls, then my dress was way more than I would've ever paid on my own, even with the gross salary I was getting working with Julian. Madame Sinclair covered the number quickly, so I don't know for sure what it cost, but I was going to kill Julian. Okay, I wouldn't, but... I sighed, and she gave me a look that meant she was very sorry. I just muttered, "What Julian wants, Julian gets." She gave me a sad smile.

"We will deliver the dresses and suits to you on July 1st," Madame Sinclair said.

"My residence here in Nalrin? Or to the house?" I asked.

"The house, Lady Megan," Madame Sinclair said.

"Thank you."

"You're welcome. Now, let me show you the passage to your residence, where you can head back without having to deal with the crowd outside. Once you're through the doors, I will raise the barrier, and it will show that you're no longer here. Hopefully, they will leave soon," she said, like this was an everyday occurrence.

She walked us over to a curtain in the back and mumbled something at the curtain. It sparkled and sighed.

"Walkthrough here and you will be back at your residence, Lady Megan," she said with a formal bow.

"I'll go through first," Mickel said. "Wait 30 seconds before going through." Then he walked straight through the curtain and was gone. Everyone went through after waiting, as instructed, except for Logan.

"You sure you won't tell me what the dress cost?" I asked again, my voice low so Logan couldn't hear.

Madame Sinclair gave me a small smile and slipped a scrap piece of paper in my hand as she gave me a warm hug. I looked at it when Logan turned toward the curtain, and I almost dropped to my knees. I would never have paid for a dress that expensive.

"You will be the bride of the century, Lady Megan." Her eyes twinkled as she gestured to the curtain, and a smirk crossed her lips. "I'm sorry I cannot tell you the price of the gown."

"Thank you again," I said, as Logan and I walked through the curtain back to my residence.

CHAPTER 21

CLARICE WAS THERE WAITING for us when we got back, but she was distracted. She hardly noticed us come into the room. She just sat there on the couch, knees to her chest, arms wrapped tight around them, just staring at the carpet.

"What's wrong?" I asked when everyone else was chatting among themselves.

"Don't worry about it," she mumbled.

"Clarice, don't make me hang you upside down until you tell me," I said with a smile as I elbowed her in the leg.

"I knew Chyss and Zamph. It's just a little disturbing they were both assassinated near Therth."

"What's in Therth?"

Clarice's body got still before she answered, "My father." Then she stood up and asked, "So, since we can teleport back home, do we want to head back tonight?" She smiled, but it didn't reach her eyes.

We decided that, considering the circumstances, it was probably a good idea to head back to the house. Annie and Amber said they needed to head back home, but wanted to come back as often as possible to help with the planning.

Logan was a different story. He asked if it would be okay if he just stayed here in Nalrin through the wedding. He was off work for the season now, and he didn't have any real reason to hurry back. In his words, "Everything I want right now is here," to which Lindy blushed incessantly.

I sent word to Julian that we were leaving and gathered our things. I had Physician Horan come and check on Annie one more time, and once we had the all-clear, we packed, gathered in a circle, and let the blue smoke lift us home.

Jean offered to take Annie home, then stop by and pick up some pizza on the way back. I volunteered to take Amber. It was mid-morning in the Manusia, and a day at the beach sounded wonderful.

"Sorry, Megan, I can't allow you to go off alone," Mickel said, making himself look all big and threatening.

"It will be mid-morning there, and I want to hang out at the beach for a bit. Get away from all of this for a while and just relax. I promise to be back before the night is over," I said, ignoring his demand.

"Then I'm going with. I've never seen Monterey or much of the Manusia for that matter. Maybe you can be my tour guide," he said, trying to spin it like he wasn't a babysitter.

"What part of just hanging out at the beach isn't comprehending, Mickel? Besides, it's the beginning of summer, it will be foggy and cold for hours. The sun will come out for like two, maybe three hours, and then the fog will be back in. You will freeze to death," I tried to convince him. That last bit was true. The weather in Nalrin was consistently 20 degrees warmer than what Monterey was during the summer. He would be in a heavy sweatshirt and still cold while all the locals were in a tank top and shorts.

"It's California. I thought it was all sandy beaches and bikinis?" Mickel said.

Logan, Amber, and I just looked at each other, laughed and Logan said, "Sure, that's what LA wants you to think. Monterey is a microclimate, sort of. It's beautiful, but the best time to visit is the spring and fall when the valley doesn't get so hot that it pulls the fog in. Trust us on this one, Mickel."

"Well, I've never seen Monterey either," Lindy said, facing Logan while she ran a coy finger over his chest. He completely melted to her touch. It was sickeningly cute. "Feel like being my tour guide?"

"Sounds like fun! Let's go!" he said with a wicked smirk. "Maybe I'll take you to the Aquarium. It's one of the best in the world. I bet you will love the touch pool and otters."

"See! They're going. I won't be alone," I said, putting my hand on my hip.

"But you'll be at the beach, and they will be sight-seeing," Mickel said. "Even without my power, I can still kick ass, Megan. Don't test me on this."

"Why do I feel like I'm trying to convince my parents to extend my curfew again? I shouldn't have to ask for permission. I'm a grown-ass woman!" I complained, throwing my hands in the air and stomping my feet like a two-year-old. Logan and Amber were just standing there, snickering. "I've lived there my whole life, save the last year or so."

"You're a grown woman, Lady Megan. A very important grown woman who was attacked in route to the capital just yesterday. You are a very important woman, under Nalrin protection. More importantly, you are under Head Julian's personal protection, and you will not go unaccompanied. I. Am. Going," he said in a voice that was all bodyguard.

"Fine," I said, walking up to him and putting my finger in his face. "But don't you think for one minute about ruining my relaxation. I won't think twice about dumping your ass in the ocean."

"I can swim," he said with a shrug.

"You don't know much about the Monterey Bay riptides, do you?" Amber said, laughing. "Come on Megan. I'll help you pack a beach bag."

"Besides, you won't use your power in front of others," Mickel said, almost like he was trying to convince himself.

"HA! I don't go to the beach where there are others. I will use my power to dump you in the fucking ocean if you disturb my chill," I said as Amber grabbed my hand, laughing. Then I said over my shoulder, "And you don't have yours back yet, so I can do what I want."

We walked down the hall and she gripped my hand tighter. I squeezed it back and when we got to my room, I turned to her and asked, "Are you ok? You can tell me the truth. I have subjected you to a whole bunch of crazy shit since you got here."

"I am. I think," she said as she sat down on my bed.

I sat down and scooted up, folded my hands in my lap. "Look, Amber. If this is all too much for you and you want to back out of the wedding. It is ok. It's..."

"Ohh no! You don't get rid of me that easily. We've been friends way too long. Sorry. Not happening," she said firmly.

I was instantly relieved. "Good, because I've always pictured you up there with me. I love Becca, but she and I never connected like you and I did."

"That's not what I wanted to talk to you about. Yes, you have subjected me to a whole bucket full of fucking crazy in the last couple of days. I'm ok though. I will probably break at some point, but right now I'm probably in too much shock. Dress shopping helped. It was something normal. Plus, I'm working on my thesis paper, so I can dive into that to filter through it. Check-in on me in a few days?"

"Done deal," I said. "So, what did you want to talk about?"

"It's Clarice," she said, playing with her fingers. "Something is going on there. I'm not sure what. I asked her if she was upset because she wasn't in the wedding party, and she said no because she had told you she didn't want to be in it. She told me she couldn't wait to take part in sharing that day with you, but that she didn't feel comfortable being a bridesmaid."

"That's true. She told me it would just be too strange for her," I told her. "Too many lost memories or something like that."

"Okay. When we were in Nalrin, she kept getting notes from runners and I noticed it affected her mood, more and more," she said and then dropped her voice. "Then I overheard her having a conversation about darkness and something about that Ardith thing you were talking about with your dad's heritage? She was really concerned that they couldn't confirm something for her. It almost sounded like she was trying to confirm whether or not your dad had gone through it."

"Don't worry about it. It's just more family drama bullshit." If Ansel hadn't gone through it yet, that could be a problem. He had to be 90, 95 by now, if I went through the timeline right. Future me problems.

"What worries me is that last night, when we were in the cots, I overheard her talking in her sleep, or at least talking quietly in her sleep."

"What did she say?" I played with a stray thread on the duvet, trying to sound like I wasn't getting worried.

"She kept mumbling about the darkness calling to her, and it sounded like she was trying to convince the darkness to go away," Amber explained. When I looked into her eyes, I could see the concern there.

"I'll talk to her about it." I said and reached over and hugged her. If Clarice can sense darkness coming, that wasn't a good thing. Things were rising quickly, and I selfishly hoped it would at least wait until after the wedding. At the very least, until CJ got home.

"Ok. I really like her, and she is usually so cheerful when I'm around. It scares me to see her like this," she said as she stood up.

"I will talk to her. She knows more about darkness than any of us, though, because she grew up in a very dark region of this world. I'm sure it's nothing, but I will talk to her, I promise," I said, as I got up and packed for a day in Monterey.

After getting Amber home, Lindy and Logan headed off to Cannery Row to go to the Aquarium. Lindy was so excited to see the otters and Logan told me later that she was just like all the kindergarteners at the touch pool. I, however, spent the day, just as planned, with my feet either in the sand or walking the beach in Seaside by the Monterey Beach Hotel.

I loved Monterey, but it was strange to be back. Even though I had lived here my whole life, it didn't feel like home anymore. I could picture the nights out at the pullouts in Pacific Grove watching the stars on the rare clear night, listening to the waves with CJ, or the nights across the bay at the Santa Cruz Boardwalk with our friends, and the time in the arcade there.

I smiled at the memory of when CJ had asked me to go to prom with him. It was at the park halfway between the Aquarium and Lover's Point. I was so surprised that I asked him if he was serious. His only reply was that he couldn't imagine going with anyone other than his best friend. I had, of course, said yes. I laughed at how I had the same reaction to him asking me out twice. Both for prom and for our first date. Both times, I had asked him if he was serious. Angels, I really was about as sharp as a bowling ball.

Looking out over the bay, I took a deep breath, inhaled the briny air, and instantly felt my shoulders relax. There were so many fond memories of growing up here, but there were also really bad ones. Namely, my parents faking their deaths, and the painful memory of losing Matt. The more I thought about it, the madder I got. Subconsciously, I started playing with the sand in my fingers and toes and didn't notice when the sand had started to ripple away from me until Mickel came up and put his hand on my shoulder.

"Lady Megan? Are you ok?" he said, breaking my thoughts, sand settling back onto the beach. He was indeed in a sweatshirt and jacket and had still shivered occasionally.

I shook it off, and before I could answer yes, the word caught in my throat. "No. I'm not," I said, with a tear rolling down my cheek. I looked up at him. "I love this place. It is home, but it isn't anymore. Except, Matt. I feel like I'm leaving him behind."

He crouched beside me for a minute before settling in next to me, almost touching my shoulder. "You aren't leaving Matt behind. He is within you always. When a person dies, a piece of them stays with us, forever."

"I probably got stuck with his stinky feet," I said, wiping my tears and runny nose on the arm of my sweater.

"If he was half as exceptional as you are, Lady Megan—"

"If he was half as exceptional as me?" I interrupted him. "Underworlds tits! I'd be lucky to be half as exceptional as he was. He could always make me, or anyone for that matter, smile. No matter what was going on."

"Did he have a power too?" he asked quietly.

"He could feel what others were feeling," I said, watching the sand fall between my toes. "As for his power range, or how strong his ember was? I don't know. He never knew about Nalrin. He died before my parents faked their deaths here in Seaside," I said, jerking my head behind me.

"Oh. I'm so sorry," he said, and I could tell he meant it.

"Mom and Dad's house, well I guess I should say the lot since the house isn't there anymore, is only a few blocks from here. I need to just sell it off, or maybe I'll give it to Amber or something. I don't know." I sighed. "Listen to me. Seems like a stupid thing to think about considering all the other bullshit we are dealing with."

"For the record, lots of officials have homes in other dimensions. You could build something for you and CJ there," he said.

"I don't know." I played with a broken bit of shell in the sand. "I'm not even sure if I will live through this. I don't know where this is going, and I'm not making plans for anything past stopping my father. I've already told the estate attorney that if I die, the land goes to CJ."

"Are you and CJ planning on staying in Nalsar?" he asked.

"For now, that is the plan. But will he stay if I die? Will I stay if he does?" I said with a small shrug. The thought made me stop though, and a hard knot settled in my throat. "I'm not so sure I could survive CJ dying though."

He just gave me a sad smile that told me he understood all too well. Then he leaned back in the sand, looking out at the waves for a long time. He didn't need to say anything. He was just there. He could be a sounding board.

We sat there long enough that the fog rolled back out to sea; we basked in the sun; and the fog rolled back in. When I got chilled, I looked up past him and saw Lindy and Logan walking hand in hand toward us. Lindy with a very large otter stuffy and Logan with a huge shit-eating grin on his face. It filled me with hope. Hope that good could thrive in the world, even with the darkness that we were dealing with.

I turned back toward the water and watched the sunset over the horizon. I just kept breathing in the salty air, really committing it to memory. I'm not sure how long they let me stay like that, but eventually, Mickel walked up, "Lady Megan. It's time."

I sighed, got up, and brushed off as much sand as I could.

"Ready?" I said. When everyone nodded, I turned to Mickel. "Mickel, you want to do the honors of getting us back home?"

He narrowed his eyes, and I smiled brightly, trying to be as innocent as possible.

"You know I don't have my power back. Now, Lindy please take us home so I can get sand out of places that it doesn't belong and warm up?" he growled at me.

We laughed loudly at that.

"Told you it was colder here, Mickel," Logan said, slapping him on the back laughing.

We took each other's hands and the next thing I knew, I was standing in our front yard. The weight that instantly fell atop me when we landed back in Nalrin almost brought me to my knees. I caught myself by grabbing onto Mickel's arm.

"Whoa, there," Mickel said, grabbing me before I hit the ground. "You okay?"

I nodded and flat out lied, "Yeah. Just a long day is all." It had been a long couple of days, but this was different. I just wanted to go to bed and rest.

Mickel, Lindy, and Logan looked at me carefully before Lindy said, "It's not-"

"No. It's nothing. Like I said, been a long day. Long few days actually. I'm heading to bed. I'll see you guys in the morning." And without another word, I walked straight to my bedroom, ignoring everyone and everything else.

CHAPTER 22

I WOKE UP LATE the next morning, still feeling dark and heavy. I hauled my legs over the edge of the bed, which felt like lead weights hanging there. It took all of my concentration just to move. I forced my hands into balls and then sprawled them out. I stretched each finger as far as I could and felt them stretch through my palms. I tried to shake my legs out and even tried massaging them. They were just one step shy of being completely unusable. Even my head was clouded and disjointed.

Every time this feeling hit me; it was different. Some days it was just this light thing pressing on my shoulders, others it was almost debilitating. I tried to massage my muscles like they were tired and sore, but that wasn't working. There wasn't that pain that felt so good when you worked out a knot or just the pain of a hurt muscle. My legs didn't respond.

I knew it was the darkness calling to Clarice, but I wish it would stop. I slowly forced myself into the shower, but had to concentrate on every step. Each step was like pulling my legs through quicksand, and my hands and arms felt like they had fallen asleep. This was for sure the worst that it had been.

I forced myself to think about CJ. I tried to focus on how he could be home soon, and everything that was good and brought happiness into my new life. My family. The wedding. Jean. Owen. Clarice. Lindy. Amber. George and Annie. Logan. Logan and Lindy becoming… something. The laughs we have as a family. I even tried visualizing the hot water in the shower washing all the dark away, but nothing worked. I ended up just filling the bathtub and laying there until the heaviness eased. At least now I could hide it from the others.

I finished up and headed to the living room, where I planned on diving into my book for the foreseeable future. Just as I sat down and grabbed it off the table, Owen came in waving an envelope in his hand.

"Megan, this came for you earlier today." He handed it to me with a smile on his face.

I looked at the envelope for a long time, just smiling from ear to ear. I could feel the heaviness of darkness, but it lifted the longer I looked at the envelope. That handwriting that I would know anywhere. That blue seal with the three vertically alternating swords with a laurel surrounding them. That seal that marked it came from one place in particular. The one place my heart was. The Curtails of the North and the Office of the Vernadali.

I ripped open the envelope and read the short message.

Megs:
I love and miss you every day.
I can't wait to have you in my arms and make you my wife.
Three days. I will be home in three days.
Keep the bed warm and my heart safe.
Love,
CJ

I looked at when it was dated. Yesterday.

"Tomorrow! He comes home tomorrow." I shouted. Tomorrow. CJ was coming home tomorrow and in 38 hours, I could hug and kiss him. I was going to have my CJ back.

I danced around the living room, looking like a complete fool. I didn't care, and that heavy feeling that I felt earlier was still there, but CJ was on his way home and I was on cloud nine!

Hours later, I was still walking on air. I had loads of extra energy and I needed to get it out. I'd done all my chores in record time, and even re-hayed the stables. Even with all that, my power was still playfully bouncing up and down my spine.

"Lindy! Clarice!" I yelled, as I bounced into the living room.

"Yes, Megan?" they said in unison, both startled momentarily. Both of them had their heads deep in their books.

"Who wants to spar? I need to work some of this adrenaline out," I said, bouncing on my toes but trying not to.

"Wow, Megan. What a change from yesterday when you got home," Lindy said.

"Ceej is coming home tomorrow, and so, yes, I am just a tad bit excited. Now, whose ass am I going to kick?" I let out, as I heard Mickel snicker behind me.

"Okay, Mickel. I guess it's you," I said, turning on my heels and putting my hands on my hips. "Come on, let's go. Get those syths and meet me outside."

"Ahh, Lady Megan… are you sure you want to do that?" he asked. When I kept staring at him, he continued, "I'm a trained Nalrin Guard."

"Most decorated in all of the Nalrin Guard at that, Megan," Clarice said.

"Are you forgetting that I'm one of the most powerful Sangra that Nalrin has seen in centuries? Plus, I've been trained by Clarice, Lindy, and said Nalrin Guard. You've even given me some pointers while we were bored off our ass in Nalrin. Oh, and did I mention Remi has even found time to spar with me?" I said, trying to make it sound like I was super confident, but Mickel just looked at me.

"No, I didn't know you had snuck off with Remi," Mickel said, narrowing his eyes. "And when did this happen?"

"You have to sleep sometime. You also have meetings I don't go to." I shrugged, secretly satisfied with the fact that I had indeed done something behind his ever-watchful eye. "Come on, let's see what the most powerful Sangra can do against the Head of the Nalrin Guard," I said, pushing him towards the door.

"Most powerful Sangra? To hear you say that, when we all know you don't believe it, is... well... quite hilarious. So just for that, You're on!" Mickel said as a slow snide smile crossed his lips and his eyes glittered with the promise of a serious as whooping.

SHIT! What was I getting myself into? Lindy ran to the back and got Jean and Owen, because as she said, "I don't think anyone would miss this for all the realms." If they could, they would probably have invited Julian, the entire guard, and all the Vernadali and the Curtails of the North military to see.

I walked outside with my head held high, though. I would not back down. Heck, I was still trying to figure out what made me think this was even remotely a good idea. Even if I could land a few hits, it would make it worth it.

I walked out to the open area behind the house before the tree line, where we had created a makeshift training center. With me still having to learn so much, we needed a good place to train that didn't destroy the garden. I stretched and tried to calm my nerves. If I had half a chance at this, I knew I had to be totally focused.

"Seriously, Megan. Are you sure about this?" Lindy asked.

"Ahh... Yeah... Sure. Why not?" I said, not so confident this time, my eyes flicking toward Mickel.

"CJ will be home tomorrow; do you want all the bruises?" she said, raising an eyebrow.

"Well, let's hope the Sa Ra will heal me up in time," I said, showing her the necklace. I still haven't gone without wearing it. Just didn't feel right not to. "Or if not, I'd love to see Mickel and CJ go at it." I winked at her.

She sighed and threw her hands up in frustration. "Fine, it's your funeral. Guess I'll start canceling the wedding plans and reconstructing them to a funeral pyre."

I took a string of leather and tied my hair back tight and turned to Mickel. I noticed he had done the same, and when he looked at me, he smiled.

"You still sure about this, Lady Megan?"

"So, you're about to spar with me, at my house, where you basically live right now, and you're still going with the formalities?"

"Okay. Let me rephrase then," that wicked smirk was coming back. "Let's go, little girl. I'm going to show you what years of training and experience are like."

"Bring it on!" I said as I grabbed my syths and twirled them in my hands. I took a deep breath and then it wasn't Mickel anymore, just his ember, and I was ready.

We circled each other twice as we slowly got closer to each other, and I could see his ember pulse in his arms, his power fully returned to him. I could still see him as a person, but I tried to focus on his ember. He made the first move and lunged, but just before he did, I turned, sticking my leg out to trip him, but he flipped up and over my leg.

"Such a predictable move, but good recovery, Mickel," I teased.

He launched for me, and I ducked out of the way. I focused on slowing things down and watched for minute changes. He didn't wait a single moment before moving again. I ducked and kicked. Swinging, I hit nothing but air. Neither of us made contact for a long time. He hadn't once touched his power. Jumping back slightly, I studied him. Why hadn't he used his power?

"You're a good fighter. I'll give you that," he said, his breathing not as fluid.

"I've learned from the best. And ya'know, having to fight for your life helps too."

When he moved this time, I wasn't able to get out of the way and he landed a shot on my left side. It hurt like hell, but I whirled around, jumping into the air and kicked him in the hip. Before I landed, I used my power to push myself back upright and stood on my feet.

"Ahh, relying on your power already?" he teased, smirking with a fire in his eyes. "Tisk. Tisk."

I took a deep breath, coiling that power back into its cocoon. He wanted to do this without power? Okay. Let's go, fucker.

He jumped and kicked out toward my chest. I stepped back out of the way, taking my syths and slicing open his shirt with my right hand, careful to make contact, but not injure him. There was still a well of blood that came to the surface.

As he went to stand, I swung my leg up over his shoulder, which he grabbed holding me in place. OH ANGELS! I forgot how tall he was!

Straddling his shoulder, I swung my other leg up and around his neck so that I was facing him, threw myself backward, punching his knees. He broke his hold on my leg and I flipped back to my feet.

The look in his eyes was pure determination, and with a sly smile he said, "Oh, this is fun. I don't think I've had to try this hard in a long time. Most fall within the first couple of minutes. Weapon change?" he said, breathing heavily and wiping the sweat from his brow.

At that moment, I could see why Clarice and Lindy were so flustered over him. He had a rough sexuality to him that was very hot. None of them had said a word, but I saw their embers there, nonetheless.

I nodded and put my syths down, picked up the bow staff that was leaning against the weapons rack that was now a permanent fixture on the side of the house. I twirled it around my back, then did some figure eights to warm myself up before settling into my right hand to face him.

After he rubbed his knees, he lunged, trying to catch me off guard. The staffs clashed, stinging my hands, but neither of us stopped. I feinted to the right and whacked his right shoulder with a swing to the left. He tried to do the same, but I ducked and twisted out of the way.

Swing and duck.

Swing and duck.

It was like a dance that we had been doing for years. There were a couple of close calls where he almost tripped me up, but I flipped over the top of him to avoid the hit. There. He was breathing heavily and favoring the left side.

I twitched to the right, and as he went to protect it, I turned and hit him on the left side as I moved behind him. He whirled around and thrusting low for my knees. I stepped on the staff, jumped up, and brought my staff up and around his neck on the way back down.

He bent backward to keep from getting strangled. When I landed, I caught the back of his head with my knee and secured the staff on both sides of his neck.

"Give?"

"Nope, not yet!" he said breathlessly, twisting out of my hold. I just barely took a step up before he took my front leg out from under me.

"Nice," I said, studying him. His ember was still strong, and he still hadn't used an ounce of his power. I sure wasn't going to use mine if he didn't. No way did I want him to say I won because I was stronger power-wise. He wants a physical fight? I'll give it to him. I wanted to win this fight fair and square.

I punched the bow to the left, and our staffs clashed. Over and over again. Each connection stung my hand. He moved too quick for me to get under him and hit his forearm. I jabbed the end of my staff into his shoulder again and he whirled, shoving the end of his in just under my ribs. I coughed in pain as I stumbled back. I sputtered and gasped a couple more times, and Mickel jabbed at my left side. I blocked it, but it stung hard in my hands.

I needed to get a kill shot in. One that he wouldn't be able to get around. First though, I needed to get the staff out of his hands. If he wouldn't let me get to his forearms... I struck closer to the hands. When he let go with his left, I flipped the staff out of his right hand, where it landed a few feet away. He lunged for me, but

I tripped him at the last minute with the staff and he skittered to his hands and knees. I swung around and brought the bow staff down swiftly for his neck, stopping just before impacting his neck where I would've hit his spinal cord.

"DEAD," I said. He sighed, nodded, and collapsed on the ground, panting heavily.

"You're a better fighter than you let on. Angels, my knees are going to hurt for a long while. That hurt like the underworld."

Slowly, he pulled himself up from the ground and looked at his shirt. "Maaan, I really liked this shirt."

"I'll buy you a new one," I said, bumping into him. I had connected with my syths more than I thought. It was slit from his waist up to his shoulder blade in the back, and lots of other smaller cuts were splattered across the front. "To be fair, I thought you were going to handle me pretty quickly. I'm surprised I won."

I stopped short. "You didn't let me win, did you?"

"Oh, Angels no. It's not in my nature to let someone win in a fight. I'm in to win every time. They kind of drill that into your head when you're training in the Guard. So, let me reiterate; I did not let you win. If I lose, it's because I was bested." He shook his head. "I haven't lost a spar in a very long time. My pride is irrevocably damaged."

"Oh, don't take it personally. Great trainers. Plus, as a general rule, I pick things up really quick. Been driving them a bit crazy," I said, jerking my head toward my family, then sighed. "If I'm being honest, it is almost like sometimes it is a bit *too* easy to pick up new incantations. It doesn't seem right. A bit storybook cliché actually."

"Don't forget the way you can just manipulate your power to do whatever you want," he said. "I am proud of you for not just taking me with your power, though. I know you could have, but you resisted."

"It was obvious that since you hadn't used yours, and trust me, I was watching for it, that you wanted a physical fight. So, I tried to give it to you, win or lose."

"Just don't tell anyone. Any of you! If word got out I was beatable, they may, gasp, take my medals away." He laughed as we met up with the others.

My family just stared between the two of us.

"What?" I asked and looked at Mickel, who was looking just as perplexed as the rest of us.

"What did I just watch?" Jean asked, drawing out each word.

"Likely, the best duel we will ever see," Owen said, almost in awe.

"What are you talking about?" I was very, very confused.

Clarice and Lindy looked at each other, and Logan just slowly took Lindy's hand.

"Megan," Lindy said carefully. "You didn't access any of your abilities while fighting Mickel?"

"Just watched his ember," I said as Mickel tossed me a towel and I wiped the sweat off my face. "Why?"

My family looked at each other again and just shook their heads.

"If you aren't going to tell me, then I'm going to take a shower," I said and headed into the house.

Just as I was closing the door behind me, I saw Mickel staring each of them down and heard him ask, "What did you see?"

CHAPTER 23

THAT NIGHT, AS I laid in bed and tried to get to sleep, I just tossed and turned. I knew that in the less than 38 hours I would be with CJ. That thought alone kept me up for hours before I finally just passed out from exhaustion. Sadly, my brain didn't let me sleep. I dreamed of my father pulling me over the edge of the cliff again. I keep fighting the chain, keep fighting the pull to the edge of the cliff, but every time I see my father's wide smile as I reach the edge, it breaks all concentration, and I tumble over into the darkness.

There had to be a connection between my dreams and father. That weight and pull to the edge had felt so much like the weight that pulled me under after Noctulanar Castle last year. I just couldn't find a connection.

After lying in bed for an hour, I gave up and jumped in the shower. As I stepped in and into the water, that same dark and heavy feeling settled over me again, but this time it was like short little tugs instead of a constant gloom. I set my mind to happier things and tried to ignore it. I finished up and headed to the living room.

Clarice was sitting out with the book on Obsecuritan on her lap.

"Clarice?" I asked quietly.

She looked up and there were dark circles under her eyes. I wondered how much sleep she was getting nowadays.

"You okay?"

"Yeah," she said, shaking her head. "Just couldn't sleep. What are you doing up? It's a little early even for you."

"Couldn't sleep. Bad dreams," I said, flopping into the chair.

"Still don't think it's a vision?" she asked carefully.

"Not unless an oversized version of my father is going to wrap a chain around me and pull me off a cliff," I said, trying to say it lightly, but it just came off tired and exhausted.

"You were in a coma. Maybe the way they feel has changed as part of it," she said, cocking her head to the side.

I shook my head. "I don't think so."

"I have to say, it would be very convenient to get some idea of what we are going to be facing after the wedding regarding Ansel. Just a glimpse of what we could face, just to help prepare, would be nice."

"Clarice. I would love for them to come back, but they aren't right now. I'm sorry. I can't control it." I didn't realize how viciously I had said it until I felt a tear fall to my cheek.

"Oh, Megan, I'm sorry. I didn't mean..."

"It's ok. I know you didn't. It's just, I want them back. I didn't realize how much they were a part of me until I stopped having them." I took a deep breath and studied her for a few minutes. She just sat there looking at the book and then out the window.

I looked down the hallway, and then asked as I played with my fingers, "Since it's just us right now, can I talk to you about something?"

"Of course."

"When we were in Nalrin, you were getting lots of notes from runners, and you seem pretty down. Are you ok? Is there anything we need to be concerned about?"

"No. My father's health is rapidly declining and since I was there, it was easier to get messages to and from Therth. So just old family stuff."

I looked at her for a moment longer and decided that was enough digging for now. "Okay, well I'm here to talk if you need to." She nodded. "Wanna help me find out more about the Ja'Nee?"

"Why? Isn't that what we have been trying to work out since the attack?"

"Julian said they have to have a connection to Ansel. I think so too. I don't know why or how, but we know nothing about them, so, time to do what we always do, research," I told her, shrugging.

"Fair enough. Where should we start?" she asked.

"The book on Noctulanar?" I shrugged, but she shook her head. "The Obsecuritan book?"

"Nah. We were through those books cover to cover last year. I don't remember anything about them in there." She got up and started looking through the bookcase. "Here, try this one on Ancient Incantations. I'll look through Ancient Runes, see if there is any connection to the Ash'bani."

I started in and next thing I knew, my stomach was growling, reminding me I need nourishment to think clearly. When I looked up at the clock, it was past lunch already.

"Is everyone still in bed?" I asked Clarice, who was still in her book.

"Jean and Owen went to work on the garden after tending to the stable. Mickel should be back any time from his run. Lindy is..."

"Right here, of course," she said, bouncing into the living room. "So, what have you guys got your noses into today? Megan, you aren't reading that book series again, are you?"

"No. Well, yes. I'm on book five again, but not the point," I said. "We both woke up early this morning, and so we decided to see if we could find out anything about the Ja'Nee. There has to be a connection to Ansel somehow."

"About all I know is that they are assassins, creepy assassins at that, but we already knew that from the attacks at Nalsar River," Lindy explained.

"Speaking of creepy. Where is Logan?" I asked her and her face turned beat red.

"In the shower," she said with a sheepish, guilty look. I swear her face turned pink from the thoughts.

"Hey! You guys are adults." I looked up at her. "I'm just glad you're happy, Lindy. You really do deserve it."

"Thanks. I've been thinking about what you said before, about how it will be different this time, and I think you're right. I love him, Megs, but don't say anything. I haven't told him yet," she said whispering so quietly I'm not sure Clarice heard her.

"Cross my heart," I said, crossing my heart and heading into the kitchen. "I need a break and some substance or my body is going to rebel against me."

I rifled through the cabinets and decided that a grilled cheese sandwich was in order. I grabbed the bread, butter, and cheese and started heating the pan. My mind was racing so fast, trying to process everything I read this morning that when I heard footsteps behind me it was instinct to grab the pan and swing back toward the intruder.

"Woooh. Megan! Didn't you beat me enough yesterday?" Mickel said as he grabbed my hand where the pan was just inches from his face. He gently placed it back on the burner for me.

"Sorry," I said, turning back to the pan. "Guess reading up on ancient incantations and the creepy origin stories behind them leave you a little on edge."

Mickel looked at me with concern. "Are you sure that's all?"

"Yes. No." I sighed. "Look, don't make anything of it. I've been getting this dark feeling come over me and I don't know what it means. With the wedding, CJ coming home, and everything else going on, I don't want to add something else to the pile of things to figure out."

He nodded and sat down at the table.

I ended up making a sandwich for him too, and was surprised that he had never had one. "You've been around me for months and you haven't had a grilled cheese sandwich? Angels, have I wronged you."

"You have. This is really good," he mumbled through his bite.

"Not the healthiest because it's just butter, bread, and cheese, but you could add some meat to it, and at least get some protein out of it."

"Ohh, I bet Yonklier meat would be good. I'll pick some up next time we are in Nalrin," he said, taking the last bite and putting his plate away.

"Not sure when that will be. I got a message from Julian yesterday afternoon. He is letting me off work until after the wedding," I said, savoring every bite of my sandwich.

He leaned against the counter and stared at his feet. I knew that look. He was thinking about why Julian would let me off work when there was so much to do.

"It's probably to keep me in one place since the Ja'Nee attacked me," I said, as Owen and Jean came in from the garden. "He is a wee bit overprotective of me."

"He feels responsible for you. I think he cares for you like his own daughter. He lost his when she was about your age. You remind him of her in a lot of ways. Strong willed, mouthy..." Owen said, smiling.

"That would explain why he paid for the dresses and suits for the wedding," I said.

"What?" Owen and Jean shouted.

"Yeah. Madame Sinclair wouldn't tell me who, but she didn't correct me when I cursed Julian's name under my breath," I said, putting my dish away. "I'm going to go for a run. Anyone want to join me?"

"I will," Mickel said.

"You just got back from one," I protested, but he gave me that bodyguard look again, and I just didn't have it in me to fight him. "Okay. I'm going to go change quick, and meet you out front in five?"

As I walked through the living room, there were two quick bright flashes out by the garden. My body instinctively went on the defensive. I grabbed my syths from the rack by the front door and ran outside, already searching for embers that were unfamiliar. The ember standing by the garden was one I would know even in the deepest depths of the Underworld.

There, standing at the entrance to the garden, was my CJ.

Next thing I knew, I was wrapped in his arms. When his lips crashed onto mine, all was right in the world. My body filled with electricity, and I grabbed his shirt at the shoulders and tried to pull him closer to me. I would not let one speck of dust come between us at this point. He kissed me back with a vigor that would make a porn star blush. The feel of his hands through my thin shirt was hot and greedy. When our kiss broke, I whispered breathlessly against his lips, "Hey."

"Hey yourself," he whispered back, his eyes lighting up, leaning his forehead to mine. "That has to be the best welcome home I have ever had."

"I missed you so much, Ceej."

"Not nearly as much as I missed you," he whispered, then he kissed me quickly as he held me tight.

"Oh Angels! Get a room!" I heard Owen say behind us.

CJ put me down, though I hadn't even realized my feet were off the ground. He smiled and pulled me close, kissing me again. The world disappeared, and there was nothing but him. The warmth of his hands on the small of my back lit a fire in the pit of my stomach, and that heat was making its way through my whole body. Screw that. Every inch of me lit on fire. When our kiss broke, I was having to take deep breaths to get the air back. It amazed me that even after all this time, he could still take my breath away.

"Again, I'll say get a room!" Owen said with much delight in his voice. He walked up and gave CJ a big hug. "Though, to be honest, I've missed having you around the house. All the girls, Mickel's been some help, but man, we need some more testosterone."

"Missed you too buddy."

I couldn't take my eyes off CJ. His hair was shorter, and he was still my stalky man, but all that training had defined his arms, and gave his legs some more definition. It was a slight change because it wasn't like he was ripped or anything, but you could tell they were working them out pretty hard. I circled him with a smirk on my face.

"Damn babe. Liking the butt," I said as I gave it a pinch and gave him another quick kiss on the cheek, leaving my arm around his waist. He smiled, wrapping one around me, pulling me closer.

Clarice, Lindy, and Jean came running up to him and engulfed him in a big group hug.

Mickel walked up and bowed. "The famous Vernadali CJ Mathewson, I presume. I have had the pleasure of watching over your soon-to-be wife over the past months. I'm Mickel de Seduisant."

"*The* Mickel de Seduisant?" he said, looking at me. I rolled my eyes and nodded.

"Nice to meet you, sir," CJ said, bowing formally. "I have to say, when they told me about you up there, I wasn't sure if you weren't just a legend."

"No legend here. Just a regular Sangra doing his job," he said uncomfortably.

"As he said, Mickel is my bodyguard," I said carefully. "Julian appointed him after we got back from the Christmas holiday, just as a precaution. And don't you worry. He even said that you'll be able to protect my body in ways that he can't," I added, curling up to him, trying to make it sound like no big deal.

"Was he there with you when the Ja'Nee attacked you earlier this week?" he said seriously.

"How?"

"Julian," he said, giving me a knowing look.

"Of course," I said. "Yes, he was. I had been making the trips to Nalrin alone, and it seems Julian had Mickel start 'escorting' me back about the right time. Regardless. I don't want to talk about that now. Let's go inside. Oh, and Lindy, why don't you go get your boyfriend."

"Boyfriend?" he said with his eyebrows high. I nodded and smiled.

Lindy ran inside and, in a flash, came out with Logan.

"Logan?" CJ said when he saw his brother come through the front door, then looked at me. "Seriously!?"

"Oh, it's *very* serious," I told him, shoving him toward his brother.

"Cory!" Logan shouted, and it was like a cheesy, romantic scene seeing those two run to each other.

One second, I was watching CJ and Logan reunite, the next I felt like I'd been hit by a wall. When I put my hands on my knees, I realized Clarice was doing the same thing.

"Wow. This one is strong. It's not letting up either," she mumbled.

"What is going on?" I heard CJ ask as he returned to my side.

Lindy filled him in, but I not wanting to ruin his homecoming, I gave her a pointed look. "Clarice's father isn't doing so hot and the darkness of Obsecuritan is calling her and Megan."

"Why, Megan?" CJ asked as he put his hand on my back. The warmth of his hand felt so good and eased the feeling a bit for me.

"She used her blood as a sacrifice at Noctulanar Castle. To open the gates. It's connected to the darkness of Obsecuritan. That same darkness is already in my blood." Clarice paused and let that sink in a little.

"Is it going to hurt her?" There was an edge to his voice.

Clarice actually giggled as she straightened up. It was already letting up, and she put her hands on her hips. "She's fine. She's just sensitive to it now is all."

"Looks like she's a little more than sensitive to it," CJ said and put his hands around my waist and helped me into the house, even though I didn't need it. I let him. His strength warmed me, and I craved his touch.

"It's fine CJ. Really. Just happens every once in a while," I told him as he set me on his lap in my favorite chair. I curled up and in what seemed like no time at all, I wasn't feeling any darkness at all.

Clarice, however, said she wanted to lie down for a while. The others had made themselves comfortable and were listening to CJ tell stories about what it was like in the Curtails of the North. Cold was all I got out of that conversation, and how much he enjoyed the training. I was paying attention, but not really. He had wrapped his Vernadali jacket with fur lining in the hood over me like a blanket, and if I wasn't so excited that he was home, I could have easily fallen asleep. I just stayed curled up in his arms, listened to the sound of his heartbeat, and inhaled his scent. It was richer somehow. Spicier.

This wasn't how I had imagined the first few hours after he got home, but my CJ was home, and he never had to leave my side again.

CHAPTER 24

LINDY AND JEAN HAD gone back to the Manusia to get Annie so they could work on the wedding a few times over the last month since CJ had gotten back. Annie was thrilled to see CJ again and used the wedding as an excuse just to come and see him. Lindy, Jean and Annie caught CJ up on what plans they had made for the wedding and made a few suggestions based on the Vernadali traditions, such as him wearing his Vernadali uniform, which he looked marvelous in. Of course, I was just a tad biased.

We were only a couple of weeks out from the wedding, and I was getting nervous. Not because of the wedding per se, but because Julian had increased security for miles and miles around the property. I tried to tell him when he visited a couple of weeks ago that if Ansel or the Ja'Nee, which we still knew next to nothing about, wanted to get through, they would.

Julian's visit wasn't completely worthless, though. He had brought some books on the Ja'Nee from Head Researcher

Bonak. We were slowly going through them, but not finding much more than what we already knew.

While Jean, Lindy, and Annie were selecting table cloths and seating decorations for the reception this morning, I was reading through one that I thought had the most promise. I was about three-quarters of the way through when I found what I was looking for under a section entitled *Darkness Rising*.

"Guys." They weren't listening. "Yo people!" I shouted louder and everyone turned to me.

"Here is a section on the Ja'Nee." Mickel and CJ dropped what they were doing, and when I looked at them, they were both standing like mirrored bodyguards, right down to where their hands were placed. I just sat there and stared.

"What?" CJ asked, relaxing a bit.

"You and Mickel..." I said, smiling. I saw Lindy smile, too. "Nothing, never mind."

"So, what did you find out?" Owen asked.

"They're in a section called *Darkness Rising*," I started. "It says that the Ja'Nee, a misty figure who take on a humanoid form with a bark-like textured face under their hood, are made of pure darkness and therefore do not actually hold a true physical form." I paused and thought about the attack at the river.

"That makes sense since when I stabbed the one in the back it just flipped around and shot darkness at me," I said, looking at Mickel, "but Mickel..."

"Logan and I beheaded one, and it totally disappeared," Mickel finished. I turned back to the book.

CJ's eyebrows shot up. "Logan?" Mickel nodded. "Logan. My dipshit brother, beheaded one of the things that attacked you?"

"Yes," I said like it was nothing and continued. "The Ja'Nee are assassins from the deepest parts of the Underworld and do not leave unless ordered to do so by one who controls pure darkness. The Angel of Death, who created them to guard the deepest parts of the Underworld, does not control them, for the Angel of Death is still filled with much light. The only way to discharge a Ja'Nee is by beheading. That's it. That's all it says."

"Beheading just about anything is going to kill it," CJ said, half paying attention.

"Who controls pure darkness, though?" Lindy asked.

"I don't know," Jean said.

"What about Clarice's family? You said there is a connection to darkness there, right?" Annie offered.

"That's a logical assumption, Mom, but it said one who controls pure darkness. Her family has darkness within them, just because of the region they were born in. They aren't darkness itself, let alone pure darkness," I said.

"Logical?" CJ said with a smirk. "Did you turn into a Vulcan while I was gone?"

I rolled my eyes at him and then sighed. "I know you've been gone a lot of the last year babe, but I thought I showed you just how unlike a Vulcan I am last night. Be careful or I'll have to, ya know, show you again how unlike a Vulcan I..." Then I stopped because well, his Mom and brother are standing right there, and there are some things that should just be kept in the bedroom.

He winked at me and just said, "Promises. Promises." I couldn't help but smile.

"Seriously! Star Trek innuendo?" Logan said. "You guys are such geeks."

CJ smiled and said, "Vulcan sex can be quite —"

"Anyways, Clarice. Thoughts?" I asked, my face bright red from embarrassment.

"You're right, my family couldn't control them. The darkness that's with us differs from the darkness in the deepest part of the Underworld. It's pure and untainted by light. That makes it the cruelest and unforgiving kind of darkness. The Gatekeeper to the Underworld can't even control that darkness, and he can control things no one else can, short of the Five Angels themselves. In short: These creatures are not to be messed with. If someone has called forth that kind of darkness, then the realms have a serious problem," she explained.

"The realms?" I asked, glancing at Annie, whose eyes were wide. Was she terrified or just shocked? She gulped. Terrified, I decided.

"The underworld spans across every dimension, Megan. If that darkness is rising, it can enter any realm," Clarice said, staring off out the window in a way that made a chill go up my spine.

"I... I don't understand," Annie said with a slight tremor to her voice.

"The Underworld is where every being in any realm goes when they pass on. There are different levels to it. Think of it like in..." she thought for a moment before coming up with her analogy. "Like in Greek Mythology. Everyone goes to Hades' realm, right? There are places of paradise, and places of pure torture within. In the Underworld, the Angels decide to what level, or land, you go to live out your eternity. Much like the Judges do in Greek Mythology."

Annie said, "So no heaven or hell?"

"No," she said, smiling softly. "Life is too gray for things to be so black and white. No one is purely good, and rarely is someone purely bad. It's..." She trailed off and I could see her warring with herself, as she chewed on her thumb and her leg bounced up and down.

"How do you know so much about the workings of the Underworld, Clarice?" Owen said quietly, but she just pointedly ignored him.

"Should I get a message to Julian?" Mickel asked when it was clear Clarice was done discussing the matter.

"No. We haven't heard of any other attacks using the Ja'Nee. Until we do, let's continue with the wedding. Besides, I don't want to incur Jean or Annie's wrath by canceling the wedding this close," Clarice said with a tight laugh.

"And what of Megan and I's wrath! I have waited years for her to be mine, and you're worried about her aunt and my mother?!" CJ fired back.

"Oh, trust me, we are worried about you two, but seriously, look at your Mom and Jean," Lindy said. "Moreover, when we were in Nalrin, you didn't hear her go all mother-in-law from hell."

He turned to his mom. She had her hands on her hips, and her eyebrows raised. "Hi Mom! I love you! Thank you!"

"Damn straight, mister. You may be some all-powerful Verna... Verb... whatever, some super bodyguard and stuff now, but I'm still your mother and I will still knock you to next Tuesday and back. You and Megan are getting married on July 2nd. We have waited way too long for this to happen, so it is happening," she said with her hand on her hip.

I loved having her here. It was like being back in the Manusia and hanging out at his house again. The only one missing was CJ's dad, but he said someone had to pay for the wedding. I think that was just his excuse not to be dragged into all the planning details. Though, to be fair, Annie hadn't told him about the attack and so he didn't know about any of the craziness that had happened on the trip to Nalrin.

"Yes, Mom," CJ and I said in unison.

"CJ, I heard a rumor that I needed to brush up on my skills because you would—what was it they said, Megan?" Mickel said to change the subject.

"Ahhh," I had to think for a second, "I believe his words were, *'That soon-to-be-husband of yours can kick some serious ass,'* and that if you were going to stay my bodyguard, you would need to brush up on your skills. I could be wrong though." I smiled, knowing I wasn't.

"Oh, they did, huh? And who told you that?" CJ said, laughing as he kissed the top of my head and sat down.

"Remi," Mickel said, saying like it was no big deal.

"Well, Remi would know. I missed him when he got reassigned, though I guess that was partly my fault." Then he looked up at me quickly and back to Mickel.

"Why was that your fault?" I asked.

"Ahh nothing. Don't worry about it," he said, not looking at me.

"If it's about what they said and what happened after, I know already," I said, leaning over and putting my hand on his arm.

He just looked at me. There was something like fear, but also determination in his eyes.

"Why don't you guys go clean up the sparring area, while I have a quick chat with Mickel and CJ," I said to the others, not letting my eyes move from CJ's.

When it was only the three of us in the room, CJ broke his stare and asked, "How did you find out? Did Julian?"

"Remi," I said. "Ceej, honey. First rule of this whole bodyguard thing is no secrets. You can't keep shit like this from me."

He looked at me for a second, and said, "There are some things that I won't tell you, but I get what you're saying."

"Look, I appreciate you standing up for me and everything, but do you really think I care what some guys popped up on testosterone think?" I said, putting my hand on his cheek.

"No, it's just," CJ started.

"Besides, shouldn't you take it as a boost to your ego that others think I'm hot enough to fuck?" I asked, trying to lighten the mood. "Underworlds being, I'd fuck me. I'm sexy as hell!"

"Megan, I don't think that's what CJ means," Mickel said, looking at CJ. "Vernadali are more than just a little protective over their charge. It's chemical. That chemical is released and amps up the protective instinct in that person. It allows them to very literally think of their Charge before themselves. That's why a Vernadali will take a syth for their charge without blinking an eye. That chemical overrides any self-preservation."

"Only it's amplified by a billion times for me. They tested it. They don't know if it's because we are romantically involved or if it's because I'm Angel blessed, or what. They suspect that it may have even manifested itself before we went to the Garden of the Angels. There is also the added issue that my Charge was already determined by the Angels. No one else has their Charge assigned yet, so their epinephetrocal chemical, they call it '*The Charge*', doesn't kick in like mine does. So, when they were... talking about you, I got supercharged, and well, that's why they spent time in the hospital."

"So why was Remi's reassignment your fault?" I asked.

"He tried to cover for me," he said, sighing and running his hand through his hair. "They said it was because they had a better option for him at Nalrin, but I know it was because he covered for me. When Vernadali Samuel asked what had happened, he tried to say that it was just a practice session gone to extremes, but the Commander said I was uncontrollable. Said that it took four other Vernadali to get me off them. Four, Megan. Four fully trained, long-standing Vernadali. That's when they did the test and found my Charge off the chart, even hours later."

"Oh, Ceej,"

"I didn't get in trouble because they said I was charged up and therefore I couldn't control it. I was protecting my charge," CJ said. "Only, I shattered a Vernadali's arm, and it delayed his training by six months. They said it may never be the same. I hurt one of my fellow Vernadali's and that's going to stay with me."

He turned to me, and I could see the pain in his eyes. Then he took a deep breath and changed the subject. "Well Mickel, you challenged me to a spar, right?"

"That I did," he said, smiling.

"Even after knowing what happened up there, you still wanna spar?" CJ asked.

"Well, I won't be trash talking your woman. Straight fight. No Charge. No Power. Just straight fighting," Mickel said.

"A chance to spar with the legend. Ain't no way I'm passing that one up," CJ said, smiling brightly. "Grabbing my syths and I'll meet you out back."

I walked out back with Mickel. "My bodyguards sparring each other? Do I even want to watch this?"

"Maybe. Maybe not. I guess the question is, are you going to stay on the sidelines and keep from protecting him? I know how your mind works. I will land hit him and he will get hurt. Are you going to watch that and stay away?" Mickel said as CJ came out, twirling his syths in his hands.

"*I guess we will see. Mickel, please be careful,*" I pushed to him as CJ joined us. He just gave me a meaningful look as to say, 'I'm not going to kill him, but hurt him a bit for sure.'

"Nice syths babe. Know how to use them?" I teased CJ.

"What do you think I was doing for the last three months? Basket-weaving?" he chuckled.

CJ stood in position as Mickel tied his hair back and stripped down to a white, tight-fitting tank top. I heard Lindy and Clarice whistle at him, but my eyes were solely on CJ. He too had stripped to a tight-fitting tank, and it showed off just how fit he was. His skin was still somehow tanned even after being in the north. That tank hugging the muscles on his chest and gripping his abs made my stomach tighten. When my eyes fell to where his Vernadali tattoo was, there was an almost audible pulsing between my legs. I clenched my legs together and bit my thumb. In the span of one second, I saw myself in the bedroom, running my hands up and down that body, memorizing each and every inch. With my tongue. I shuddered with my next breath and took another one to center my power, bringing both their physical beings and their power embers into view.

"Megan. Whatever it was that just went through your head right now," CJ said, almost with a growl. "Stop. It's distracting."

Mickel just chuckled under his breath as I looked at him carefully. How? What?

Once they were both ready, Owen started the fight.

Just like when I fought Mickel, they circled each other. CJ's movements were slow and methodical, while Mickel's were jumpy and scattered. He was playing with CJ, and I resisted the urge to tell him so mentally.

"Come on, boys, stop playing around and just duke it out already!" Logan shouted, as his mother smacked him on the chest.

"If CJ gets hurt, Logan, I'm holding you responsible," she said.

I couldn't help but laugh, but apparently that was the push they needed. CJ lunged for Mickel. When Mickel got a slice into CJ on the shoulder, it was a good thing that Logan was there to hold me back. Out of instinct, I wanted to go in there and protect him. I heard Annie cringe and hiss through her teeth, but she stayed in where she was.

"Annie, how are you not jumping in the middle of this?" I whispered to her.

"I raised CJ and Logan. Sometimes I just shoved them outside the door and said fight it out. Twenty minutes later, they would come in with broken noses and fat lips. I would patch them up. Sometimes boys just have to work their differences out with fists. This is a little harder though, with the knives," she said, cringing as another slice went into CJ's forearm.

Their arms and legs were moving so fast I had to watch their embers in order to keep up with them. Like really fast. I don't remember Mickel moving that fast with me.

That SHIT!

He did let me win.

"Mickel, you're a fucking jerk" I shouted. "Ceej. Kick his ass for me."

"Babe, I appreciate the permission, but I'm a bit busy here," he shouted back to me as his arm was forced behind his head and he dropped his syth onto Mickel's foot and it stayed *in* his foot, to which Mickel cussed under his breath and I smiled gleefully.

At that point, their arms and pants were cut to shreds, and Mickel called the syths out and said body only. They put their syths up and cleaned away the blood that was seeping from both of their wounds before they walked back to the center to face each other.

"Straight hand-to-hand combat," CJ said, smiling.

I watched as they punched, kicked, and jumped each other. It was more like an MMA fight than anything else now.

There was more blood, but for some reason, this was easier to watch.

They could still kill each other, syths or not. I knew that, but this was easier.

At least that's what I kept telling myself.

Fifteen minutes later, they called a draw.

"Megan, at least you know you can be protected," Logan said, then whistling appreciatively. "I couldn't even see them at times they were moving so fast."

"Mickel de Seduisant. You're such a lying mother fucking asshole," I said, power surging to my fingertips.

He spit blood off to the side and gave me a questioning look.

"You said that you didn't let me win our spar," I said through gritted teeth.

"Wait, you sparred with him?" CJ said. "And you won?"

"Well, he let me think I did," I fired back. I could feel the muscles in my arm tighten and my hand clenched into a fist. If he didn't answer me properly, someone was going to have to pull me off of him.

"I did not let you win," he said, pointing at me and wiping his face with his shirt. Then turned to clean up a slice in his side that CJ had made with his syth. Jean waved her hand, healed it for him, and he gave her a small, appreciative smile.

"Really? Because I don't remember you moving that fast with me. I had to track embers, you guys were moving so fast."

"Megan. You moved that fast. Jean and I discussed it the whole time you two were fighting. It was like watching a fight in fast forward," Owen said, holding my forearm. He had seen me preparing to punch him.

"Don't you cover for him!" I said through gritted teeth.

"No, seriously, he isn't covering for him. When you two fought, it was incredibly fast," Lindy said. "That is why we stared at you two afterward. In fact, Mickel asked us not to say anything to you."

"I don't believe you," I said in a huff and I stormed toward the house. If I didn't leave, not even Owen would have been able to hold me back.

"Seriously? She sparred with you, and kicked your ass?" I heard CJ say behind me.

As I strode to the back door, I saw Mickel nod his head and say, "Yes. Hard on the ego. I hadn't lost a fight in a very long time. You're a lucky bastard. She can take care of herself, that's for sure. Then to have us and this family to back her up. Ansel would be stupid to try anything."

I slammed the door behind me and sighed, leaning against it. I knew I was being a serious drama queen, but my stomach dropped as Mickels' words settled within me. Mickel was wrong. He was so, so wrong. Ansel was reckless and stupid. It was going to take everything that this family had to fight him off, and I didn't want to think about what that cost would be.

CHAPTER 25

I WOKE UP SNUGGLED tight against CJ's frame and sighed. I slept the night through again. I hadn't had the dream of Ansel pulling me over that cliff since he had been home. My Vernadali was protecting me even in my dreams. I cherished the feel of his chest rising and falling against my back, the feel of his arm around my waist, and how his legs curled up into me. Angels, I missed this.

The time he was gone made me realize just how much I love him, not that it was in question, but I felt different without him here. I was still me. Powerful, self-reliant, and all those things that make me Megan, but when he is here, I just feel stronger. We aren't different people when we are apart, and I don't need him to make me complete, but we are better together. That alone would get me through anything.

I laid there for a long time just letting him sleep. When he rolled over onto his back, I rolled over just to watch him. There wasn't anyone I wanted to marry more in two days. I ran my finger over his Vernadali tattoo on the underneath of his forearm that he got when he finished training. It was the Vernadali herald: three alternating vertical swords surrounded by the laurel. Underneath was a scroll with the name of his Charge; my name, Megan. I giggled as quietly as I could.

"What's so funny?" he said, his eyes still closed.

"Thought you were still asleep."

"Nah, been awake for a while. You were talking in your sleep. Yelling at Mickel for something."

"Humm. I don't know. I don't remember it," I said.

"So, what's so funny?" he asked again.

"I was just thinking that I'm your Charge."

"Yes. I would've been more than a little pissed if they were cruel enough to Charge me with someone else," he said deliberately.

"Yeah, but now you're really stuck with me. You can't get rid of me even if you wanted to."

"And what makes you think I want to get rid of you?"

"I know you don't. It was just a silly thought, that's all."

He rolled on top of me. "Yes, it was silly." Then he kissed me and I wrapped my arms around his neck, pulling him closer. We had taken every opportunity we had to have sex since he returned. There was so much time to make up, and there was nothing like the feeling of him inside me.

He moved the hair out of my face and then kissed my nose. "Man, I would love to just stay here in bed with you all day."

"Maybe we should. Just you, me, the sheets. We could 'playhouse' and enjoy each other," I said, as he reached down and kissed just below my ear. The movement had him pressing against me, the thin material the only thing keeping him from entering me.

"Build a pillow fort!" he said, his head popping up excitedly.

I laughed. "Yup, and stay all day fending off the Lindy and Jean dragons who force us to make decisions about the wedding!" Then there was a soft knock on the door, and I sighed. "Or not."

CJ climbed off of me and went to answer the door. "Ceej! You're just in your boxers sporting an impressive hard on!"

"That's what they get for interrupting my private time with my fiancé." He opened the door, and I heard Logan say, "Ahh dude! Clothes please!"

"Logan! If you don't have a fabulous reason for interrupting, I'm gonna leave you hanging upside down inside a flower in the garden. I was about to have my way with your brother, and you know I get cranky when I don't get my way," I said loud enough for him to hear, but not the whole house.

"Well, it's a good thing that I have a good reason then."

"What is it?" CJ asked with a groan.

"Julian is here," Logan said, cringing a bit. He knew Julian was the last person we wanted to see today. I searched out the embers in the house and low and behold, Julian was sitting in the living room.

"AHHH Angels! Now what?" I said, as I heard CJ cuss under his breath.

"Ok fine. We will be out in a few minutes," CJ told him and shut the door.

"Raincheck on the pillow fort?"

"Tonight?" I asked excitedly.

"It's a date," he said with a smile, and leaned down to kiss me. It was soft and gentle. Warmth spreading through me, melting me like butter. When he broke our kiss he whispered, "I love you, but first dibs on the shower."

"Oh, not if I don't get there first," I said, but before I could get the blankets off, he wrapped me up like a cocoon.

He was almost done in the shower before I could get out of that thing. When I stepped in the shower behind him I told him, "You can tell Julian why it took me so long to get ready." Then I pushed him out of the shower.

"Man, you're cranky when you don't get your way," he said with a smile, sticking his head back in to stick his tongue out at me. When I turned to get my hair wet, he reached in and turned the hot water off. I yipped, cussed him out and turned it back on as he laughed hysterically.

Grumbling, I showered quickly and got dressed to meet the others in the living room. When I saw Julian there, he wasn't in his usual formal attire.

"Julian. What can we do for you?" I asked.

"I'm on my way to my sister's house and figured now would be a good time to go over some pre-wedding formalities with you," he said.

"Ok, like what?" I asked.

"First the vows. Are you going with Manusia tradition or Nalrin tradition?"

"Crap, I hadn't even thought of those," I said, somewhat embarrassed. "What is Nalrin tradition?"

"The Bride and Groom write their own."

I looked at CJ, shrugging.

"We can do that. I never liked the Manusia vows, anyway. Besides, it's not like you would say obey. Not that I would expect you to either," he added quickly when he saw the look on my face.

"There are two things you should know. The first and last lines have to be read in a certain way to be bound by Nalrin law. The first 'I take you, the other's full name, as my husband or wife.' The last, 'I give you my heart, forever to hold,'" Julian explained.

"Done deal," I said. "What else do we need to iron out?"

"The next, you probably already know, and I have to insist," he said. "Nalrin marriage laws state you must sleep in separate bedrooms and abstain for the two full nights before the wedding."

"I'm sorry! What?" I said, dumbfounded.

"You have to be kidding me. I just spent months away from her. The last thing I want to do is spend two more nights without her by my side."

"In order for it to be legal, I must insist." Julian's eyes narrowed at the rest of my family.

I looked at Jean, Owen, and Lindy, who were trying very hard not to make eye contact. "We have spent how long planning this wedding? You have planned every detail down to the exact size of the napkins for the reception, and you couldn't mention this to me once?!" I could feel my power pulsing inside me and my fingers felt very electrified. CJ slid his hand into mine, intertwining our fingers, and I relaxed slightly.

"We were going to tell you tonight. We just didn't want to deal with the fight," Lindy said.

"So, you were going to wait until the last minute," I said, and she nodded.

I took a deep breath and looked at CJ as he said, "I want this legal. I mean, I've already got you in every way possible except on paper, so if this is what we have to do, fine, but I don't like it."

"What is next on the list?" I asked grumpily.

Julian pulled some paperwork out of his jacket and said that we needed to sign the official forms stating our agreement to the two-night exclusion, we agreed Julian would perform the ceremony, making our marriage binding in all realms since it was performed by the Head of this dimension, and stating the location of our honeymoon, in case of emergency.

"Now, that's an excellent question," I asked, turning to CJ. He had told me before he left for the Curtails of the North, that he would handle the planning of our honeymoon, and never once had given me an ounce of an idea of where we were going. "Where are we going?"

"That's for me to know and you to just have to wait and find out," he said with a kid's voice.

"Seriously? You aren't going to tell me where we are going?"

"Nope," he said with a pop.

"Have I been there before?"

"Megs. I'm not telling."

"Whatever."

"Megan, will you be taking CJ's last name?" Julian asked, interrupting us being children.

"Of course!" I said so fast that Julian could hardly finish the question.

"Reason?" Julian pressed. He looked genuinely confused.

"Most importantly, because I want to be his. I want to be part of his family, to make it our family."

"But you have created a name for yourself here in Nalrin. The whole Nalsar realm knows of Megan Keller."

"I want my name to have meaning on an intimate scale. I can't wait to rid myself of a name that's plagued with hate and vengeance. I want my name to mean love and dedication," I said fiercely, but quietly.

I turned to look at CJ, whose eyes were lined with silver. The entire room was quiet for a long time before Julian spoke. "Very well then. That's all I have, but I believe there is something Lindy wanted to discuss with me?"

Lindy stepped forward and handed him a piece of paper. "Yes. This is the guest list for those from the Manusia that will need to be transported here. I have talked to Madame Sinclair, and she has agreed to let us use her passageway, instead of having half the Nalrin Guard transporting people back and forth..."

"But you need my approval and incantation to have it work between the dimensions," he finished for her.

"Yes, sir," Lindy said cheerfully.

"What of confidentiality?" he asked.

Annie stepped forward. "In the invitations to the wedding, and as part of the RSVP, we included a confidentiality clause whereby they're to ask no questions about the actual location, or arrival to the wedding. In fact, they're not to talk to anyone about the wedding unless it is with someone who was actually there."

"Jean and I cast an incantation on the RSVP cards, that if they signed them stating they would be here, then when they did speak to someone about the wedding to another attendee, they would actually speak in Ancient Nalrin, but hear it in their native tongue," Lindy said.

My gaze went to each of my family. They had been busy, but I didn't realize the lengths that they had taken to keep both dimensions happy to keep the secret that Nalrin existed. I was impressed, and when I looked at CJ, I could tell he was, too.

"All that for our wedding?" CJ asked.

"Yes," Annie said, smiling at her son and standing tall. "When you said you wanted your wedding here, I went to Jean to see if there was any way we could get the extended family and, of course, George's business partners and friends here, without causing an issue. Jean and Owen set to find out just how we could make that happen."

"Mom, I'm so sorry. I didn't even think about the logistics of all that for having the wedding here. I'm sure if you had said something, we would've moved the wedding to somewhere in the Manusia," CJ told his mother. "Or had a Manusian wedding in a few months."

"Absolutely, I'm sorry you guys had to go through so much trouble," I added.

"Really, it wasn't that big of a deal." Owen said. "Ok, yes, it was, and I'm very proud of us for finding that incantation to make it happen, but that's not the point. Megan, CJ, you are family, and to do this, it is just part of giving you the wedding that you rightfully deserve."

"Where will the entrances be located?" Julian asked.

"Here, it will be at the tree line with a hedge on either side to block the view from out of the forest, and in the Manusia it will be placed at Amber's grandparent's house in Carmel Valley. They have acres of land against the Ventana Wilderness, and we will do the same hedge there at the tree line behind their house. The thought is that they will think they're going from one side of the hedge to the other by going through the passageway."

"And I will appoint security. Annie, can you make sure that Amber knows I will send some Nalrin guards to be at that location at her parents' house?" Julian said.

Annie nodded.

"Great, I already have Nalrin guards at the entrance here, and surrounding the property," Julian continued. "Mickel, can you take me to the site location in the forest and we can discuss the strategy?"

"Julian, why are CJ and I getting the royal treatment?" I asked quietly.

"You are royals in my eyes, Megan. What you have done for this dimension can never be repaid, and thus you are, as you put it, Royal," he said softly. *For such a small person, he sure has a big heart.*

"We never wanted that though, Julian," I said.

"I know, but that is not relevant," he said, standing. "Now Mickel, with me. Oh, and Madame Sinclair will be here by midafternoon tomorrow with your dress, bridesmaids' dresses, and various suits. It is quite a beautiful dress, Megan. Worth every kinl." He winked at me as he slipped out the door as I just glared at him, trying very hard not to send a shock of my power to his ass.

"What does he mean worth every kinl?" CJ said, staring after Julian.

"That was the benefactor who paid for all the wedding attire," I said, my blood pressure spiking.

"Even the custom Vernadali uniform?" CJ asked, surprised.

"Even your uniform. You don't even want to know what he paid for the dress." I wanted to scream. "I'm going for a run. Anyone care to join me?"

"Yes," CJ said.

I got up and stomped off to the bedroom to put some running shoes on, and in five minutes, CJ and I were out the door.

CHAPTER 26

THE NEXT TWO DAYS were filled with last-minute preparations, set up, and the amount of Nalrin Guard in the area rivaled what I saw every day in Nalrin. I had next to no privacy and to top it all off; I slept horribly. I had nightmares all night, both nights. In the last two nights alone, my father pulled me off the cliff no less than four times.

The morning of the wedding, I had such a wonderful dream of CJ and me, much older than we are now. *We were hanging out on a warm beach with Lindy and Logan watching Bluchree playing in the waves, while a broad of children played in the sand.*

A brown-haired, brown-eyed little girl, who couldn't have been more than four years old, came running up to Lindy, "Mommy, Brannen won't let me play with the filka."

"You tell him that Mommy said to share or she'll make Uncle CJ spar with him again," Lindy told her. The little girl's eyes brightened and ran screaming back toward the waves.

"Lindy, honey, stop scaring that boy," Logan said, kissing the top of her head.

"Well, seems CJ is the only one that boy fears," she said as the four of us burst into laughter and I woke up smiling from ear to ear.

My smile faltered as I reached over to an empty bed. I stared at it for a moment, and then the smile was back on my face.

Today is July 2nd and I will be marrying Cory James Mathewson. The one person who knew everything about me. Knew every secret, every piece of my history, and who, when my world was literally thrown into chaos, grabbed ahold of it, and rode through it with me. He left everyone and everything behind to stay with me. ME. He stayed, and accepted everything that has happened to me, to him, and to us with grace, and never once complained.

I took a deep breath, got up, and put on my running clothes. My nerves were making my power bounce wildly and, therefore, made my skin crawl so much that I had decided a good run was in order to help clear my head.

When I reached the kitchen to have a bagel, Amber and Lindy were each eating a bowl of my cereal.

"Um, where do you think you're going?" Amber said, looking me up and down.

"To the fridge to get some cream cheese to put on this bagel?" I said with sass.

"Okay, and after that, where do you think you're going?" she clarified, as Lindy tried to stifle a laugh.

"I'm going for a run. The wedding isn't until twilight, which is like what, a hundred hours from now? I think I can afford a little time to go for a run," I said, smirking slightly at her.

"We still have hair, makeup, and need to get dressed. There is so much to do. Not even including the fact we need to double-check to make sure that everything is set up right in the meadow, double-check to see if the incantation is working on the waterfall, etc., etc., etc.," Lindy added waving her hand in circles.

"Well, it sounds like you have a full day ahead of you. I, however, have to go for a run. Then, sit down and read while you decide to dress me up like a Barbie and, most importantly, come twilight, marry the man of my dreams. None of that needs to happen for at least another..." I made a show of counting off my fingers, "Four to eight hours at minimum, so yes. I'm going for a run," I said, as I took a bite of my bagel, smiling.

"Did I hear my name?" Logan said, walking in, looking a little worse for the wear.

"No, I was talking about your brother, AND what did you do last night... More importantly, what did you do to CJ?" I asked, just as Owen walked in and looked like someone had hit him with a shovel.

"He took us to Las Vegas," Owen mumbled. "Where is that Manusia drink... coffee. I think I need some of it."

"What you need, Owen, is to go back to bed and sleep that shit off," I said, shoving him back toward the bedroom. Lindy and Amber were trying not to burst up laughing.

I turned on Logan. "Seriously! Vegas? You and CJ can handle Vegas. Fuck! Amber, Clarice, and Lindy can handle Vegas. Owen and Mickel? They don't have alcohol here. He can't handle that shit!"

"Yeah, no kidding. Owen is the lightest lightweight I have ever seen in my life. Mickel did pretty good, though. He said that the Nalrin Guard has a brew that isn't the same, but causes intoxication," Logan said. Amber started busting up laughing. "One of the waitresses at the Rio had a thing for Owen though. Or was it at Planet Hollywood, or Ceaser's, or Bally's? Oh no, it was at the MGM. Hell, I don't remember."

"Logan Francies Mathewson!" I screamed at him. He cringed, and Lindy laughed out loud.

"Francies?" she said, trying to stifle her giggles. I just gave her a look.

"If you broke my bodyguard, uncle, and your brother, I swear, with every ounce of power in me, Lindy teasing you about your middle name is going to be the *least* of your worries," I told him with my sparkling finger in his face.

And that's how Annie found us. Him standing there hungover to the nines, and me with my finger in his face, knowing that my power could zap him, which it did, right on the very tip of his nose. I smirked, and he just jumped back and rubbed the tip, glaring at me.

"Oh GOD! Logan, what did you do?" she said with a sigh and trying to pull me further away from him. "Did you miss the memo about not pissing the bride off on the day of her wedding?"

"I'm going for my run. Annie, kill him for me please, and then can you check on CJ to make sure Logan didn't kill him. Owen, stop standing there giggling. Go back to bed and sleep it off," I said as I jogged out the door and slammed it behind me.

What an idiot that man is! Seriously? Owen in Vegas? I love my uncle, but he has never been there and ugggggg.... seriously! I darted for the forest.

When I reached the clearing, workers were setting up the seating and the wedding bell flowers in the aisle. Jean was barking orders left and right and smiled when she saw me. I ran over to her and gave her a big hug.

"Thank you," I said.

"For what, sweetheart?"

"Everything. All of this. Taking me in. Last year. Literally, everything," I said and hugged her tight again.

"It is Owen and I's pleasure. We love you sweety and you deserve your very special day."

"I love you too," I told her, wiping a tear from my eyes.

"Now go. I don't want you to see what this looks like until it's time."

"Okay. Okay." I kissed her on the cheek and headed back out.

I ran through the forest and just concentrated on the feel of the air against my face and the feel of my muscles propelling me along. I wasn't paying attention and almost ran straight into a Nalrin Guard.

"Lady Megan!" he said.

"Oh, I'm so sorry. I guess I've reached the perimeter."

"You have," he confirmed, looking at me. "Not running from the wedding, I assume."

"No, no, I can't wait. Just out for a morning run."

"Head Julian has made it very clear that no one is to go past the perimeter, in or out, unless by his permission."

"Very well. I'll run the perimeter. How far apart are the guards?"

"Point seven, give or take," he said, nodding in each direction.

I did the math in my head and figured that if I ran the whole thing, I could be done in time for Lindy and Amber to make me into a Barbie doll. Maybe I could even kill some more time and stop by the creek for a serene moment before continuing on. "Ok, I'll run it."

"Lindy, I'm going to run the perimeter. Be back in a few hours," I told her mentally. Hopefully, she got the message. No doubt she was going to be mad as a hornet's nest, but it gave me a couple of hours to just get away.

I thanked the Guard and headed out. As I ran, I visually imagined taking everything that weighed on me and throwing it from my body. I wanted to sit back and enjoy today when I got back. I passed the first guard, who nodded and then flipped his wrist. His ember pulsed just slightly. That must have been the signal to the next guard, and sure enough, when I reached the second, he did the same thing.

I ran up the hill past the third guard and stopped at the top for a moment, taking a drink from my water bottle. It didn't seem like long before I got to the next guard, and he nodded at me and signaled the next in line. When my watch told me I should be at the next check in point, I didn't see him. Maybe I was off route, so I pushed on and a few minutes later, I got to the next guard.

"Lady Megan. I didn't get the signal that you were approaching," the Guard said.

"I must have missed one or gotten off course and didn't meet up."

"Well, congratulations Lady Megan and have a good day."

"You too," I pushed off and headed for the creek, where I sat down and splashed my face with some of the cool water.

I looked down at my hands, and they looked fuzzy, dark, and hazy. Oh, not today. I sat down and took a few deep breaths. It felt as though there were ten sandbags on my shoulders. I tried to center myself and felt out. Everything looked normal. I could just see the two guards on either side of me. Stupid darkness. I sat there concentrating on pushing it away and listening to the creek.

I tried to visualize the darkness being washed from me and flowing on down the river. It took a while, but it worked. Though maybe it just wore off. When I looked down at my watch, I had been sitting there for nearly 45 minutes. The guard next up was looking out my way, so I sent him a message. "*I stopped at the creek. I'm fine. On my way to you now.*" I saw his ember stop and relax a bit, so I knew he got it. I put my shoes back on, though I didn't remember taking them off, and headed out. Great, now I'm losing my mind.

I completed the rest of my run without incident until I got back to the house where her Royal Highness Lindy aka my hairdresser aka maid of honor aka best friend aka wedding planner aka all things obnoxious was standing there waiting for my return arms crossed and looking very cranky.

"I know I took longer than expected, but we still have all kinds of time," I said.

"We have less than 6 hours!"

"Lindy. Stop," I said, putting my hands on her shoulder. "First, we are where we need to be and there is no travel time save maybe a 15-minute walk from the house to the meadow. Everything we need is here. Second. Do you hear yourself? You're the one acting all crazy, and usually, that's the bride. Maybe you needed to go for a run."

She looked at me for a moment and then sighed. "I know I'm acting all crazy, and I have totally taken over everything. I just want it to be perfect for you."

"I know you do," I said as Amber came over to join us. "You, Amber, Jean, and Annie. You guys have done more than I ever could have dreamed. Growing up, I wanted a simple family-style wedding. I know that isn't feasible here, considering Julian, but whatever. You guys have listened to what I want, and when CJ came home, you even incorporated his ideas, even when the wedding was knocking on our front door. I really can't thank you enough."

Amber and Lindy smiled. "Like she said, we just want everything to be perfect for you."

"And you have. Thank you." I gave them each an enormous hug. "Now I'm going to jump in the shower. Did anyone go to make sure Logan didn't kill Mickel and CJ last night?"

"CJ is fine. Said something about Jose something..." Lindy said.

"Cuervo. Jose Cuervo, Lindy," Amber said, then turned to me. "CJ said he and Logan did Fireball shots as well. Boys," Amber said, rolling her eyes. "CJ is fine. Not even hungover. Took it like a champ."

"Tequila and Fireball? How did they make it back standing?" I said, shaking my head. "They're adults, but seriously? Vegas? I really could kill Logan."

"Go easy on him. After you left, Annie gave him the riot act pretty hard," Lindy said as we headed back into the house.

"Still, he could have told me beforehand. Where's CJ?" I asked. They stopped dead in their tracks.

"George and Annie are holding him hostage until showtime. They seem to think that they're going to follow our tradition that the Groom doesn't see the bride on the wedding day before," Amber said warily.

I just looked at her. What was it with this? CJ and I have been around each other for as long as either of us can remember, and on the day of our wedding, they were going to hold us apart?

Six hours.

Only six hours. Then he really doesn't have to be out of my sight ever again.

"Fine, I'm going to take a bath then instead of a shower. I want to soak my legs after that run," I said, as Lindy growled in frustration.

When I got to my room, there was a note from CJ.

My love,

I tried to sneak in to see you this morning, but Dad found me and I got sent to the quarantine unit, aka Logan's room, for the day. Mom said that you went for a run, so I'm leaving this note just to tell you I love you with all my heart. I truly cannot wait until this evening when I get to officially give it to you for safekeeping.

Thank you for believing in me.

~CJ

I smiled and held it close to my heart, trying not to cry for a few minutes before I stripped and got into the bath.

CHAPTER 27

ONE THING I LOVED about the water here in Nalrin, the bathwater never gets cold. That pretty much meant that I would sit there and just soak in the hot water until I shriveled up and became a raisin. On a normal day, I wouldn't care, but it may not be the best idea for my wedding day. Frankly, it was hard to relax with Madame Sinclair, Lindy, and Amber planning everything else that they thought need to be done before showtime. Each time I would get my shoulders to relax, I could hear them chattering in the other room, and they would tighten up again.

I stood up, rinsed, and toweled off as I heard them disagreeing on how I should have my hair done. It wasn't like we hadn't discussed it, and I thought we had decided it was going to be up, even though I had a sleeveless dress, but apparently, they didn't think that was going to be the case, or rather, they didn't agree on *how* it should be up.

"To tie in with the scenery it needs to be, down, loose with pieces of wedding bells in it," Madame Sinclair said.

"It doesn't go with her dress, though. It should be up and slick. Refined and glamorous," Lindy said.

I rolled my hair up, on the top of my head, threw my bathrobe on, and as I walked out of the bathroom, I said with a smile, "Or you could let the Bride at least have some say in her own wedding."

"Of course, Lady Megan," Madame Sinclair said quickly. "What would you like to do?"

They had completely transformed CJ and I's bedroom. I walked over to a huge elaborate vanity where our bed used to be and looked down at the assortments of make-up set up there. Bronzers were every shade of brown for Amber, to the fairest of colors for Lindy. Eyeshadow pallets were sprawled across one corner of the desk in reds, browns, pinks, yellows, white, black, purples, and every variation you could think of. There were liquid and pencil eyeliners and so many lipstick vials I didn't even try to count them.

They had extended out our room to make it bigger to accommodate all the extra furniture and space needed in here. Along the wall opposite the vanity stood three mannequins.

In the center, on a three-step-up platform, was my dress, with the train spread behind it and down the stairs of the backside. Lindy and Amber's bridesmaid dresses were on their own mannequins on either side, shoes sitting at the base. The wall with the door had two more dresses, one for Jean and one for Clarice.

My heart skipped a couple of beats as I realized this was really happening. My eyes flickered to the vanity and then back to my dress. I could feel my power pulse against its cocoon, and I clenched my hands into a tight fist to hide any electricity that wanted to show itself. Closing my eyes and concentrating on breathing in and out, I coiled up all but a tiny amount into that cocoon. I could feel it press against me resisting being put away, but today was not the day to lose my cool. There were way too many high-profile guests and too many people from the Manusia who knew absolutely nothing of what was here.

I searched out CJ's ember and found him in Logan's room. I pushed to him, *"I love you Ceej."* I saw him freeze for a moment, his ember flare slightly, and I could only take that as a good sign.

"Megan?" Lindy said, lightly touching my elbow. "You okay?"

"Yeah. Just pulling my power into its cocoon for safekeeping," I said, forcing a smile. "I'm sorry, where were we?"

"Your hair."

"Right. Sorry. How about we meet in the middle?" I said, as Jean walked in. "Have it up, but soft." I strode over to the vanity and took my hair out of the wrap on the top of my head and put it up into a ponytail. "Like this. Then put it into a loose braid. Then wrap it up sort of like a bun. It will be loose and soft. I don't want it slicked back tight." I took a couple of bobby pins and secured it loosely. It would need to be redone properly after it had fully dried, but this would give them an idea of what I was thinking, at least. "Madame Sinclair, do you have any of the same silver cord that was used for CJ's uniform?"

"I do." She went to her bag and after a moment of searching, she pulled it out and handed it to me.

"We could help secure the hair and give the bobby pins something to hold on to by wrapping it here around the bun, then twice around my head, separating it a little at the top of my head like two headbands... like this," I said, maneuvering the cord around until I got it the way I wanted. I ended up holding it in place while they looked at it. Amber was smiling and nodding excitedly, and Lindy and Madame Sinclair were thinking it over.

"It is a great compromise. It will work well with the dress," Madame Sinclair said.

"It's beautiful, but it needs a clip or something. Oh!!! How about some wedding bells!" Lindy said.

"Wedding bells?" Amber said.

"Baby's breath," I told her.

"Right! I forget sometimes that we aren't back at home and things aren't called the same," she said as she went to sit down on one of the chairs. Jean was going to do Amber and Lindy's in a simple low ponytail with a twist where some of the wedding bells would sit in the crease. They had hounded me about how I wanted their hair, but I really didn't care. I wanted them to be comfortable.

I pulled my hair out of the loose set up and let Madame Sinclair work on drying my hair so that she could make sure the hairstyle would hold. With a wave of her hand, bottles and bottles of various hair products showed up along with a table next to her with pins, brushes, combs, curlers, wands, and a blow dryer.

I grabbed my book from the table and leaned back. When Madame Sinclair was done with drying my hair, she spent the next hour and a half on getting my hair just right.

Then Lindy went to work on my face. I begged her not to do too much. I wanted an elegant, natural look.

"If I go too natural, the guests around the outer edge of the ring will not be able to see your face. So yes, it has to be a little heavier than you would like. Get over it," she said sternly. I glared at her as she attacked my face.

CHAPTER 28

AN HOUR BEFORE THE wedding, I could hear masses of people being ushered outside to the meadow. I was standing in front of a full view mirror while Madame Sinclair laced and cinched the red tie to the corset in the back of my dress. I started panicking. I kept shaking my head and taking a deep breath.

"Megan, you need to relax," Madame Sinclair said.

"What's wrong, Megs?" Amber said, taking my hand.

"What if all those people down there scare CJ off? What if it is finally enough to break him and he doesn't want to go through with this?" I said, panic rising in my chest.

"Seriously?!" Amber looked at me, shocked. "That's what you're worried about?"

I looked at her.

"Do you have any idea how absolutely, totally, and completely absurd that sounds?" Lindy said, laughing hysterically.

"Yes, there are an insane amount of people down there, and most of them you probably don't even know because they're

George's business associates or part of the Council. However, CJ? CJ is the very last thing you should be worried about. Though I see what you meant by those Ralvin's being scary creatures," Amber said.

"WHAT?! Ratulk is here?" I said, my eyes as big as saucers. Madame Sinclair pulled tight just as I exhaled and I looked at her over my shoulder. "Am I still going to be able to breathe?"

"Lady Megan, the corset is all in the lower back. Your ribcage and lungs are perfectly free to move. Breathe properly and it won't be an issue."

"Megan, the entire council was invited. Julian practically made your wedding a mandatory event for all Heads and TakeOvers. He didn't, but I can't imagine that any of them would not be here for fear of making Julian mad, or that you would take it as a personal affront, without prior approval or a damn good reason," Lindy said.

"Oh my Angels," I said under my breath.

"We set aside half of the circle of guest seating, just for diplomats. Also, I should probably warn you that because so many of them here, there are much more Nalrin Guard here than anywhere else in the dimension, besides the fact that most of the Vernadali are here to support CJ," Jean explained. "If you're worried about Ansel showing up, that would be very poor judgment on his part. He could never get to you."

"Strange enough, I haven't thought about Ansel at all today." I looked up at Jean through the mirror's reflection. "Is that wrong of me?"

"No," she said, coming to stand in front of me and taking both hands. "That's one thing that you can put out of your mind."

"Okay, all tightened up," Madame Sinclair said, and I stood in front of the mirror. I loved the dress. She had even ensured that the red ribbon lacing the corset was the same as the red in the tulips in my bouquet.

"Where are my shoes?" I said, looking at Madame Sinclair.

"Ask Lindy. She said she was going to get them."

I looked to Lindy, and she was holding out a pair of beautiful peep toe high heels that were heavily sparkled at the toe but faded to straight white satin in the back. "Lindy, those are beautiful, but I have a question."

"Yes?"

"How am I going to walk in those in the meadow? The heals are going to sink the second I put any pressure on them," I said, raising my eyebrows.

She just looked at me and smiled. "Incantations of course!"

I rolled my eyes. "Of course."

"Wait, on just the shoes or on the meadow?" Amber asked. "Lindy, you and I both have a pair of heels sitting over there that are going to do the same thing."

"There is an incantation on the whole area today. When you walk on the grass, it will be like walking on carpet, to make wearing dress shoes easier for everyone today," Jean said.

There was a soft knock on the door, and Lindy let Clarice and Annie in.

"Sorry I haven't been here. I've been a diplomat greeter downstairs. You know that one of the Ralvins showed up?" Clarice said.

"Head Ratulk is a delightful man... considering the reputations of Ralvins," I said. "We have talked occasionally, and he has been very, what's the word, respectful, I guess you could say. You just have to get over the very creepy wings that pulse and give you shivers. Once you do, it is like talking to anyone else. Frankly, I like him more than some of the less creeper-looking beings that I'm sure are going to be here today."

"Oh, and Julian asked me to thank you for the Ash'bani reviews. He wanted me to let you know he has chosen Titus as Head and considering the situation, As'nal and Tarol will be Co-Takeovers," she said.

"Titus, I think was a better fit, but Julian is the one to work with them, so." I played with my hands for a minute and tried to settle down. Amber and I did them last night before bed, and I tried not to pick at the lacquer. They looked nice. I just wasn't used to having nails of any sort.

Lindy and Amber got dressed and put on their black high heels that I just loved. When I saw them, I demanded that they wore them. The heel was the stem of a tulip that sat on the heel of the shoe. They looked great with the retro black dress they had picked out and tied in with our bouquets.

Clarice walked up and handed me a small velvet green box. "Megan, I have something for you, for your something old and something blue."

"Really?"

"Is it not a tradition in the Manusia to have something old and something blue?" she sought an answer.

"It is, but there is little of the Manusia traditions in the wedding."

"Open it," Clarice said.

When I did, there was a pair of earrings inside that were beautifully simple. The earrings had a dewdrop shape of clear stone that hung down from a small blue stone that covered the stud. "Clarice, they're beautiful!"

"They were my mother's. It was one of the few things I brought with me from home when I left. I know I haven't been too involved with the planning and such, but I wanted to help out in some way."

"Thank you!" I said, as I gave her a big hug.

I put the earrings on and clasped the Sa Ra to my neck and turned to Lindy. "Ok. You're up. I hope all that practice paid off."

"It's not easy turning an Angel object colors," Lindy said. Clarice and Jean put their hand on her shoulders to help steady her and Lindy took the Sa Ra in her hand, focused, and muttered a whole bunch of words so quietly that I couldn't make them out. There was a flash of light and when I looked down, the Golden Medallion of Sa Ra was the perfect shade of silver to match my dress and cord in my hair.

"You are miracle workers," I said. Tutting the necklace back on, I then turned to Madame Sinclair, "Madame Sinclair, could you place my veil, please?"

"Of course, Lady Megan." She secured it with some pins in the cord that surrounded the braided bun at the back of my head. Then she adjusted it a little more.

I looked in the mirror. I loved that the veil was virtually see-through. It brought that elegance of a traditional bride without deterring from the dress. I started to get tears in my eyes, and when Lindy saw, she freaked.

"Oh! Don't you dare let that makeup run, missy! No crying for you today," she scolded.

"It's my wedding. I think I'm entitled to a few tears."

Then I heard Julian outside the door, "Lady Megan, it is time to head to the meadow."

"Ok girls, let's go get me married," I said with the biggest smile on my face.

I was going to marry CJ, and the thought made me feel like my heart was going to burst.

CHAPTER 29

AT THE EDGE OF the tree line, I saw Logan and Owen. George was walking down the aisle on the far side that separated the circle of our friends and family. He soon took his place in the first row of seating. In the center, I could see CJ in his Vernadali uniform and the cape over his right shoulder, secured with the same cord that matched the one in my hair. It was just as I had in my vision a year ago. I looked for Lindy, but I couldn't see her. Where did she go?

"Attention! Attention!" Julian announced. "Please take your places. It is time to begin."

The seats were filled quickly, and when I looked to the side of the circle that the Nalsar Council sat on, I noticed that even though there was no seating chart, they sat just as they did while in the council chambers. I smiled at that. Creatures of habit, I suppose.

"*Lindy, Jean, Annie, Amber, you did perfectly!*" I pushed to them.

Once everyone was settled and at their seats, Julian nodded to someone off to the right and music started playing. I saw Amber and Owen make their way from the left aisle to the center, separating and standing on the bottom step of the center stage. Just as Amber and Owen took their places on the bottom step, Lindy and Logan came from the right aisle and stepped onto the second step of the stage.

CJ walked his mom down the aisle directly opposite of me and escorted her to her seat next to George. When he reached the stage, he turned, formally bowed to Julian, with his fist over his heart, and took the steps up to the top of the stage. I saw him take a very large deep breath before he turned in my direction. He couldn't see me, but I held my breath as everyone stood at attention and turned in my direction as the music played the traditional Nalsar tune.

The elegant notes rose and fell as I rounded the barrier and stopped at the edge of the aisle. My heart started racing faster as I looked down at the bunch of red tulips in my hands and then slowly up the aisle. There were wedding bells in the aisle and red tulips with more wedding bells and fairy lights strung within at the edge of each aisle. Perfect.

Julian's eyes met mine and gave me an almost imperceptible nod.

I slowly lifted one foot and took a step. I couldn't look at CJ yet.

Another slow, methodical step.

I was almost regretting not having George walk me down the aisle now. I could have used someone to hold on to.

Another step.

I looked up and scanned the crowd. Clarice and Lindy were right about the Council. The entire Council was here. The Nalrin Guard and Vernadali encompassed the outside circle of those who were seated, and there was not an empty seat. George's business associates filled a large section of the family seats. Our high school friends were here, sitting just behind the family. My old office where I used to work were here. So were people who used to work with CJ. When I looked to the

Guard and Vernadali again, they were standing at full attention. I wondered how many were here for the wedding, and how many were here because their Charge was here.

I had stopped moving. I blinked at the sheer number of people that had made the trip.

Then my eyes fell upon CJ. He was standing there, beaming from ear to ear. He wiped his cheek and then, very clearly, muttered for Logan to shut the fuck up, which made me smile. His eyes met mine, and my heart sang.

CJ was waiting for me. Waiting for me to make it down this blasted aisle and make me his wife.

ME. Not anyone else.

In all the realms, he chose *me*!

"Ceej," I pushed to him and smiled. *"Damn, you look good."*

He raised one eyebrow, looked me up and down, and then smirked.

That smirk had everything melting away. I picked up that foot and continued to put one foot in front of the other. I was going faster now, and by the time I got up to the center podium, I was not so sure I hadn't run toward it.

I was so ready to become Mrs. Megan Mathewson.

CJ stepped down from the podium, which was surrounded by miniature versions of the Five Angels, and took my hand. When his hand reached mine, the electricity in my cocoon jumped through that small hole I had and wrapped around his wrist. He looked at it, looked at me, and there was a small chuckle that came from him.

He gripped my hand tighter and walked me up the stairs. I glanced down at his hand and tried to bring my power back, but it wouldn't listen to me. When I tried again, I realized it wasn't burning him. It was sitting there, binding our hands together. We presented our hands out before us, electricity weaving itself around our fingers and wrists toward Julian.

Julian looked at our raised hands, saw my power there, and the corner of his lip twisted up in a smile that lit up his face. Then, in a voice so quiet CJ and I were the only ones to hear it, he remarked, "It seems even the Angels bind you two together."

Julian winked and then said loud enough for everyone to hear, "*Motival Centelial Bonkifar.*"

The pillars of the arches separated at the top and sunk into the ground, giving everyone who was there a perfect view of the ceremony. No one would have a bad seat here.

I looked back at CJ and smiled. He had tears in his eyes and they sparkled as he whispered, "Beautiful." I couldn't help but blush.

"Thank you all for gathering here. Family, friends, diplomats, Guard, and Vernadali," Julian said. "Cory James Mathewson and Megan Isabel Keller have vowed to give their hearts to each other for love. For those who are not familiar with the customs of Nalrin, it is no small thing to give your heart to another. For here, when you bind your love and give your heart, their heart resides in you," he stated. He continued to talk and talk, but I couldn't comprehend anything he was saying. I heard him talking, but all I could see was CJ.

Then Julian stopped. There was nothing but silence. I looked at him, and his eyes were as big as saucers. I followed his gaze. Instantly going on the defensive, mentally checking to make sure my syth was still attached to my thigh. The guests had even gone dead silent as well.

The statues of the Five Angels were... they were growing. The stone sculptures of the Five Angels slowly morphed into full-sized figures. When they reached full height, just as the Angel of Beauty in the Garden had, five white marble–like figures stood before us.

I blinked. The only emotion I was willing to show, but the Five Angels were surrounding us. My heart raced. This couldn't be good. Why now? What was so pressing they had to show up in the middle of our wedding ceremony?

I looked at CJ, who I could tell was having the same thoughts. His hand gripped mine harder as we stepped back to allow them to gather in front of us. We bowed our heads as they passed. Julian moved to stand behind, just off of the stage. It was the Angel of Beauty who spoke first.

Dearest Sangra Megan. Vernadali CJ. It is so nice to see you again.

"It is good to see you again, Angel of Beauty," CJ and I said as we bowed formally to them, which I had to admit was no small feat in these heels and dress.

Head Julian, please step forward.

Julian took a tentative step forward before saying with a shaky voice, "Angel of Remembrance. What can I do for the Five Angels?"

The Five would like to perform this ceremony. Do you have any objections?

"I do not, Angel. I cannot see anyone claiming invalidity when performed by the Five Angels themselves."

The Angel of Love, who resembled pictures of the Goddess Aphrodite, stepped forward and the Angels of Healing, Remembrance, Death, and Beauty each took one step back. As I scanned them, the Angel of Death smiled softly and winked at us. There was a knowing light in his eye that put me on edge. Then he turned to Clarice, who looked like a deer in headlights.

Please step forward Cory James, Vernadali of Megan Isabel, and Megan Isabel, Protector of Light.

Then she looked out to the audience and continued in a voice that was soothing and musical:

For those not of this realm, I am the Angel of Love. My brothers and sisters, the Angels of Healing, Remembrance, Death, and Beauty, carry much stake in the wellness and love of these two beings. Their love for each other makes strength and power. Their love has the power to cleanse and heal this world of pure darkness. To have this love is to be filled with nothing but concern for the other being's happiness.

Today, the Angels make an appearance to cement their love, as you have come on this day to share in their commitment to each other.

Cory James, your vows to Megan Isabel are...

I turned back to CJ, and the electricity holding our hands together seeped into our skin. He pulled a small sheet of paper from behind the cloak, and with a lump in his throat, he slipped the ring on my left hand and said:

I take you, Megan Isabel Keller, as my wife.

I promise to love you always and no matter what the realms

may throw at us, I shall be at your side, and

we shall always be equals.

I promise to protect your heart, body, and soul.

To love you in every faucet,

You are my bright light in the past, present, and future.

I will love you in every lifetime.

I give you my heart, forever to hold.

My eyes were filled with tears and I swallowed them. Lindy handed me a tissue, CJ's ring, and vows as I handed her my bouquet.

Megan Isabel, your vows to Cory James are...

Then I turned to CJ and took a deep breath. As I slid on his ring, that electricity going with it on his left hand, I said:

I take you, Cory James Mathewson, as my husband.

Not only for who you are, but also for what I am with you.

I'm stronger, fiercer, and better *with* you and

I promise to keep your heart safe.

From the start, it has always been you.

And through everything we have been through,

It has always been your light

that has led me from the darkness.

Each and every time, your light saves me.

In every lifetime, I give you my heart, forever to hold.

As we gazed into each other's eyes, I felt my electricity wrap around our hands, binding them back together. Then, just as it had been when we were in the Garden of Beauty in the Manusia, we were surrounded by blue sparkles and lightly lifted off the ground. We turned in place for all to see as we hovered for a moment. I felt the Golden Medallion of Sa Ra tingle and warm on my chest and could hear gasps and sounds of amazement under our feet.

We were gently placed back down, but when our feet hit the stage, the Five Angels surrounded us. Speaking in unison, their eyes changing to balls of light:

Cory James and Megan Isabel Mathewson,

You shall face incredible amounts of darkness in your future.

The purest of darkness will be met with sacrifice and a love as pure and bright as yours.

It is only the brightness of your love that will cleanse this world.

Remember and cherish your pure love, for you are strong as individuals, however, infinitely stronger together.

Their eyes faded back to soft embers and then the Angel of Love spoke again:

Your union and commitment to each other is now bound by the Five.

I looked at CJ and even through all our happiness; I heard the warning they were giving. They wouldn't waste an appearance in the realms. No way they would waste an appearance. Of course, there was an alternative motive to them being here. I spread the golden protection to him and pushed, *"Did that just sound like a warning?"*

He made a quick nod and added, *"Later. We will deal with that later."*

The Angels then stepped back, the Angel of Beauty nodding to Julian, The Angel of Death looking to Clarice and then to us giving us another wink, small smile and a nod, before they all slowly absorbed back into the statues which represented them surrounding our podium. We stood there in silence for a long, long moment.

Julian stood from the audience and said, "I proudly present to you, as bound by the Five Angels, Mr. and Mrs. Mathewson. Vernadali CJ, you may kiss your bride." Out of the corner of my eye, I saw all of Nalsar's guests bow to us. Our human friends however, I'm sure, were a bit more confused.

"Finally," CJ whispered as he lifted the veil. Then he pulled me close, and I threw my arms around his neck. We leaned in close and just before our lips touched, I whispered, "I love you."

"I love you more," he said, and I smiled as his lips touched mine. Feather–light and sweet at first. Then he crashed into me. All the worry, stress, and even the confusing message from the Angels vanished that very second. All there was, was us. His hand on my back sent chills down my spine, reaching all the way to my toes, which were gently lifted off the ground as he held me tight. I kissed him harder and pressed against him, willing us to become one.

When we broke our kiss, there was a cheer that was loud enough to rival anything else I had ever heard. I vaguely heard our friends from the Manusia shout, *"It's about time!"* through the cheer from our human side of the crowd. I couldn't help but huff a laugh out at it. I felt him do the same.

"That's right. It is about time," he said as I looked deep into his eyes and only saw happiness and his love for me. Nothing else mattered at that moment.

CHAPTER 30

As we greeted our guests, the Vernadali came through first. CJ greeted each one with a hand clapped over their mutual tattoo on their forearms, the other in a fist over their heart with a short bend at the waist. There was one, however, that CJ didn't. Not out of disrespect, but because his arm was in a sling and bound tight to his chest. When he reached us, he bowed formally to CJ, and me and said, "Forgive me Vernadali CJ, for not greeting you properly, for my arm, is not available."

"Paul, I..." CJ said stuttering slightly, but stopped.

"CJ, we hadn't been able to talk after, but I should have known better. It was inappropriate, and..." He stopped and stood up straight. "A Vernadali should never speak of another's Charge in such a manner. Please forgive me. It shall not happen again."

"What is in the past, stays in the past, Paul. Thank you for coming."

Then Paul faced me and bowed. "Lady Megan, you're the picture of perfection. Vernadali CJ has truly received a beauty to rival the Angels. After all, after today, no one can argue that he and your union are indeed Angel Blessed. I also wish to apologize for the wrongs I have committed against you. Do not hesitate to call upon me in your time of need." Then he turned and walked out.

"That was weird," I whispered to CJ. "And yes, I pieced together who he is."

"Well, considering the circumstances, I didn't even expect him to be here," he whispered back, watching him walk away.

"Maybe he was ordered here," I said with a light laugh.

"I wouldn't be surprised. Most of the camp is here save a few." He paused for a moment, looking back at Paul and pondered something he didn't voice. While his face didn't register any confusion, I could see it in his eyes. "Megs, I shattered that arm. It's not fixed yet because they needed to regrow bones. That apology, there was weight in it. I could feel the bond it carried. If I asked, he would come. No matter what. I could *feel* it."

I took his hand and squeezed it. "We will worry about that later."

When the Vernadali had passed through, the dignitaries were next. The last of which was Ratulk, Head of the Ralvins. I could feel CJ's protective side rise, so I took the lead.

"Ratulk! I'm so glad you could come. I wasn't sure you would make such a long trip since you have had such a problem with your wing as of late," I said, bowing to him.

"Oh, Lady Megan, ye shall never bow to me again. Everyone shall bow in ye presence," Ratulk said, his voice deep as if it was stuck in the back of his throat, but there was reverence in his voice. He bowed deeply and was careful to keep his wings in close.

"Thank you, Ratulk," I said, tipping my head to him.

"Bakluar apologizes for not being able to come. Their eggs are hatching."

"Oh! Tell him I said congratulations. I hope the little ones behave."

"I will do, Lady Megan. I won't monopolize your time any longer. Good day to you. Long life and prosperity."

"And to you," I said.

"I didn't realize you had gotten so comfortable with the Ralvins?" CJ said quietly as we greeted a few of his father's business associates, most of whom I'm not sure CJ even knew.

"He actually came to me for some guidance and I helped. It broke the ice between us, I guess. I just try to ignore the eeriness of the wings, and it becomes just like talking to anyone else. You know what I would really like right now?" CJ looked me up and down, licked his lips, and gave me a look that did nothing but make my nipples harden and have me squeezing my legs shut. When I didn't answer right away, he raised his eyebrows at me to continue, and I blinked before shaking my head slightly. "I would really like to get out of these shoes! They're beautiful, but they're also killing my feet. I have some slippers back at the house, but..."

"Maid of Honor to the rescue," Lindy said from behind me. Amber handed me some water, too.

"Ohh, I love you two," I told them and stepped out of the heels and into the slippers.

"We know you do. Now hold on a second and I'll get this veil out so it won't catch on anything and everything. You will have to wear the shoes for dancing though," she said, taking out the veil, and looping the train on a hook in the back so it would be easier to walk. I couldn't imagine wearing those heals dancing. Wonder if I can sneak out without them on?

"What? No character slippers?" CJ asked, just as his cousin walked up.

"No. No character slippers. The only ones available in white were bunny ones. I didn't want those, and Amber told me no Marvin the Martian slippers," I said, laughing. I turned to his cousin. "Hi, Curt. Look at how much you have grown. It's been forever, it seems."

"It's only been what, five years? I know I'm not supposed to ask how or ask you to explain what happened today. I'm sure some of the guest list is on the non-disclosure too," he said as he glanced at Raltuk, and CJ and I just looked at each other. "So,

I'll just say that I don't think anyone is ever going to top this wedding. It was beautiful."

"Thanks, Curt. I'm really glad you guys came all the way out here," CJ said.

"Well, it wasn't that far, I guess. Remember, we moved to San Jose a couple years ago, so it's only a couple hours' drive," Curt said like it was nothing.

"Right, sorry, I forgot," CJ said, covering his mistake.

"I guess we will talk later," Curt said, waving and trotting off toward Raltuk. The thought made me smile.

For the most part, that's how it went with our human family and friends. The others from Nalsar and the council were pretty much in awe that the Angels appeared to officiate our wedding. They just didn't appear at all for anyone for thousands and thousands of years, and they just made a random stop to officiate our wedding? We blew it off and said that we were deeply honored and were still in shock at it all. This was true, but they also didn't need to know that we have seen the Angel of Beauty once before. If they had been paying attention, then they may have figured it out during the ceremony, but I think most were just in awe that the Angels were there.

At the end of the line was my family. George and Annie were still talking to one of George's business associates.

"What do you make of what the Angel's said?" CJ asked.

"It was beautiful. Though I've been running through what they said and there wasn't any hint of a warning or anything. I can't imagine there not being some sort of hidden message in what they said," Lindy said.

I looked at CJ, confused. His eyes narrowed slightly and said, "Their statements were laced with warning."

"What?" Jean said, but Clarice stiffened.

"You didn't hear what they said when their eyes glowed?" I asked, and when I was met with blank stares, I continued, "When we were raised above the ground."

"No. There was a musical chiming, then they declared you bound by the Five, and that was it," Owen said quietly.

"You shall face incredible amounts of darkness in your future. The purest of darkness will be met with sacrifice and a love as pure and bright as yours. It is only the brightness of your love that will cleanse this world. Remember and cherish your pure love, for you are strong as individuals, however, infinitely stronger together," CJ recited for them.

They looked at each other. "We didn't hear that," Clarice whispered as George and Annie came up with the rest of us.

"We can talk about it while they're on their honeymoon. I mean, it's not like we didn't know there was going to be darkness involved. It is Ansel," Lindy said.

"I'm sorry. Am I missing something?" George said.

"No, honey. It is just Lindy and Clarice's job they're talking about," Annie said to him, and I gave her a thankful look for covering it up like that.

"Megan, I'm so glad that you're now part of our family. I mean, you have been for years anyway, but it's nice to have it official," George said.

"Thanks Dad," I said and gave him a huge hug.

"Megan honey?" Jean said, looking at me with her eyebrows scrunched together.

"Yes?"

"Um... Your necklace..."

I reached up, panicking that I had lost it, or that the Angel of Healing took it back, but when my hand touched it, it didn't feel like it used to. I pulled it out farther to look at it. The clump of twisted and mangled metal that was the Golden Medallion of Sa Ra, was back to its original form and golden color. The metal was shaped like a heart and filled in with a swirling pattern that never touched or met anywhere. Just like it had been when Symatha wore it.

"Guess the Angel of Healing really didn't like the fact it had been mutilated. She must have fixed it during the ceremony," she said, smiling.

"Well, I'm starved. Let's go get some grub!" Logan said, patting his dad on the back.

"Logan, do you ever think without your stomach being involved?" I said, giving him a sighing chuckle.

"Not really. Well, except for when it comes to Lindy." Then he turned bright red when he realized how that sounded. I burst out in a fit of giggles, and CJ was trying not to do the same. He turned around quickly and her face was as red as the tulips in our bouquets. "I meant, I think with my heart when it comes to you, babe. Geesh. Get your minds out of the gutter."

"Annie, what happened to him? Did he get dropped out of a building when he was younger or something?" Clarice said.

That made us all laugh. "No, Clarice dear. That's just the way of human boys. They think with the wrong head. You just saw CJ after he was all la la over Megan. So, you didn't hear it so much."

"We do actually. They just clean it up when you two visit," Clarice chuckled.

"Oh geezers! I'm with Logan on this one. Food sounds good. I haven't had much of anything since that bagel this morning," I said, trying to change the subject.

Once the photographer was done getting the pictures she wanted, we waited for Julian to announce us at the reception area. It was nice to have a few moments just for CJ and me. He turned me to face him, put his finger under my chin, and brought me in for a kiss. It was soft, gentle and made me completely weak in the knees.

"Ceej," I breathed when our lips separated.

"Yes, Mrs. Mathewson?" he said, and I shuddered.

"Angels, I like the sound of that," I said, pulling him closer to me. "By the way, you look amazing in this uniform. I know I said that at the beginning of the ceremony, but damn babe. You look good."

"Thank you, but I can guarantee that there isn't a Bride that has ever looked as sexy as you do right now," he said with a sly smile, and then whistled. "Logan told me the dress was amazing, but..."

"Logan? How? Oh, right, the dress shop," I said. "I forgot about that."

"Seriously. Wow." Then he kissed me again. This time, though, there was a hunger to it that made my gut pulse.

"Do you think they would be mad if we ditched the reception, and went straight to the honeymoon?" I whispered, and eyed him hungrily. "Maybe I could just wear it as you—" I trailed off as someone passed us.

"You may be the most powerful Sangra to have walked these lands, and I, your Angel Blessed Vernadali, but I don't think even Ansel could hold a candle to the wrath we would incur from Jean or Mom if we did," he said laughing, but that didn't negate the seriousness of his words. "And when you say things like that..." He adjusted the front of his pants as I giggled.

"Owen and Jean Tudor, Uncle and Aunt of the Bride!" I heard Julian announce to the crowd of people.

"George and Anastasia Mathewson, Father and Mother of the Groom!" Julian said a minute later.

"CJ, what the Angels said," I whispered as we made our way to stand behind Lindy and Logan.

"Let's talk about it later." Then he turned to face me again. "For the next few hours, let's just forget all about that. Then we are going to be selfish and think of nothing but ourselves while on our honeymoon. We are going to celebrate the fact I finally conned you into agreeing to be my wife. Deal?"

"Deal," I said, rolling my eyes as I vaguely heard Julian announce Amber. Then I reached up and kissed him softly. "I love you, my husband."

He smiled as big as the stars. "You're right. That does sound nice."

"Best Man and Matron of Honor. Logan Mathewson, brother of the Groom, and Lindy Keller, Aunt to the Bride." The last name threw me off. I had forgotten that technically she was my aunt by marriage. What a turn of events if she were to become my sister-in-law. I wouldn't be too surprised at the way those two are going. They made their way to the head table and sat down.

I took a deep breath and grabbed CJ's hand. This time, I allowed that thread of electricity to bind our hands together as I waited for Julian. "Now, I present to you, as Bound by the Angels, Mr. and Mrs. Mathewson."

As we walked out, our human friends and family clapped and cheered, while everyone else from Nalrin formally bowed. I think I was getting bowed to enough today to fill me for a lifetime.

The amount of food that was available was insane. There was something from everywhere. Two lines of tables, a "human" side, which had all of CJ and I's favorite from the Manusia, including the finest steaks to enchiladas to sushi. The Nalrin table had everything from Gurglin squid to Fairy Balifin stew, which if you knew what was in it, you wouldn't want to have it, but let's just say it's got more inners than Scottish haggis. I didn't care for it, but since there were representatives from portions of the Cinder lands, we wanted to ensure that everyone had food of their lands here as well.

I sat down, and CJ brought me a plate of food. I was starved. When he sat it down, there was a steak, mashed potatoes, and a kichbin, a small pastry from one of the northern Nalrin providences. I looked out over the guests once I had my fill and just smiled at how wonderful things had turned out. The ten-foot-long tables had small black wood boxes with tulips in them every few feet, with garland and wedding bells running down the center, that hung over the edges slightly. Garland and white fabric hung from the awnings with intertwined fairy lights that twinkled.

After everyone ate, Julian announced it was time for the first dance. CJ was standing and taking my hand before I had a chance to object. A look of mischief all over his face.

"What are you up to?" I asked as we headed to the floor.

"Just wait and see," he said as he picked me up enough to whirl and twirl me onto the floor. Then he gently put me down and pulled me in close as the music started. Becca, James, and Amber, our friends from the Manusia, whooped and hollered as it came on. CJ gave them a little wink, and I blinked.

The first few notes were familiar, and when I realized what it was, I asked a little surprised, "*I knew I loved you,* by Savage Garden?"

"Yup."

"I haven't heard this song in a long time."

"Now, do you know why I chose this song?"

"Give me a minute." I moved in closer to him and let the music wash over me as I thought back through time. It was much older, so there had to be a reason for it from a long time ago. Then I remembered and took half a step back. I looked up and smiled at him, picturing him years younger and in a rented tux. "Man, this song was old when we danced to it at prom."

He laughed and pulled me closer, then twirled me around as the chorus started.

"I'm surprised you remembered," I said, smiling as I rested my head on his chest.

"Babe. That was the moment that I knew you were the measure. I knew I was seriously 'friend zoned' so I had no chance, but you were going to be the one that everyone else had to measure up to."

"You thought you were friend zoned?"

"Oh yeah," he said, smiling down at me. "I think I knew I cared for you beyond our friendship, but I don't think I really knew. James told me I was whipped, but I didn't believe him. Little did I know."

"When was it you realized no one could live up to my awesomeness, then?"

"When you were in the coma the first time," he said seriously, and without hesitation, as he looked down at me and I met his eyes. "Well, okay, it was before that, but that was when I knew I needed to stop kidding myself and just accept the fact that it was you or no one." His breath hitched, and I studied him. His eyes were full of tears. "I was so scared you would never wake up. I couldn't bring myself to leave you."

"Why didn't you tell me after I woke up?" I said, almost stopping in the middle of the dance floor. I had already known at that point how much I was in love with him. Angels, we could have been on this path so much sooner.

"Because I was a chicken shit," he said, laughing. "Then almost two years ago, when we fought, I went to work and just sat there staring at my computer screen without turning it on. I couldn't think of the reason we had fought. My only thought was that I loved you and couldn't lose you. It had physically hurt in my chest just to think of it. I knew I needed to tell you how much I loved you and risk everything. So, when the boss came into the office that morning, I stood up and quit."

"You told me you put in for a transfer!"

"Sue me. I lied, but I went home, packed my stuff, told Mom where I was going, and booked the flight to where my heart was."

"Then everything changed," I said, sighing heavily. "Literally."

He reached up and pulled my chin so I was facing him. "Yes, but in ways that I never could have imagined. Yes, there is crazy stuff happening, but right now, I have never been happier. There isn't a day in all of our history that has made me happier than I am right now. Not even on our first date where you told me you love me. You, you handing your heart to me? You being my wife. Angels. Megan. You're mine. You're really mine and I'm yours. Forever."

"In every lifetime," I said, reaching up on my toes to kiss him, and we danced to the last beat.

When the music stopped, CJ danced with his mom while I danced with Logan.

Then Julian asked for me to enter the center of the floor. "Lady Megan has requested this next dance. The Father–Daughter Dance." There were gasps and murmurs throughout the group. CJ looked at me bunching his eyebrows together, and Annie stood there smiling as she and Julian were the only ones who knew what I was up to. Our Nalrin guests looking at me with worried expressions written all over their face, and our human friends looking for my father. As far as they were concerned, he had been dead for a few years. The Vernadali and Nalrin Guard, however, were reaching for their syths.

"She has also requested that halfway through the dance, for any other fathers and daughters, or mothers and sons that wish to join her, please do so. Now, Lady Megan, the floor is yours," Julian said with a smile.

"George," I began, "would you do me the honor of dancing with me... please?"

George's eyes shot up in shock and with a dry croak, he said, "Me?" as he slowly stepped out. Annie and CJ stood there next to each other, smiling from ear to ear.

"Yes. Would you do me the honor of sharing this dance with me?" I asked, formally bowing to him.

"Megan. It would be my honor!" Then he took my hand and danced with a smile that stayed throughout the whole song. When it ended, I felt light and refreshed. I was overjoyed at his reaction. I wasn't sure how he was going to react, but I loved George and wanted to honor him at the wedding as well.

"Thank you, Dad."

"Thank you. Just take care of my boy, ok?" he said with light laughter.

"Oh, I think he will be the one taking care of me," I said, hugging him again.

The rest of the evening was filled with dancing, socializing, and celebration. CJ and I spent as much time as we could with Amber, Becca, and James. It didn't matter how long it had been; it was just like old times, regardless of how much had changed.

By the end of the night, the lines between the Nalrin guests and human guests blurred, and I even saw Raltuk interacting with a few of the humans, including Curt. Curt had always been an open-minded human, so it shouldn't have surprised me, but it did. Even Julian had noticed Curt's ability to talk to Raltuk easily. Julian had spent a lot of time talking to Curt over the evening and had even mentioned to me he thought Curt would be a great ambassador for Nalrin. I knew Curt would be in the Council's employ before too long. There was a small part of me that looked forward to seeing Curt in the Nalrin Council halls.

I couldn't have imagined a better way to celebrate CJ and I's marriage. The night went by so fast that before we knew it, Julian was telling us that the carriage was ready to take us to our first stop of the night.

I turned to CJ, practically bouncing on the balls of my feet. "Mind telling me where we were going?"

"Oh no, ain't going to happen. You're going to love it though," he said, kissing me on my temple. There were lines of our Manusian guests going by us, making their way through the portal in sections. We waved quickly to Curt as he disappeared behind the veil.

"So, Julian, why do we have to take a carriage? Why can't we just take the horses? You know I love riding."

"That isn't going to happen. You will be gone for over a month, and you will have everything provided for you. This is your time to just relax and... well, put aside everything else for now."

"A month?" I exclaimed, surprised. "But what about Ansel?"

"A month. Don't you dare show up in Nalrin before the first of September," he said, leaving no room for discussion. "As for Ansel, we have already talked about this. If something comes up, we will tell you."

"But do we really need the guard?" I pleaded.

"You will be under the best of care, under the best guard we have."

"Oh. No. You don't mean..." I groaned, looking from Julian to CJ with pleading eyes.

"I've already tried to talk him out of it. I'm now under orders to accompany you with twenty other guards and Vernadali," Mickel said, walking up with his head low. There was a major apology in his eyes that assured me he had fought back on this order, but what Julian wants, Julian gets.

"But what if where CJ is planning on taking me doesn't have room? How am I supposed to enjoy my honeymoon with all the Guard and Vernadali hanging around? And no, I don't care if some of them are women too."

"Where you're going, you will have your privacy, but protected. I don't want anything interrupting your honeymoon. Ansel especially," Julian said in a voice that once again left no room for compromise or negotiation.

"But the fewer people that are around to protect me, the less conspicuous we will be traveling," I tried to point out.

He looked at me with a raised eyebrow, and I stared him down. There were a lot of people around us who gawked or pointedly tried to ignore the interaction. Mickel even tried to poke my side in a reminder of just *who* I was staring down. Someone coughed behind me. He smirked after we stared at each other for a good, solid minute.

"As you said earlier, you're getting the royal treatment. That includes being protected like one. The Guard is going. Is that understood, *Lady* Megan?" he said, standing up taller.

"Would it do any good if I formally declined?" I whined.

"No." While he may allow my rebellious side to fight him on occasion, even I knew there was a line.

"Great. Even my bodyguard gets to share in my most intimate moments. No offense Mickel. I love you and all, but..." I said.

"No, I completely understand Lady Megan. I was in your corner on this one. I've heard enough of you and CJ in the last month, and yes, once was enough, so trust me, I fought hard. Julian's orders," he finished for me, and Julian nodded in agreement. I smirked at the memory of him accidentally walking into the bedroom, just as CJ and I were tearing each other's clothes off. So, while he didn't find us in full swing, it was enough to keep him apologizing for the rest of that day.

I turned back to CJ, "Since we are going by carriage, and two full squads of Nalrin's best protectors, I guess we aren't going anywhere in the Manusia as you lead me to believe."

"That would also be correct. Though it will now take about three days to get there since Julian is insisting on..." he finished by jerking his head toward the carriage.

"Three days?" I stomped my foot. Yes, I fully realized that I looked like a two-year-old. The carriage was half hidden from where I was standing, but there were four gray horses hitched up and one was pawing at the ground, eager to get going.

"Don't worry. I have arranged for the carriage to move silently and quickly. After a couple of hours, you will fall asleep and when you wake up, you will be at your destination. The incantation is only for the trip there," Julian said.

"What if Ansel does attack, or someone else?" I asked, hoping he would read between the lines.

"The Guards will wake you. I've taken every precaution," he beamed, obviously proud of himself.

"Guess I should go change into something else then." I turned to kiss CJ, "Ready to be selfish for once, and start our new lives together?"

"I'm so ready to be selfish," he said, and then he kissed my temple as we headed to the house.

After we changed, we said our goodbyes to our families and headed out the door. When we walked through the crowd of people, bubbles flew everywhere, including one that went up my nose, and I smiled and laughed lightly. It was almost strange to just sit back and enjoy myself. The guard opened the door to the carriage, and I leaped in, CJ right behind me.

I had to admit, it was like being a princess. The carriages are usually only reserved for the diplomats, and while I didn't like that Julian was pampering me like such, I knew I would cherish this day and appreciate how much he ensured that happened.

I know I've complained, but thank you for everything, Julian." I pushed toward him. I saw him smile and give me a quick nod to let me know he heard me.

I took CJ's hand and waved to all of our friends and family as the carriage took off. When I couldn't see them anymore, I turned to CJ and found him staring at me. "What?"

"You really are mine. I have loved you for so long, I keep expecting to wake up and realize it was all a dream, and I'm lying in my bed in Chicago." His hand was on my cheek, his eyes wide in amazement.

"Believe me when I say that I know what you mean. I never in a million years thought I would ever become Mrs. Cory James Mathewson." I felt tears fill my eyes, and I blinked. CJ reached over and wiped the tear from my cheek. "I love you Ceej."

He leaned in and kissed me. I pressed into him and let myself be swallowed up in his love.

CHAPTER 31

I WOKE UP TO CJ kissing me. "Wake up, my Sleeping Beauty. We're here."

I threw my arms over him and pulled him on top of me. "Who says we have to go anywhere?" I said as I wrapped my legs around his waist just as the door opened to the carriage.

"Oh! I'm so sorry," the guard said, a blush rising in her cheeks.

"That's why we have to get up," CJ said with a smile. "Don't worry about it, Janet."

"Where are we?" I asked as I sat up and tried to look out the window, but they were all shut.

"Take a deep breath and tell me what you smell?"

Umm okay. I'll play along. I closed my eyes and inhaled. I could smell him, but that was only because he was so close. The smell of the carriage, the horses... clean crisp air... the forest and... I smiled brightly and my eyes flew open. "The ocean."

"Come on," he said as he climbed out, then turned to offer me his hand. I took it and stepped outside.

When I did, my bare feet immediately sank into a white sand beach with water the color of turquoise, jade, and light blues. I looked around to the forest right up against the beach and once again inhaled to take in the crisp, clean air. The sky was bright with a few white puffy decorator clouds with trees that stretched to the sky. I let go of CJ's hand and ran out toward the water.

"Janet, take the carriage up to the compound and tell Mickel we will be up there in a bit," I heard CJ say behind me.

I rolled up my pants to my knees and stepped into the water. When my feet touched the cool, soothing water, I had flashbacks of all the times that CJ and I had hung out at the beach back in the Manusia. I stood there letting the waves wash over my feet as they slowly sunk in the sand and I just breathed. It was so relaxing that even my power just swam in its cocoon.

CJ came up behind me and put his arms around my waist, which made me jump a little because I hadn't heard him. "So," he said, drawing out the word as he nibbled on my ear, making me smile and lean back into him.

"So what?"

"Did I do good?"

"You done good," I said, letting out a deep sigh. "It's perfect."

"I promised you back in Sao Tome that you would see the ocean again. This is one of the few Vernadali resorts in the realm. One of only two that have a beach, and the only one on the Nalrin continent. There is a complete wait staff to take care of everything for us, including a masseuse, if you want a massage. There is snorkeling and diving equipment if we want to use it, and in the Tes Forest behind us, there are some great hiking trails, so I've been told. We can hit those up too if I can ever pull you off the beach," he said with a smile at the end. His hand had started making circles on my stomach, and he nipped my ear again. He wasn't playing fair. Not at all.

"I'm sure you could," I said, turning to face him and putting my arms over his shoulders. "This is our honeymoon. It's not all about me, ya know. We can do whatever you want to do too."

"Well, since all I want to do is make you happy, then I'm good," he said, smiling.

"You already do that, Mr. Mathewson. Stop being all sacrificial. Tell me what you want to do," I whispered, and kissed him. He pulled me closer and kissed me harder. His hands were so soft and strong on my back. I opened my eyes as I pulled back and his eyes had a hunger in them that made me weak in the knees. "Ceej."

He smiled a sly smile. "We have time, babe. Let's walk the beach for a bit before we head up to the compound. Give them a chance to get everything else set up."

"Everything else?"

"Hey, I've thought it all out. I wasn't just training up there. I was able to get this all organized. Except for the guards. I wasn't exactly planning on having chaperons on our honeymoon."

We walked down the beach hand in hand to a small, protected cove where CJ had a beach picnic set up. I looked at him and smiled. "You really had this all planned out, didn't you?"

He shrugged, "Well, what better way to start a vacation than a picnic on the beach?"

I jogged over to the blanket and sat down to look at what was in the basket. When I did, I couldn't help but smile. "Strawberries?!" I said, pulling one out. "How did you get strawberries?"

He just smiled and joined me on the blanket as I took a bite, juice running down my chin. As I tried to catch it with my other hand, CJ caught my hand and proceeded to lick the juice from my chin and lips, before licking them clean as well.

For all that was holy.

CJ pulled the rest of our picnic out, which seemed like way too much food. He had the strawberries of course, turkey sandwiches on rolls from the best bakery in Nalrin, tulberries which are a raspberry like berry that are specially grown in Cinder, and cristena, a chocolate buttercream-like cake, and one of my favorite desserts from the same bakery the rolls came from in Nalrin.

Afterward, we ate it all; though, I guess after being asleep for three days, you are hungrier than you think you should be. Now, as I sat between his legs, leaning into him, I just enjoyed the scenery. His arms rested on his knees and occasionally his hand roamed up and down my arm absent-mindedly. Each time my stomach tightened, and there was no doubt he knew just how much he was turning me on with each pass.

I sighed and took his arms to wrap around me. "I could sit like this for the whole time we are here."

"I know you could," he said in my ear. "And you know what. We can."

"Except..."

"Except what?"

I turned around to face him and sat on my knees. "Except that you've been driving me crazy since we woke up here."

"Oh, have I?" He cocked an eyebrow and then took a hold of my chin and brought me in for the lightest of a kiss.

"Yes. Yes, you have," I said against his lips and when I tried to push him down onto the blanket, he wrapped his legs around me and rolled me onto my back.

"Don't you think you haven't been doing just that since the very moment I saw you in that wedding dress?" he said, or at least I think that's what he said. I was lost. Lost in the touch of his lips on my neck as he kissed me ever so lightly. Lost in the feel of his body against mine. Every small touch was like a wildfire being lit on my skin. He leaned back and looked deep into my eyes. "I love you Mrs. Mathewson."

I moaned and raised my hips to meet his. He chuckled as he worked his way down, undoing each button of my shirt with slow, precise movements. Each pop sent a jolt through me. He was being unbearably slow, and I felt that all too familiar pulse between my legs.

I reached down and pulled his shirt over his head as he worked his way down. With a quick flip of his wrist, he had my bra undone and off to the side along the cliff face. He had always been so good at that. He ran his tongue along my breast line, and then slowly around each nipple before closing his mouth around each and flicking it.

His tongue continued down between my breast and to the waistband of my pants. His hands slipped below the waistband and with a lift of my hips, he was slowly sliding them down my legs, kissing every inch of the way down to my feet, where he completely froze.

His eyes bounced up to mine, and I smiled at him. When he looked at it again, he lightly ran his finger along it before his gaze go from me to my ankle and back, lines of silver in his eyes.

"A small thing to show you I'm just as committed to you, as that tattoo on your forearm says you're committed to me," I whispered. I had snuck away four days ago to meet the tattoo artist at the Nalrin River port to have it done. A small syth with his initials, CJM, sat tattooed between my ankle and the back of my foot. It had hurt like hell in the tender flesh, but worth every moment. The hardest part was hiding it from him until now.

He gently kissed it before moving up, his shoulders widening my legs. He kissed each side, and there was a moaning growl that emanated from him before his tongue circled that bundle of nerves and flicking it. I twitched at the action, my back arching, as his tongue moved and explored every inch of flesh. My hips moved of their own accord, and he allowed each movement.

"Mr. Mathewson," I breathed.

His eyes lifted to meet mine, but he didn't stop. His eyes were full of a heat that could have started a wildfire in the forest behind us. It almost undid me right there. He slid his tongue from one end of me to the other before flicking my clit and moving back up my body.

When he kissed me, I kissed him with an urgency that I didn't suppress. I reached down and undid his pants and slipped them off, with his help. He kicked them off to the side and rolled me over so that I was poised above him. I smirked and slowly rubbed myself up and down his length. He let out a small whimper that had me biting my lip in appreciation.

I took his arm, kissed his Vernadali tattoo, and said, "I love you, CJ," as I slowly lowered myself on him, never taking my eyes from his. His mouth opened slightly as I took him all the way. I gently started rocking my hips, and he matched my movement. The hunger in his eyes matched my own as he pulled me down, rolling me as he went. He leaned down to kiss me, never breaking our rhythm. We matched each other perfectly. His movements were precise and conveyed the love we felt for each other.

I ran my fingers over his abs as he bent down to kiss me. He held my face in his hand and said, "My heart is yours. In every lifetime." Each word was enunciated with a deep thrust of his hips. "Never forget it."

I felt the ocean breeze blow across us, and my nipples hardened even more. When I moaned at the sensation, CJ smirked and reached down to take one into his mouth, nibbling gently. I moaned again as I arched my back and I thrust myself against him. He kissed his way up to my neck and then thrust into me hard, over and over again, as I met him for each and every deep thrust of his hips. He growled as he thrust into me again, the blanket under us now nowhere to be seen and sand getting everywhere, but we didn't care.

I opened my eyes and met his as he pounded into me repeatedly. I was so close, and he knew it. He let an evil smirk spread across his lips as he slowed and brought himself out to just the head of him before quickly entering me, grinding against my nub, slowly retreating to the head of him, and repeating the motion.

"Ceej," I begged. He loved to bring me to the edge, slowly and repeatedly. I writhed under him. He kept repeating the motions until I couldn't take it anymore. I rolled him onto his back, sand spraying and sticking to our bodies. I pinned his hands next to his head and rode him hard.

His eyes met mine, and he bucked under me, meeting me stroke for stroke. The guttural moan that escaped was quickly followed up with, "Fuck Megs."

He bucked under me. Our moans carried away in the breeze. He reached up and pinched each of my nipples as we released in unison, neither one of us being quiet about it. I collapsed on top of him, covered in sand and sweat.

CHAPTER 32

I WOKE UP TO CJ tracing the fingers of his right hand up and down my bare back, and his left hand entwined with my right. My leg was laying over his and I was curled up as close as I could be to him. The sun was warm on our skin, and the blanket had somehow ended up under us again. When I opened my eyes, his bare chest was hard and solid under my hand that he held gently. I looked up as he leaned over and kissed my forehead softly. Total bliss.

"I could lie like this forever," he said with a sigh.

"Humm hummm," I murmured, just enjoying the touch of his fingers on my back and the feel of us laying in the sun skin to skin.

"We should probably get dressed before we get a sunburn, ya know," he whispered before kissing the top of my head again.

"Fine. Be mister sensible."

I sat up and looked down at him, every indecent thought going through my head before I whispered, "Thank you."

"What for?"

"Everything. Not running off when I first brought you to Nalrin, for not running for the hills after my parents took off with you last year, for staying with me at the hospital, *both* times, and for enduring everything my life has thrown at you with the most amazing amount of courage and strength." I sighed again, glimpsing my ring out of the corner of my eye, "But most of all, for choosing me, out of everyone in *two* dimensions, *me,* to be your wife."

He sat up, took my face in his hands, and looked at me fiercely. "Megan Isabel Mathewson," my gut tightened as he said my new name, "there is no one, no one anywhere, I would rather have stand at my side as my equal and share my life with than you. You're by far the strongest person I know. I'm the one who should thank you for showing me just how strong I can be. For showing me that even when there is nothing but evil and hate surrounding you, that goodness, light and love, most of all your love for me, can, and does still exist." Then he kissed me, and I could feel the truth of his words and the ferocity of it. He honestly meant them. I felt like the luckiest woman in all the realms as I felt tears fall to my cheeks.

CJ wiped the tears from my face. "No crying on your honeymoon."

"Not even happy tears?"

"Okay, happy tears exempted," he said, smiling brightly. "But we should probably get over to the compound before Mickel sends a search and rescue team out for us. To be honest, while I like the look of you naked, covered in sand, I don't want to have him or any of the Vernadali or Guard finding us like this."

"AGREED!" I said, laughing.

We got up, dusted off as much of the sand as we could, threw our clothes on, and cleaned up our picnic. We headed back to the compound, as he called it, hand in hand and with our feet in the water.

As we got closer to where the carriage had dropped us off, I saw a rough stone staircase up to a large two-story stone building with terraces overlooking a bluff to the ocean and beach.

CJ pointed up to the compound. "Up there on the second floor facing the ocean is the Mathewson Suite," he said lightly. "There is also a pool, big open lawns to lounge on, though I suspect you won't use either of them. Why should you when you have the beach to lounge on?"

We made our way up the stairs and at the top were greeted by Mickel. Some silent signal sent the Guard and Vernadali, standing about 15 feet behind him, lining either side of the pathway to the door into full attention. I inwardly groaned.

"Lady Megan and Vernadali CJ Mathewson, welcome to Hartwood Citadel, a Vernadali Resort. You're nestled between the Tes Forest and the Lucent Gulf," he said with a formal bow.

"Mickel..." I said, my hand on my hip.

"Yes, Lady Megan," he said, trying to suppress a smile.

"I believe she is about to tell you to stop being so... fucking damn formal and bowing to her, for fuck's sake. You are family," CJ said.

"That may be true Vernadali CJ, however, as I have told Lady Megan before—" he started to say before I interrupted him.

"You're working right now, and there are others around. Yeah, yeah, yeah," I said while waving my hands up in the air. Then I looked at the other guard and Vernadali standing at full attention along the pathway. "You are all excused. You may do... well, something. Relax and have fun. If you're required to be here, at least try to have some fun and do your jobs without being all formal about it. You can still do your job without walking around like you have sticks up your asses."

Mickel and CJ laughed as the Guard and Vernadali tried to keep straight faces as they looked to Mickel for instructions.

"You heard the Lady. Be present, but don't be. I believe there was a pool game that the Guard had issued the Vernadali? Go play it," he said, giggling. Then he turned to me, "Megan, I know you don't like this."

"Damn straight, I don't like this. I'm on my *honeymoon*! We don't need a babysitter," I said, stomping up to the front door, but before I could turn the handle, the door was opened for me. I sighed in frustration, but when I saw the inside of the main room, I stopped, speechless.

The room was open to the second floor, with an open hallway on the second floor to the rooms up there. The main floor was decked out in traditional Vernadali leather and furs. It reminded me of the hunting cabin, well, this would be an Estate based on the pure size of it that CJ's uncle had taken us to up in the mountains. There were big, soft, light brown leather couches, wood paneling, and a giant stone fireplace with a couple of loveseats angled and arranged close to the fire. It was a huge room, but the way it was set up made it feel so warm and cozy.

"This part of the compound is all yours and CJ's. There is a full kitchen staff on call for all hours of the night and day. All you have to do is tell them what you want to have and they will make it happen. The stores have been stocked with all kinds of food from here in Nalsar and the Manusia. Want a grilled cheese? They will make it. Want a Larkspur Cocoa? They will make it. Want a steak with Cinder rice and that horrible broccoli stuff? They will make it," Mickel said behind me.

"Oh, come on, broccoli isn't that bad," I said under my breath as I took in the details of the room. The pelts, pillows, and blankets. I could curl up here for days with a good book, and CJ beside me. Maybe I would.

"Whatever you say, Megan." He laughed.

"Babe, I know I keep saying this, but seriously, you have set this up to be the most heartwarming, relaxing time I could have imagined." I reached over and kissed him on the cheek.

"Well, then I have succeeded. I wanted something that would remind you of happy times. When they showed me pictures of this place, I thought it would remind you of the time Uncle Elias took us up to Yosemite," he said, putting his arm around my waist. "The only thing unplanned was Mickel and crew."

"I know CJ, but Julian," Mickel said uncomfortably. "However, there is a whole residence section behind the war room door that has all the amenities for the Guard and Vernadali to use that are separate from the rest of the living quarters. They built it to be self-contained in case of an attack. You shouldn't have to worry too much. We will stick inside here," he said, leading us to the door to the backside of the living room near the staircase entrance.

"We will try to stay in there as much as possible to give you privacy, but still available should you need us," he said.

"Need you? Hello... Angel Blessed Vernadali and most powerful Sangra!!" I said, objecting to the whole notion.

"Megan, you're doing it again. You can't disregard that all the time, then whip it out when it's convenient," he said.

"Well, why not? It suits its purpose."

"And what purpose is that, Lady Megan?"

"The point of *go away*. I want to have loud, obnoxious, voracious sex with my husband without my bodyguard and half of the Nalrin Guard and Vernadali overhearing it! That point," I said with my arms crossed. I knew he was just following orders, which kept my temper from completely boiling over.

"Man, you are sexy when you're pissed," Mickel said as CJ laughed. I glared at CJ, and he wiped smile off faster than you could say thank you.

CJ cleared his throat, trying to get back on my good side. "Isn't there something you guys can do? I mean, this is supposed to be our honeymoon, and when I planned this, the Nalrin Army and certainly not you, Mickel, don't take offense, weren't in the plans. It was supposed to be just me, her, us being totally selfish, a few staff to get us food, and lots and lots of beach sexy time."

"We will stick to the war room and facilities, CJ. That's all we can promise. When the door is shut to the room, it becomes soundproof, so we won't be able to hear outside or anything else that's going on, so it needs to stay open," Mickel explained.

"What about Cognitis proof?" I smiled at my idea.

Mickel looked at me, then smiled. He knew what I was thinking. "Well, since we haven't ever had one around here, I don't know, but the walls are really thick. Do you think it's strong enough?"

"Mickel, the months we have been non-stop at each other's side have made me super in tune to you. I can push messages to you as easily as I can to any of my family." I shoved him behind the door to the war room and shut the door.

I kissed CJ and grabbed his ass to make Mickel sweat it out. CJ took the opportunity to push me against the wall, play with my boobs, and nibble at my ear. He reached down and rubbed me through my pants. "Fuck," I whispered as I ground against him.

Yeah, round two, as husband and wife, was going to have to happen very soon. CJ, in a staggering amount of control that I did not have, stepped back and jerked his head toward the closed door. I made a face and pushed. *"Mickel. You're such a stubborn ass. Great bodyguard, but would it freaking kill you to tell Julian to fuck off?! Oh, and your zipper was down."*

A moment later, he opened the door. "How were you even able to tell that my zipper was down?"

"Please, I can look into your eyes and be able to tell that your zipper was down," I told him.

"Dude. I could have told you, but ya, it was funnier just to let you walk around," CJ said, slapping him on the shoulder. "Well, at least we know that works. So, door closed at all times."

"Megan can tell me when to shut the door. Otherwise, it stays open."

"But what if we're in the moment, walk in and decide to have a go right there on that couch, where you could totally see it? The last thing I'm going to be thinking is *'Oh I better tell Mickel and the Guard not to look.'* I'm on my FLIPPING HONEYMOON, not a supervised date, where the supervisor looks the other way during sex," I complained.

"Megan, I don't know how many times it has to be said. This is the last time. I'm under orders not even CJ can override. I will try to stay out of your and CJ's way as much as possible, but there is going to be a presence, and you can't change that. I'm your friend, but on this trip, I'm your bodyguard first. And this bodyguard has orders. End of discussion. Nothing we can do about it."

"Fine," I said. "But just fair warning, you may end up seeing more of me than you want."

"Lady Megan, it's not seeing more of you I'm worried about," he said, laughing as a couple of the guards inside the war room gave him a look that clearly said they couldn't believe they just heard him say that. "Now, CJ, I'll leave that sight for you only."

I just rolled my eyes and CJ laughed. There were a lot of wide eyes watching our discussion, but at least, we were comfortable enough with each other that we can joke around.

"Lady Megan," one of the guards said, and I looked at her. "Your belongings are on the second floor, double doors at the end of the hall. Vernadali CJ asked for the room overlooking the ocean." Then she bowed and left the room before I could say thank you.

"This way babe," CJ said, taking my hand and leading me upstairs. Just before he opened the door, though, he bent down and swung his arms under my legs and picked me up.

"What are you doing?" I said, laughing.

"Isn't it tradition for the husband to carry his wife over the threshold?" he said as he opened the door and carried me inside to a room that was covered with red tulip petals. That included the very large canopy bed with sheer fabric laid over the top. We walked past the double doors with sheer white curtains that opened up to a large balcony where CJ laid me down on the bed and whispered things in my ear that made my body warm and tingle from head to toe. My shirt disappeared, and my bra was in shredded pieces on the floor before I knew what happened.

CJ had my nipple in his mouth, pumping two fingers in me as I stroked him with my hand. A moment later moaning, I threw my power at the door, shutting it, and pushed, *"Mickel, shut that fucking door."*

CHAPTER 33

THE NEXT DAY, WE woke up quite a bit later than usual, but a little extra rest was in order. We headed down for breakfast, me in only my robe and CJ in lounge pants and a tight-fitting t-shirt. He is the one that insisted on the t-shirt. There were a few bite and scratch marks from last night, and he didn't want everyone else to gawk. I would've been perfectly happy with him walking around shirtless, but then again, we may not have made it through breakfast without another round, and we needed something to eat. We sort of missed dinner last night. Mickel had tried to tell us that dinner was ready and CJ sent him away, as my mouth was very full at the time. I vaguely remember hearing him bellowing in laughter as he walked away.

At the base of the stairs, the door to the war room was open, cheering and teasing spilling out. I turned to CJ and put my finger to my lips. I peeked my head around the corner and saw Mickel trying to throw darts blindfolded. I snuck in and when some guards behind him noticed me, I shooshed them too. When I was standing just behind Mickel, one of the female guards, I think CJ had called her Janet yesterday, winked at me and said, "Come on, Mickel. Prove you can hit the bullseye blindfolded. One shot, it's all you get."

"Shut it Borsky," he said as he lined up his shot, and just before he let go of the dart I blew on his neck, which sent the dart sailing off to the left and sticking in the window's windowsill, narrowly missing a guard who had just moved to avoid it.

"What the... Who the..." he stuttered, turning to wrap his arms around the offending party. I dodged out of the way, kicking his feet out from under him, but before he hit the ground, I caught him by the shoulders, much like I had done in the fighting ring at the house.

The room ruptured with laughter as Mickel took the blindfold off, and I smiled down at him.

"Megan," he growled.

"Good morning, Mickel," I said with a smirk.

"Oh, didn't you notice? It's almost lunch," he said, standing up and crossing his arms, matching my smirk.

"Yeah, well, I needed the sleep," I said, as CJ came and stood against the table just behind me.

"After last night, I guess you would," Mickel had a mischievous glint in his eye as he continued, "I have to give CJ props, though. You guys kept busy well past midnight."

"Not that hard when I have a sexy wife like this," CJ said, wrapping his arms around my waist and kissing my cheek, making me blush uncontrollably.

"Okay, you two. That's enough," I said, looking at Mickel. "I warned you, and technically, it was our first night together since our wedding, so what did you expect. Just for us to sleep all night? PLEASE! You know me better than that, Mickel."

Mickel just nodded and chuckled. Then my stomach reminded me that eating would probably be a good thing. "Come on Ceej, let's go get some breakfast."

"Lunch!" Mickel yelled after me. I extended a single finger over my shoulder and heard his deep chuckle behind me. CJ shook his head and took my hand as we headed for food.

When we got to the kitchen, we rounded up enough o last us the day at the beach. Then we headed up to the bedroom, cleaned up, grabbed a blanket, and headed down to the water.

It was a beautiful sunny day and even though I noticed the Guard and Vernadali were consistently watching over us; they did stay quite a distance away and were trying to give us our time alone.

I spent most of the next two days wrapped up in CJ's arms, swimming, snorkeling, laying on the beach, letting the sand flow through my toes, or in the water. They were days full of nothing but us. Absolute fucking nothing, and that was the best thing about it.

When we headed back up to the compound on the third day, after a long hike, I was completely relaxed. Halfway up the long stone stairway, I got a whiff of barbeque. "Oh! Damn, that smells good," I moaned and looked at CJ.

CJ inhaled, and I could have sworn I saw him wipe the drool from his lips. "Yes, it does."

We headed to the kitchen, and I smiled. "HAMBURGERS!"

"Yes, Lady Megan," one of the kitchen ladies said. "Mickel said they are your favorite and they will be ready in about 20 minutes. The Guard and Vernadali were eyeing them with question, but we told them they can eat them or go hungry. We also have some... onion rings, I think they're called, and a variety of BBQ sauces."

This time it was me who had to wipe to drool from my lips.

"Sounds fantastic." I turned to CJ. "What do you think about just lighting the fire pit on the beachside balcony and hanging out there tonight?"

"Sounds good," CJ said. "I need to run up and shower quick though. I've got sand in places that really shouldn't have sand."

I smiled, kissed him on the cheek, and told him I would see him when dinner was ready. I flopped into one of the oversized chairs and closed my eyes. "I wish I could spend the rest of my life like this," I whispered to no one. I sat there enjoying the quiet time when I heard Mickel in the war room.

"No, we will not tell them. I promised Julian, and more importantly, Jean and the family, that they weren't going to be disturbed unless it was an emergency. These are only rumors. No need to let them know of it now. They will enjoy their time here," I heard Mickel say quietly, but with authority. The door to the war room was open, but only a crack. I tried to listen more carefully, but one of the Nalrin guard came and swung the door shut, effectively ending my eavesdropping.

"Damn it!" I said in frustration.

"What's wrong babe?" CJ said behind me. His hair was still wet and his shirt stuck to him where he wasn't fully dry before putting it on.

"Mickel is keeping something from us, and he has ordered the guard not to tell us," I said, glaring at the door.

"The door is shut, though. What could you have heard?"

"Just that there are rumors about something and that he promised Jean and everyone that we would have our quiet time without the world interfering, basically." I sighed. "I appreciate him trying to let us have our time, though. I really do, but I just don't like secrets."

"That's not a bad thing, babe," he said, sitting down and moving me, so I was sitting across his lap. I could feel my power stirring, but it still sat there. It had been very quiet and almost non-existent since we arrived here. It obeyed any command I gave it, but it didn't jump out nor beg to be released.

"I know, it's just..."

"Just that you still feel you have all the responsibility to save Nalrin."

"Yes, but now that you say that out loud, I feel guilty for breaking my promise to you to just be selfish and not think about all of that other stuff."

"Don't worry your pretty little head about it. I understand," he said as he kissed my wedding ring, just as the Head Chef came out and said that dinner was ready.

I got up and as I walked toward the kitchen, I pushed to Mickel, *"If you're done hiding what is going on from us, dinner is ready."*

The door to the war room flew open, and the look on Mickel's face was mixed with frustration and shame. When his eyes met mine, he mouthed that he was sorry. I just went to make my burger. I placed a couple of onion rings on my patty and looked over the BBQ sauces they had when I saw my favorite from the Manusia. I grabbed it and squeezed a little too hard. "UGGG!"

"Megs..." CJ said in a way that warned me not to let my temper get the best of me.

I just shook my head. CJ turned to Mickel and the guard and sighed. "Look, if you have to keep things from us, that's fine. Whatever man, but just make sure that if you're talking about it, to keep that door shut. We know shit is happening out there, but to know that you're purposely hiding it from us is a bit frustrating."

The Guard and Vernadali froze, eyeing Mickel. Telling us was not something he wanted to do. Mickel sighed. "Ok, look, it is only rumor. We are getting reports that the Ja'Nee are roaming through Obsecuritan. We don't have anything confirmed, and I want you guys just to enjoy your time here without the other stuff interfering, so I won't tell you rumors or anything that isn't confirmed."

"You mean there are more than the ones we fought at the Nalsar River?" I said, shaking my head, feeling stupid and then going back to making my plate. "Of course, there are."

"Megan, I'm sorry if you're mad because we are keeping reports from you..." Mickel tried to say, but stopped when he realized he didn't really know what to say. He wasn't sorry, but he also didn't want to worry us when we were supposed to be relaxing. I understood that, but I didn't have to like it.

I sighed heavily and put my knife down. "Mickel, I understand. I'm sorry for being a bitch."

He nodded.

"Now, I'm going to go outside and eat this delicious, yummy burger." For the first time since I got here, a wave of that heavy dark feeling hit me. I tried to shake it off, but just as I stepped outside, I felt my knees buckled underneath me. "Oh, for Angels' sake!"

CJ dropped his plate and caught me just before I hit the ground. "Babe. Look at me," he said, placing his hand on my cheek. I couldn't move. It was so heavy it was almost paralyzing. "Focus on me."

I did. I looked into his eyes and tried to push the heaviness and darkness that had washed over me away, but there was a pull at the back of my head, making it hard to keep my head up. Even my vision was flittering at the edges. I could see him, but it took all my concentration. I felt like I had every ounce of energy pulled from my body. I even tried to rally my power to help push it away, but it just suck deeper into in its cocoon. I felt my heart race. This wasn't normal. Even the worst of it back at home hadn't left me like this. Nothing had paralyzed me so much.

"Focus on me babes," he said more forcefully, a spark of lightning just outside of the pupil of his eye, kept my focus. I felt myself feeling lighter the longer I looked into his eyes, and when I felt somewhat reasonable again, he picked me up and placed me in one of the chairs by the fire pit. It took a few minutes, but then I felt like nothing had happened. Just like that, I was feeling normal. Only a little more drained, like I had just had a long day.

"I'm ok. Really, I am," I told CJ, over and over again. To prove it, I said, "What I want right now is my damn burger."

"Well, ok then," he said laughing and got up to make us new ones as ours had sprawled out on the ground. One of the guards must have picked up the pieces for us as CJ and Mickel made sure I was ok.

"Look, you don't have to get all light-headed and stuff just because I keep some information from you," Mickel teased.

I gave him the evil eye. "Ya. That's it."

"Want to tell me what that was about?" Mickel asked when no one was close enough to hear.

I just sat there, staring into the fire, wondering how Clarice was doing. If the darkness calling was affecting me still so strongly, how was she fairing? She didn't seem to be as affected by it as I was, though. Maybe she was just better at hiding it.

"Lady Megan," he said all business, "I'm your bodyguard. I need to know what is affecting you that way."

"Shortest story ever, okay?" I said, and he nodded. "At Noctulanar Castle I fed the darkness some of my blood. It's somehow tied to the darkness that's in Clarice's blood, and her father is trying to call her home. Period. That's all you're getting for now."

CJ showed up with my hamburger then, and I dove in. I was ravenous. The hike, the collapse. It just sucked all the energy from me and, honestly, this was probably the best burger I had ever had.

Luckily, the rest of the night was fairly uneventful. We just sat outside and snuggled by the fire. I could feel CJ being a little more protective over me, and while that normally would've driven me crazy, I let him do it tonight. Whether it was that Vernadali Charge, or a husband protecting and worried about his wife, I didn't care. I just wanted to be wrapped up in his arms. Mickel however, seemed to station himself a little closer, which made me briefly wonder what else he knew that had been confirmed, but didn't tell us.

CHAPTER 34

THE NEXT COUPLE OF days were split between the beach and hiking through the Tes Forest. We hit up the trails that CJ had heard of, and we found some beautiful spots along the way. There was a meadow that I felt a little bad for, as there were parts that weren't so neat and pristine after we left. I blamed CJ, of course. He was the one who was touching me so that it caused my electricity to awaken and fire throughout my body. Okay, fine, call it the honeymoon hormones.

The forest and beach here were truly a magical place. The smell of the ocean, the feel of the sand between my toes, and the shade of the trees just relaxed me in ways I hadn't been in what felt like a very long time. I found it so much easier to center myself and let all those dimensional worries float away.

CJ and I took advantage of each other everywhere we could. And I mean everywhere. We had come up the stairs from another day of lounging at the beach to the estate, but when we entered the main room, I looked at CJ and said, "They're learning."

"War Room is shut," he said and immediately started stripping right there.

I pulled the shirt I had on over my swimsuit off, and then his hands were on me, removing my top so he could knead my breasts. There was a quick check around the room to verify that the room was indeed empty, and he untied my bottoms, leaving them by the entry door, and lifted me to carry me to the loveseat in front of the fire.

At first, he just ran his hands up and down my body, as if memorizing each and every curve it provided, as if he didn't already know each inch of me. When I palmed him in my hand, there was a needy moan that emanated deep within him. I pushed him back and straddled him for a moment, before kissing down his chest, and then licking down his stomach to where his length stood tall and proud.

Stroking him again, his head rolled back as I took him fully into my mouth. His hand rested lightly on the back of my head, and I bobbed up and down a few times before releasing him. I stroked him, fingered the head of him, and took his balls into my mouth. Swirling my tongue around each of them, I moaned. His cock twitched and grew harder.

"Fuck, I love when you do that," he said to the room.

I repeated it a few more times, and once he was seconds from coming, I stopped. There was a whimper from him as he looked down with pleading eyes. Smiling, I licked my way back up his full hardness and flicked my tongue over the head. Slowly, I was taking his full length into my mouth and down my throat.

His hand was again on my head as I bobbed up and down, his hand guiding the tempo. He didn't force it, just guided me. I hummed into him and he moaned, low and guttural, "Mrs. Mathewson."

That had me with my hand between my own legs, rubbing my clit as I sucked his cock. "Stick a finger in. Suck my cock as you finger yourself. I want to see it," he commanded.

I happily obliged, and he moaned at the sight. When his hand on my head moved faster, I sucked him harder and moaned into him. That was all he needed. There were a few short thrusting movements before I swallowed him whole again and he came down my throat, my name loud in the space around us.

I gently licked him clean, and just before I rose, I gave him a quick extra suck. He popped out of my mouth, and his body twitched. I kissed his chest as he gathered me in his arms and set me across his lap.

His head rested on the back of the couch, and when his eyes met mine, they were glazed over. We sat there for about ten minutes, just content in each other's arms, when a guard walked through the back of the room.

She was still about ten feet from the war room door when she stopped. "My apologies, Lady Megan and Vernadali CJ." She couldn't see anything, except for maybe our bare shoulders, but I doubt she missed the line of clothes on the floor from the front door. That didn't stop CJ from grabbing my boob and running his thumb over my nipple, tweaking it, all while I tried to keep a straight face. He chuckled under me.

"It's okay, Antal," I said, trying to keep my voice light. We had gotten to know just about each of the Guards and Vernadali that were stationed here by this point. "Give us a few minutes and the room will be open."

She bowed and agreed, "Yes, Lady."

"Please stop bowing," I half growled, but there wasn't any real bite to it because CJ was now running his fingers through the folds of me between my legs and flicking my clit.

She stood up, smiled, and nodded as she made her way to the War Room door and hurriedly slid in and made sure it was firmly shut.

When I looked at CJ, he grinned.

"Asshole," I said, thumping him on the chest.

"What?" he asked, trying to sound innocent.

"How would you like it if I ran my fingers over your dick while you were trying to talk to someone?" His eyes widened at that, but I felt him twitch under my leg. I smiled and said, "Or maybe you would like that."

His hand ran down my side and cupped my as, squeezed it, and his eyes filled with a mischievous heat when he said, "So, if this room needs to be clear in a few minutes. That doesn't leave me time to repay the favor you just gave me."

I felt him stiffening again under my leg and I cocked an eyebrow. "There are no favors to repay. We give and take. Equal partnering. If I want to give you a blow job and that's all we have time for, then that's what I am going to do, because I love sucking you off," I said, nibbling his ear.

"But we have nothing but time, love," he said against my neck as he kissed it. "So, I think I will take you upstairs and ravish you. Take my time, and enjoy every inch of the woman I get to call my wife."

I had to consciously not curl my toes at how he said that. "You haven't had enough today?" I said, my breath short as I recalled the beach that morning, the tree I was against just before lunch, and the very extensive session on the cliff a mile or two up overlooking the ocean.

He brazenly looked me over and I felt him firmly harden. "Nope. Not in the littlest bit."

With that, he stood, picking me up with him, and carried me off to the bedroom.

"What about our clothes?" I asked.

"Later," he purred, taking the stairs as quickly as he could.

CHAPTER 35

"WE HAVE TO GO."

"Clarice, wait, what's wrong?"

"The darkness is pulling. We have to go." Her voice wasn't right. It seemed so monotone, so distant.

"Okay. We will go. When do you want to leave?" I asked her as darkness was closing in around us.

"Well," she said, not making eye contact and staring straight ahead, "Tomorrow morning. I will send a message ahead that we will be on our way."

She turned on her heels and walked away from me.

Then the darkness' tendrils closed in around me and licked at my skin. I tried to scream, but I couldn't. I kicked, punched, and swatted at the tendrils to stop touching me, but they just kept licking at my skin. I tried to use my power, but there were only small wisps of power that flung from my hands. They crawled up my neck and licked at my lips and nose. I screamed and —

"Megan, wake up," CJ pleaded, shaking me awake. "You're thrashing."

"What do you mean I was thrashing?" I said, after I realized I was safe with CJ.

"Thrashing. As in, I may have bruises on my ankles from you kicking me. What were you dreaming about?"

I thought about it for a minute. The air felt dark and heavy again. "Darkness and Clarice."

"What about it?"

"No, it's calling Clarice."

"Megs, I'm really confused. You need to explain."

"Remember how when you got home from up north, Clarice and I felt darkness calling to her?"

"Yes," he said. I felt the Vernadali Charge instantly put his muscles into alert mode. I traced his tattoo on his forearm for a minute, and then finally sighed. That was going to take some getting used to.

"Megan, I'm trying to be patient here," he said gruffly.

"I'm feeling it stronger than I have before. I've gotten pretty good at hiding it. Felt it a few times while here at the beach after the burger incident, and once much on one of the hikes yesterday. Her father must be getting worse," I said.

CJ sat there, looking at me with concern written all over his face. Even though I hadn't had a vision in so long, it felt more like a premonition, a feeling like something was going to happen. It couldn't be though, because it just was this strange open space, with black tendrils to it. I shivered, and CJ started rubbing my arms and wrapping the blankets around me.

"Ceej. It wasn't just darkness. In my dream, Clarice was telling me we had to go, and no, I don't know where to. Then once the decision was made to go, the darkness tendrils started..." I shivered again.

He studied me for a long moment before he said, "Maybe we need to head home. I'm going to talk to Mickel."

I could see the difference in his movements. He wasn't CJ, my husband. He was Vernadali CJ. His Vernadali Charge in full swing. He was up and out the bedroom door before I could say anything else.

"CJ. Wait." I threw the blanket off, grabbed my robe and his pajama pants off the edge of the bed, and headed down the hall after him.

"Ceej," I called.

"We are in here, Lady Megan," Mickel said.

Lady Megan. Shit!

I sighed and walked into the War Room. CJ was standing there, in his boxers, talking to Mickel with no less than eight other Nalrin Guard and two Vernadali in the room, all standing at full attention. Double shit.

"CJ, I'd like the others in here not to be too jealous of that body of yours." I smiled slyly and tossed him his pants. One of the guards' eyes met mine, and he gave me an apologetic look as his cheeks heated. I pushed to him, *"Not even mad."* With a small smile.

CJ caught them in one hand and put them on, while Mickel just laughed. I turned back to CJ and said, "Honey, we don't have to go. It was only a bad dream."

"If it was only a bad dream, then why did this arrive from Clarice this morning?" he said, handing me a sheet of paper. His eyes were full of worry. "It may not have been a vision, but babe..."

"Mickel:

I received a letter that my father is going to die very soon. I can feel it pulling stronger and stronger every day. I thought I could resist it.

We are heading for Therth and leaving in three days. A few arrangements need to be made beforehand. Please tell Megan and CJ to take the boat from Mirklinar to Chastdane. Then meet us in Therth. Ask them not to be mad. Beg them if you have to. I promise to make it up to them.

-Clarice"

My heart sank. He's right, we have to go. She wouldn't ask us to leave early if it wasn't important. Poor Clarice. Mirklinar, that was a two-and-a-half-day hard ride south, and the transport across the channel would take us four days to Chastdane. Depending on how often we could get fresh horses, it was going to take a week to go from Chastdane to Therth. The terrain wouldn't allow us to get to Therth any faster than that.

If we head back now, we could get home before they leave and go with them. I read the note from Clarice again and looked back up at CJ. He had done the math, too. I gave him a quick nod as I chewed on my thumb.

"We are heading home. Tell everyone to pack up," he said with a command in his voice that had everyone scrambling. I gave him a questioning look. Then looked at Mickel.

"They all just instantly took his orders?" I said quietly to Mickel.

"Sorry, Mickel," CJ said, just as quietly.

"Don't be. You outrank me by virtue of the Vernadali status alone. The Vernadali that are here are under orders from Julian to heed my orders, which is why they follow mine," he said. I looked at both of them.

"But they are yours to command. Even the Vernadali. I overstepped. I apologize."

Mickel put his hand on CJ's shoulder and said, "You're the highest-ranking person here. We are here for your protection, and we have orders from Julian, that you can't overwrite, but otherwise, what you say goes."

"How is CJ the highest-ranking Vernadali, though? There must be someone here who has higher rank or status than him. He only just left the Curtails of the North." I said.

CJ wouldn't look at me and just stared at Mickel. "You didn't tell her?" Mickel said, cocking his head to the side. Then laughed. "You prick."

"She doesn't need to know about rank status," CJ growled. "Sorry babe. I don't mean to keep shit from you, it's just I've been afforded things I don't feel I've earned, so I don't think or talk about them."

"Okay." I understood where he came from. "But neither of you answered me. Why did they all took his orders?"

"CJ is Angels Blessed." Mickel said.

"I don't see how that changes anything." I looked between them, and CJ still wouldn't look at me.

"They created a new rank for CJ. The Angels or what we know as the '*A Rank*'." Mickel explained. "It will also be given to any Vernadali children you may have."

"Our children will have a special rank because of who created them?" I couldn't believe what I was hearing. "Mickel, that is total and utter bullshit."

"I agree." CJ said through gritted teeth, and then finally looking at me, he said, "It was ruled by the Council of Vernadali and Julian that an Angels' ranking would outrank any other person short of Julian. Which is understandable, but that is why everyone took my orders."

I looked at Mickel, then to CJ.

"I don't like it. If Vernadali Samuel, or Mickel gave me orders, I'd follow them. I don't like that my Angels Blessed rank insinuates I'm the best person to make decisions."

"Experience is something that will take time, but you will continue to outrank everyone short of the dimensional head. Technically, you will have authority anywhere in the dimension. It will just depend on whether those Heads will honor the Vernadali." Mickel said.

CJ nodded and looked at me. Concern in his eyes.

"It's fine. Details to sort out later," I said. My stomach was so tied up in knots, I was on the verge of crying, so I turned on my heels and went back to the bedroom.

When I got there, I plopped on the bed and tried very hard not to cry. I was mad that we had to head back early, and it felt selfish. CJ and I will have the rest of our lives together and here she was, about to lose her father. Estranged father, yes, but still her father. I sniffled a tear away just as CJ walked back into the bedroom.

"Babe, I'm a bit confused. I know that you're feeling bad for Clarice, but you're actually feeling... selfish?"

"Ok, I know you've known me for like ever, and there isn't another person alive who knows me as well as you do, but how did you nail that so perfectly?" I asked.

He suddenly looked very uncomfortable. "It's part of the, ahh, Charge. I can tell what you're feeling. Remember when I fought Mickel, and I told you that whatever you were feeling was distracting?"

I thought back and remembered how amazing he looked. I had gotten very turned on at that sight. "Yes."

"I just felt a wave of tingling heat from you that settled deep in my core. It's the best way I can describe it," he said. "What was it you were feeling, anyway?"

"I was thinking how incredibly sexy you were standing there in a tank ready to fight. I was really turned on by it. I sort of imagined you in bed," I said, smiling slightly. He came over and kissed my temple. "Anything else that you need to tell me about this Charge thing?" I asked.

"You already know that it makes me super protective over you, super emotional connection, over and above my love for you, and the ultimate protector. There are some other nuances, but don't worry about those right now."

"That scares the underworld out of me, Ceej. Let's get packed up," I said, wiping a tear that managed to escape.

"Not going to lie; that selfishness that you're feeling? I find very satisfying," he said as he headed into the bathroom to get his things.

I just sat there on the bed and played with my fingers. When he came out, he sat back down with me and took my hands.

"Babe, what else are you thinking?" he asked carefully.

"I just don't like feeling this conflicted. I totally want to be there for Clarice. We need to be there for Clarice. She has stood by and helped us through everything with Ansel and Symatha."

"But," he said when I didn't continue right away.

"Ceej, this was our one time to be totally and completely selfish. Just us. Really, just you and me time. We got what six, seven days!" I said, as I threw my hands up in the air and stomped them back onto the bed. CJ was trying not to laugh at me, because, let's admit, it is very silly. Most people in the Manusia would be thrilled with a week-long honeymoon.

"I know it's selfish, but that's what our honeymoon is supposed to be, right? Just time for the new husband and wife to just hang back and do whatever they want. Once we get back, it all becomes about stopping Ansel again. While we are in Therth, and Clarice is spending time with her father, we will be looking for more clues on how to stop him. We will research the libraries, we will talk to whomever we can, to find out what we can. Clarice and I had already decided that when the darkness got too strong, we would have to head to Obsecuritan. We just figured it would be after our honeymoon."

"How about this? When all this craziness settles, you and I will come back here, or wherever you want to go, and we will go for as long as you want," he said, looking me straight in the eyes.

"Promise?"

"Promise. You're right. This was our one time to be selfish, and I'm a little irked about it too. That being said, we have, actually and surprisingly, been able to do whatever we want and whenever we want considering the Guard are here," he said, as he smeared the last tear from my cheek and ran his hand down my neck then to the space between my breasts.

It was the lightest of touches like this that drove me crazy, and he knew it. I closed my eyes, and a breath caught. He took his hand under my chin and kissed me ever so lightly that if I didn't feel the shock of his lips run down to the pit of my stomach, I could have missed it. "I love you, Mrs. Mathewson," he breathed.

"How is a girl not to smile at that?" I said, and before he could pull too far back, I threw my arms around him and pulled him closer.

"Mickel and the Guard will be waiting," he said with a mischievous grin.

"Mickel, don't rush. I want one more honeymoon rendezvous with my husband before we leave," I pushed toward him, then I heard the door to the war room shut and I smiled at CJ.

"You are..." he started to say as he ripped my robe off.

"Wonderful!" I finished for him as I pulled his pants down and kissed his chest.

Then he took my head in his hands, kissed me hard, and pressed against me. When I opened my eyes, I saw that appetite in his eyes that mirrored mine.

"One last honeymoon rendezvous," I whispered as he kissed my neck, tore my thin silk nightdress off, and entered me in one forceful stroke.

CHAPTER 36

ONCE EVERYTHING WAS LOADED in the carriage, the guard opened the door to let us in. I hesitated, trying to think how we could get there faster.

"Do you have a couple of horses so we can ride on ahead?" I asked.

"Lady Megan, Julian wants you protected by the Guard in your travels back. He was very specific about you and Vernadali CJ taking the carriage," the guard said carefully.

"Yeah. Yeah. Yeah. Orders. I got it. But, we need to get back quickly. My family is leaving in a few days, and it is a three-day trip the way we came. If CJ and I ride through Tes Forest instead of going around it, then we could cut at least a day off the trip. Maybe even cut it in half." When he didn't move, I continued, "Mickel and a few others could go with us, giving us the protection that Julian had required. Plus, if this is Ansel trying to spring a trap, he will have no doubt heard of Julian's demand for us to travel via carriage during our honeymoon with the Nalrin Guard and Vernadali. In essence, you will be a decoy. Mickel and a few Guard could surely keep up with me and CJ."

"As you wish, my lady. I will inform Mickel of your change of plans," he said, bowing formally.

"I'll be so glad when we get back home, and the only Guard we have to worry about is Mickel. He is much more like family, so I don't mind him around as much. However, all this extra, makes me feel like... I don't like it. It's just more people to protect. We know he will attack. We just don't know when," I said to CJ, as I gathered a few of our things.

"I agree. Mickel is a good guy, and he at least tries to let us have our privacy."

"Lady Megan, I have your horses," one of the Guards said, leading two horses. "Mickel said he will be just a minute. He is sending a message to Nalrin via Lark Messenger that you are returning to the family early."

"Thank you," CJ said for me, and I frowned. His charge had taken over and now he was answering questions for me too? I sighed and climbed to the top of the carriage to grab our backup syths, my syth belt from one of our bags, and a few other things we would need for the trip.

I secured my syths to my thigh and saw CJ do the same, just as Mickel walked over from around the corner.

"Julian won't be happy you're going by horseback and not the carriage," he said firmly, but with a hint of teasing.

"He can get the fuck over it. If I'm leaving my honeymoon early for a family emergency, and he still has teleporting locked down, I'm going the fastest way possible, and that is not by snail-carriage," I said as another wave of darkness fell over me, causing my leg to miss as I tried to swing up into the saddle. I looked at CJ and pushed, *"We need to get moving."*

"How fast do you think we can get there?" CJ asked, and moved over to help me up.

"It's still early in the day, so we should get there by the day after tomorrow?" Mickel said. "That is, if we ride hard, but the horses are going to need to rest. They may be quick, but..."

"Calling?" CJ asked in my ear as he helped me up.

"Yeah," I whispered.

"Lady Megan, are you ok?" Mickel asked.

"I'm fine," I said as I straightened up.

"You sure? It's not like you to miss..."

"She is fine, Mickel," CJ interrupted him.

"Very well." He nodded and swung up onto his horse.

"Relax, babe. You're charged more than a power plant. Breathe," I pushed. He glanced back at me, and I saw him visibly take a couple of deep breaths. *"Breathe. He's just doing his job."*

Those two are going to need to work on their communication.

We rode hard and pushed the horses, but let them rest as we could. We made camp at nightfall and I insisted upon sleeping under the stars. It would make for faster clean-up in the morning, thus more time on the road. Besides, it was a warm clear night, and the stars were beautiful. I stared at them most of the night. The darkness was weighing so heavily that I couldn't fall asleep for a long while. I did finally crash due to exhaustion, but I think I got only a couple of hours. When I woke up before daybreak, I went to the horses.

As I patted their backs and soothed their sighs, I tried to figure out a way to get home sooner. There was something telling me we had to get there today, but we were too far away. I couldn't transport without causing an inter-dimensional issue, and we were already taking the shortest route through the forest. The carriage would need to take the northern route up and around and wouldn't arrive at home for another three days.

SNAP.

I whirled around, syths in hand.

"Whoo, babe. Shhh," CJ said, catching my hand inches from his face.

"Ceej. What are you doing up?" I asked, putting my syths back in their sheaths.

"Well, I could ask you the same thing? But you asked first. My answer is simple. A wife doesn't climb out of the sleeping bag she shares with her husband without her husband waking up," he said quietly. "Plus, I can feel your anxiety. I hate that. I'm sure in a fight it would be or could be useful, but it does make it hard to sleep."

"Why are you all charged up?" I asked him, avoiding the obvious question.

"We are on the road. I'm going to be somewhat charged," he said, shrugging off the question. "Now, your turn to answer."

"Thinking of Clarice. We need to get home," I said.

"You keep saying that," CJ said, teasing me a little.

"I know. I just don't know how to do it. Darkness... I don't like it. It's just..." I couldn't even put together a whole sentence. I took a deep breath and ran my hand over the flank of one of the silver mares and said, "Here I am supposedly the most powerful Sangra in recent history and I can't do anything to speed the journey up."

"There you go, Megan. Denying yourself when it doesn't suit you," Mickel said, stepping out from behind a tree. "And before you ask, I was already awake when you got up. I just wanted to give you space."

I tried to ignore him and thought back to the horses. "For such an advanced society, we still traveled by foot or by horse. Nalrin has medical breakthroughs in cancer research that the Manuisa only wished it had. They have a cure for HIV, do heart surgery without cutting someone open more than an inch, all of which are light years ahead of the Manusia. Yet there are no cars, no planes, no helicopters, no anything. Still, just travel by good old-fashioned horse. Don't get me wrong, I love the simple living. It's one reason I want to live here. It can just be so darn inconvenient is all."

"There have been discussions, serious discussions, for modernized transportation, but after seeing the effects in the Manusia and Rhodem, this dimension has decided to keep the use of technology for the good of people. Medical advances, research, some kinds of telecommunications, those types of things. There are no military contracts for technology. No advanced weapons of any kind. Besides," he said, patting one of the horses, "this keeps us in touch with the ground, and by extension our power. It also helps to remind us that we are all connected. We need the ground just as the ground needs us to keep it safe. One cannot live without the other. So, we use our power to manipulate what we can without harming what we need the most."

"That's so beautiful," I said in a whisper. It really was. For all the convenience that fast transportation has brought us in the Manusia, it is easy to forget how connected we all are. We really can't have one without the other. Then it hit me. "If I am the most powerful Sangra in recent history..."

"And you are," said Mickel and CJ in unison.

"Anyway, and taking what Mickel said..." I tried to think it through. If I use my power to strengthen the horses, maybe we could ride faster and get to the house sooner. Clarice and Lindy put an endurance incantation on CJ last year so he could do that very thing. I knew the incantation too. I had studied it when we got back. Why couldn't it work on the horses?

"Megs, what are you thinking?" CJ said, as I smiled.

"It could work."

"What could work?" CJ asked hesitantly.

"Last year, when we had to... well, amid everything else, CJ was worried that in one of the travels that he would be a liability because he was human," I tried to explain to them.

"I'm still human, but I know what you're saying. And you think it could work?" he said.

"Again, what could work?" Mickel asked, getting impatient.

"There is an incantation they put on CJ to help him keep up with the hikes and traveling we needed to do. Why can't I put that on the horses to get us to the house faster?" I said.

Mickel thought hard on it. "I can't think of a reason, but what of the guard. It wears on them too to travel that long and hard."

"So, I cast it on the whole camp. Everyone will get the benefit," I said and turned to the horses, not waiting for them to talk me out of it. I took a deep breath, centering my power, brought my hands out to my side, up above my head, and back down into a prayer position. I opened my eyes and moved my hand to form a triangle and flat again repeatedly, as I repeated the words, *Gil mah re spree en phis,* over and over again.

Soon there was a blue-green film that settled over each of the horses. I felt my Maltal warm and said the incantation once for each horse in our group and when I stopped, the blue film absorbed into each horse. I looked at each of the horses and they were awake and ready to go. One even looked at me, pawed at the ground, and gave a soft huff.

"The horses are ready. Time to do the Guard," I said, turning back to CJ, but I could feel the pressure of darkness settling over me again. I grabbed his hand and concentrated on pushing it away. *"DAMN IT! Not now. Every minute we aren't on the move, that incantation wears off the horses and we are trying to get home so she can answer your call,"* I said under my breath. No sooner was I finished did the darkness let up just as quick as it came on.

"Get me to the guards and start getting them up so we can head out. I'll cast the incantation while they pack up," I said.

"Honey, don't you need to rest. That looked like it took a bit out of you," CJ said.

"No," I told him. He didn't miss a damn thing.

"The darkness is pushing on you again, isn't it?" CJ asked, stiffening.

"Is that what caused you to miss the mount back at the estate?" Mickel asked.

"Yes. It is getting stronger. That's another reason she is so insistent on getting going. Please Mickel, get the others up," CJ told him, and I made a mental note that we are going to have to talk about that Vernadali charge, and soon.

I stood up straight and started in on the incantation for us. Again, I repeated the incantation for each of the riders, including CJ and Mickel. Once finished, the Guard who were traveling with us moved faster and we were on our way before the sun was fully up.

We stopped at the planned night stop just after mid-day and got some lunch, let the horses rest, and get water. I thought for sure we were going to have to get fresh horses, but once they were done drinking, they were the ones urging us on. The incantation worked so much better than expected. At this rate, we should be at the house just after nightfall. I had my power open to watch for any unwanted embers, and watch to make sure weren't being followed.

Once we were through the forest, the horses picked up the pace since we didn't have to weave and watch for trees and branches, so we made even better time across the grasslands. Just as the sun was falling behind the trees, I could see the tree line to the forest that was just behind our home. I chirped and put my heels to my horse, leaning down to streamline the airflow.

Once we reached the tree line, we slowed down again. The trees were closer together here than in the Tes Forest. I felt out and saw some embers and smoke from within the trees to the northeast of us.

"Mickel, head north slightly. There is smoke burning. It shouldn't take long to get there!" I pushed to him.

He nodded, and we rode as quickly as we could, weaving through the trees. We arrived 20 minutes later, and the sight took the breath straight from my lungs.

Remi was standing over Raltuk, covered in blood, not moving.

"Remi!" CJ shouted as we dismounted, and I ran over to Raltuk. His wings were limp and still and there was a huge wet spot in his chest where a sword had gone through it. His chest wasn't moving, and there wasn't a flicker to his wings. He was gone.

"Oh, Raltuk," I breathed. His hand was already cold as I took it. I hung my head, a lump tight in my throat as I wiped a tear. I crossed his arms over his stomach and pulled his wings in tight. A bandage already had one wing secured tight against his left side.

"... That's when they jumped from the trees and attacked the carriage," Remi explained. The carriage, which looked exactly like the one I had taken from home to the beach at Hartwood Citadel, was shattered and burning. "The Ja'Nee just jumped from the trees directly into the carriage. They didn't even try for the guard. Just swooped in, pulled Raltuk out with a sword through his chest. Then they destroyed the carriage and took off. We tried to fight them, but they just evaded us and left us alone."

"Did Raltuk have anyone else with him?" I asked.

"No, Lady Megan. After the wedding, he went back to Nalrin, and he was on his way home to meet up with his mate for some time off before the next council meeting," he explained, but hesitated.

"Remi, what is it?" CJ asked.

"It's just that I've been running it over in my head. When the Ja'Nee came out of the carriage with Raltuk, he looked to another one of the Ja'Nee, and it surprised them who was in the carriage."

"What makes you say that?" CJ asked.

"I can't explain it. It's not like they have faces you can read. Just a feeling I have based on how they moved afterward and how they didn't pay us any attention. Like their only target was whoever was in that carriage, but it wasn't who it was supposed to be."

I looked at CJ, and he was already putting it together, but I said, "They were looking for us."

"I was afraid you were going to say that," CJ said, running his hand through his hair.

"If that's true, Lady Megan, then why be surprised by who was in the carriage. Why not figure out for sure which one you were in? There were a hundred of them at your wedding. All the diplomats arrived in one, then returned to Nalrin," Remi said.

"But how many of them are still being used other than the one for CJ and I?" I asked.

"Only five," he said, realizing what I meant. "Raltuk's wing was recovering from some surgery right after your wedding, which is why he didn't fly home. I need to get back to Nalrin so we can warn the other carriages."

"We are only a couple of hours' ride to our house. Come with us, rest for the night and then you can leave in the morning. You can send a message ahead from there," I said.

"As you wish, ma'lady," he said bowing. Then, turning to the other Vernadali, he spoke, "Let's get that fire out and get moving. We are going to Vernadali CJ and Lady Megan's for the evening. You have five minutes."

"What about Raltuk?" CJ asked.

Remi turned to me. "Lady Megan, I don't have enough power on my own to send his body to Nalrin. I'm depleted from attacking the Ja'Nee. Can you help me please?"

I nodded. "Wait, let's place a note for Julian in his hand, and we will send him directly there. I don't think that it would be smart considering the circumstances to send him directly to the morgue," I said and headed to my horse to retrieve a pen and paper.

Julian:

Raltuk's carriage was attacked by Ja'Nee. Remi and the accompanying Vernadali were avoided and are uninjured. The carriage is destroyed. Remi and the other two Vernadali are heading to the house. Remi will send more information directly to you from there.

-M. Mathewson

I took some cord from my pack and tied it to Raltuk's hands, then sent a silent prayer to the Angels asking them to guide him to rest. I reached up and took Remi's hand with my left, raised my right hand over Raltuk, pictured where I wanted Raltuk to be placed in Julian's office, and muttered the incantation with Remi. With a pop, Raltuk was gone.

"Ok, let's move. Mickel, stay with Megan and stay in the middle of the group," My Vernadali ordered, as I climbed up onto my horse. He looked at me and there were unspoken words of loss and worry between us. Then he chirped and took up the front line with Remi.

CHAPTER 37

I FELT US CROSS the warning incantations at the property line and when we broke the tree line, I saw Owen standing out in front of the house, syths out. *"Owen, it's Megan and CJ. And a few friends,"* I pushed to him. He sheathed his syths, and by the time we rode up, the rest of my family was standing there looking very confused.

"What in the Underworld's name are you doing here?" Jean yelled at us.

I looked to Clarice whose eyes narrowed at me as she grumbled, "She didn't follow my instructions to meet us in Therth."

"Well, that would've taken us longer than meeting you here before you left," I bit back at her as I dismounted and handed my reins to Mickel. "Mickel, can you get the Guard and Vernadali set up near the stables?"

"I'll help you, Mickel," CJ said as he dismounted and started leading the horse to the stable.

While CJ and Mickel got the Vernadali and Nalrin Guard settled for the night, and Owen and Remi sent a warning to Nalrin, I went inside and brought the others up to date on what was going on.

"Why attack a Ralvin though? What would be the point? They are creepy, but they pretty much keep to themselves, and don't make enemies," Lindy asked.

"That's just it. I'm not so sure they were looking for Raltuk. Remi said that, after the wedding, all the diplomats returned to Nalrin in their respective carriages. Only five were being used to transport anyone. One of which was CJ and me," I explained.

"They were after you two," Jean said. "DAMN IT! We can't catch a break. If dealing with Ansel and trying to figure out how to destroy him wasn't enough, now we have to deal with the Ja'Nee?"

"I was kind of hoping that the attack at the Nalsar River would've been an isolated incident," Clarice said. "Maybe we can find out more about them when we get to Therth."

Mickel walked into the living room and stripped his jacket off, hanging it on one of the pegs by the door. "The guys are showering, and Remi got a message off to Julian. I set them up in the extra rooms in the stable house for tonight."

Owen said, "I'll take some extra towels out there soon."

"If the Ja'Nee are pure darkness, didn't the book say that they can only be controlled by someone who *is* pure darkness?" CJ asked.

"Yeah. The problem is we just don't know who that is?" Jean said.

"Who could wield that much darkness and survive it?" Lindy said.

"What do you mean survive it?" Logan said.

"My understanding is that pure darkness would literally rip someone apart from the inside. To wield that kind of darkness..." she said, as Clarice came and sat down on the couch next to her.

"Logan, you know how in the Manusia it's said someone is pure evil and has no soul?" Logan nodded slowly and Clarice continued, "Let's just say that the mass murders, the Hannibal Lectors, the Adolf Hitlers of your world, they wouldn't hold a candle to this type of person."

"So, you don't think it's Megan's dad?" he asked.

"No. We've known Ansel for a long time. He has known love and is acting out of revenge," Lindy said. "Whoever is controlling this pure darkness, the Ja'Nee, has been to the Underworld and embraced that darkness."

I thought I saw Clarice stiffen slightly and then looked at Lindy again, as if she was assessing her words.

"Well, then," Logan said. "Guess that's going to make life interesting."

"Clarice?" I said, calling her from her thoughts. When she turned to me, I asked, "What are you thinking?"

"Just a theory, but I'll have to verify it in Therth," she said with a distant anger I wasn't going to touch. Give her space. Got it.

Turning to Logan, I stared him down and when he gave me a questioning look, I said, "Ummm, I thought you were going to head home after the wedding?" I had to admit, though, it wasn't that much of a surprise to see him still here.

"Well, I got a little caught up in wedding fever," he said with a smile, then turning a wonderful shade of red. "Not that I wouldn't have asked her to marry me eventually anyway, but..."

I looked over at Lindy, who was blushing brightly. "Seriously? He popped the question?" I asked excitedly.

She held up her hand and smiled the biggest smile I've seen from her in a very long time. "It was a big surprise. We were talking and he just casually mentioned that he wanted us to have a small house along a river so our kids could torture your kids in it all day. Then he stopped when he realized what he said."

"That runs in the family," I said, chuckling and thinking of CJ back at the beach that first night. Mickel chuckled, remembering how I told him about it.

"He just stood up, went to his bag, pulled out the little black box, and asked me to marry him," she said.

"She didn't even hesitate," Logan said. "Thank the Gods and Angels. I saw the ring in a little antique shop out near Mom and Dad's and I knew it needed to be Lindy's."

I bounced up and gave Lindy a hug just as CJ walked in. "I'm so happy for you!"

"Why are you so happy for her?" CJ said, unbuckling his syth belt and hanging it on the hook next to the door.

"Because now you're never getting rid of me," Lindy said, smiling and holding her hand up for him to see. His eyes went wide with shock, then he rolled them dramatically.

"Logan... dude. Are you sure you want to do that? I mean its LINDY! She's a nut ca...oomppffff." I didn't see her throw the pillow, but it landed straight in his face. "Ok, fine. Congrats, man," he finally said and stuck his tongue out at Lindy.

"I had to watch you for years with Megan. Give me this, you little fuck!" Logan said. CJ just laughed and hugged his brother.

"Megan, CJ, can I talk to you in the kitchen for a minute?" Clarice said, standing by the kitchen door, once everyone stopped teasing each other.

We headed into the kitchen, and she closed the door. When she turned around, tears were streaming down her face.

"I'm so sorry!" she sobbed. "I shouldn't have had you guys leave your honeymoon early. I feel horrible. I just wanted to say I'm sorry."

"I've been feeling it too, Clarice. I know how strong it is, and you're feeling it a hundred times more than I am. I would've done the same thing. You're family. This is what we do," I said, pulling her into my arms and hugging her.

"Clarice. It's your father. We need to go," CJ said.

"You guys are letting me off the hook too easy," she sniffled.

"Oh, you just wait. Don't you worry about it. We will hold this over your head for years to come," I told her, pulling back as I smiled brightly.

"I would expect nothing less." She smiled a little and blew her nose.

"Every little comment about how we get all lovey and mushy? I'm going to blame it on the fact that we couldn't get it out of our systems on our honeymoon," I said, trying to keep a light sound to my voice, even though there was a part of me that was still peeved, but I also knew it wasn't her fault.

"Thank you, guys. You really are the best family ever," she blubbered.

"Now, look who's all mushy and lovey," CJ said, rolling his eyes.

"Ceej, I'm hungry. Can you cook up something please?" I asked.

"Planning on it. I'm starved. The Guard and Vernadali, Mickel included, need something more than that prepackaged crap they've been eating on. You know they wouldn't take anything from the kitchens, even when we told the cook to send something into them after the burger incident. Even though there was plenty of food. Something about not wanting to eat us out of our food stores or some crap. Stubborn bastards," he said, then headed into the living room. "Owen, Jean, can you guys come into the kitchen and help me out, please?"

"Come on Clarice. Let's go get that face washed up. If Lindy sees all that running mascara, well, you know Lindy," I said, giggling.

CHAPTER 38

CJ, OWEN, AND JEAN made up all the food that was in the house. There was so much of it. We set tables up outside and created a huge buffet. There were about 25 of us circling a big campfire that one of the Vernadali had started behind the house in the sparring arena.

It felt good to relax with all my friends and family, and listen to some stories that the Vernadali had. Mickel and Remi told of a story where they shared an assignment, where they had to go to the Cinder Lands and retrieve a Sangra who was attempting to hide out with the fairies.

"He was so high off the drinks that he kept asking, '*Why did you pluck my wings? Why did you pluck my wings?*' the whole way back to Nalrin," Remi said in a high-pitched voice and fluttering his arms off to the side.

"Seriously?!" I asked, almost spitting out my drink.

"Yeah. When the physicians at Nalrin gave him the cure for it, he looked like Owen and me after Vegas for a week," Mickel said.

"Speaking of. Logan..." I said, drawing out his name and turning to him.

"Megs, honey," CJ said, trying to keep me calm. "Mom already practically beat him sober that morning."

"Yes, my favorite sister-in-law of all the realms," he said, sweet as candy. The Nalrin Guard and Vernadali were leaning in, listening carefully, while my family was trying to contain their laughter.

I stood and went to stand in front of him, putting my electrified finger in his face, just as I had that morning. His eyes were wide as saucers. I made sure some of that electricity jumped from my finger at each point, "First of all, I'm the *only* sister-in-law."

Zap.

"Second, if you *ever* pull a stunt like that again, I will beat you within an inch of your being."

Zap.

"What if they had gotten alcohol poisoning, or they got hurt or anything else that could have happened in Vegas?"

Zap.

"The night before the wedding?! Really?!"

I zapped him multiple times at that one.

In a brotherly effort to save Logan from my wrath, CJ came over, picked me up, and forced me to sit in his lap. He gave me a stern warning, "Babe. Don't embarrass him before everyone here please."

"You're just protecting him," I said, glaring at him.

"I don't need you to protect me from Megan! I've known her my entire life. I can handle her!" Logan said defensively to CJ.

The entire group went dead silent as I whipped my head around toward him. I lifted my hand and electricity swirled around each of my fingers.

"Logan, I would quit while ahead," Remi said.

"But-" Logan said.

"Honey," Lindy put a hand on his arm when he sat back down next to her, "if even Remi is telling you to stop..."

"Logan, you know how much power and destruction can be wrought with just a few of us in this circle. The Guard and Vernadali even froze at your statement," Mickel said, begging Logan to shut up.

Logan, not willing to back down, strode over to me. When he was about three steps from me, I smiled at him, twisted my fingers, and he flipped upside down and hovered there. The look on his face was priceless.

"Logan," CJ said with an exasperated sigh, "Can't say you were not extensively warned. We are hereby not responsible for your stupidity or what my wife aka Lady Megan does."

I swear I saw Mickel roll his eyes and the Guard and Vernadali sit a little straighter. He had basically said that anything that happens, I am not legally responsible for it.

I stood up, pushed him back a couple steps, so he was more in the middle of the circle, and crouched before him, looking at him eye to eye. "You're my brother. You always have been. Back home, I was just a girl. Just your little brother's bratty little friend. Someone you could pick on because I was just that bratty little girl. You have known me since before your scrawny ass went through puberty. We have basically grown up together. Now, I am your brother's wife. I carry his heart within me, Logan Francies Matthewson. Putting all that aside, I am also a Sangra who carries more power in her than any other in living memory in all of Nalsar. Everyone in this circle would take my command without hesitation. Take your brother's too," I said seriously.

"Megan, you're choosing when to wield it again..." Mickel chastised.

"I'm making a point, Mickel. Now, shut the fuck up," I said and wrinkled my nose at him. The Vernadali and Guard went deathly silent and still again.

"Yes, Lady Megan," Mickel said.

Raising my eyebrow and smiling back at Logan, who was still hanging upside down, I said, "Now, who is the highest-ranking person here?"

"Mickel," Logan said without hesitation, and I could feel Mickel, CJ, and all of the Guard and Vernadali stare at my back. I wasn't going to correct him, because while the Guard and Vernadali knew different, I didn't want to put CJ in that position.

"Note how even the highest-ranking person here backed down from me?" Logan nodded. "Now, stop being a stubborn ass. I love you too much to beat the shit out of you right now. And I'm tired and cranky."

This time, he looked at me and stuck his tongue out at me. I let him drop to the ground in a heap.

"You let him off easy," one of the Vernadali said, almost disappointed.

"Like I said, he's family and I love the shit for brains. Don't get me wrong, he is one of the most intellectual people I know, but he is still a shit for brains," I said, shrugging and sitting back down on CJ's lap, holding me tighter than he had before. I kissed him on the temple and I felt him relax a bit under my touch.

I looked back at Logan and said, "Seriously though, Logan, for all the love of the Angels, will you please be careful where you take these guys. The Guard has an intoxication drink, but it isn't the same as alcohol."

"Yes ma'am." He was rubbing a spot on his shoulder where he landed.

"Manusian alcohol for sure hits you different," Owen said, rubbing his head, surely remembering the hangover he had that morning.

"Owen, you sobered up very well, all things considering. Doesn't excuse Logan from trashing you guys the night before the wedding," I said pointedly.

"Fair enough. Fair enough," he said. Then he turned back to the group and tried very hard to change the subject. "What other stories do you have to tell?"

For the next four hours, they sat around telling stories. CJ even told them about our time in the Manusia. It was a great way to spend the last night before we were all business again.

CHAPTER 39

"GOOD MORNING, BEAUTIFUL," CJ said the next morning as I laid there snuggled up next to him with my arm draped over his stomach.

"Morning," I said, refusing to open my eyes and scooting closer to him, if that were possible.

"Other than the nightmare again, how did you sleep?" he asked. I dreamed of my father pulling me over the cliff again, and CJ stayed up for over an hour with me while I calmed down.

"Great, once I got back to sleep. I was wrapped in your arms, so how could I not." I smiled and kissed his chest. "My husband, my Vernadali, keeping me safe, even in my dreams."

We laid there like that for a long time. I kept pushing away all the thoughts of what today was going to entail when he sighed heavily.

"What was that big sigh for?"

"Just thinking."

"About?" I said as I got up and sat straddled over his hips.

"Well, for one, how lucky I am to call you my wife?" he said, putting his hand on my hip, looking down at me with a hunger I knew all too well.

"Flattery will get you everywhere, dear husband, but what were you *really* thinking about?"

He sighed again. "Logan and Lindy."

"What about them?"

"I'm happy for them and all, but I'm worried about Logan. I would prefer if he didn't go to Therth with us. I know that sounds horrible because I would've been royally pissed if you had dumped me back in the Manusia while all that crap was going on."

"Well, you were *part* of all that crap and the Angels were involved," I said, trying to sound convincing.

"Still. He is going to be pissed, but I'm afraid he will get killed if he goes with us. He's my brother, babe. I don't want to lose him."

"Ahh, look at my macho man getting all sentimental about his big brother," I teased him a little, but the haunted look in his eyes wasn't difficult to see. "Don't worry about it, though. He's heading home today before we head out."

"Really?" he said, surprised.

"Yup. Lindy is taking him. Said he could likely get back to work early, and he knows there is a lot we need to deal with here. He knows all about it. Remember, I had to tell him, Annie, and Amber, when the Ja'Nee attacked us in the marketplace. So, he will wait as patiently as possible back in the Manusia for us to get back. He also said something about not wanting to be a liability, but he wasn't going to tell Lindy that," I told him, and I felt his whole body relax. "He really loves her, you know. I don't think I've ever seen him this happy."

"He hasn't. I was telling Dad the same thing during the reception. He was worried that Logan was chasing a girl that would never be his, and I tried to tell him that Lindy was indeed complicated, but that he shouldn't worry because she cares for him deeply."

I waited a moment before continuing. "Lindy and I talked about it a lot. She was worried that she couldn't love him like she should because of Auturno. I told her that no love is the same. She would not love Logan the same as she did Auturno. I think once she accepted that, she could open her heart and love Logan fully."

"I was beginning to think he wouldn't be serious about anyone after Rebecca. He's had girlfriends, but," he looked at me, shook off the thoughts, and added, "I'm glad that they're happy, and I won't have to worry about him on the road." He got a very mischievous smile on his face. "So..."

"Sooo," I smiled back.

"Do you think they would be mad if we were late for breakfast?" he said, removing my nightshirt.

"Oh, and miss an opportunity to give Clarice grief?" I bent down to kiss him, but just before I could reach his lips, there was a soft knock on the door.

"Lady Megan?" Mickel said.

"*Mickel, go away, we are busy, or about to be anyway,*" I told him mentally.

"Very well," he replied, and walked back down the hallway.

"So, where were we?"

"I love that you can tell him to go away, without ruining the mood," he said, "and I think we were right about here."

He kissed me and tried to flip me onto my back, but I forced him to stay where he was.

"I love you, but my mouth is watering looking at you like this," I said, kissing him again as a guttural groan reverberated from his chest.

I slowly kissed my way down his chest and ran my tongue along the waistline of his pants. I grabbed them, looked up at him where his eyes met mine, and a wicked grin crossed his lips. A moment later, they were in a pile on the floor and I had taken the head of him in my mouth. He hissed in pleasure as I ran my tongue along the ridge, and lightly put his hand on my head, then I sucked just the tip of him.

I ran my tongue down his length slowly as I stroked him. When I took his balls into my mouth, he moaned loud enough that I was very glad I had remembered the silence incantation on the room. I ran my tongue greedily up and around him, swallowing him whole. I moaned in delight, which sent a vibration through him that made him hiss, "Shit Megan." When I released him a few strokes later, with a pop, he pulled me up and settled me onto my stomach.

Lifting my ass so I was on my knees, he spread my legs far enough that I felt long caressing licks that made me shudder in pleasure. When he sucked down on my clit, the moan that came out of me was anything but human. I lost any resemblance of control as I ground my hips on his face. He moaned into me as he gripped my hips and ate like a starved creature.

When he slipped a finger into both parts of me, my release came hard and fast. He drank up each and every ounce of it, and when I came down from that place so high in the sky, I rolled over to face him. He met me with a kiss as he slid himself into me and I wrapped my legs around his waist.

There were no hurried movements, just us. The next time I found release, CJ swallowed my moan with a kiss releasing into me.

He collapsed on top of me and slowly I felt him leave my body.

"I don't think I will ever get enough of you," he whispered in my ear. I smiled at that.

CJ rolled to the side of me, but made me face him. "I love you, Mrs. Mathewson."

"I love you too, Mr. Mathewson," I said, content.

We laid there for a few more minutes, just staring at each other before there was a banging on the door. We both sighed.

"Guess the world isn't going to wait any longer," I said, smirking at him.

"All right. All right. We will be ready in 20 minutes!" CJ shouted after I waved the silence incantation off.

"You missed breakfast, so you're going to have to fend for yourself before we get on the road," Jean said.

"Ahh, Jean, don't give them too much of a bad time. They're still in honeymoon mode," Owen said, defending us.

I just blushed and went straight for the kitchen. CJ, however, threw a pillow at Mickel. "We need a new rule. No bothering us in the morning unless we have to fight or it's after 10 am."

"Hey! I was on orders from the Aunt on high!" he said, throwing his hands up in surrender mode. "She's the one who told me to go get you guys out of bed for breakfast."

"Jean, I love you, but the rule applies to you too!" I shouted from the kitchen. I could only imagine the heavy sigh in response.

"Logan's outside. Make me one up too please?" CJ said as he walked in and saw I was pulling the bagel and cream cheese out. I nodded as he kissed me on my cheek and smacked my ass. "Meet us out there. Lindy and Clarice are gonna take Logan home."

"Yes, dear." I laughed. While I waited for the bagels to toast, I looked down at my hand and smiled. I could get used to this. Waking up every morning next to CJ, sharing a house, making each other food, doing normal things. He is mine for eternity, and I'm his. If you would've asked me three years ago, if I thought I could stand here and feel this happy, I would've told you, you were smoking crack, but here I am.

"That is one shit-eating grin you got there on your face," Mickel said, interrupting my thoughts.

"Just thinking about how happy I am this morning," I said to him as the toaster popped our bagels out.

"I'm happy for your happiness," he said.

"I know total bliss will not last, though. Today we leave for Therth and get back to the grind of finding out what Ansel is up to. Then the impossible task of actually figuring out how to stop it, then actually stopping it. You know, normal things that couples have to deal with," I said, laughing slightly and pulling the bagels out of the toaster. "So, what's on your mind?"

"Actually, I was wondering if you would mind if I headed back to Nalrin with the Vernadali and Guard. There are some things I need to discuss with Julian," he said in a hurry. Fear filled me, and I took a quick breath.

"Mickel, I'm going to ask you something, and I want you to answer me honestly," I said, putting the knife down carefully, trying to hide the shaking I felt, and walking up to him.

"Of course."

"Why are you really leaving?" I asked quietly.

"I need to speak to Julian," he said as I searched for any clue he was lying. His ember was steady, and there was nothing there.

Then I saw it, the flicker in his ember, the twitch of the eyebrow. "What about?"

"I prefer not to answer," he said, knowing I had caught him.

"Is it because of Jean?" I whispered as quietly as I could.

"No, I have loved being here, and I meant what I said before. Plus, I have felt more alive than ever since being assigned to you. I can never thank you enough for that." And he meant it too. I could see that fire in his eyes.

"Mickel, please. What are you not telling me? I can see all your tells. You're keeping something from me. What is it?"

He looked at me for a moment, then sighed. "Let me ask you this: If I were to be permanently assigned to you for life, how would that affect our relationship? How would that work with you having the only Angels Blessed Vernadali in recorded history?"

"I don't know. There would be bumps in the road, but we would work through it. Just like this morning. We would make and modify ground rules." I shrugged. Then I thought about it. "Is this about not feeling like you can protect me anymore?"

He looked at me with pleading eyes. "Why would I need to when you have an Angel Blessed Vernadali? Vernadali out rank the Nalrin Guard. I am the highest ranking Nalrin Guard, and your husband outranks me. CJ outranks everyone, save Julian, and that's only because he's Head of the dimension. I... I don't need to be here. You have CJ."

My heart sank. He was going to ask Julian for another assignment. He was going to leave us. I didn't want Mickel to go. He was such an important part of my life now. A lump formed in my throat and tears welled in my eyes. "But I don't want you to leave. I love you and don't want you to leave," I said in a small voice.

He paused at that. Slowly, he came over and took my hands. "Lady Megan, I don't want to leave, but my high rank requires me to protect those who can't protect themselves. You can protect yourself. You have CJ to protect you as well."

We stood there like that for a minute, my mind racing with what I could say to make him stay. He couldn't leave. He was wrong; I do need him. He's part of my life now. I knew it was selfish, but I couldn't let him go. Then it hit me.

"I have an idea," I said, wiping my tears. "What if I ask Julian to assign you to the family?"

He looked at me, his eyes still sad. "You still have the most powerful Sangra alive, and the Angel Blessed Vernadali to protect them. Denied."

"But we will be out and running into all kinds of dangers, but there is one family member who needs protection. He won't be with us," I said, as the idea fully came together in my head.

"Who is that?"

"The dip head who got you drunk in Vegas," I said, smiling as he sagged and groaned into his hands. "You could be the family bodyguard, with a special assignment to me, just as Julian would want. So, you wouldn't have to leave. See, once Ansel finds out that CJ and I are married, which I can't imagine he doesn't already know, and more importantly, once he finds out that Lindy is engaged to marry Logan, he is going to go for him."

"Really? You want me stationed to boredom in the Manusia? What did I do to you to deserve that kind of punishment?" Mickel had resorted to flat out whining now, and I found it quiet humorous.

"Actually, I was thinking, you're right. I need to own up to the power I have. Both physically within me, and the political pull I have. So, it's time to use it. In the Manusia, Logan is an independent contractor as a Military Training Coordinator. I could try to use some of the weight and influence I have with Julian by asking him to give Logan a job here in Nalrin. Maybe even within the Guard division. Nalrin City is about as safe as a place as you're going to get. While he is there, I want him learning everything there is to know about this dimension. Traditions, races, everything. When this is all said and done, you *both* can move back here. From there, Logan and Lindy can sort out what they want to do next."

He thought about it for a minute. "It could work. Do you think you could persuade Julian?"

"I'll send a message with you. You can hand deliver it, tell him you were following my direct orders, CJ's even, if you need to pull the rank, and tell him that shall he have any questions, I'll be in Therth with the family. I'm assuming that he knows Clarice's family and where to find us there. Even if we don't have a clue," I said and got up to write the letter. Mickel watched me the entire time, dumbfounded at how I had laid out the entire plan.

When it was done, I sealed it with wax and pinched the ends together to close them off. It was a real old-fashioned way of sealing an envelope, but Julian had taught me how to do it so that if I did have to send a message to him that had to travel a long way, he would be assured it came from me, and that it was of high importance. When I handed it to him, he slid it inside his jacket.

"So, who wants to go tell him I'm his new babysitter?" he said with a smirk that made me laugh.

"Are you ok with this? I still prefer you to be with us, but I am legitimately worried about Logan's safety too. Even more so now that he is officially going to be part of this craziness," I said, as we walked out the back door.

"It is a compromise, Lady Megan."

"What is? It's never good when Mickel goes all *Lady Megan* on us," CJ said.

"What I have decided to do with your brother as punishment for getting my family toasted in Vegas," I said, as Clarice giggled.

"You aren't going to let this go, are you?" Logan said.

"Come on, Megan," Lindy said, holding onto his hand like it was for her life. I'm sure her imagination was running wild right now.

"I hereby sentence you to an eternity in our dimension, living out your life with Lindy, safe and sound. I also want to give you an extravagant wedding." I saw them all relax, except for Logan and CJ. They knew me better than that, and I smiled.

"Oh no. What's the catch?" Logan and CJ asked in unison. Logan cringed as possibilities raged through his head.

"While we are out doing what we have to do, as you so eloquently put it, I have given Mickel a scroll with instructions for Julian."

"You're giving Julian instructions?" Clarice said incredulously. Owen and Jean had similar looks on their faces.

"Well, it's about time I use all this weight people say I have. I am basically asking, by telling him, I want him to give Logan a job in the Nalrin Guard, using his current skills as a training coordinator, and to be stationed in Nalrin," I started.

"Seriously?! You're giving me a job as punishment? Hell, I'll take it."

"And now for the catch," I said, smiling from ear to ear. "After much discussion with Mickel, and for various reasons that shall be unstated, Mickel is going to be your babysitter. Oh, I'm sorry, his official title would be your temporary bodyguard."

CJ started chuckling, and Clarice was trying not to laugh hysterically herself. Logan and Lindy, however, just stared at me.

"A babysitter?" Lindy said. "He's older than you."

"Can you not put two and two together, Lindy?" I looked at her, willing her to understand. She just stared at me, trying, but not getting anywhere.

"Ok, fine. I'll connect the dots for you. You and Ansel have history. The second he realizes you guys are engaged, he is going to go after him. Mickel can protect him. Plus, they will be at Nalrin, which is the safest place I know. Safer than anywhere in the Manusia, even if Mickel went with him."

I could see her thinking it through, and slowly, reasoning crossed her face. "You're right. He would be safer in Nalrin City."

"In the letter, I asked him to be treated as I have. Basically, that means you will be waited on hand and foot, but you will have to learn the customs, greetings, etc. of what it means to live in Nalrin. When you're first there, you're going to be learning a lot. You can stay in my residence for the time being," I said, turning to Logan.

"Do I have much of a choice in the matter?" he asked, almost smiling.

"Not really." This is the best solution to a few issues. "To be honest, it really is about your safety more than it is about me paying you back. I want you and Lindy to live a long and happy life, and you can't do that if Ansel kills you in the Manusia."

He reached over and hugged me tightly. "Thank you, Megs. I truly mean it."

"I protect my family, even when it's from the hands of my parents," I told him as I held him tight.

"You're not going home. You're riding with Mickel back to Nalrin. Get your pack secured," I said, pushing him that way. "Mickel, can you have a message sent to Annie and George that he will stay in Nalrin for the time being? Will probably miss some holidays and birthdays and not to hold that against him. Us too." My eyes flickered to CJ, who nodded in agreement.

"Depending on how this goes, it might be after the new year before we see them again," CJ said.

Mickel nodded and went to finish preparing for the trip to Nalrin.

Lindy hung back a bit and when everyone else was out of earshot, she said, "Megs, thank you. I don't know how I can repay you for this."

"I meant what I said. He is family. He needs to be protected, and it covers some miscellaneous issues." I told her and looped her arm through mine. "You don't have to pay me back. Consider this me paying you back for that beautiful wedding you guys threw for CJ and me. Besides, I want you guys happy. That can't happen if he's dead."

"Yeah, that would make it difficult," she said, laughing.

CHAPTER 40

WE SAID OUR GOODBYES and when they were nothing but dots in the distance, we turned to head into the house to get ready for our own departure. The world spun as a wave of darkness hit. I sat, well, more like plopped down on the ground. I grabbed onto my knees and tried to focus on CJ's face, right in front of me. It didn't work too well.

It was letting up, but this time was different. It felt like the darkness was coming toward us. I closed my eyes and put my head between my knees to stop the world from spinning and felt out. There, not people, but... what were they? I searched my memory for what was heading our way. They look like lionesses, but beefier. Prowlers. "In the distance... Through the trees. Prowlers are coming."

I forced myself back up and reached for my syths and saw the others do the same.

"Wait, did you say prowlers?" Clarice asked.

"Yeah. Through the trees, should be here... now," I said, as they passed the tree line and headed directly for us. I was instantly on guard, and I could feel CJ's charge next to me. I could feel the energy radiating off of him in waves. I took a sideways glance at him and his ember was a yellow orange color. Not the burning coals of fire like everyone else's. How had I not noticed that before?

When I looked back to Clarice, who was squinting at the prowlers, she laughed. "Put those away. Squeesha! Come to Mommy!"

The purple prowler instantly transformed into what was more of a puppy who was way too excited to see his people come home from a day at work. While Clarice petted and tried to get Squeesha to calm down, the other five prowlers relaxed and laid down behind the one Clarice was loving so adorably.

I walked up to one prowler and admired how magnificent they were. These cats were as big as horses, hair smooth like a horse, but they had a pattern in the coat all over their bodies. As the prowlers relaxed, so did the heavy and dark feeling that had filled us. It wasn't much longer before the feeling was gone. Completely.

When Clarice had finally gotten Squeesha to calm down, it was Jean who spoke up next. "Um, sweety, mind telling us why prowlers are here?"

"To take us to my father," she said, reading from a piece of scroll that was attached to Squeesha's saddle. She eyed me quickly out of the corner of her eye, and I just nodded in understanding. We needed to go, and now.

"How did they know we were going to come?" Owen asked.

Clarice didn't answer any of them, but just stayed quiet.

"Clarice sent word out last night when we got back that we would head out in the morning," I said, covering for her. She had already told me she would not send word of our arrival, but there was no need to worry the others.

"Let's get our packs secured so we can get on the road," Lindy said. "I'm glad that we don't have to hike it through the mountains. That was going to be a long trip."

"We wouldn't have. I could have arranged for transportation through the Marsh and Obsecuritan," Clarice said quietly.

"Doesn't matter, the prowlers are here, and it's a long hard ride. Let's get going before it gets much darker," CJ said and took my hand and led me inside to get our things.

I looked back to Clarice and pushed, "*Who could have sent them?*"

She just shook her head, in either denial to answer, or her not knowing.

I walked up to one of the silver-blue-colored prowlers that purred under the touch of my hand running up and down her neck. Her fur was soft and smooth like fleece, even with the swirls and glyphs in the patterns of her fur.

"Thank you, CJ. I know that you guys just got home," Clarice said again.

"Seriously, no worries, Clarice. You're part of my family and you should see him before. Maybe things can be said to give you peace," he said as he secured his bag to the saddle on the prowler next to mine.

She thought about that for a minute. "I don't know about peace, but... the prowlers will get us to the mountains bordering the Seltic Marsh and Obsecuritan by midnight if we leave soon.

"The channel is a full day ride away. And I mean a full day hard ride." I looked at her like she was a little crazy, then looked to the prowlers. "Are they that quick?"

"Yes, they're that fast. The fastest ground creatures in Nalsar. The trick will be getting across the channel. I think I know some Gurglin's that should be able to help us out. As long as we can secure getting across the channel, we should be able to make it to a spot to camp by midnight. It won't leave much time for sleep, but hopefully, if we make good time, we should be with my father by tomorrow night, but it will be a long, hard ride once we get up in the morning and through the mountains. Otherwise, we will need to stay the night in the Noctulanar providence before moving farther south. If we don't have time to get from Noctulanar to Therth before nightfall, we stay the night."

"That's a long stretch of land," I told her. "What's out there?"

"Not anything that will be a friend of ours if we stop, and we really should try to be through there by dark," she said, as she grabbed the reins and positioned Squeesha. The others were almost done securing their packs on the fronts of their saddles and were lost in their own thoughts.

I mounted my prowler and secured myself to the saddle. Clarice had told all of us we needed to strap ourselves with not only the waist strap but also the leg straps. With the speed that we were going to be going, it would help with fatigue and keep us from flying off the back end of them.

As I did, I thought back at all Clarice had told us about her life before living here. There wasn't much, and the only thing I could remember was that she and her father had a major falling out, which had eventually landed her here with Jean and Owen. She never talked about what exactly it was, and wouldn't even talk about Obsecuritan. But someone had sent the prowlers and wanted her back, and BAD. Someone other than her father, since it was our understanding that he didn't know where she was. Everyone else was securing their pack or mounted and ready to go.

"Clarice?" I asked hesitantly.

"Ya'um?" she said distantly.

"I know you don't talk about home, and what happened, but since we are going there..." the others had joined us, mounted and ready to go, "What happened?"

Everyone froze.

She paused, took a deep breath, swung up on Squeesha, buckled the fastenings, and said, "Get on, we need to head out."

When no one moved, she took another deep breath, and with a chirp to get Squeesha moving, she snapped, "He used me to help kill my mother."

CHAPTER 41

WE RODE FOR HOURS. The prowlers were indeed fast. Not as fast as the dragons we rode last year, but damn fast. The straps securing us to the specially made saddles helped keep us from flying off, but I still leaned forward into the wind to keep the aerodynamics and keep myself from wearing out just from staying on the saddle. It reminded me a lot of riding a motorcycle. The ground was a swift blur around us, and there was no way to carry on a conversation without the words being left in the wind.

It was mid-afternoon when we reached the Whispering Channel that separated the Nalrin providence from the Seltic Marsh. I never would've imagined us getting this far today, let alone with so many hours of light still available to us.

I had forgotten how the sky changed colors from the blue I was used to back in the Manusia to the red in the marsh. Even though there were still quite a few hours of sun, the light over the Seltic Marsh was sunset-like, no matter what time of day it was. It was stunning to watch.

Clarice dismounted and went to speak to the Gurglin's she knew and came back a few minutes later to tell us they will give us a ride over the channel. We dismounted and handed the prowlers over to the Gurglin's who then attempted to load them onto the ferry.

Attempt being the keyword. I watched as they tried and tried again, trying not to giggle. The prowlers certainly did not like this one bit. I admit the boat wasn't anywhere near as nice as the ones we took to Nalrin from the river port. This one was rickety and reminded me of something I'd seen on a survival show back in the Manusia. It was just a bunch of tree branches together with vines. The only difference was that this had a motor and some kind of siding to it.

The area was nothing more than a mud pit with a shack. I couldn't smell much more than dirt, but I wasn't sure whether that was from all the mud, or from being on the prowlers for hours and having dust infiltrated every crevice of my nasal cavity. There was a faint sour note to the air, though, and I couldn't place what or where exactly it was coming from.

The Gurglin's who were handling the prowlers were a little worn and shady looking, so maybe that had something to do with it. I had seen Gurglin's while in Nalrin, but these Gurglins weren't like the privileged ones that were on the Council. In fact, according to my studies, most Gurglin's lived much as these did. Poor. Living in small huts and makeshift homes. Scavenging for food. Only eating what they could grow or catch. Nalrin supply routes didn't run down this close to the channel, and they were too far north and on the wrong side of the channel for the Seltic Marsh traders to have access to the supplies that are available for purchase from the vendors. These two traded what they could off of people trying to get into the Seltic Marsh without using the usual Nalrin transports. We could have taken those transports, but they would've dropped us on the western ridge of the continent and that would not be conducive to us getting to Therth immediately. This was faster, though I was wondering if it was the safest way to go.

The brown Gurglin who was trying to get Squeesha onto the ferry was older than the blue one, and his skin was peeling and blistered on his back. The blue one's small eyes kept shifting from us to the prowlers and to the small shack. Something was off and I didn't like it.

Clarice walked up. "Tryh and Fong's family have been doing this for a long time. We will get across safely."

"The blue one keeps eyeing us and the shack. What's his deal?" I said harshly. Even I had to admit, I had said it harsher than I had intended. "Something isn't right about this."

"Like a vision feeling?" she asked.

I looked at her evenly. "No. Not like a vision. Gut. My gut tells me something isn't right."

"Ok, I'll go check it out," she said, clearly annoyed as she took off for the shack.

I just couldn't figure it out. Something is wrong with this whole thing. The blue Gurglin looked at me, narrowed his eyes, and then took off to the shack with Clarice. When he walked in, I saw they were yelling at each other. There was a lot of jabbing and pointing involved, and I wished I could hear what they were saying.

I turned my back on them and decided I needed to just let it go for now. Clarice knew them, so I had to trust them. Well, at least trust in her. I spotted CJ and Owen off toward the ferry, talking and laughing. The prowlers finally got loaded when Lindy walked up.

"Where is Jean?"

"She went inside to get us some food for the ferry ride. Well, if you can call that a ferry," Lindy said, gesturing to the ferry, but glancing back to Clarice in the window.

"I just hope we get across alive."

"Clarice says we will. I trust her. The Gurglin's... well..."

"Not so much," Lindy said, finishing my sentence. "I agree. That blue one has been overly shifty. Though they look like they're yelling more than anything."

"You noticed too, huh? Clarice went to talk to him and find out what their problem is." I saw Owen and CJ motion for us to get on board. "Well, here we go I guess."

Clarice and the Gurglins stormed out of the building and Clarice stomped onto the ferry. When the ferry moved off from the shore, the prowlers shifted a bit, which rocked the whole ferry back and forth. Clarice ran over and was making chirping and clicking sounds that seemed to soothe them, all the while giving the Gurglin driving the ferry a wary eye.

I had to admit that the boat seemed a lot sturdier than it looked once we were on the water. The prowlers were laying down, huddled together and shaking. Clarice assured me it would be a quiet trip, but they did not like being on this thing. I walked around a bit, and I saw Clarice staring at the scroll that she had taken off Squeesha. She signed heavily and looked out across the channel.

We walked up beside her, and CJ actually leaned on the railing. Brave bastard.

"Hey," I said gently. "I'm, I am really sorry for pushing into your past."

"No, I'm the one who should be sorry. I shouldn't have snapped like that. It's justifiable to want to know. I have told none of you anything, and even heading there now, you're just blindly following me. It's just II know I said I wasn't going to, but sent word I was coming, but it was before breakfast this morning..."

"This morning? There is no way there was enough time for the message to get there, send the prowlers out, let alone time for the prowlers to arrive. Something isn't right."

"I agree, but this scroll was tied to Squeesha... She's my prowler. My personal prowler. She won't allow anyone else to ride her.... Father says there are no strings attached. He just wants to see me."

"I thought he didn't know where you were," I said carefully.

"He doesn't, but... someone does," she said with a sigh that left her heavy in thought. I couldn't tell if she knew who it was, or if she was trying to figure it out.

"It's said that when people are about to die, they don't think about what they did with their lives, they think about what they didn't do. Maybe he is trying to at least make amends?" I suggested.

Clarice chuckled darkly at that. "If you knew my father, you wouldn't even ask that question. I just hope this isn't some trick to have me take his place."

I let the silence linger between us. I still wanted to know what caused such a rift, but I would not force her into telling us. We would find out eventually. By tomorrow night, her secrets would be out.

When Jean, Owen, and Lindy came to stand with us, she sighed heavily. "Mom and Dad had been fighting a lot over my sister and me. My sister always thought I was the favorite, and that she had gotten the short end of the stick." She smiled at the memory.

"I guess most siblings do, though. Always think that the other is more privileged... But, in this case, it was true. I got more extravagant gifts, more attention, people to cater to my every whim. After all, I'm the oldest. The one destined to take my father's place. She, however, had the friends, the chance to play games, the ability to be anything she wanted to be."

"While she was jealous of you, you were jealous of her freedom," Jean said softly.

Clarice nodded. "She was free. I was being groomed for greatness. I was also the one who didn't want it. My sister, however, did. She wanted to take his place. She wants his power."

We all looked at each other, knowing this was hard for her, but we all wanted to know what the hell they had groomed Clarice for.

"The night that my mother died, I was studying the ancient language of Arili. I could hear my father and mother fighting in the room across the hall. The more they yelled, the weaker I felt. Since I was to inherit, the darkness that runs through our blood linked us. It's what allows us to control it. Through that link, I could feel his anger, his rage..."

She shook her head, and a tear ran down her cheek. "Sorry."

"It's ok. If it's too painful..." CJ said.

"I just haven't spoken about it in a very long time. You guys need to know now." She smiled faintly and continued, "I got up, went, and peeked through the doors from the hall. I could see a dark haze building around him, but there was also a faint haze linked from him to me. As the link grew stronger, I was getting weaker. He was using the darkness in me to strengthen himself.

"The more they yelled, the stronger the haze around him and then the surrounding haze engulfed my mother and pulled her heart straight from her chest. Her heart hovered over her body, beat twice, and stopped, and then I saw her crumble to the ground. I ran out to her and looked at my father. There was nothing but rage in his eyes. He inhaled deeply, drawing more darkness from me, and I passed out. I woke up the next morning in my bed.

"My mother's death was ruled accidental, and my sister believed him and the reports over me. There was no funeral, no memorial, no anything. He buried her in a black stone coffin over the blood-stained ground where he had ripped her heart out of her chest. We were forbidden to speak of her death ever again." She looked out over the channel and took a few deep breaths.

I remembered what she said; *He used me to help kill my mother,* and my heart broke for her. I squeezed CJ's hand, not recalling when he took it. No wonder she left and never went back. No wonder she never wanted to talk about it.

"I avoided him for a very long time after that. I saw him occasionally, and he continued to have everyone pamper and groom me to take his place. When the time came for the ceremony where I would become his..." She looked at me, then at Lindy before sighing and continuing, "Suk'Natal, I declined to complete the ritual. My sister was furious. Here she was, wanting to do exactly what I was being forced to do, and I declined. No one ever declined. It was a birthright requirement. Well, until me." She let out a little smirk.

Lindy's eyes went wide as she was putting it all together. I narrowed my eyes at her in question, but she was just staring at Clarice in awe. She mouthed some words I couldn't make out.

"My father, trying to save face, asked for an official declaration. I said I could not serve under the murderer of my mother. I can still hear the gasp and murmurs and instant silence that followed." She was pointedly not looking at Lindy now and said, "To say that there was a fight after that would be an understatement. I went back to my room, packed everything I could carry and headed to Nalrin, swearing to never return or use that darkness. That's where I met Owen and Jean, who took me in like family."

I stood there in stunned silence.

"Clarice, what does your father do?" CJ asked slowly. Lindy's face was still just staring at Clarice, like she couldn't believe it.

"Lindy, what have you figured out?" Jean asked, still just as confused as the rest of us.

Clarice's eyes looked out over the channel again. She took a deep breath, and then she said, "Who my father is."

"Who is your father, Clarice?" Owen said carefully after no no one spoke.

"He's the Gatekeeper to the Underworld," Lindy said, her eyes wide and shaking her head in amazement.

We just stared at Clarice. Unable to keep his smart ass in check, CJ said, "So we are going to hell. Literally?"

"Well, the Gate of Hell, as you so eloquently put it. My father is the Gatekeeper to the Underworld, not the Angel of Death," Clarice said with a sly smile as the boat pulled up to the shore. She turned and walked toward the prowlers as we just stared at her in shock, unable to say anything at all.

CHAPTER 42

THE SQUELCHY POUNDING OF the prowler's giant paws hitting the ground as we had made our way through the marsh reminded me of last year as we walked through the forest to Noctulanar Castle. I tried to push the memory away, but it wouldn't budge. I wished we could have used the dragons from Nalrin, but there wasn't time to get permission, and teleporting still wasn't an option.

We camped at the base of the pass to the Obsecuritan mountains that night. Seeing it from this angle made the pass look so much more ominous. Sharp shale-looking hills rose before us. Barren jagged peaks jutted into the sky. Nothing about the pass said it would be an easy crossing in the morning. The moons were high and bright enough that they had allowed us to travel longer into the night than we normally would have.

We were still technically in the marsh, so we found the driest area, set up in a circle with our heads together, and settled in for the night. We talked for hours about the bombshell Clarice had dropped on us, but she spoke in general terms. There were still things that she hadn't told us, and we didn't press her about it.

When we decided to get some sleep, the Marsh ground was so soft you could almost forget you weren't lying in a bed. It was musky, but I curled up next to CJ and was out. Not sure if it was how comfortable I was, or because I was so tired from the ride, but for the first time since we left Hartwood Citadel, I slept solidly through the night.

We woke up to the skies dark and heavy with rain clouds that were heading right toward us. I turned to CJ and we each let out a grown. "This is going to suck monkey..." I whispered, but stopped when he shook his head.

I loved the rain, but not when I was traveling. You end up drenched through and where we were going, it was going to be bone chilling cold even if we were dry. Now we were going to be wet on top of it. Not something we were looking forward to in the least.

"The rain is going to make getting through the pass a lot slower," Clarice said. "Sections get... a bit slick."

"Let's get going. We need to cover as much as possible before it rains," Lindy said as she mounted her prowler.

We pushed the prowlers hard before the rain started. We were only about a quarter of the way up the mountain when it started sprinkling on us. We slowed so that the prowlers wouldn't lose their footing. The last thing we needed was for one of them to fall and get hurt, or worse, break their leg.

When we reached the peak, we stopped to let the prowlers rest and get some water. I drank deeply from my water bottle and looked out over Obsecuritan when a chill that had nothing to do with the weather shuddered through me. Looking off in the direction of Noctulanar Castle, memories of what happened there flooded through me. My power roiled as visions of Penny laying in the hallway, CJ... CJ laying on that stone table, my father standing over him with a knife ready to pierce his heart, CJ sliced and diced...

CJ's face filled my vision, breaking my train of thought for just that second. Then I saw him on that table again and I started to hyperventilate. My chest had a tight band that was being cinched tighter and tighter, and I faintly registered that my hands were shaking. CJ took my hand and kissed me on the cheek. I saw my father swinging that blade toward CJ's chest on repeat as CJ tried to get me to calm down.

"Megs, breathe in and out," he said, bringing his forehead to mine to make me focus on him. "That's in the past. It is not real. I am here. I am whole. I am safe. We are all safe," he said firmly, squeezing my hand again.

It took a few minutes, but with him reminding me to breathe normally and focus on him, I settled down. Once I had pulled myself together, we headed back down the pass. Owen kept turning to check on me, and CJ kept a little closer than he had been.

As we made our way further down the pass, the rain fell steadily, and we finally just dismounted to walk the prowlers down. It was safer to just hike it. As it was, we all slipped and fell on our butts a few times. Jean's prowler was limping slightly after taking a pretty nasty slide down and slamming into the hillside. Squeesha had slid down about fifty feet before gaining her footing, standing and huffing at Clarice. Clarice had just walked over to her, scratched her behind the ears, and murmured to her in a language I didn't understand.

We knew we wouldn't make it to Therth by nightfall, not with the rain delaying us so much. We pushed through Noctulanar and stopped at the edge of the bluff at the edge of Gendril. We wanted to push through. A warm bed, clean clothes, and most of all, a warm bath sounded fantastic right now. I had mud in places that mud was not supposed to be when you were fully clothed.

"No, we stop here for the night," Clarice had said when Owen had asked her for the fifth time why we shouldn't push through.

"Clarice..." Owen whined.

"No," she said firmly. She turned to look out over the plains and when her face drained of color, we dropped it.

So, we set up camp. The perpetual twilight in Obsecuritan made it hard to judge the time, so I had no idea what time it really was. There were noticeable differences during the day, but it was not like back home, where there was a clear morning, day, evening, and night.

We pulled off the muddy clothes and cleaned up as best we could and got into some clean and dry clothes. The rain had stopped, so at least there was that small blessing.

A couple of hours later, I sat wrapped up in a blanket, looking out over the expanse from the edge of our campsite after everyone else had gone to bed. It was beautiful. Even though the whole of Obsecuritan holds the darkest, weirdest, and in some cases, evilest creatures known in all of Nalsar, there was a beauty to the way everything looked. Dark rocks covered the landscape, the multi-colored twilight sky, the moons lighting your way... Were they waxing or waning? I could never keep that straight. I giggled just as CJ came over and handed me some hot cocoa.

"What's so funny?" he asked, grabbing part of the blanket and joining me.

"I was just thinking how beautiful the view is, and how the moons are just spectacular," I said.

"And that was funny?" he asked, raising his eyebrows.

"Well, no," I said, shoulder bumping him as he wrapped an arm around me. "I was just laughing at myself because I can never remember which is a waxing moon, and which is a waning moon."

"The waning moon is after a new moon or no moon," he said, looking up at them in the sky. "The waxing is after the full moon."

I looked at him. "Seriously? You can keep that straight?"

"I didn't use to, but when I was training, that was something we had to know. They drilled it into us during field medical training." He shrugged like it was no big deal.

I shook my head and rested it on his shoulder. We stayed like that for a long time before I sighed contently.

"What was that for?" CJ whispered.

"I know it sounds crazy, but I'm actually really relaxed," I said softly. "It's nice."

He let out a small laugh. "What is wrong with us that amid turmoil we are actually finding a way to be relaxed?"

"Maybe we have just gotten used to it. So even when things feel out of control, and even when bad things happen, we are just able to relish the calmer parts of it," I said with a small smile. Then I saw the shadows of the expanse twist and dance, and I stiffened. "Ceej..."

"I saw it too," he said, his arm tightening around me. "Must be whatever Clarice wanted us to stay away from."

"Any idea what it is?"

"Not a clue. You did more research on Obsecuritan than I have. Cinder, Lankspur Frozen Islands, Underworld, even what lies in the Slumbering Expanse sure, but Obsecuritan, that's your specialty."

"Not hardly. Clarice is the specialist on that," I said with a light giggle. "Though I have to admit the shadows have a mesmerizing quality to them. The allure is probably what makes them so dangerous."

We sat in silence for a long while, watching those shadows dance across the plain. My head rested against his shoulder as his fingers drew slow, lazy lines on my ribs, along my back and hip.

"What are you thinking?" I asked quietly when I felt him sigh against me. He took his finger and placed it under my chin and turned me to face him. I looked deep into his eyes as he whispered, "Megan Mathewson. I just love how that sounds."

He leaned in and kissed me, light as a feather. It made my whole body tingle and come alive. When he pulled away, he rested his forehead on mine, his hand still on my cheek. My breath caught, and I could not speak. He ran his thumb across my cheek. It was those smallest touches from him that made my core melt. His energy, his touch, affected me in ways I couldn't explain. Would it ever stop?

Before opening my eyes, I tried to concentrate on breathing and when I was sure I could breathe again, I opened them.

"You know exactly how to drive me crazy, don't you, Mr. Mathewson?" I whispered.

A big smile crossed his face as he leaned back. "Well, that was sort of in the job description."

"Which one? Vernadali or Husband?" I said, laughing.

"Both, but in different aspects."

"You succeed in BOTH," I said, reaching forward and kissing him again. I turned to look back at the others, who were all asleep already. "What time is it?"

CJ shrugged. "Doesn't matter. We will be up at dawn regardless of how much sleep we get."

"They're all asleep and since you started something, are you going to finish it?" I whispered along his jaw and kissed just under his ear.

"Megan?" he said tentatively, and when my eyes met his, they sparkled in the moonlight.

He stood me up and led me behind one of the rock formations away from the others and pushed me against the rock. I pulled his belt loose and kissed him. I felt him moan deeply under the kiss as he started undoing my pants. The efficiency with which he had them off and pushing me back up against the rock face was impressive. He kissed me again as I wrapped my legs around him. After a few adjustments, he sprung free.

"Eager, are you, babe?" I teased in his ear.

"I always want you. I don't know how many times I have to tell you that. How many times I have to show you. Now, be quiet and let me fuck you?" His voice was full of heat and I shuddered as two fingers slid into me as a third slid into my ass, and I had to bite on his shoulder to keep from screaming. His eyes held mine while he pumped those fingers in and out of me, and a mischievous look crossed his face as he kissed me again. My back scraped on the rock against my back as he moved me to sit higher.

"What do you want, Megan?" The domination in that statement was fierce.

"You, Ceej. I need you inside me."

"Do you now?" he said as he moved to let gravity lower me onto him. I was splintering in pleasure as he held me against the rock and slowly filled me. Pulling out just as slowly, he waited just a moment, waiting until I squirmed under him, begging.

There was a mischievous chuckle as he said in that demanding, controlling voice, "Tell me what you want."

"You. Always you," I said. He kissed me and plunged in. It was his kiss that absorbed the moan that escaped me.

"Like this?" he said, breaking the kiss and moving against that interior spot that brought another wave of pleasure. A hotty moan escaped from my lips.

I was trying to be quiet, but the only thing I could get out of my mouth was, "Fuck me, Ceej."

He grabbed my hips and thrust into me deeper, harder and faster each time. My nails raked over his neck and I bit into his shoulder again to keep the sounds down. His whispers of pleasure in my ear turned me on to a new level. My back arched as he reached down and fingered my clit. CJ's eyes stayed on mine as he purposefully pounded into me over and over again. The domination and intent in his eyes undid me. I could feel him tightening and when he released, he bit down on my neck, sending me over the edge with him.

We just stayed there panting until he slid out of me. He kissed me as he closed up his pants, then said, "Do not move from that spot. Be right back."

When he returned, he had a rag and a water bottle. He used it to help clean me up and made me stand there. The entire time, he looked me up and down, doing nothing but turning me on again. He slowly lifted my panties and had me step back in them, then caressed my legs every inch up as he put them back in place. He repeated the motion with my pants, but just before he buttoned and zippered them, he kissed my pelvis. That kiss lingered for a long moment before he stood up and closed my pants up.

He had the most peculiar look on his face. I turned to head back to where we were sleeping, but he pushed me back against the rock, wrapped one arm around my waist, and the other behind my neck, wrapping my hair into his fingers, and kissed me hard. He leaned back slightly and then just held me with his forehead to mine.

I was so taken aback by the domination that I just stood there holding him. It was one of the most erotic things he had done. We stood like that, just staring at each other for a few minutes before he released me and led us back to the sleeping bags to get some sleep without another word.

CHAPTER 43

I WOKE WITH A start, grabbing my syths automatically, as CJ, in our shared sleeping bag, rolled over on top of me without putting any weight on me. He put his hand over my mouth.

"Shhh!" he whispered in my ear. "Ja'Nee. Sky."

I looked up, my power jumping to my fingertips, and froze. Hundreds of Ja'Nee were flying on birds that resembled giant ravens. My heart dropped through my stomach, leaving a gaping pit. We assumed there were more, but... there were so many of them.

I could feel his charge pulsing off his body. I looked at his ember and it was bright and fluid as he hovered just above me, balancing on his toes and forearms. I felt out, and checking on my family, they were awake too, with their hands on their syths. Clarice, however, had her head in her hands, her ember totally erratic.

"Clarice's ember is erratic," I pushed to CJ.

"She's what woke me up. She must have felt them coming before they got here."

"They're heading northwest. The only thing out there is..." My eyes snapped to his.

"Noctulanar Castle." He nodded. "What would they be doing there? It's deserted."

"I don't know."

We all laid still while the Ja'Nee flew overhead. There was very little light in the sky, and once they had passed, CJ and I sprung up and went to check on Clarice. When I looked down at her, my breath hitched. Her eyes were black as night from eyelid to eyelid.

I bent down and put my hands on both sides of her head. "Ceej, put your hands over mine." When he did, I concentrated on calming her mind. Her body, however, was still writhing.

"Angel of Healing, please help Clarice," I prayed. I focused all my energy on trying to calm Clarice down. Slowly her body relaxed, but her eyes still looked straight to the sky and were black as night.

"Come on Clarice. You can push through this. Push the darkness away," I pushed towards her.

Her eyes met mine, and I was unable to look away. She stopped blinking. Her breath hitched with every intake, and her lips moved quickly. I couldn't make out what she was saying, but her black eyes had flickers of dark starlight in them that seemed to reach inside of me. There was a strange pull to them and I twitched, falling into their blackness.

When the lights flickered on, I was standing in a room next to a teenage version of Clarice. The room was filled with dark tendrils that reached out toward us, lapping at my feet. I grabbed her hand, the electrical current within me springing to life, I could feel it coating my hands. There was no reaction from her as she looked at me, her eyes still black as night. "Push it away Clarice. It doesn't control you. You control it."

"No, it controls me. It always has," she said in the same hoarse deadpan voice from the dream I had back at Hartwood. "I can't escape it. It flows within me. I can't run from it anymore. I have to accept my place. This is where the darkness needs me."

"Yes, you can. Focus on my voice. Envision your light. Light will push the darkness away. Just focus, Clarice," I said, each phrase slowly, trying to will her into believing the words.

When I turned to look around the room again, a man was standing to the left, but he had no face. He was wearing an elegant red robe with silver runes all over it. I turned to teenage Clarice, who was now looking straight at the man, eyes wide, hands shaking and balled up into tight fists.

"Who is that?" I asked.

She shook her head, defying my question.

"Clarice. Who is that man?"

She just shook her head again, but faster this time. Ok, fine then, let's get out of here. Wherever here is.

"Clarice, focus on the light," I told her again.

She cocked her head and looked at me.

"Your inner light Clarice. Find it and hold on to it tight."

I could see her trying. I took a step forward and moved her with me. The darkness moved back to reveal a wall with an ancient, beat up door. It looked like an army of dwarves had taken their axes to it over the years, but weren't able to break through it.

When we were standing at the door, I reached for the handle and I saw her do the same. The door opened just before we touched it, and I was back, looking into her black eyes. CJ's hands were fully encased in flowing ribbons of electricity, and were the only thing that kept me from jumping up and away from Clarice. I shook my head.

Focus on Clarice.

"Come on Clarice. Focus on the light. The door will lead you out," I pushed toward her. Slowly, her eyes returned to normal, and she took a long ragged deep breath.

When her eyes met mine, she sat up quickly and scooted back. "How did you get in there?"

"I... I don't know."

CJ looked at me. Fear and confusion written all over his face.

"She pulled me away from..." She stopped, wrapped her arms around her knees, and changed the subject. "The Ja'Nee. There were so many of them. The darkness... Why were there so many of them?"

Everyone looked at each other, but no one said a word. After a moment of silence, Jean stood up. "It's light enough to see. The creatures of the night between here and Therth will have retreated to their caves for the day." I looked at her. So, she knew what was out there, too?

Clarice nodded and stood up, brushing the ground from her clothing, then jerking her head up. "Squeesha!"

She rushed over to where they were huddled so close together that if it were not for the color differences, you wouldn't have been able to figure out where one began and one ended. They were shivering in fear. When we approached, they pounced in fear and stood up, snarling and growling. We stopped.

"Squeesha, it's Mommy. It's ok. They're gone." Squeesha looked around and shook her head and snorted. The others mirrored her, relaxing slightly, but their eyes were darting all over the place. Clarice walked up to her and tried to calm her, but they were still on edge.

"The darkness in them must have made them more aware of the Ja'Nee too... But Clarice had said that darkness flows in me now too, even to a lesser degree, and I'd been feeling her father call, but I didn't feel this? Why?" I asked quietly as I pulled CJ away so we could talk in private.

"I don't know Megs, but I'm more concerned about what she said about you going somewhere?" He looked at me sternly, "Physically, you didn't go anywhere, you were right there."

I didn't know how to explain it to him. I looked down at his hands. "Your hands!"

"I don't care about my hands. Megan, tell me what Clarice was talking about."

I took his hands in mine and cast the incantation to heal them. "I'm sorry, Ceej. I keep burning you. I don't know how to not do it."

"Again, I don't care about my fucking hands. They will heal, or you will heal them for me. Now, tell me. What was Clarice talking about?" There was a command in his voice that made me look up at him. He was all Vernadali.

I looked over to see Clarice, who continued to calm the prowlers, while the others cleaned up camp. I didn't know how to explain it to him. I really didn't. I don't even know what happened.

"Megan Isabel Mathewson," he said, half growling. "Answer me. What did Clarice mean?"

"I don't..." I trailed off as he took my face in his hands and looked at me.

"I was holding your hands, which were on her head. My hands were bound in your electricity. You were here. You were anxious, worried, and trying to calm yourself to help her. Then there was nothing. I couldn't *feel* you anymore."

"What?" I said, finally meeting his eyes.

"The Charge gives me insight into your feelings, remember? I was there, feeling what you were feeling, but then there was nothing. I could see you there, feel your electricity biting into my hand. I could feel your body there, but the Charge couldn't feel *you* anymore. It was as if you were an empty husk." His voice broke as he stepped away from me and ran his hand through his hair. "So, please tell me what the fuck happened."

"I can't explain it to you, Ceej. One moment I was there, looking into her eyes, the next we were in a bright white room, tendrils of darkness lapping at our feet. There was a faceless man there, teenage Clarice was terrified of him, whoever he was, and I just kept trying to get her to find her light, so we could leave the room. We got to a door, it opened, and I was not *there* anymore."

He looked to Clarice, then to me, then back to Clarice.

"What the fuck, Megs?" he whispered, then pulled me into a bear hug. "You scared the shit out of me."

I just held him and saw Clarice eye me carefully over CJ's shoulder.

"We will figure it out," I said, giving him a quick kiss on the cheek before I turned and headed back to where Jean and the others were finishing up. They were loading the prowlers with our stuff, but each of their eyes had flickered to me at one point or another.

"Jean, how long of a ride is it?" I asked quietly. With the Ja'Nee out and flying around, we needed to get to Therth as soon as possible.

"We will have to take a more covered route now that the Ja'Nee are out. So half a day?" she whispered back.

"Not quick enough," I said, grabbing and tossing my pack to CJ. Then I ducked back behind a rock formation so that the others couldn't see me. I had to be quick, and I had to focus. I raised my arms to my side, over my head, focused on centering myself, and bringing my hands into prayer position, elbows high. I opened my eyes and said the incantation as I repeated the words. CJ's eyes met mine and when he realized what I was doing, he shook his head and smirked. I repeated them once for every prowler and once for each of us. Just as before, when I was done, the blue haze settled into each of them.

When I walked out from behind the rock, I saw the prowlers stand up tall and ready to go. "What were you doing back there?" Owen asked.

"Potty break," I said, not making eye contact.

He grabbed my arm and made me turn to face him. "Potty break? That's your best answer, when all of us, including the prowlers, now suddenly have the energy to run a marathon?"

"Well, I guess the Ja'Nee got the adrenaline pumping. Your embers are stronger, too. So, let's put it to good use and get on the road."

"Megan..." he said, looking at me pointedly.

"Owen," I said, looking at him with my face as straight as possible.

"Fine. Just remember you're messing with physics," he said, dropping my arm.

"No, I'm using what power the Angels gave me to protect my family," I said through my teeth, dropping my voice, and moved closer to him. "That includes you, Jean, Lindy, and Clarice. We need to get Clarice to Therth. Something happened to her. I can't explain it, but we need to get there. Fastest way possible. I'm one powerful bitch, Owen. I'm going to use it every way I know how."

"There is nature's balance when we use power, Megan," he tried to say, but I interrupted him.

"No, there is a nature's balance when witches use their power. Ours is our own. We don't need nature to make our power work. That's something I'm realizing more and more. I draw strength from myself, my love for CJ, my love for my *family*. I wasn't raised to think of limits. Maybe that's the difference. I'm not scared to use mine in whatever fashion I can in order to protect everyone else."

Hurt flashed hard in his eyes, and then anger, before he said, "Are you saying I wouldn't use every ounce of my power to save each of you? To protect everyone I hold dear? Do you think I wouldn't give my life to give you one extra second to live? Do you seriously think that I wouldn't stand between you and sure death to allow you moments to get to safety?"

"No, I know you would," I said and sighed. "I'm sorry. I really am. I didn't mean for it to come across that way. I'm just trying to have a logical, rational reason I have more power than others."

"You do, that's been proven."

"I am accepting that. I just want a logical reason for it. It's still hard for me to think the Angels are just giving me something when I have done nothing to deserve it." I stopped him before he could interrupt. "I had this power and free will of it before we stopped my parents from creating the weapon."

"You're right. You did," he said and before he could say anything more, Jean came over to tell us that the prowlers were ready.

"You guys, ok?" she asked.

"Yup. Just having a chat," Owen said, putting his arm around me as we headed to the prowlers.

"No hard feelings, Megan," Owen said whispering in my ear as he gave me a tight hug. I hugged him tight.

"I love you, Owen," I whispered to him.

"We love you too, sweetheart," he whispered back. "But Jean and I feel responsible for you. We want to protect you too."

When we let go, he looked at me and smiled. I wiped the tears from my eyes and climbed up on my prowler. They were pawing at the ground and you could feel the restraint in the tension in their legs.

"Lean in tight to their shoulders," I told them before we took off. I looked at CJ, and he smiled brightly at me and winked.

"Why?" Lindy asked.

"Do you trust me?"

"With my life, but that doesn't... Oh, Megan, what did you do?"

"Just lean in tight," I chirped, smiling.

"Oh Mega—" I heard behind me as the prowlers took off like a bullet train.

CHAPTER 44

As we approached Therth, the prowlers skidded, pounced, and slid down the side of the bluff. Each time they landed, you could feel it in your bones. Each landing crushing into our joints. They were close to home and knew it. When they hit the bottom of the bluff, they lowered their heads to bolt for the doors to the City.

"Hold up!" the sound came booming from the tower on the right.

We pulled to a stop, dismounted, and waited as instructed. The walls were solid stone, rough, and meticulously placed, so there was next to no sealant to secure it in place. The doors, which had to be at least 3 stories tall of solid wood, opened silently and quickly to eight guards standing at attention. CJ moved his prowler to come and stand closer to me, his hand twitching closer and closer to his syths. I took his hand to keep him from looking aggressive. These Guard weren't dressed in the same uniform as Nalrin Guard, and they had a unique symbol on their shoulder which looked just like a prowler head.

"There is no entry to Therth," the Guard said from outside the gate. He stood with his hands behind his back and a good fifty feet away, his voice amplified by his power. I heard Clarice let out a gasping sob behind me.

"We are just passing through. We will be of no concern to anyone," I said confidently.

"Then you will need to go around the city. It is only a half-day ride," he said. "You have time before nightfall, but I suggest you obtain shelter before then."

I looked sideways to Clarice, who had pulled her blue cape from her pack and put the hood up, hiding her face. "We have business in Therth, and it is imperative that we are allowed passage into the city," I said, using my professional voice I reserved for when working with Julian.

"The King has taken ill and is not allowing anyone in or out of the Therth. Your trip has been wasted. You may turn around and head back from where you came," he said and turned on his heel.

"Do you not know who she is?" CJ said.

"I do not, nor do I care. The city is on lockdown. If she doesn't know who she is, she should seek a physician!" he shouted back over his shoulder.

There was a gust of wind and a blue blur that blew past me, instantly putting me on guard. Then I noticed Clarice facing us, but with the guard standing between her and us. How had she moved that fast?

The Guard seemed to stagger for a moment. He reached out tentatively to touch Clarice's cheek and paused. I could not hear what she said, but the Guard stepped back and bowed to her with his feet together, bending at the waist so that he was perpendicular to the ground.

"Let them through," he said when he rose. The eight guards who were blocking the entrance slowly moved to each side of the gate to let us by.

I looked at CJ, who was trying very hard to hide his confusion, and if I didn't know him like I do, I may not have seen it. Jean was looking at Lindy and they were just as confused as I was feeling.

We started toward the gate, and when I got to where the Guard was, he turned to me and shouted, "Lady Megan with Vernadali CJ and..." His eyes flicked to Clarice before he continued, "companions have free passage through the City of Therth." Then he bowed to us before standing up, moved back and out of the way.

I looked at CJ again, and he sighed and shrugged, rolling his eyes this time. I couldn't help but giggle. I lead my prowler through the very large stable area. Both sides of the road were lined with stables, which were three to four stalls deep. When we reached the end of the stables, there was an iron gate blocking the way. I stopped and looked back to the Guard, reaching for my syth to my side. The wooden doors to the outside edge of the city closed, and I noticed CJ had dropped the reins to the prowler and had both of his syths in his hands.

Clarice flashed by me and was standing in front of CJ, with her hands on his forearm. Seriously, how in the Underworld was she moving so fast? "They have to close the outer wall gates before the iron gate will open. It's a protection to the city," she whispered.

"It's a bottleneck strategy," CJ said, growling. "We are trapped in here. We couldn't get out if we tried."

Clarice nodded. "It has saved the city on more than one occasion."

She was right, though. Once the outer gate was closed, the iron gate flashed up with a wave of her hand. Her hand. What was going on here? I gave her an assessing look, and she just shook her head and said, "Later, Megan."

The guard came and stood at the iron gate, and once again announced us. A couple of them looked to Clarice, and I swore they bowed even lower as we passed by.

"Lady Megan with Vernadali CJ and companions. Please clear the way to allow passage," the head Guard shouted with a voice that had been obviously amplified by his power. The whole town stopped and turned to face the gate.

"Seriously?!" I groaned and turned to him. "Did you have to do that?"

"Yes, Lady Megan. The City has been on lockdown for over a month. No one in or out," he said. "They have a right to know why an exception is being made."

"And why is that?" Owen asked at the same time that I asked, "And why was the exception being made?"

"There are rumors of a dark force traveling through the lower, darker portions of Obsecuritan," the Guard said as we entered what could only be described as a marketplace area. I looked at CJ, who just shook his head at me to not say anything. He continued to talk to Owen about it, but I was taking in the sight of the town.

The town was super run down. It reminded me of a really poor medieval village, with dirt roads, dirty people, threadbare clothes, and barefoot. It was like someone had parted the seas for us as we made our way through. The other eerie thing was that the whole city had gone completely silent. Not a person dared to make a noise.

In the center of the marketplace was a platform where a guard was standing next to a woman in a ragged dress, knotted hair, and of course, barefoot, like most everyone else. Her hands were tied together high above her head, causing her to stand on her tiptoes.

"Natasha?!" Clarice hissed, looking at the woman. Her head twisted to the guard, who refused to meet her eye. Then Clarice ran up the stairs to the top of the platform, where she immediately attempted to untie the woman's hands, but the guard was there trying to stop her. The problem was, he didn't realize who he was standing before. Clarice was one of the most badass fighters I had seen this side of the Manusia. No one could get past her if she was determined enough.

With her cloak and hood still concealing who she was, Clarice ducked the swing of the sword and used her whip to remove it from the guard's hand. She tripped him up, and he fell flat on his back. If the town had been quiet before, you couldn't even hear anyone breathing now.

She kept her head down and turned to the guard, who was standing as though he was trying to decide whether to attack her. "Remove her binds. She comes with us."

A large, oversized guard, with a ridiculous mustache and dressed in a fancier version than the others, came out from under the platform.

"Under whose authority do you claim her release?" he said, circling around and up the platform. "Certainly not Lady Megan's. Her authority does not reach Gendril, girl. Her authority stopped once she left the Nalrin continent. As for Vernadali CJ, we do not recognize the authority of the Vernadali here in Therth. They have never given their assistance in our time of need."

"Under whose authority is not of your concern," she said, still trying to hide her face, but I could see the grimace under there.

"It very much is of my concern. This woman is a harlot. She showed her knees to the market. She is serving her time. One week in the hanger," the Head Guard said, crossing his arms over his chest, which made his potbelly stick out even more. I tried to stifle a giggle but walked up closer to the platform so that I could see Clarice's face without having to have her lookup.

"Clarice honey. I don't know what standing you have here, but it's obviously something. If you want this woman released, you're going to have to reveal yourself. Not only to us but to them," I told her mentally, and she quickly shook her head.

"I know it's scary. Whatever it is, you know we will not judge you. We love you for who you are. Not what any stupid title is, but if you want her released... I know it's forcing your hand. I know you don't want to," I pushed toward her as I looked at her pointedly.

Clarice kneeled to me and whispered, "Promise me this will not change how you think of me? I have never..."

"Of course, it will not," I said, surprised she would even ask. She studied me for a long moment, looked to the rest of our family, then nodded, took another deep breath as a black haze covering her as she rose.

"By order of Princess Clarice, Eldest Daughter of King Babak and Queen Selene, the rightful heir to the Gate of the Underworld," she said, throwing back her hood and standing tall. Everyone in the town dropped to their knees and put their head to the ground. Well, except for us and the one defiant Head Guard.

"Princess?" CJ mouthed to me. I just stood there, stunned. Did she just say *Princess Clarice?* Whatever title I had been thinking, it was not Princess.

While she had stated that her father was the Gatekeeper to the Underworld, I still did not expect those words to come out of her mouth. In retrospect... The boys from Gendril had called her Princess, which she immediately demanded they not call her. I had thought it was just a term of endearment, but they were literally using her formal title.

Even when we met with the Council, the Takeover had bowed to her. She did not bow to him. No, she had stood tall and proud as he did so.

What the ever-living hell. Clarice was a real life fucking princess, for Underworld's sake. Literally.

"Princess Clarice hasn't been seen for decades. How do I know you are who you say you are?"

The guard from the front gate stood up. "Sir, I will vouch for her. She is the reason I granted them access to the city. I have known her since I was a child. This is Princess Clarice. She had asked that I keep her identity a secret, for she did not want..." He looked at her with warmer eyes than he had before. "Well, this."

"Thank you, my dear Alexei," Clarice said softly with eyes and reached over and cut the ropes to Natasha's bindings.

I blinked.

"Very well. She is of no consequence to me. Take her, but she is not to return," he said and stomped off back under the platform.

"That shall not be a problem," Clarice said, the black haze dissipating.

"Her rat children too," he said with vile in his voice.

Natasha stopped dead in her tracks. "Sima and Max, Sasho's boys," Natasha whispered.

"Very well, go get them and ask them and Sasho to pack their belongings. They will stay at the castle," Clarice ordered the guard. When he didn't move, she turned to face him and with a voice that you could feel the shock wave of power, she said, "Do you dare defy me?!"

I was just at the right angle to see her eyes turn black again and the guard take a step back with his face in shock. "No, Princess. Immediately Princess. We will have them delivered before nightfall. Unharmed."

Clarice helped Natasha off the platform and set her on Squeesha. "Owen, Jean, can you look after her for a minute? Get her some water. There is a food pack in the right back flank pouch." Jean nodded and moved to get the food pack from Clarice's bags.

The man she called Alexei came up to us, "I'm sorry for all of this."

"It is not your fault, Alexei. I should've known coming back here would've turned out this way." Her eyes had mostly returned to normal, but considering what had happened out on the bluff, I was not going to relax that easy.

"I haven't seen you use that power since..."

"Yeah. I know," she said, hanging her head and putting the hood of the cloak back on. She took a step toward him and took his hands. Under the circumstances, I would have thought he would have twitched at her touch or something, but instead, he pulled her close and hugged her.

"I've missed you, my Silnaree," I heard him tell her.

"Ok. What's the deal here?" I asked in a rushed whisper.

Alexei stepped back and put a finger up. "Marketplace is closed. Return to your residence for the evening."

CHAPTER 45

ALEXEI HAD DRINKS AND food brought out to the platform for us to eat. It only took about 15 minutes and the whole marketplace was empty. The guards were standing outside the gates to the residence portion of the town and enforcing the new curfew.

"Don't worry. The curfew will be lifted in the morning and the marketplace will once again be busy," Alexei said, though he hadn't let go of Clarice's hand the entire time.

"Clarice, do you wish to explain what in the world just happened and why you two are all lovey dovey? I mean, apart from the obvious that you guys were sweethearts at one time," I tried to keep it light.

"We were, are, more than just sweethearts, Megan. We are Silnaree." Her smile brighter than I have ever seen from her.

"Silnaree? Seriously?" Lindy said, her voice high and excited. "Was it approved by your father?"

"I'm sorry, what is a Silnaree?" I asked.

"An engagement bond bound by the darkness of the Underworld. The same darkness that runs through her blood. It's unbreakable," Alexei said.

"We were engaged to be wed on our 25th birthday. Only..." Clarice's voice caught.

"You needed to leave," he said softly.

"It wasn't easy to do. Not only had there been my turning down my father's position, but there was also Alexei."

"Alexei, you knew what and who her father is?" Jean asked.

"I do. My mother worked in the kitchens of the castle, so I spent a lot of time there, which is how we met. When she was 16, I finally had the nerve to ask her for a walk in the gardens, and when we were 18, we solidified our engagement. And yes, King Babak approved it," he said, smiling brightly.

"Then at 21, I declined my birthright, and left," Clarice said quietly. "It has been 53 years since I saw this place."

"53 years, 28 days, and," he looked at his watch, "17 hours, to be exact. I wanted to go with her. My heart and the darkness kept urging me to go after her. My mother, she was kicked out of the kitchens after she helped protect Clarice from one of her father's tirades, and so there was no one else to provide for the family. My sister was still in schooling, so..."

"You did what you needed to," I said quietly, knowing how he felt. I turned to CJ and smiled slightly. "You put family before your own happiness."

"I did," he said. "But see, here is the thing that I don't know if King Babak knows. The darkness that he bound us with, it works like a witch's locator spell. I've always known that Clarice was alive, safe, and where she was. Until last year. There were a few times I felt the ties weaken. I was fearing the worst, but then they came back stronger."

He sighed and continued, "When King Babak got worse, I sent Clarice news. I knew I couldn't send too many updates, because they would figure out where she was and I feared what the King would do if he found her. Let alone her sister. There was a rumor he had sent some associates of his to find her, but they returned saying they never found her. King Babak didn't believe them. They disappeared shortly after."

"I may have had something to do with that," I said under my breath, and CJ squeezed my hand. I remembered how they had shown up at the house and I shredded their clothes off in that fight. Clarice and Lindy had given me quite the tongue lashing over it. I had been showing off and left their clothes in ruin.

I studied Clarice. Her eyes were brighter, her smile more vibrant, and she stood taller. She looked... happy. Was it the bond between her and Alexei? Was their engagement why she was so distant in the planning of CJ and I's wedding?

Jean walked over to Clarice and took her hand. "Why didn't you tell us who your father was? That he was King, and you the rightful heir to the crown? Whether you wanted the position, why didn't you tell us, sweety?"

"I didn't want you to look at me differently. The last few decades, being part of your family has been the best in my life," she said, a tear slipping down her cheek.

"You're a Princess Clarice. A bonafide princess," Owen said, still in shock. "It won't get you out of doing your chores around the house, but Angels Clarice... A little warning would've been nice."

"Well, you were told my father was the Gatekeeper to the Underworld back when we were going across the channel. I thought maybe you would've pieced it together."

"How were we to know that the King of Obsecuritan was also the Gatekeeper of the Underworld. That's not a detail that is known. Who would have known that?" Lindy said.

"That's why Julian never enforced protocol with you and Benedict, was it? You..." Jean said, her eyes wide. "Clarice, you outrank everyone on the Council except for Julian."

"In some ways, I outrank him, but I would never pull rank," Clarice said with a heavy sigh. "As I told you on the channel, I didn't want any of this. The only thing I want out of Obsecuritan is Alexei. The rest can all fall through the gate and burn for all I care."

Everyone was quiet for a long moment before CJ asked Alexei, "How did you find out King Babak was so ill?"

"I still have friends in the castle. When I found out he had been asking for her to return before his death, I requested an audience with King Babak. It took a couple of weeks for me to even get the request in. When I did, I told him I wanted to send the prowlers to her, but that I wouldn't tell him where she was. He agreed but asked to write a note to her, so he did, and I sent it with Squeesha. I wasn't sure she would even come, but I pulled on the bond between us as often as I dared."

I looked at Clarice, who just smirked at me.

"I hate you right now, Clarice," I said, smirking and shaking my head. "I really hate your guts. The very fiber of your being."

"I didn't lie to you. The darkness that's in my blood bound me and Alexei. It also runs in Noctulanar Castle. So, it is within you."

Alexei looked at me, confused. "You could feel my tugs on the bond?"

"Apparently," I said slowly, narrowing my eyes at Clarice.

"I couldn't tell you what it was without explaining everything. Alexei was tugging at the bond. Tugging on the darkness. So the darkness was calling me home. So, technically, I didn't lie to you."

"You could have just said that you were mated, and your mate was pulling on the bond. I could feel it because the bond was encased with the same darkness in Noctulanar," I said, trying to keep my voice low. "That's how you could have explained it without the Gatekeeper or Princess shit."

"Still doesn't explain why you get the headaches with them, though, or why it makes you so light-headed," CJ said, pulling me closer.

"Yeah. That I don't have an answer for." She shrugged. "I've been trying to sort that out. All I could think was that because it was not naturally in your blood, it affected you differently, but it still doesn't exactly work that way."

"Why is the town so runned down? I thought Therth was a prosperous capital?" Jean said, changing the subject.

"There isn't much interaction between the castle and the city. The city itself has a ruling council of governors for each section of the city, but the King doesn't have much authority here. They don't like to share their resources, I'm afraid. The Governor's hold on to what money they can get because there isn't much here," Alexei said. He looked to Clarice and a small smile tipped the left side of his mouth before he said, "Frankly, I'm not sure the Governors have any knowledge of the King's illness, but they recognize that when your bloodline is handpicked by the Angel of Death to watch over the entrance to the Underworld, you're pretty much royalty. Clarice's orders will always be followed in the City itself."

"Yeah, tell me about it," I said under my breath.

"See, Megan, I told you I knew what you meant about it being a pain in the butt," Clarice said, laughing, then she stopped and sighed. "Alexei..."

"I know, my Silnaree. I know what you guys are doing. Just stay alive, okay. I plan on holding you to it, even if it takes 100 years." Then he pulled her close and kissed her.

My jaw dropped. Clarice... was being kissed, and kissing him back, with enthusiasm, I might add. I looked to the rest of my family, who were also in shock. CJ's jaw was on the floor. Lindy's eyes were about to bug out of her head, and Owen and Jean were staring at each other in shock.

I turned to let them have their moment and checked on Natasha. She was finishing up the food packet that Jean had given her and smiling at Clarice. "It's good to see her again." She looked at me and smiled. "And not just because she saved me. She has been missed. I know she won't stay, and some won't want her to, but some men would love it if she did. Other than Alexei."

I nodded and looked back at Alexei and Clarice. I felt for her. She left her love just to escape her father. Then guilt washed over me as I thought about CJ, and my heart sank.

"We are ready to go. Alexei is going to make sure Natasha's family arrives safely and gets them settled. I'll make the arrangements when we get inside the castle," Clarice said, grabbing Squeesha's reins. "Let's go."

"Clarice. Are..." I started, then dropped my voice down to a whisper. "Are you ok? I saw your eyes turn black again like up on the bluff."

She sighed and moved closer. "It's my power. The darkness, I mean. It is stronger here because this is where I'm supposed to use it. My inner power doesn't work like yours. Mine is fueled by the Underworld's darkness. That's why I'm such a good fighter in hand to hand. The farther away from Therth, and the gate I get, the weaker my power is. The closer I am, the faster and more powerful I am."

I nodded and followed the rest out of the city walls and across the stretch of land that separated the City and the Castle. It was only about a mile across, but it felt like so much farther. The closer we got, the heavier the air got. It wasn't causing dizziness or anything, but I just felt heavier.

CJ asked me if I was okay a couple of times and I just waved him off, but he knew something was wrong. That blasted Vernadali link. That was kind of annoying. How am I supposed to keep from worrying him when he is now super in tune with me?

When we got to the gates, the gate looked exactly like the one at Noctulanar Castle. There was even a black haze on the gate and walls that I recognized as the darkness. I shivered at the memory. While the walls and gates weren't as tall as the ones that surrounded the city, I don't think many would be dumb enough to tangle with the darkness that covered them.

The Castle Guards let us in and once inside the grounds, we dismounted and handed the prowlers to the caretakers. Clarice gave the Guards instructions for Natasha to be taken to her private guest house, where she and her family would be living. She sighed and lead us to the main doors while I slowed my walk to drop to the back of the group. The grounds were beautiful, even though it was all in shades of black, white, gray, and gray-purple. The grass was even perfectly manicured. It was so different from what we saw back in the town. Everything here was clean and pristine. There were flowers of just about every variety planted around the edge along the Castle walls, and the cobblestone pathway was lined with big gray-purple bushes every few feet from each other.

Halfway between the gate and the doors, there was a statue that looked extremely familiar. It was huge and gave off an eerie soft light that was coming from a ball of gray and black that swirled and moved like lava drying in the air. The whole thing moved as if it were alive, but it was soothing to watch. I didn't get the feeling it was darkness, which is what I thought it was from the start. Lindy was also examining it closely, but was being very careful not to touch it. The substance was being held up by five dark-colored statues joined at the hands, which when I looked closer, I recognized as the Five Angels.

"Lindy..." I said. "This looks familiar."

"It should. You saw it in Nalrin, in the library. Remember?" she said, her voice full of excitement.

"Oh!" I said. "But... the one in Nalrin had a bright center."

"Exactly, which is why this one is so interesting. The fact that even I didn't know there was a sister statue like the one..." she said as she stood back, looked to Clarice, back at the statue, and sighed.

"Stories say that it was given to my ancestors by the Angel of Death himself when he assigned us the duties of Gatekeeper. I didn't know there was anything else like it," Clarice said, running her fingertips over the image of the Angel of Death, before sighing and lowering her voice. "Come on, let's get this meeting over with. I'm not looking forward to it at all."

It was weird to see Clarice like this. She had always been the one in the background, our support system. Now here she was, thrust to the forefront. She knew the ins and outs of this place and the people here. She was our guide.

When we got to the front doors of the castle, the Guards opened them, and we walked into a huge entrance hall with a double staircase on either side. At the top of the landing on the 2nd floor where the staircases met was a woman in a floor-length red dress, with sleeves that widened at the wrist to a point where they hung down halfway down her thigh with silver trim. She looked down at us with hate in her eyes, but a sweet smile fixed upon her face.

Her brown hair flowed down in ringlets from the bun in her hair, and she held her hands just in front of her, fingertips touching. Her whole body was tense, but her shoulders and head were thrown back in dominance.

"Ahh... The deserter has returned," she said with a sickly, sweet voice.

"Erida," Clarice said, looking up at the woman.

CHAPTER 46

THE WOMAN, ERIDA, SLOWLY made her way down the right staircase, watching us as she did so.

"Erida, don't," Clarice said.

"Don't what my sister?" she said, overly sweet.

"Stop trying to make my family feel uncomfortable by trying to show you have all the power here. You don't have a drop until—"

"Father dies. Which won't be too far away," she said way too comfortably. Then her face twisted and she spat, "Then, I will assure you will never step foot on these grounds again."

"Well, luckily I didn't come here for you, or your perceived thought of importance," Clarice said flippantly. I looked to Lindy, whose jaw was on the ground, and Jean, who was fighting the urge to ask Clarice to be nice. I hadn't realized I had taken a step forward until CJ grabbed my hand and held me back.

"AHHH, yes, *Lady* Megan and her sorry excuse for a Vernadali." Erida turned to face me.

"Excuse me?" I said. "I don't care who you think you are, but you have no right..."

"Oh, I have every right. See, here I am Queen or will be shortly, so I can say and do whatever I want," Erida said.

"So, you decided to be a royal bitch," I said, feeling CJ's grip on my arm tighten. He had stepped just behind me and I felt his hands tight on my arms. How dare she threaten my family? Her sister was back, and she was treating her like trash off the street. I would be ecstatic to see Matt again. "Clarice, I can see why you *just* couldn't wait to come back here."

She eyed me as she continued down the stairs. "Such the drama queen *Lady Megan*."

"Erida," Clarice warned. She had taken a step to stand at my side.

"What? Boohoo, she had a bad deal with her parents? Do you think any of that matters to me? She's been parading outside of these walls around like a princess under the protection of the mighty Head Julian." She laughed.

"Must have been so hard being pampered, just like you had always wanted after I left. Sorry to tell you, but not being under someone's thumb all the time is a better way to go. That is, unless you have no soul or self-worth and need other's validations to make yourself feel like something other than a cold-hearted snake." Clarice spat the last three words like they were bile in her mouth.

I moved to take a step back when Erida shot towards me and her eyes flashed black, but I stood my ground and didn't flinch. Granted, my syths had instantly ended up in my hands, my power running through them, but I stood there and stared her down. I was surprised that CJ or Clarice didn't stop her before reaching me.

"You know nothing of who I am. Neither of you do," Erida said, turning to glare at Clarice.

I raised my eyebrows at her. Before I said something I probably shouldn't, Clarice said, "Megan has earned her title with loss and a dedication you shall never know. You're an evil, vile woman who will never know the importance of love or light.

You let that darkness flow through you and consume your heart in the darkest of ways."

"You abandoned your duties. You abandoned father," Erida spat.

"Clarice left the murderer of her mother. Clarice chose to do something meaningful with her life for the good of all beings. To save lives, while you hole up here waiting for the day where you can just be a vindictive, ruthless... bitch," I said.

"You know *nothing* but the lies that Clarice has told you."

"That's just it. She has told us nothing about this place, but I can see it. I can see it in your eyes, and I can see it in your ember." She stepped back with a questioning look on her face. "Yes, your ember. Your power. It always shows your true colors. It's dark, full of jealousy, hatred, and untouched by love. I pity you for that last bit. You want nothing more than power and the ability to throw it over others. I can only hope that someday that will change because love and a genuine sense of family, is the most powerful thing in the realms," I said as I stared back into her pitch-black eyes, which flickered and returned to their normal color.

"You know nothing," she snarled, turning her back from us. Before she went back up the stairs, she stopped, took a deep breath, and said, "Father is in his bathing chambers. They sealed your room shut when you left. The rest of you can stay in the north wing, and rooms should be ready. I will tell Father that you're here and we will meet you in the throne room tomorrow morning. I'm sure you are tired from your travels and want to bathe and sleep."

When she disappeared down the hall at the top of the stairs, everyone turned and looked at me.

"Wow, Megan," Clarice said, turning to me, astonished.

"She's not very nice, is she?" Lindy said.

"Well, no, but damn! That was harsh, even by my standards," Clarice said, smiling. "I'm not complaining. It isn't like I was all lovely and nice to her. She needed to be put in her place."

"I'm sorry if I overstepped, Clarice. Though I'm shocked that you or CJ didn't jump in to stop her when she ran in front of me," I said as CJ squeeze my hand.

"Not going to lie. It was hard, but I really try to let you fight your own battles, love," CJ said, whispering in my ear with a nibble. The tone of that voice indicated something else entirely, and it made my pulse quicken and my stomach tighten.

"Clarice, don't you want to go see your father?" Jean asked, trying to change the subject. Though she gave me a look that we may have words later. Probably wasn't one of the smartest things I've done. I pushed to her, "*I know, I know. Way to go, Megan, piss off the future Gatekeeper to the Underworld.*"

Jean nodded and smirked.

"Yes," Clarice sighed. "No, I don't know. Now that I'm here, it brings all kinds of things back I don't really want to remember."

She looked around the entryway and I could imagine what the walls were telling her now. The memories flooding her, both the good and the bad, had to weigh on her. Finally, she sighed again and said, "Ok, let's get settled. I would like a shower, and *then* I want to sleep. It's probably a good thing we don't meet with King Babak until the morning. Gives me time to process being back within these walls."

A small girl who couldn't have been more than eight came forward and bowed. "Princess Clarice, do you want to have dinner in the study with your guests, or in your rooms tonight."

She looked at us, and we must have looked worse than we thought, because she said, "Please have meals brought to us in our respective rooms tonight. Something to break our fast in the morn as well please."

Her cadence was so much more formal and traditional that I just looked at her. The girl simply gave her a small curtsy and trotted off down the hallway.

Clarice sighed as she turned to head up the stairs and said, "Things are pretty old-fashioned around here."

We headed up the stairs and down the hall. "Go ahead there to the right, and I'll meet you back downstairs around nine in the morning. I'm sure all the rooms are proper. CJ and Megan, you take the farthest one down the hall. The rest take the ones closer to this side. I kind of promised them some alone time. I'm going to head to my old room, see if I can even enter it."

"Want me to go with you?" I asked.

"No, I need to go myself," she breathed, as she looked down the hall.

I took her hand and pulled her into a hug. "I'm sorry if I overstepped. You know you have us to talk to, right?" I whispered to her.

"Yeah. I do. It's just I never planned on coming back here is all." She pulled back and looked at us. "I love you guys, and thank you for being here for me. I really appreciate it. I'll see you in tomorrow."

She turned around and walked down the hall with a new sense of determination. When I turned to the rest of my family, Lindy and Jean had tears in their eyes. "What's wrong?"

"I just feel so bad for her. I mean, when she became part of our family, she told us she came from a powerful part of Obsecuritan, that her family was broken, and she wanted nothing to do with it anymore, we just had no idea," Jean said, as Owen put his arm over her shoulders.

"We have found out more about her in the last few days than we had for all the years she has been with us," Owen said sadly, as we all headed down the hall. "We just had no idea. Had we known, we still would've taken her in, don't get us wrong. We may have just handled this trip differently is all."

"That may have been the point, Owen," I said. "Remember how she hid from the guards in Therth. She didn't want anyone to know who she was."

"I guess you're right," he said thoughtfully. "She *really* did want to leave this all behind, and telling us about it would've kept this part of her life alive. I suspect she never thought her journey would lead her back here."

"No, I don't either," I said, squeezing CJ's hand.

"I don't think any of us would've thought our lives would've taken the path they have. We are in the middle of Psychoville,"

CJ said, his fingers intertwining with mine and he rubbed his thumb back and forth over the back of my hand.

Owen and Jean went into the third bedroom on the right and Lindy said she was going to bathe and sleep in the room one down and across from them. When Lindy shut her door, CJ swung around and picked me up off the ground.

"Now, you missy," he said, kissing me.

"What was that for?" I said, smiling for the first time since we walked into this place.

"There is just something so sexy about you taking command and putting people into their place," he said as he continued down the hall.

"Seriously? With all the heavy that's going on, you're going all mushy honeymoon on me?"

"Is there a problem with that Mrs. Mathewson, because fuck, that was sexy as hell."

"Well…" I wasn't able to finish my sentence, because he kissed me again, put me down, and swung open the door to one of the bedrooms. We dropped our bags as I kicked the door shut behind us.

CJ's hand was on my chest as he pushed me up against the wall. Our kiss broke. He deliberately looked me up and down, before meeting my eyes and said, "Now, you, Mrs. Mathewson, are to get out of those clothes and then I'm going to worship every inch of that body."

Heat pulsed through me, and a familiar throbbing was bursting between my legs. There was nothing I could do but start slowly undressing as he took a few steps back to watch me. When I slowly took off my panties, I flung them at him, which he caught before they hit him in the face. I stood there naked, leaned against the wall so my chest stuck out, and said, "Now you were going to do what?"

His eyes roamed over me, and there was a shuddering breath that came from him. I took one single step toward him, and he instantly started stripping. As that last piece of clothing was strung on the floor, he took two long strides toward me, swooped me up, and carried me to the large, canopied king bed.

"As I said, Lady Megan," he smirked a bit as he said with heat in every word, "I am going to worship every inch of you."

He kissed my neck as his fingers ran lightly down my sides, making my back arch, my breasts pushing against his chest. My body filled with a lustful hunger that would not be contained until it was satisfied.

"So, do it," I panted.

"Your wish is my command," he said huskily in my ear.

CHAPTER 47

THE NEXT MORNING, WE were running down the stairs apologizing for being late. CJ was running his fingers through his hair and I was buckling my syth strap to my thigh, blushing as we met up with our family.

"Honeymooners." Owen rolled his eyes and sighed as Lindy, Jean, and Clarice giggled.

"That's enough, you guys," I said, looking at them pointedly.

"Well, it's true," Clarice said, smiling brightly. She looked so much better than she did when we had left her last night. "This way."

We walked down a large corridor that had windows open to the outside, letting a soft gentle breeze flow through the space. There was a hint of mint and something deeply earthy in the air that I couldn't place. Eventually, it turned and wrapped around back toward the center of the castle. Clarice nodded to the guards that stood at the massive stone doors and when they realized who she was, they bowed to her.

"Princess Clarice, it is good to see you again." She stood, staring at them. They stayed bowed for a long moment before saying anything.

"Thank you," Clarice said, allowing them to rise.

When we walked into the room, I faltered at the sheer size of it. There were black shining pillars lining the sides of the room that reached the ceiling to a curved peak at the top. The floors and walls were made of white marble, making the room look bright, clean, and massive. We walked to where King Babak was sitting on the throne, a vacant chair next to him. Erida stood to the right of the queen's empty seat, head held high and smug.

On the opposite side, just out of the shadows, was a woman dressed in gypsy clothing. Her skirts patched and a little raggedy. She had a white capped-sleeved billowy shirt under a leather corseted vest that cradled her breast, which only helped to accentuate them. She had a red bandana holding her jet-black hair back and simple gold hoops in her ears. Other than the hoops in her ears, there wasn't any other jewelry except for a ring on her right pinky and a simple threaded bracelet on her left wrist.

Clarice's father, King Babak, sat tall in his chair, though it looked as if it took all his strength to do so. His face was thinning at the cheeks and his eyes were hollowing. His hair thin and dry to where if anyone tried to touch it, it may have just crumbled to dust. When I looked at his ember, it was fading, and I had the feeling he was days from passing. I took Clarice's hand and squeezed it; she squeezed it back. She sighed and took a step forward.

"King Babak," Clarice said, bowing. The rest of us followed suit, and I could hear Erida click her tongue in displeasure. "I'm sorry for the delay. I wanted to ensure we were all here to greet you."

"Clarice, my eldest daughter. I am so glad that you have come." His voice was strong, but it crackled at the end, and he broke into a wet coughing fit.

"Why doesn't your mistress come out of the shadows and stand next to you?" Clarice said, looking at the woman.

"I have no mistress. She is a witch from Alnwick," he said and leaned forward to look at her. "Dorith, you may come stand next to me."

"An Alnwick witch?" Lindy asked. "What would be the reason for an Alnwick witch to be at your side?"

"She is finding the source of my sickness," he said.

"Why not just call for Nalrin Physicians to come and do an assessment?" Clarice asked.

"The Nalrin Physicians said that it is an incurable, inoperable mass within my lungs," he scoffed. "I am the Gatekeeper of the Underworld. I do not have anything that's incurable."

CJ looked at me and I spread the golden protection. *"Lung cancer."* I heard him say, and I nodded. *"Poor Clarice,"* he continued, and hung his head.

"But..." Clarice said but then the doors to the chambers burst open, and a man with enormous eyes, ragged clothes, greasy hair, barefoot, and dirty from head to toe came barging in. I froze. I looked at Lindy and Jean.

"Ash'bani?" I mouthed. My father had never looked like that. I could only tell by the oversized eyes.

"King Babak! King Babak! King Babak! I must speak with you immediately," the Ash'bani shrieked down the hall.

"You will need to wait, Fargo."

"You don't understand!" he begged.

"No, you don't understand. I am in council, and I will speak to you later."

I thought the man named Fargo was going to explode. "But..."

"But nothing," King Babak said, his voice rattling the whole room. "I will meet with you when I am done speaking-"

"Ansel Keller completed the Ardith," Fargo interrupted quickly. I perked up. The sound of my father's name made me instantly more attentive.

"Lots of Ash'bani complete the Ardith," King Babak said with a wave of his hand, rolling his eyes.

"Your Highness, you don't understand. He traveled to the Underworld just over a month ago, and not to The Five Angels," the creature said, almost curling into a ball when he finished the statement.

King Babak went still and silent. There was not so much as a muscle twitch. His eyes then started moving about the room quickly and he cocked his head to the side, as if listening carefully to a sound none of us could hear.

I looked to my family for answers, but they looked as lost as I felt, except for Clarice. Her face filled in concentration, her lips moved so fast I couldn't make out what she was saying. She was thinking through possibilities.

"What would that do?" I asked, my voice soft as a feather. It still sounded too loud for the room. I knew that when one traveled to the Angels all darkness would be expelled from them, but if they traveled to the Underworld? There was only one answer going through my mind, and I immediately wanted to reject it.

"It was a theory I wanted to look into when we got here, but... I don't know of anyone who has ever done it, but..." Clarice said, but trailed off, deep in thought. "When we were in Nalrin, there was a rumor that someone close to the limiting age hadn't gone through the Ardith, and I wondered if Ansel had. I couldn't find anything on it. I was going to check the Underworld records here."

"You knew my father hadn't completed the Ardith? And you said nothing?" I said, almost grinding the words out of my throat.

"I said there had been rumors that someone was reaching the limiting age, who hadn't. I didn't know whether Ansel had or not. I didn't want to worry you until I found out more," Clarice said, her eyes wide, looking at me.

"Clarice," I said carefully. There was an awful oily feeling filling me, and when I did speak again, dread coated each word. "What would happen if my father went to the Underworld and not the Angels?"

King Babak continued for her after a few seconds in thought, "If Ansel Keller traveled to the Underworld then that would mean that he didn't expel the darkness, the darkness would expel the light... Which would mean, that he is quite literally, pure evil."

CJ turned to me.

"Then he could control pure darkness," I stated, knowing that King Babak would confirm it.

"Theoretically, yes," King Babak said.

"The Ja'Nee," CJ said. "That's how he sent them after you."

"Sir, there is more," Fargo said in a meek voice and hunched over like he was scared he was going to get hit. That made my stomach drop. What could be more devastating than knowing my father is pure evil, but also controlled it?

"Continue," King Babak commanded.

"When Ansel awoke from his meditation, he had a black aura to him..." Fargo looked to us, and then back to the King.

"Spit it out!" the King snapped.

"When he walked out of the temple, the temple collapsed in a heap of rubble and tar oozed from the center. Then it... It covered the city... Ghant is destroyed... We tried to fight him off... We tried. We did. I swear, King Babak, but we couldn't fight it off. Anyone who tried, they... they became part of the substance." Fargo was trying to talk slower, but he was shaking.

"The tar covered everything and everyone in its path. No one in town survived. When the tar consumed one of us, they melted to the bone, so they were nothing but a tar covered skeleton, which also became part of the substance. The people of the city are now under his control. He is controlling this substance to wipe out everything and everyone in his path."

"Wait a minute," Jean said, her voice unsure of itself. I could swear I felt her go on the defensive. "If no one survived, how did you get out?"

"When Vicar Alard came out of the temple after overseeing the Ardith as he does for every Ash'bani who completes it..."

"I'm sorry, what is a vicar?" CJ asked.

"Like a priest, pastor, basically the head of a specific church, in this case, Vicar Alard is head of the temple in Ghant well—was head of the temple. Guess Ghant isn't there anymore," I told him, trying to absorb what Fargo was telling us. It couldn't be real. This was something out of a horror story.

"Anyway, go on. What happened when he left the temple?" I needed to know what I was up against.

"He knew something was wrong. Usually, when someone travels to the Five Angels, there is a soft white glow about them. Vicar Alard said Ansel had a dark haze and when he got closer, he saw what was more like black thin strings flickering around him. He told everyone in town to leave. Some did, most did not, and those who didn't were consumed by the tar."

I knew what he meant by the dark strings. It was just like at Noctulanar Castle, and the gate here. Instead of the light and benevolence from the Five Angels, the darkness had consumed him. I thought about my father and his last words to me.

"When we were in Noctulanar Castle, he said that I would pay for what I've done. Is this what he meant?" I said, looking at my family.

Clarice spoke carefully while looking just at me, but her voice was quick and was bordering on the line of hysteria. "Father, I know we have had our differences, and that I vowed to never return to this place, but I pushed that aside to see you one more time. These people are my family, as much, if not more, than you are. I am sure you know who Lady Megan is. He's coming for her. It sounds as if he is destroying Obsecuritan in his path to get to her. We have to stop him."

King Babak sat in deep thought for a while, studied me intently, and then looked up to Fargo. "You know the one thing that can destroy Ash'bani other than old age and the Angels."

"Yes, but no one has ever attempted such a feat. Let alone know where to start. Her trail is littered with old legends," Fargo said.

I thought I saw Witch Dorith flinch. King Babak looked at Fargo and raised his eyebrows. "No one had tried to assemble the weapon of the Five Angels either, and Ansel and Symatha certainly tried."

"But they failed," Fargo said.

I interrupted this time, "Only because I have the Golden Amulet of Sa Ra. They had everything else." My fingers played with the amulet around my neck, newly repaired by the Angel of Healing herself. I also squeezed CJ's hand hard enough that I could feel him wince through the golden protection.

That seemed to make Fargo hesitate. Word had spread, but just not the details of just how close my parents had been.

"Humm," King Babak stroked his beard thoughtfully.

"Your Highness?" Lindy asked.

He didn't answer. His mind seemed in a far-off place, thinking about something intently. He continued to mutter and think to himself, and I was trying to be patient. Just when I couldn't take it anymore, Clarice spoke up, "Father... what are you thinking about?"

"Helena."

"Father, that's a story you and Mother used to tell me to make sure Erida and I behaved."

"And wasn't the Five Angels weapon only a bedtime story?" I hissed.

"Megan, sometimes a bedtime story is just a bedtime story," she quipped.

"It's more than a bedtime story," King Babak said quietly. Witch Dorith looked at him and her expression was one that I couldn't place.

I sighed deeply. "Okay, so spill it. Who is Helena? Where can we find her? And how exactly is she going to stop Ansel?"

Through the golden glow of protection, I could hear CJ ridicule me for talking to a King like that, but he kept his mouth shut.

King Babak looked to Clarice. "Why don't you tell it?" It was formed as a question, but it was definitely more of a statement. He started coughing again, and Witch Dorith gave him a cup with some water and a rag.

"Short story?" We all nodded, and she continued, "Helena Rowland. Long before the Ash'bani war, another war left the landscape across all continents scorched and barren. See, Helena was a very powerful witch, a really, really powerful one, as the story goes. Its rumored she might have been born of the original witch. Her lover was destroying the world and so she crafted a spell to rid the world of him."

Witch Dorith looked at her and there was a flash of something in her face that I couldn't place.

"Legend says that she scaled the highest mountain in the land of Cinder, while the Cinder Fairies held off her lover at the base, giving her time to cast the spell. The spell was to heal the damage to the world, but also to take away its darkest of darkness. Once the incantation was completed, her lover shriveled to dust, and the land touched by his evil healed. When she didn't return from the top of the mountain, the Cinder Fairies climbed the mountain to retrieve her. What they found was Helena sitting at its peak with a crystal in each hand; one red and the other black."

"Why?" Jean asked.

Witch Dorith turned from King Babak and said, "See, in magic, especially magic that powerful, nature must find a balance. Yes, she defeated her lover but for her to defeat him, she had to split her soul in two."

"That's terrible," I heard Jean say.

"What happened to her?" Owen asked.

"She became an empty shell. Her soul had split and left her body with no resident," King Babak told him. "Her body did not wither. It did not age. It simply, over time, turned to stone. To my knowledge, Helena still sits at the top of Cinder Mountain."

"So, what happened to the pieces of her soul?" I asked.

"All her light was put into the black crystal," Witch Dorith said.

"And everything bad about her?" CJ asked.

"Well, legend says that when her soul split, the good went into the black crystal, which the Fairies named Helena, the Crystal of Pureness. Any darkness in her was contained in a ruby. They immediately shattered it for fear it would be used to commit harm. It is said that the ruby bled for 13 days before drying up and every particle of dust from the ruby was absorbed into the ground," King Babak said.

"Thirteen days. Why is it always 13?" I mumbled under my breath.

"It is the pure number," King Babak said, like all the energy had been drained from within him.

"You think we need to find Helena?" CJ said quietly.

"Yes, but I must warn you that should you use her, it will kill any Ash'bani near him. Find her, but make sure that you are not near others when you use it." His voice was growing weaker and weaker.

CJ looked at me from the corner of his eye. I could feel his Vernadali Charge tighten around me as he squeezed tightly.

"Don't ask. You know the answer," I pushed toward him.

With a strained voice, staring directly at me, he asked what everyone else was thinking, "And what of someone of mixed blood?"

"Anyone with any trace of Ash'bani will be destroyed." He paused, twitched a few times, then stood with the strength a man in his condition should not command and said with an eerie voice that sounded as if it came from all the shadows in the hall, "Megan Isabel Mathewson, you must find Helena and use her to stop this from occurring. The Angels will not intervene in taking his life force from him. I will not intervene in taking his life force from him, for stopping Symatha and Ansel is the task afforded by the Five Angels to you. Find Helena. Only once Ansel has been defeated can the damage be repaired upon the land that he taints."

King Babak collapsed back into the throne's chair, Witch Dorith rushing to his aid, while Erida just stood there staring at him, eyes wide.

I felt eyes on me, but couldn't see anything but a future that I had secretly feared. The Angel of Beauty had said that stopping my parents was the task demanded by the Angels, and I had hardly heard anything after he said any trace of Ash'bani would be killed. The only thing I could think of was that I was going to have to die to save my family and the world. What surprised me even more? I knew that when the time came, I would be ready and willing to do it.

"No," CJ said in a thundering voice.

I jumped back, and as our hands dropped, I saw the golden protection drop off the tips of our fingers. Shit!

I turned and strode out of the room.

CHAPTER 48

"WHY ARE YOU ASSUMING you have to die?" CJ paced our bedroom.

"It just doesn't surprise me that whatever or whomever Helena is used against will die and there will be casualties," I said in a low voice. "Besides, the Angel of Beauty had already told us it was my responsibility to stop my parents. Did you think that was going to stop with just the weapon of the Five Angels? So, no, it doesn't surprise me."

We had been fighting for over an hour. He yelled and screamed the entire way back to our room after I stormed out of the throne room. I didn't want to talk about it. I just wanted to move on and work on finding out where we could find this Helena stone, and then we could work out the rest of the mess.

"Megan, you are *not* going to be a casualty! You're my wife, my Charge, my responsibility," he said; the last word filled with more authority than he should have.

I stood up and yelled at him, "Excuse me? I am *not,* anyone's responsibility. Don't you dare get on your Vernadali high horse. I'm not a child. I don't *need* a Vernadali. I am perfectly capable of taking care of myself."

"This isn't about me being a Vernadali. This is about me protecting my wife," he said, almost hissing the words. He was trying not to yell, but was not doing a great job of it.

"Really? Because your words were *'my Charge, my responsibility.'* Cory James, I am your wife, and I understand you don't want me going and putting myself in harm's way. You want me safe. I get that, but your words and the way you're saying these things are pure *vernadali* and that is *not* going to fly in this marriage," I said, straining not to yell myself. "Be worried as a husband all you fucking want. You're entitled to that, but that Vernadali needs to back the fuck off."

I could feel my power sizzling at my fingertips. I flopped on the bed and coiled it back into its cocoon.

"Ceej," I said, much calmer. He had his back to me and was taking slow, measured breaths. His charge filled the room, and it kept my power peeking out of its cocoon. He was trying to pull it back, but he was struggling.

I got out of the bed and walked over to him. I gently put my hand on his forearm, running my thumb over that tattoo, and said, "What I need is my husband. I know this whole Vernadali thing complicates us. Underworld's darkness, all this, complicates our marriage. Being a Vernadali is part of who you are. I understand that. I'm not trying to take that away from you. Heck, it is going to come in handy way more often than not. I also know that makes you want to protect me even more, and there is no doubt it gives you more ability to do so, but..."

"But you're right," he said, with a heavy sigh. "You always have been able to take care of yourself."

"Well, not always. I can remember lots of times the only thing that kept me together was because you were by my side."
"Yeah?"
"Yup."

"Like when?" he said as he put his arms around my waist and pulled me close. Both of us needed the contact.

"Let's see. Well, getting through high school in general," I said, as he chuckled.

"Well, I'm sure the only reason I got through Mrs. DuBois' drama class was because of you, but you know that's not what I meant, Megs."

"Okay, in all seriousness. I'm not sure I would've come out of the coma if you had not been there."

"Which one?" he teased.

"Both! For sure, not the one last year. It was your voice that kept pushing through the pain that kept me from going under again."

"That's just the Angel Blessed thing."

"No. It wasn't. It was you. All the memories of us, all the love, and your unwavering commitment to me, even when things went from usual Megan crazy to Hollywood can't make this shit up kind of crazy." I wasn't going to let him object, so I threw my arms around his neck and kissed him.

There was a loud crash from the hallway, and I looked to CJ and grabbed my syths from my thighs. I saw him grab his from his bag, twirl them in his hands and crack his neck. The whole movement made me smile. His Charge filled the air, and I felt it envelope me. My electricity was already at my fingertips and running down the blades of my syths.

I stood by the door and when I turned around, I said, "Ready?"

"Ready. I got your back."

"I know you do." There was something in his eyes. A fierceness I hadn't seen before. A louder crash, closer now, came from the hall and a scream of one of the servants.

"Now, let's move," he said.

I threw the door open and ran down the hall. When we got to the center corridor, Clarice was fighting with a Ja'Nee down the south wing. With CJ right behind me, we ran to help her. There was a table just close enough to Clarice and the fighting Ja'Nee that when I got to it, I jumped up on it to propel myself higher into the air. Just as I got above the Ja'Nee, it flipped its head around and roared as I slid my syths through its neck, decapitating it. I landed on the floor, bouncing up just as it disappeared in a poof of smoke.

"Thanks. That was kind of an awesome move," Clarice said.

"Thank Mickel," I said, smiling.

She ran into her room to grab her whips.

"Looks like Mickel was teaching you a thing or two while I was gone," CJ said as we waited for Clarice.

"What did you think we were doing? Baking all day?"

"You, bake? No way," CJ said, smiling. "Just glad to hear that he was doing some training too."

"Hand to hand. Dagger throwing. Archery. Power exercises. Trust me, I wasn't just planning a wedding," I shrugged.

Clarice came out of her room at a full run and continued down the hall. She shouted over her shoulder, "They weren't going down your hallway, so they must be after my father. Come on."

We ran down the hallway and into the main hall when we saw Owen, Jean, and Alexei fighting off six more Ja'Nee. I heard Clarice swear under her breath, and we ran down the stairs, skipping as many as we could on the way down.

Before hitting ground level, Clarice jumped over the banister and cracked her whip at the Ja'Nee fighting Alexei. It was enough of a distraction that it gave Alexei the chance to decapitate it, where it disappeared with a pop.

Owen and Jean were landing stabs and hits on theirs, but it was doing no good.

"Decapitate it!" I shouted at them as I made my way over. I jumped on the table nearest to Owen and just as I was about to decapitate him, the Ja'Nee turned and threw me back up against the back wall.

I landed flat against the wall and fell to the floor, gasping for air.

All the air was forcefully removed from my lungs.

Gasping, I stared out in front of me, seeing nothing. I had no airflow. My power was scrambling and jumping out of its cocoon.

My vision was getting black around the edges.

Calm Megan.

Calm the fuck down. Stop panicking.

Breathe, Megan. Breathe.

I had to center myself. I closed my eyes and tried to imagine the air flowing in and out of me. There was a loud crack in my head, and air rushed back into my lungs.

Gulping it down, I shook my head, trying to clear my vision. I had to gulp down a few more breaths before it cleared.

"Megan!" CJ was backing toward me.

"I'm fine... air... knocked out of me," I told him silently.

CJ nodded and went back to helping Jean. I got up and went to help Owen. My lungs still burned, but I tried to push the pain away.

I came up back behind one of the Ja'Nee, decapitating it while I went for another one, but only stabbing it in the leg. The Ja'Nee threw Owen behind him, and I ceased the small window of opportunity to keep its attention on me. Owen threw his syth at the perfect angle to slice right through his neck. I ducked and caught the syth in my hand, before I heard the pop of it disappearing. I twirled around again and sliced through one that was coming up behind me.

I turned to look at Jean and CJ who were just removing the head of their Ja'Nee.

"The King!" Alexei shouted. "Clarice went after him."

"Where are his chambers?" I asked.

"The last room in the south wing," he said, running up the stairs. We followed him up and through the corridor, where we met Clarice.

"He isn't in his chambers," Clarice said.

Just then, Dorith came around the corner. "King Babak asked me to come and get you. He's at the Gate. The Ja'Nee are escaping through there. He needs Princess Clarice's help to close it. Princess Erida is already on her way."

Clarice froze.

"Princess Clarice, we must hurry."

I could see the look of confusion and conflict on her face. Jean walked up to her, put both of her hands on her face, and forced Clarice to look at her. "Honey. What is it?"

Clarice put her hand on Jean's shoulder and looked deep into Jean's eyes. Jean shook her head, sighed, then nodded.

"I understand, but honey, the Ja'Nee."

Clarice nodded. "Okay, let's go." She turned on her heels and started in the opposite direction than Witch Dorith did.

"Princess, where are you going?" she asked.

"I think I know this castle better than you. There is a passage from the King's chambers directly to the gate," she said.

As we ran toward the King's chambers, we passed an open room, and when I looked into it, I stopped. There was a black stone coffin in the center. The longer I looked at it, the more I could see something rising out of the top. I took a step into the room when CJ took my hand, stopping me in my tracks.

"Megs, what is it?" he asked.

"There is darkness rising from the coffin," I said, tilting my head to the side.

"That's impossible," Clarice said, but the look on her face said that she saw the same thing I did.

"Clarice," Witch Dorith said in a voice that was much too musical to be her own.

"Mother?"

"I'm trying to help, but don't have much time. We must hurry to your father. He is holding off the Ja'Nee as long as he can, but won't be able to hold out much longer," she said, not giving her a chance to ask questions.

Clarice nodded, and we started running. The King's Chambers was lined with large black drapes from the ceiling to about four feet up from the ground, plush gray carpet, and a massive bed that could easily fit my entire family.

Clarice rushed to the dressing area and pushed on the wall, where the door opened. Clarice didn't pause as she launched herself down the rough, narrow stone stairway leading down.

We took off after her and when we reached the base of the stairs; the air was heavy and dark. It was so close to the feeling

I'd been getting for months, but different somehow. The closer we got to the gate, the stronger the pull to it. I pushed it aside and pulled my syths back from their sheaths.

When we walked in, the room was all white marble, except for the ceiling, which was of flawless pitch-black marble, with a square pool in the center of the room. Only the water looked more like the veil at my wedding. It was there, but it was so sheer, you almost couldn't see it. I'd seen this place before. But when?

My eyes widened. I had seen this room. Last year. I had seen the Gate to the Underworld. I looked around the room and saw the statues of the Five Angels in a gray-purple smooth stone circling the room, but where the four angels were looking straight out, the Angel of Death on the far wall looked down into the pool. My heart sank as I thought through the rest of that dream. I hadn't shared it with anyone, because none of it had made sense until now.

All I needed to know what would happen next was to see that King Babak was indeed standing on the north side of the pool, throwing darkness like daggers at the Ja'Nee that continued to fly from the center of the gate. Princess Erida was on the opposite side, doing nothing more than standing there frozen in fear. The Ja'Nee were flying out from the center of the gate so quick that I lost count of how many had passed through.

"Okay, this isn't what I expected the Gates of Hell to look like," CJ said. I couldn't help but smile.

Witch Dorith went to stand on the far side of the pool. "Clarice, honey, stand on that side."

"Selene?" King Babak said at the same time Princess Erida said, "Mother?"

"Yes. There is no time. We have to concentrate," she said.

"What can we do to help?" I asked.

"Keep the Ja'Nee busy. They won't like us closing the Gate," King Babak said, his voice stronger than it was earlier, and I suspected he was pooling all his power to make this happen. My eyes flicked to Clarice, and I wondered how she was going to handle this.

As they started their spell, their hands outreaching to the other, a diamond forming to connect each of them together. Once the diamond snapped into place, the Ja'Nee screamed and started for the four of them. That was our queue.

I ran for one that was heading straight for King Babak, and stabbed it in its side to distract it. Instead, it turned to face me; the hood reached to cover my face, ice-cold filled my head. I ducked and swung back around, decapitating it. When it popped out, more came to take its place. I swung, ducked, dove, and decapitated as many as I could.

I had settled into an eerie calm. I could feel my power within me pulse and thrive, but it didn't feel erratic for once. Fighting and using my power against the Ja'Nee was... Soothing. I glimpsed CJ out of the corner of my eye, and as our eyes met, his eyes filled with an unspoken question. I gave him a smile of wicked enjoyment.

The popping of Ja'Nee being dispatched throughout the room continued as I let my power fill every inch of me and run free. I let out a laugh at the release in my gut and kept on swinging. I decapitated Ja'Nee after Ja'Nee. I was strong, sure, and swift.

There was a hollowing out in the room when all that heavy air just disappeared. As one, the Ja'Nee roared and fled through the corridors. King Babak screamed just as Witch Dorith, Princess Erida, and Clarice fell to their knees.

I turned to go to King Babak but there was a konarak pierced straight through his chest. Almost instantly, there was a pop and Clarice was landing on her feet at her father's side, the Ja'Nee now gone as its konarak fell to the ground. Witch Dorith collapsed on the ground, and stayed there. Princess Erida was on her knees across from where Clarice and King Babak were with a silent scream on her face.

Darkness rose high above King Babak's body, circling the room, gathering the loose tendrils from the air. It flew through Princess Erida, whose body bowed with the force of it as it passed through her.

Circling the room twice more before smashing into Clarice, she threw her arms out wide, flung her head back, and screamed in pain.

No one moved.

I wasn't so sure that anyone was even breathing.

It was as if time stopped, except for what was happening to Clarice.

Erida stared, tears streaming down her face. Her eyes had flicked to Witch Dorith, then back to where Clarice and her father were. Clarice pulsed. Her entire body pulsed.

As the darkness was absorbed into Clarice, she screamed and flinched. That darkness circled her again and speared for her chest. The room hollowed out again as Clarice let out an ear-splitting scream before it was silent and still in the room.

Clarice sat on her knees, arms hanging at her sides, as she took a few heavy breaths.

My eyes widened when I saw the change in her ember. It was a living black flame. "Clarice?" I said tentatively.

She leveled her head and looked at me, her eyes. I froze completely at that point.

Her eyes matched that swirling, living black flame.

CHAPTER 49

CLARICE STOOD UP AND calmly walked out of the room toward the Ja'Nee. The Ja'Nee in the room rushed her and as they touched the darkness slowly covering her skin like armor, there was a soft popping sound and a puff of dust. Whatever traces of darkness left in the room began billowing in a trail behind her like a cape.

I turned to CJ, whose eyes met mine. There was a quick silent conversation between us, and we took off after her. As I left the room, I yelled back to the others, "Stay here. Watch over Witch Dorith and Princess Erida."

Clarice took small, short deliberate steps up the path to the courtyard that didn't match her quick pace on the ground. She moved much faster than her strides. CJ and I jogged to keep pace with her.

When we broke through the path to the courtyard, everyone stopped and froze at the sight of Clarice. Guards and Ja'Nee alike turned to face her. Guards fell to their knees, their heads bent down in supplication, even as the Ja'Nee floated before them, roaring at Clarice and shooting toward her.

I lunged forward, syths in hand, CJ on my heels without thinking. However, just as we got to her side, there was an invisible wall blocking us.

"Clarice! Remove it now!" I shouted, heart racing.

Clarice turned and gave us a sweet smile. Then, in a voice of pure power and command, she said, "Megan, you have always protected us. Let me protect you now."

The Ja'Nee were almost to her. "Clarice, you can't possibly stop them all. Let CJ and I help you."

"I am Gatekeeper of the Underworld. I have power you have never seen. Stay here. Stay safe," she said with love and kindness, but I felt the command within me to stay where I was. To stay safe. She turned back toward the incoming Ja'Nee, raised her hands, and as darkness gathered at her fingertips, she stood tall and proud.

What happened next was nothing short of amazing. She shaped the darkness into knives, daggers, swords, and flung them at each of the Ja'Nee with inconceivable accuracy. Not a single Ja'Nee was able to avoid her attack. Ja'Nee after Ja'Nee vanished with a pop as she decapitated them. If any made it within five feet of her, the long sword made of that darkness she wielded in her hand would decapitate them before they could get much closer.

I turned to CJ, and his face was blank in amazement.

"I've never seen anyone move like that before," I heard Owen say behind me.

"She's absorbed the darkness that our father controlled. She's... she's becoming the Gatekeeper to the Underworld," Erida said quietly behind us.

Jean pushed against the wall that separated us from her, but it held. I looked across the courtyard and not a single guard had moved from their knees. They still kneeled, arms now outstretched to her, palms up.

"Why aren't they helping her?" CJ asked.

"She has ordered them to stay where they are. She does not need the help. Even I felt the order," Erida said.

"I don't—"

"Understand. Of course you don't," she spat, and I glared at her. Now was not the time for a pissing contest. "When a guard is sworn in, as part of taking their oaths to protect Obsecuritan, they drink from a cup of the Gatekeeper's blood. The darkness is their blood bond to the Gatekeeper. It continues through succession. She can order them through the darkness they drank from our father or our father's father." She was almost yelling to be heard over the popping sounds around us.

I turned to Clarice, and she had nearly dispatched each and every Ja'Nee, darkness pulsing in the armor it had created around her. When the last of the Ja'Nee had vanished, she rose from the ground, becoming completely encased in a black haze, and turned toward us.

When she threw out her power, my eyes widened at the sight. Her features had shifted. Not drastically, but the lines on her face were sharper. Her cheekbones became more predominant, and her skin smoothed out. Her eyes were still pitch black and pulsed, and her hair was no longer to her butt, but was now cropped short and had changed from her brown–black hue to a bright vibrant red. What I had known at home as the soft coals of her ember were now a raging, living black flame with glowing embers that were as vibrant as the red that colored her head.

The wind picked up in the courtyard, and I grabbed CJ's hand to help stay standing. My hair whipped across my face so fast it stung. Jean, Owen, and Lindy had taken to kneeling. The Guard stayed where they were, and I could see them struggling to do so.

"She's... accepting the darkness. Accepting the control. Accepting... The power," Erida said in awe as she too kneeled on both knees and raised her hands toward Clarice.

"Clarice," Alexei said softly.

Nothing.

The wind howled. I leaned into the wind to stay standing. I didn't want to just stay there, but I couldn't do anything. I felt the command to stay where I was. It pressed against my bones. Besides, the wall was still in place, and we couldn't get past it, anyway.

"Clarice!" I yelled as she raised herself from the ground, circling in place for all to see who she was.

"Clarice," Alexei said softly, forehead against the barrier. The wind did not affect him, and I stared at him. Not a hair moved as loose strands of my own still whipped around my face.

CJ pulled me down to my knees. The wind stripped the trees of their foliage, bent plants at odd angles, and the wind still grew stronger.

I stole a glance at the guards, where they kneeled in front of Clarice. Their hands had lowered, but their heads faced Clarice. Their eyes black as hers.

"Clarice," Alexei said again against the barrier and then passed through it. I strained to go with him, but CJ held me tight in place, his charge lending him additional strength.

We watched as Alexei stood in front of Clarice, looked up to her, and reached a hand out toward her, "My Silnaree."

She looked down at him with an inquisitive look, then slowly raised her hand just halfway to his.

"Clarice, my Silnaree," Alexei said with emotion in his voice that the tears in his eyes couldn't convey. He reached up and took her hand. Once their hands touched, the wind instantly stopped and Clarice fell from the air, landing perfectly in Alexei's arms.

CHAPTER 50

CLARICE HAD SLEPT FOR a full day before she woke up. Alexei never once left her side. It reminded me so much of CJ. He wanted to make sure she would see his face first, that their bond was stronger than ever, and that things haven't changed because she had now become who she was is.

When she did finally venture down from her rooms, she explained that all of her father's knowledge and memories had transferred to her, along with all that darkness.

"I don't understand why I had inherited upon his death. Erida was supposed to take it. I renounced it. Formally with witnesses. I don't want it. I don't want the responsibility, the crown, the darkness, and I especially don't want his memories," she had said when she slumped into the armchair in one of the lounges.

That was the hardest part for her. The assumption of her father's memories. There were some that she cherished, like the day he met Queen Selene, their Silnaree bond, their marriage, but with those memories also came the torment of how it felt when her father killed her and the days afterward. There was the anger when Clarice rejected her place as his successor and the one that surprised her most was the disappointment in Erida's inability to comprehend everything that had come so naturally to Clarice. Her father didn't want Erida to become Gatekeeper. He would've rather had a new family line taken over.

Clarice hated her father even more now that she had his memories. She realized just how bitter, angry, vicious, uncaring, nasty, and cruel he was. It was a reality she had known and thought she had accepted, but she hated having to relive it all again.

It took two weeks for Clarice to recover enough for us to prepare to leave. She would have to return to Therth, eventually, but had set up a system that would work for now. Since the Gate was closed anyway, there wasn't much she could do.

Witch Dorith had been invaluable in helping with the translation of the texts of Helena. We knew Helena needed to be on our radar, but we didn't know where to start.

"You will need to speak to High Witch Kaige in Alnwick. She can arrange for you to meet with the Fairies of Cinder that are said to protect Helena. They will teach you more about her as well."

"What if she won't meet with us?" Jean asked.

"Here," she said, taking off a bracelet and handing it to Jean. "Give that to her and she will know I sent you. I will create a portal for you to get there and into the Coven's home. High Witch Kaige will meet you on the other side. I will see you outside in fifteen minutes to open the portal."

"Why don't you go with us?"

"I'm going to stay here and help Princess Erida. She's all alone now," she said, hanging her head. "And I made a promise to her mother. Part of the deal I made for her... to help. No matter what happened, I don't leave King Babak or Princess Erika. I must stay here and care for them."

"Why did you?" I asked.

"I've assisted King Babak for decades. I knew Queen Selene when she was little. She was one rightful powerful witch." When she saw the shock on my face, she elaborated, "Yes, she was a witch. She had to give up her power when she married King Babak. I knew I wanted to help, but to close the Gate, it has to be a blood power diamond."

"You didn't think that King Babak, Erida and Clarice could close it by themselves?" Owen said.

"Diamond Sir Owen, the Gate can only be closed with a blood power diamond. There needs to be that fourth person," she said, shaking her head and talking to him like a four-year-old. She looked back up at me, smiling, "Once King Babak sent me to find Clarice, I started channeling my power to call forth Queen Selene. I didn't hesitate when she asked it of me."

Nodding, I turned toward Alexei and Clarice, who were whispering feverishly back and forth to each other.

"Alexei, you know I have to," Clarice said.

"But you are Gatekeeper now. You need to stay." He was begging her and my heart broke for them. "I need you to stay."

"I will be back. I'll have to now. I won't be able to leave you forever again," she said, and kissed him softly.

We gathered our things and headed downstairs to meet with Witch Dorith. When we got down there, I thanked her for her help and waited for the others as she started the spell.

Alexei pulled Clarice close and kissed her hard, trying to convince her to stay. I knew I should try to convince her to stay, but I also knew she wouldn't.

"Ahh, Silnaree," he told her.

"I love you, Alexei." she whispered. "I will return. I promise you."

"I'm going to hold you to that," he said, smiling. "I can track you, so if you run off and don't come back, there is nothing to stop me from coming after you this time."

We waved our goodbyes and stepped through the portal.

Stepping through the portal was like pressing the fast-forward button on the movie. Everything was speeding by so fast. Lights streaming past, wind in your face. Then when it stopped, I threw my hand over my mouth and concentrated so as not to vomit on the spot. The air was saturated with the smell of rotting flesh.

We were in what used to be a living room. It was covered with spots of tar that burned whatever it touched. The furniture was broken, shattered, and splintered all over the room. The altar at the far end of the room had figurines that were shattered pieces of marble and the mantle of the fireplace was broken in four places.

"The Witches. Where are they?" Lindy said.

"I don't know, but pure darkness has been here. I can feel it. It's stronger than what I was feeling in Therth," Clarice said.

"Stronger than that?" I said shuttering. I felt a heavy presence, but I didn't feel anything like it was at the Gate. This was more like a tug on the back of my mind that reminded me of after Noctulanar.

"Yes, and that's about as close to pure darkness that you can get to in all the realms."

"Shhhhh. Listen," Owen said. "Hear that?"

"Screaming?" CJ said.

I looked at him. "Ansel? Ghant is along the southern coast, right? About a three-week ride south of here? Why come here? If he completed the ritual a month ago? I... I don't understand."

We slowly made our way through the house, and room after room was the same. Bedrooms were completely tossed, beds broken, blankets scorched, the bathroom porcelain shattered and scattered, the library tables broken, and books shredded and burned. My heart broke as I inspected a table leg sticking in the wall and ceiling. The knowledge lost here today was staggering. There were spots of tar everywhere, and everything was utterly destroyed. When we stepped outside the smell, well let's just say, it wasn't much better in the 'fresh air.'

"I think I heard screaming this way," Owen said.

We followed the destruction down the main road. A man burst through one shop on one of the smaller streets that hadn't been destroyed yet and ran directly into Jean.

"Get out of here. He is destroying everything and everyone in his path," the man said as more screams erupted from down the street.

"Ansel," I growled and took off running. I vaguely heard the others call for me, but I didn't slow for any of them. The screaming was getting louder, and I ran through a destroyed building covered in tar, but when I jumped into the streets, I saw a family running toward me.

"Where is he?" I yelled at one of them, flinging m power out, but unable to see anyone.

"Three streets up. You aren't going after him, are you?" he yelled back as I took off in the direction. I heard him yell, "Your funeral."

The next street up was a woman trying to get an elderly man out of one house. I ran over to help her, but he wouldn't go. "I'm not leaving," he said stubbornly.

"Popa, we have to go. The monsters are destroying everything. We are going to die if we stay," the woman pleaded with him.

"I'm not leaving your mother," he said stubbornly, looking at his daughter. She sighed and ran to one of the back rooms. I tried to get him to move. "Come on, your daughter went to go get her, let's get you outside," I told him.

"I'm not leaving without her!" he screamed at me.

"You aren't. We are just getting outside while she gets her," I told him, practically picking him up to get him out the door. I had just got him over the threshold when the woman came back with a small urn. She eyed me thankfully, and there was an apology in her eyes.

"Popa, I'm back and I have her. Now, let's go!" she said, handing him the urn. I ushered them down the street toward safety. Just as I was about to run back down, CJ caught up with me.

"What were you thinking, Megan?" he scolded as he grabbed me and pulled me close.

"I have to stop him," I replied as the others came around the corner and the look of relief on Jean's face shocked me. CJ, however, put my face in his hands and looked at me evenly. "Not at the expense of your life."

"We've discussed this," I said.

"Yes. Yes, we have," he said, his lips tight and small. "And today is not your day to die."

Then there was laughter behind us. I knew that laugh. My power burst from its cocoon, sending an electric hum into my ears, and electricity flowing quickly around my fingers.

"Ah. Megan. Come to join in my party?" a voice as cold as ice said.

CHAPTER 51

I TURNED AROUND WITH my syths in my hands, growling as I saw him at the end of the block. "Ansel."

I centered my power and waited for him to make a move. I tried to coax it into compliance, telling it I would let it out like I did at the gate. It simmered slightly, but still bounced up my back and down my arms, waiting impatiently.

"So eager for your death you are, you sought me out?" he said with a tisk, and then slowly a smirk crossed his face. "And so considerate that you brought underlings and your new husband to die with you."

I felt CJ move next to me. His charge flowing off him in waves. I smiled back as I heard Clarice's whips crack behind me.

As I focused on his ember, I saw it flicker as he threw a jab at my side. I just got a wall up before it hit, but it came so much faster than I'd seen him or anyone else before. I looked up at him with surprise.

"That's right, Megan. I'm so much more powerful than I was." He raised his hand and admired the darkness as it flickered through his fingertips.

"Ansel, if it's me you want, then fine. Take me." I felt CJ move closer, but he said nothing. "But leave the town alone. You don't need to kill all these innocents."

"Oh, sweet girl, but I need them for my army. We will march in and destroy those who have destroyed our family," he said, his eyes getting larger with every word. I felt a hot burning sensation at the base of my skull again and did everything I could to push it away. "All I wanted to do was to learn. I wanted to collect knowledge, and they punished me for that!"

"You destroyed our family. You and Symatha exacted revenge. This has nothing to do with knowledge," I said as pain pushed down my chest as I thought about Matt. "We could have continued our lives in the Manusia. None of this ever happening. You could still be with Mom."

"That Council you have grown to care for, Julian, the one who pampers you like a fucking entitled princess? They're the ones who started all of this, and you just follow their orders blindly!"

"I don't take their orders. I work within the system. I don't forget that they're responsible for Matt's death, but I also don't forget what triggered their action. Your defiance of the laws of this world. I don't forget it was you who took revenge on more than just that council, but also an entire realm of innocent people who have done nothing to us. No, it is you who has brought on this destruction. You who have brought you where you are," I said.

Ansel's whole body pulsed with a black haze. The darkness at his fingertips fingered out, and I felt a chill crawl down my back. "It is glorious too isn't it."

"Ansel, you have received a power that has no mercy. It will not hesitate to destroy you," Clarice said.

"Ahh, yes, the King's deserter," he said, turning his attention from me to Clarice. "How is King Babak these days? Oh, that's right. My Ja'Nee KILLED HIM." He smiled, showing all his teeth, which gave me a chill.

"You son of a..." Clarice said as she stepped forward, eyes turning black as night as she threw as much power as she could at him. It was dark, powerful, commanding, and I could feel the strength behind it. The darkness she had absorbed from her father and sister had made her a hundred times stronger than she was before. I felt a shred of fear as I looked at her.

Ansel laughed, and with a flick of his wrist, pushed it away. Clarice stumbled back and turned her black eyes toward me. "He shouldn't have been able to just flick that away."

"You still think you're going to stop me?" he said as the tar substance bubbled behind him, creeping forward just a few feet as he walked towards us. He laughed. "You can't, Megan. There is nothing in this realm that can stop me."

"We will, Ansel," I said, stepping towards him, bringing my power to my fingertips. I don't know where I found the strength or resolve to say it, but there I was, standing in the street, staring down my father. I pulled every ounce of power that I could from deep within me. Electricity bounced up and down my back and it took a lot of concentration not to squirm at it, but it sat ready to be released.

"You can't. You don't have the raw power. I have the unstoppable power of darkness," he said as he threw his head back in laughter and sent another blast at us. I threw a wall up and when his power ricocheted off it, it blew the roof off of the house. I put another shield up between him and the rest of my family as he threw jab after jab. Jean and Owen had done the same. Lindy tried to blast back the tar, to no effect. It took all of us to deflect the blasts, and we were losing ground.

"We have to run. I'll keep the wall up for as long as I can. I'll be right behind you. GO!" I pushed to my family. I took a deep breath and pushed my hands out from my chest, pouring all of my power into the wall to deflect the blasts. The wall hummed with electricity that fueled its boundary. That wall pulsed dark green where Ansel's hits landed. It held, but I could feel myself getting weaker by the moment. I pulled and pulled from each corner of my being as they made their way down the street, but deep in my core, I felt a sputtering in the depths. I concentrated

and poured more into the wall. I would let every ounce of my power leave me to protect them.

The others took off down the hill. Well, all except CJ. "Ceej. Go. I'm right behind you," I said, gritting through my teeth.

"Yeah, not going to happen, babe. I may not be able to fight him, but I'm not leaving your side."

"This isn't the time for you to get all Vernadali on me," I said, hissing through my teeth. Ansel was tossing blast after blast, and it was getting harder and harder to keep it up. I conceded a few steps, then a few more as he continued his assault.

"Yes, actually this is the exact time it is supposed to come into play, but I'm not leaving you because you're my wife," he said. "On the count of 3, okay?"

"1... 2..." I counted as I stepped back, getting closer to the corner, and my power sputtered again. Any moment now, and it was going to go out on me. Sweat flowed down my face, down my back, and down my arms. My arms hurt at the pressure of keeping that wall up between us.

We couldn't win today.

One more bounce of electricity bounced up my back and I threw it into that wall between us. There was just a spark left lying on the floor of that well, and I had to save enough to take off down the street. If my power goes out —

"Three," CJ said as he grabbed my hand and pulled me behind the building. Ansel had sent another blast at that very moment, and it blew off the corner of the building just behind us.

We ran down the street and saw Lindy peek her head around a building a couple of blocks up. I looked at CJ, who was keeping up with me stride for stride, and he nodded to me.

Pieces of buildings were flying and landing in the street. CJ and I ducking and swerving to keep from getting hit by the debris.

Finally, we turned the corner into an alley right behind the rest of my family.

CHAPTER 52

WE DUCKED INTO WHAT was once the bakery and tried to catch our breath. I covered my ears to stifle the screams of the villagers we couldn't save, those who were being consumed by the tar. The entire town smelled like decay and it was worse inside the buildings. I tried to breathe through my mouth to keep from gagging.

"This royally sucks," I breathed. I didn't want to be running from Ansel. It was at that moment that I realized we really had no other choice but to find Helena.

"No matter how hard we try, we can't fend him off until we get Helena," Jean said.

"Megan! Come out, come out, wherever you are!" Ansel's voice screamed down the alleyway we had just left. "Alnwick is mine. The town is mine to control."

"We have to find a way out of here," Lindy said. "We're sitting ducks."

CJ was standing at the doorway and peered around the corner, looking for an escape route. It amazed me how his Vernadali training was taking over. Then his eyes locked further down the alley. "If we hurry, we can run through the stables and back into the forest. We should be able to lose him from there."

"Once we are through the stables, we will be out in the open though," Clarice said, looking through the window.

"Guess we'll just have to haul ass," CJ said, winking at her.

Owen and Jean nodded. CJ led them out, with Clarice right on their heels. I took a deep breath. Helena is our only option. I knew that now. I looked back out the window as Jean and Owen cleared the street into the stables. We are going to have to hurry, though. I took a deep breath as that same twisted, oily feeling settled into my stomach.

"Megan, don't worry, we will find Helena. Then we can destroy him," Lindy said, trying to comfort me.

"How is it you always know what I'm thinking?" I said as I stood up and brushed the dirt off my jeans and headed out the door.

"I'm your best friend, remember?" she said, smiling brightly.

"Yes. Yes, you are. Now, let's move before Ansel finds us." Man, we sounded like a couple of teenagers.

We were a few steps behind the others, and just as we were about to sidestep into the stables, I heard him and stopped dead in my tracks.

"Ahh! There's my precious daughter!" Ansel said behind me. I turned to look at him where two Ja'Nee were at his side.

Lindy pushed me behind her, so she was standing between me and Ansel. I felt out and could see the rest of my family's embers watching from just beyond the stables. Ahead of me and just behind Ansel was nothing but darkness. The tar hung back behind Ansel, and I could see the embers of the thousands of people that the tar had consumed. The tar wasn't just darkness. Was it consuming the souls, and thus their power to do his bidding?

"Ansel," I said, trying to get Lindy to move on behind me and to the others, but she wouldn't budge. She can be so stubborn.

"Lindy, go with the others. NOW!" I pushed to her. She moved to my side, but still stayed a little in front of me. *"We can't win this until we get Helena. Go!"*

"Oh, come on, girls. We can all get along. No need for things to get messy here," he said slyly.

"You killed Arturno! Your own brother," Lindy spat at him.

"He took the council's side. I was only defending myself and my wife," Ansel said, as if he was disagreeing as to the color of the curtains on the window. "Again, there is no need for things to be messy here."

"Then why don't you release the souls you have trapped in the tar?" I said through gritted teeth.

"Oh, now, why would I want to do that? I have something that can't be stopped. I can finally take revenge..." Then his eyes narrow and his mouth spreads into a too big grin again. "Upon you for killing Symatha."

His face terrified me to the core. I had to concentrate on breathing. The smell was singing my sinuses.

I couldn't stand to keep looking at him smiling, but I knew if I looked away, I was good as dead. I could feel Lindy next to me, creeping toward the stable door. She finally got it.

"Go, Lindy. I'm right behind you. Run for the tree line and don't stop."

Ansel saw it too, and with a flick of his finger, I didn't have time to feel the fear and dread that had filled me. I just moved, but before I could do anything to help her, the tar covered her feet.

Lindy screamed in pain. I took her hand and tried to pull her out of it, but the tar kept moving further up her body.

"Get it off!" she screamed, but it just crept further up her legs the more she fought it. I pulled and pulled at her, but couldn't get her loose. I sent bursts of my power at it, and the one good burst I got, the tar turned white hot, black screaming smoke rising from it, but it didn't do anything to the tar. It just continued to crawl up her leg. I tried again, and there was nothing but puffs of power that came out. I was power dry.

My father stood there laughing and willed the tar slow. I reached for a board and tried to scrape it off, but it just burned the board to ash and left burn marks on Lindy, who continued to howl in pain. How had she not passed out from it? When it reached her chest, she turned to me and her tear–filled eyes met mine.

"Get Helena. Use her. Stop this. Tell Logan I love him. So very much. And I'm so sorry, Megs. I love you," she said as the tar encased her chest and she started shrieked again from the pain.

I felt a burst of power come from her as it threw me back and out of the other side of the stable into someone's arms, as the tar covered the rest of her body. I felt CJ's charge radiating over me, but I couldn't take my eyes from Lindy.

"Lindy!" I screamed and tried to run back to her, but CJ's arms were holding tight against my body.

"Lindy!" He picked me up as I kicked and screamed and tried to get loose. "Let me down! I need to get back and save Lindy!"

"She can't be saved! She's as good as gone," he growled.

I tried to line my power between me and him and push out, but it was no use. I heard him grunt against it, but his charge flared. He wouldn't let me go.

"LINDY!" I screamed and sobbed, the further CJ pulled me from her.

"Lindy," I whimpered.

Her screams filled the air as the tar reduced her down to a skeleton. When it finished, the tar covered skeleton of my best friend turned to face me and roared.

CHAPTER 53

CJ's ARMS WERE FIRMLY around my waist as he pulled me away from the spot where my best friend once stood.

"No. Lindy!" I screamed repeatedly. I kick again, this time making contact. He grunted, but it didn't slow him down.

"Megs. Stop. We have to get out of here," he said in my ear as he ran for the tree line.

He carried me past Clarice, who was covered in a black pulsing mist that grew with every pulse. I blinked hard twice, making sure she wasn't covered in the tar too. She was screaming something, but I couldn't hear her. I could see her lips moving, but I couldn't hear anything other than CJ begging me to stop kicking. His Vernadali charge was in full force as he carried me away from my father.

Away from Lindy.

Away from Lindy.

I needed to get back to her. She needed my help. She couldn't be dead. The tar couldn't have taken her.

My father must be inside my head. That's it. He's placing visions of things that aren't really happening in my head. None of this is happening. None of this is real.

I'm standing with everyone around me, Lindy right beside me, while my father plays mind games with all of us.

No.

He doesn't have that ability. He's not Congiti like my Mother and I.

My heart sank. If he isn't playing mind tricks on us, that means... I froze. I stopped squirming and let CJ move further toward the forest.

"Lindy's dead," I whispered, but he said nothing. Did he even hear me?

As we passed Jean and Owen, they were fending off a swarm of Ja'Nee. I felt CJ's arms tighten around me, and his charge pulsed as he jumped over a fallen tree and into the forest.

I covered my ears. All the sounds crashing down on me at once, covering me like a blanket. CJ put me down, and I just stood there. He was checking me over, head to toe.

"Lindy's dead," I whispered to him. "She's dead."

"It's okay, Megs. We will be okay," he tried to reassure me. His voice hiccupped slightly, but he continued to look me over.

"No, we won't. Lindy is dead," I said as tears flowed freely down my face. I just stood there looking off into the forest, not seeing any of it through the blurriness in my vision. "My father killed her. I was supposed to protect her. Keep her alive."

"Megs," he said carefully, cradling my head in his hands. "There is nothing you could have done to stop it."

Panic flared through me. "Jean, Owen... Clarice. We have to save them."

"Stay here," CJ said, eyeing me carefully. "I will go get them. Stay here."

I blinked. "What?"

"Stay here."

"But Lindy... The others," I said, taking a step toward them. I felt anger and adrenaline pump through me. It brought everything crashing in around me again and my hands had my syths in them before I had taken a single step. Two steps toward the fight and CJ grabbed my arm with one hand and with the other turned my face towards his.

There was a hesitation before his eyes flashed bright with lightning. "You are going to stand right here where it is safe until I come back for you. Understand?"

"Oh, the Underworld no! I'm not going to just stay here while everyone else fights. Who do you think I am?" I said, looking at him like he was crazy. He looked at me seriously, and before he could say anything else, I continued, "I'm your wife. The person who you married because I can take care of myself, not some helpless woman who is going to let her man fight all the battles."

I took another two steps toward the tree line, but then I felt the weight of his words. I would be safe here, just behind the tree line. I looked back at him. CJ's face was covered in determination and... an apology?

He shook his head, looked at me, and lightning cracked through his eyes again. With a renewed determination and with more firmness said, "Megan Isabel Mathewson, you're right. You don't need me to fight your battles for you, but your power is zapped. You will stay here and wait until I come to get you again. Until then, you will not leave this spot."

I felt the force of his words, but I still couldn't believe they were leaving his mouth. I laughed under my breath and said, "Yeah, over my dead body."

"That's what I'm trying to avoid," he growled and then again, with more force and resolve, his eyes flashing with lighting the likes only Thor could appreciate, he said, "Megan Isabel Mathewson, you are going to stay here where it is safe until I come back for you. Do. You. Understand?"

This time, I nodded my head in agreement. He kissed me quickly on the forehead and I thought I heard him mumble he was sorry under his breath as he ran out past the tree line to help Owen and Jean with the swarm of Ja'Nee that they were fighting off.

No. I need to get out there. They need my help. Come on, Megan. MOVE. I turned to head out to where they were, but when I got to the tree line, my muscles froze.

No. CJ said to stay here. I have to stay here where it is safe until he comes back for me. My muscles relaxed, and I headed back further into the forest.

What the fuck, Megan! Get your ass out there and help them! But as I turned to run back out there, my muscles froze again, and this time I tried to fight it. The problem was that it was like I was locked in a... binding spell.

"Cory. James. Matthewson," I cursed under my breath. That damn Vernadali Charge was forcing me out of the damn fight. A fight with my father. A fight, my best friend....

"No. No. No," I said, shaking my head as I crouched down, holding my hands over my ears. No. Lindy can't be gone. She's going to marry Logan. They are going to live happily ever after, have a house near to me and CJ. Our kids are going to grow up together, and... and... no, Lindy can't be gone.

I forced down the lump in my throat and the hysteria that was building in my chest. I took several deep breaths in quick succession. I didn't have time for this breakdown crap right now. My family needs my help, and I can't because CJ's Vernadali Angels be damned charge is forcing me to stay put. He *clearly* hasn't shared all of those secrets with me.

Man, was he in for one hell of an ass chewing if we lived through this.

I looked out past the tree line and saw Clarice's ember pulsing as violently as the black mist surrounding her. The black mist pulsed in time with her ember and getting stronger and stronger. I'd seen nothing like it before. Not that I'd had a lifetime of experiences to go from or anything. It was only about two years ago.

Her ember was getting stronger and stronger as the black mist that surrounded her pulsed. The pulsing was mesmerizing. She pulsed one last time and let out a roar so loud it even caused the Ja'Nee to paused and turn to her. She blasted massive amounts of darkness towards my father, where he stumbled backwards a few steps and was held in place.

Then, the Ja'Nee was pulled into the blast of darkness, and the tar that had just consumed Lindy, my best friend, retreated to my father's feet. Ansel stood there, frozen in place, arms sprawled out, head back, and mouth gaping.

Clarice gave some sort of command that left the other scrambling in my direction

Jean eyed Clarice carefully as she ran past her. When she ran behind CJ and Owen into the forest, u and when CJ grabbed my hand, I felt all that pressure to stay where I was, release from me. I looked at him, and there was sorrow in his eyes. I narrowed my eyes at him and bit back any remarks as we took off into the forest.

I felt out behind me, feeling Jean and Owen about twenty yards behind me. Clarice was not too far behind, but her ember was still pulsing irregularly.

"Are you ok?" I asked her silently and twisted my head to see her nod her head.

CJ looked at me, but I couldn't look at him. "Just run," I said, picking up the pace. We had to put distance between Ansel and us.

CHAPTER 54

As we ran through the forest, I kept a feel out for anything that may be following. I lost range on Ansel a while back, but we just kept running. I'm not sure how long we had been on the move, but the sun was starting to fall behind the trees and it was getting darker.

"We should stop for the night," Owen suggested through breathless gulps of air.

"Don't suppose Julian would mind us porting back to Nalrin, would he?" Clarice said, only half joking.

Owen picked some moss off the side of a tree and threw it at Clarice, where it hit her arm with a wet *thwap*. "Why don't you cast it and have your powers taken for a day. I am not going through that again. I felt like a baby trying to learn how to walk."

When the forest opened up to a small clearing, I flopped down on a fallen tree as Owen and Jean went to find something in the forest for us to start a fire. We had left everything back at Clarice's father's... well, I guess at Clarice's house, okay so the castle was more like it. Regardless, we didn't have much of anything on us at all.

"We need to get back to Therth," Clarice said, drinking down as much air as she could. "There will be something in the library about Helena."

"And warn the towns on the way back about Ansel," I said quietly, focusing on the ground.

There was silence for a moment before Clarice said, "I'm going to see what I can do about finding something to eat. You two need to talk." I think she had some kind of silent conversation with CJ because it took her too long to move out into the forest.

"Megs," CJ said without looking at me. I felt the last shred of my power pulse in me.

"CJ, we will talk about it more later, but if you..." I looked up at him and through my teeth continued, "If you ever do that to me again. It won't be Ansel, you have to worry about tearing you to pieces. It's me."

"Megs..." he said as he reached out to me.

I jerked my arm back. Keeping my voice low, I said, "Ceej, I'm not just your Charge. I'm your wife. I am your wife first and foremost. I can understand you using that type of ability on your Charge, someone who was just your Charge, but to use it on me?"

I screamed in frustration and kicked a rock a few feet away, before sitting back down on the log. I don't even remember standing up to yell at him.

CJ came over and kneeled in front of me, and sighed. I was holding the tears back. I knew that once they started to flow again, I wouldn't be able to stop them. The chaos back at Alnwick, Lindy, feeling hurt that CJ would resort to using his power over me, it was all too much. I mean, I've been dealing with so much in the last couple of years, but... Lindy.

"Megs. Look at me." Even the pleading in his voice hurt. "Please."

CJ took my hands in his and when I didn't answer him, he reached up and lifted my chin to make me look at him. I wanted to yell at him, to be mad at him, but I couldn't. I just didn't have it in me. I felt... I felt everything.

"Look, I don't want you to say you're sorry, because I know you're not. I just want you to promise me you will not use that on me again," I breathed.

"You're right. I'm not sorry. It kept you safe, which is my job as your Vernadali, as your protector. You are also my wife and as your husband, I want to protect you, too. Can you take care of yourself? Hell, yes you can. However, because I am your husband, I also know that through your grief, anger, and, well, fury, I knew you would go in charging. Fuck, Megs, you did go in charging." He ran his hand through his hair again, growled in anger, and chucked one of his syths. It landed with a solid thud in one of the tree trunks a few feet from us.

Taking a few deep breaths to calm himself, he said, "You weren't thinking straight, and I didn't want you to get hurt. Your power was gone. Even now, you can't even summon one spark of that electricity to zap me in protest. So, yes, I used my Charge, and it kept you safe. I am sorry that it hurt you I forced you out of the fight, but I'm not sorry that you are here and safe to yell at me about it. So yell, scream, and cuss me out about it. I will do it again if it will keep you safe."

I looked up at him and met his eyes. I sat there for a few minutes, not saying anything, just staring into his eyes. Fierce. Determined. A mountain not budging.

He was my husband, something solid and secure. I saw no lighting, no remorse, but what was there was love. Lots of his love.

Just like he knew what I needed, he leaned forward and kissed me gently on the lips. I kissed him back and whispered, "I love you Cory James, but I'm still mad as a pit viper. Do you understand?"

He nodded. "I will do my best. It's extremely hard to control."

"Have you ever used it before?" I asked, looking down and playing with my fingers.

"Not like that."

"What do you mean not like that? So, you have used it on me before? When?" Anger burst inside of me, and I felt each of my muscles go taught, but I felt empty.

"I don't know for sure, but remember over a year ago, when you were in the living room and you found out about Arturno? You were pissed that Ansel had killed him, too? You kicked everyone out of the living room?"

"Yeah. Vaguely." My head was in a fog right now. "When I first burned your hands with my power and you backed me up against the wall?"

"I may have used it then to help you calm down." He shook his head. "Like I said, it is hard to control."

"You told me to focus, and I remember feeling the command deep in my chest. That was before you knew you were a Vernadali though," I said, confused.

"I know. But today, it felt like it did then." He ran his hand through his hair, back to front this time, making it stand up on end. "And if I used it on you then, then that throws all the theories out the window about how I became one."

"My thought has always been that you were born to be my protector. The Angels had you pegged for me from the moment you took your first breath. Power or not, you have always protected me since we met." I sighed. "It doesn't matter. We have to sort out a balance between husband and protector. I know it will take a while and I don't expect you to have all the answers."

He came to crouch before me again and took my head in his hands. "I promise you Megs, I have never used it on you knowingly before today."

"You said that," I said, and put my hand on his cheek. "Still mad as a pit viper, but let's move on from it for now."

He just picked me up to make me stand so he could hold me. Everything crashed down on me again, and the tears spilled over.

"Lindy's gone, Ceej. She's really gone," I said into his chest. My power jumped but faded out. It just wasn't there.

"Yeah, babe, I know," he said as his arms tightened around me, and I could hear the lump in his throat.

"She's gone, and it's my fault," I said, my legs finally giving out under me. CJ caught me, and we gently sat down in the middle of the clearing. "Lindy's dead and it's all my fault."

"There was nothing you could have done."

I just sobbed and sobbed into his chest, and I felt him cry, too. He held me for minutes or hours. It didn't matter.

I jumped when I heard a crack behind us. CJ had his syths in his hands and I wrapped myself around him, not willing to let him go as I felt out and saw the others heading back with dinner slung over Owen's shoulder.

"It's just the others. Owen has dinner," I told him, my chest tightening and tearing all at the same time. My breathing was coming in fast, short breaths.

"Megs, calm down. Slow deep breaths."

"Ceej," I couldn't look at each of them and see the accusations that would be on their faces for letting Lindy die. "Ceej, I can't face them. They're all going to hate me. I killed Lindy. It's all my fault. It's all my fault."

"They won't hate you. They won't blame you. Again, there is nothing that you could have done that would've changed the outcome of today."

I finally raised my head to look at him. His eyes were red and puffy, and yet there was so much love and understanding in them. "I can't face them yet, Ceej. I... I can't."

He just nodded, picked me up, and carried me just outside of the clearing, where we sank back to the ground against a big tree far enough away from the clearing. He put me in between his legs and wrapped his arms around me, syths still in hand. "It's okay babe. I've got you."

So, I hid there with CJ.

My husband. My Vernadali.

The protector of both my heart and body, and cried.

⊠ THE END OF BOOK 2 ⊠

ABOUT THE AUTHOR
K.M. Ringer

K.M. Ringer lives in California with her husband, little human, and two furballs, a Jack Russell mix and a Pomeranian Terrier mix. She loves providing some spice to her stories and showing that no matter what happens in your life, you are worthy of love.

Contact K.M. Ringer:

www.kmringer.com

Instagram: @kimberlymringer
Facebook: www.facebook.com/kim.m.ringer/
TikTok: @kmringer

Sign up for her newsletter on her website
and receive freebies, coupon codes, and stay up to date
on all things Kimberly M. Ringer and K.M. Ringer

Other Books by K.M. Ringer

Weekend Series

Weekend with Rylie
Weekend with Malcom
Weekend with Desiree
Weekend with Bethany
Angel's Shadow

The Ashstrike Sanctorum

The Ashstrike Sanctorum: Orgin Story
The Astral's Bonded
The Exorci's Touch
My Kismot Savior
The Kismot's Undesirable
My Kismot's Beloveds

Other Books

Ashes and Flame
Otter Be Saved
Under the Needle
Dedicated in Ink

ASHES AND FLAME

AFTER WORKING AS AN Advisor for the Roman Empire, Tiberius Maximus Vispania returned to Herculaneum in 79AD to start over. When he meets Sidonia Regilla, a fire instantly ignites between them. She would be allowed to choose her future husband. Could Sidonia be happy with Tiberius?

Just when happiness finds a way, an epic tragedy occurs and the entire village is wiped out. Only Tiberius and his best friend survive, courtesy of a curse that's provided them with immortality.

2,000 years later, Kelsey walks into his bar and lights a desire within him that only Sidonia had ever done. When their dark worlds collide, an overwhelming need to protect her takes over, and he realizes there may be more to Kelsey's ability to get under his skin than he thought. When Kelsey is kidnapped and tortured, unknown old rivals and secrets come to light.

When Max rushes in to save her, he vows that either all of them would come out alive, or none of them.

THE ASHSTRIKE SANCTORUM

<u>THE ASHSTRIKE SANCTORUM:</u>
<u>CREATION STORY</u>

When the Dark Witches of Moesia go rogue, and start creating immortals, will the paranormal creatures allow the new beings to live, or will they be out to destroy them? They have tasked Benjamin, an Ovexa, with finding three of these immortals to be interrogated to determine if they can be trusted to keep the paranormal world a secret from the humans.

Jorgen Hegland has found himself newly made but quickly learns being an immortal isn't worth it. When Benjamin finds him and demands he meet with the other creatures of the world, he agrees, but it isn't until he finds his mate, that he decides he will fight for his right to live.

<u>The Astral's Bonded</u>
<u>The Ashstrike Sanctorum:</u>
<u>Book 1</u>
Even Alphas have to answer to someone.

It was supposed to be a simple assignment. Astral Jade Romero was supposed to fix the werewolf problem at the Porter Ranch.

Only there was a problem, she hadn't prepared herself for, the human foreman Kolton Webster. He occupied all her thoughts and sucked her in like she never had been before.

When the wolves attack and Jade is injured will it be Kolton or the wolves that destroy her?

THE EXORCI'S TOUCH
THE ASHSTRIKE SANCTORUM:
BOOK 2
WHAT DO YOU DO WHEN YOUR ASSIGNMENT
DOESN'T DIE.

Exorci Jesse Westbrook can't touch anyone with his bare skin. If he does, they die. Such is the curse of an Exorci, the executioners for the Ashstrike Sanctorum.

His job is as simple and complicated as that. Receive the name and location of the person, and with a simple touch, the extermination is complete.

Jesse's life isn't all death and destruction. He has Maddie Taylor. The woman is his forever, but he's never dared to truly touch her. When her brother dies, her life spirals out of control, to the point she pushes Jesse from her life. Now... Now she's his next assignment.

<u>MY KISMOT SAVIOR</u>
<u>THE ASHSTRIKE SANCTORUM:</u>
<u>BOOK 2.5</u>

Angelica's life has been nothing but hiding from her parents and trying to make ends meet. It's been hard, but worth the freedom it afforded her from her family.

Morgan would have never guessed he would have found his queen just walking down the streets of Carmel, California, but there she was, arguing with the most despicable of women.

When Morgan intervenes, chaos ensues and Angelica and Morgan's secrets come to light quickly. Only Angelica seems to have one more...

<u>THE KISMOT'S UNDESIRABLE</u>
<u>THE ASHSTRIKE SANCTORUM:</u>
<u>BOOK 3</u>

Masen Cartwell was the son to the pride's king. It was his responsibility to ratify the treaty by marrying the Los Padres pride's undesirable, Veronica Aktins. There is something about her though. Something that pulls at his protective instincts and calls to his tom.

Ronni was the daughter of traders to her pride, an outcast, the Undesirable. Used and assaulted by the princes, the King has demanded that she marry the rival pride's prince and kill the Ventana Prides ruling family. Only, when she meets Prince Masen, his possessiveness over her and the adoration he showers her with sings to her heart.

When Prince Edwin steals Ronni, Masen will do anything to get her back. He had promised to protect her and keep her safe from her old pride.

Masen Cartwell won't let anything happen to what is his, and will stop at nothing to have his Queen back.

<u>MY KISMOT'S BELOVEDS</u>
<u>THE ASHSTRIKE SANCTORUM:</u>
<u>BOOK 3.5</u>

Leo Banks has watched his best friend and his prince find their mates. As hand to the crown prince, he was okay with that. They found their happiness and now his princess, and a woman he considered a sister, was pregnant with twins. He vowed to be her protector through the troubled pregnancy. He was happy with just being Uncle Leo.

Then when her pregnancy takes a turn for the worse, Dr. Marie Fuller and her nurse, Hadrian Fuller, come to Landow to care for her. When they arrived, Leo was not expecting to find his mate, let alone a queen and tom.

Can he balance the stress of protecting his princess, and welcoming his mates into his life?

WEEKEND SERIES

BY K.M. RINGER

WEEKEND WITH RYLIE
Book One

Luci's whole life changes in one weekend with her boyfriend, Rylie Allen.

Of course, there was the mind-blowingly good sex. It always was, but then there are secrets revealed, and a new job opportunity that would change everything between Luci and Rylie. When her ex-boyfriend comes back to haunt her, it threatens to throw their lives into further upheaval.

WEEKEND WITH MALCOM
Book Two

Malcom Henderson has been obsessed with his Project Foreman for months. When she's disrespected at a bar he steps in and after an enjoyable night, he hopes to have it turn into something more. The next morning, she's convinced that as much as she wants him, it was only a one-night stand, and tries to protect herself by kicking him out. A torturous week pulls between them when unexpected problems are occurring on the job site that ends up being tied to the Chicago mafia families, and it's not long before Malk and Raquel find themselves in the middle of a brewing war.

WEEKEND WITH DESIREE
Book Three
With threats against the Don Supreme and his family lurking around every corner, Jensen Maloy, the most feared man in all Chicago, has been working overtime to ensure everyone stays safe and alive. Desiree Hernandez loves and trusts Jensen with every fiber of her being, and while she understands the reason, they need to live in lockdown, it doesn't mean she's happy about it. Even if she

is living with her best friend and honorary sister, and her fiance.

Jensen and Desiree aren't used to being apart for such long stretches of time, and despite all the support from friends and coworkers, tensions rise, and morale drops to an all-time low. When the enemy takes drastic actions to finish the deal, they forget to factor in two very important things. Desi is not to be underestimated, and Jensen will stop at nothing to make sure his Princess is safe and in his arms. Who will still be standing when the dust settles?

WEEKEND WITH BETHANY
Book Four
Her strength will save them all.
Weekend with Bethany is the explosive conclusion to the Weekend Series. The war between Dallas and Vaux has become deadly, and no one is safe. When Beth is captured, she was shocked to learn that her Wes was the one and only Wesley Backnoff. Sure, she knew the name. Who didn't? Can she reconcile the compassionate man with whom she fell in love, with the killer who stands before her?

After rescuing Bethany, Wesley Backnoff, second to the Don Supreme of Chicago, can't hold back his feelings for her any longer and is bound and determined to keep her.

Old secrets come to light and threaten to destroy them all. Who will pay the price? Will Beth and Wes survive the night or has their time run out?

www.ingramcontent.com/pod-product-compliance
Lightning Source LLC
Chambersburg PA
CBHW051157190726
48288CB00006B/1693